BLACK
DREAMS

Also by Kate Green

SHATTERED MOON
NIGHT ANGEL
SHOOTING STAR

BLACK DREAMS

KATE GREEN

 HarperCollins*Publishers*

ACKNOWLEDGMENTS

Special thanks to Vickie Palmquist, Cheryl Urie, Ray DiPrima, Dr. William Friedlich, Richard McCormack, Echo Bodine, Clara Rosemarda, Natalie Goldberg, Mary Logue, Peter Hautman, Mary Bendtsen, and Cathy Paulsen. And, as always, to my parents, Ken and Anne Green, for everything.

HarperCollins books may be purchased for educational, business, or sales promotional use. For information, please write: Special Markets Department, HarperCollins Publishers, Inc., 10 East 53rd Street, New York, NY 10022.

FIRST EDITION

Designed by C. Linda Dingler

Library of Congress Cataloging-in-Publication Data

Green, Kate.
    Black dreams / Kate Green. — 1st ed.
      p. cm.
    ISBN 0-06-017984-8
    I. Title.
    PS3557.R3729B53 1993
    813' .54—dc20   92-56226

93 94 95 96 97 ❖/HC 10 9 8 7 6 5 4 3 2 1

For Paul Webster Green and Martha Green Davidge,
with love

FRIDAY,
JULY 3

THE FIRST TIME she heard the child's voice it woke her. The bedroom window was open to the damp smell of rain, midsummer, Los Angeles. 4:37 A.M. The digital clock glowed green on the nightstand. She woke startled, not sure why. A few blocks away, perceptible above street traffic, the low tumbling thunder of the ocean.

Theresa scanned the black corners of the room, half expecting someone to be standing there, perfectly still, but the house was quiet. Her eyes adjusted to the dark and she made out Osiris staring from a wicker rocking chair. His white fur glowed. That was when she heard a voice, bell-clear, but with the sound of metal through the chest, the voice of a survivor carrying the tuning-fork chime of whatever it had survived. A child's voice, ever hopeful: "*Where is my mother?*"

Then the man spoke out of the black. "*Let's get you dressed,*" he said.

She knew the voices were inside her, in her mind, that the man was both nurturing and lying at the same time. She knew that much.

For some reason she expected the ground to begin to move. She glanced at the glass bottles on her dressing table to see if they would rattle toward the edge or the floor ripple under her. The earthquake out by Palm Springs had been less than a month ago, and she'd ridden through seven aftershocks in the last weeks. The ground was not solid.

Theresa sat up at the edge of the bed. The sheer curtains blew in. They billowed like skirts. She realized she was holding her breath and exhaled slowly. The conversation in her head seemed to have stopped. A car backfired, rap music booming, then fading down Washington Avenue.

That was when the images came like a childhood memory, something she'd moved on from, but had never forgotten, a scene that would never leave her, surfacing years later on this July night with the bougainvillea rustling against the windowsill, but with one difference: it was not her memory. It was someone else's.

Theresa felt herself as the child. A man hands her a twenty-dollar bill. He slips a blue dress on over her head, she puts the twenty in her pocket. *Sharp, my arm. That hurts,* she thinks.

The man picks her up, arms around her. *Muscle man, strong man.* She rests her head on his shoulder. Sense of relief and affection, but hot inside. Stomach flurry. The girl is not sure what is happening.

But he's nice, she thinks. *And I want to go home.* She nestles down in the dark place. *Why are you covering me? Little car, rolling down the hill. Going into the fog. Where is my mother?*

The scene jolted shut, snapped back to the dim room. Theresa looked at her reflection in the round dressing-table mirror, pulled her hair back, and held it at her neck with a fist. It was not particularly unusual for her to have voices or pictures in her head. Sometimes voices came to her like that, inner soundtracks cutting through her thinking in a subtle, insistent whisper, an underthought. Or they came loud, as if amplified over internal speakers.

At other times, images came as waking dreams, odd symbolic pictures to be deciphered. They flew through her, fantasies spun off to the side of everyday life while driving or doing the dishes. But after years of learning to manage and harness her strange talent and claim it as a gift, it was rare that voices came to her uninvited. Usually they left her alone unless she was conducting a professional reading or teaching a class. She'd worked hard to keep her intuitions contained so she wouldn't be flooded with them.

There had been years, long gone now, when Theresa thought for sure she was crazy. *She thinks too much, my oldest.* Her Italian mother shouting on the sidewalk outside church after mass. *She's got too much imagination, she belongs in the nuthouse. Father, maybe she's some kind of idiot saint, sees the face of Mary in a washcloth. What am I supposed to do with this girl?*

Does she see Mary? asked the priest.

No, no. Everything but.

Does she do her homework?

Yes.

Does she steal, smoke, run with boys?

No, none of that.

Leave her alone, then, Father had said.

Theresa had not known that she was psychic until her grand-mother took her on the sly to see a gypsy in Manhattan when she was fourteen. That had been the beginning, the knowing. She had her grandmother to thank for that. And the gypsy.

So this was strange, even for her, voices from the blue nowhere. And just when she thought they'd left her, the child's voice spoke again.

"Draw," said the girl.

Young, thought Theresa. Nine, ten. She'd never had a voice tell her how it should be received.

"Draw?" Theresa repeated out loud.

"YES," came the inner voice, big and silent. It pulled her out of bed with an urgency. She flicked the hall light on, headed down the hall to the desk at the back of the kitchen. Quickly, the way a good mother would rise at a child's cry, hurry to the sink for water or offer a hug, soothe the bad dream down.

"Colors," said the girl's voice.

Now where had she put those felt-tipped pens? Here was red. Purple over by the phone, the rest of the markers in the desk drawer. Theresa yanked out a few sheets of paper and sat at the round wooden table at the center of the kitchen. The overhead light beamed a circle down on her and the dark world surrounding.

She put a blue pen to paper, letting the other feeling guide her. She wasn't artistic at all, hadn't drawn anything since high school art class. Cold in her cotton nightgown, she shivered. Her thick hair fell over her shoulders, shadowing the white page.

She watched as the picture took shape, her thin hand like a sepa-rate animal with a mind of its own. The first drawing was of a bed, a crib maybe, boxed in, anyway, with railings. Outside the window, there was a street with round cars and the face of a large smiling woman with too many teeth.

Theresa sketched it, the lines sure and slow. It was almost as if she were tracing a child's drawing. She drew a twenty-dollar bill float-ing out a square window. Then a barefoot girl in a blue dress reaching out her hand for the money, which was flying away like a small green bird. She drew a pair of blue sneakers. The shoes glittered on the floor beside the bed. Tiny lines radiated out from them, as if they were shin-ing. Sapphire slippers instead of ruby. *No place like home.*

Theresa set the paper aside and immediately her hand began to move over the next clean page. She watched as the picture came into recognizable shapes, a car with a bed inside it, the girl lying down on the bed. Sensation of rolling. Big round doughnut tires, the black pen circling around and around, digging into the page. Now, in the background, she drew a ship, a small animal in a cage, a castle, pinpoint stars with rainbow trails, and, finally, a white horse. Her hand paused over the page, then added a horn to the horse's forehead.

Then Theresa felt herself slip completely inside the dream. A subtle shift in her body. Behind the child's eyes now. Standing in a midway, dusk. Pretty as the inside of a jewelry box, all the colors.

She saw neon lights whirling, blurred reflections in puddles on black tar. Lights spinning far above. *Way high,* thinks the child. Inside the child, behind her face. She was small now, looking up at a fat man with a dragon tattooed on his hairy shoulder. Up close, the green lines of the dragon's wings. *How do they get the ink in between the hairs?* Flap of rubber thongs, loose on hot pavement, and the yellow lights. *Gravitron, Quasar, Ultra Mirror Maze.*

The man takes the child's hand. He nudges her along through the crowd. She stops to look up at a huge face of an Indian. *Superstition Mountain. Club Fun.* She is reading. Rides at a midway, food booths. Smell of hot grease and sick sweet sugar. "Want to try fry bread?" the man asks. "How about a Texas Taco?"

The child's hand, writing on a napkin. Theresa tried to see it, the letters fading, running wet. "What are you doing?" asks the man. "Writing a message to put in the time capsule," she says. "In a hundred years, someone will know I was here."

He takes the napkin away and pulls her through the crowd. Dream presences pass her.

Theresa breathed deeply and sank into a listening place, the child's voice coming through her, in her mind, as if she could listen right inside her head.

I'm glad I'm out, it's not that. I hated all the shots and the tests, all the pills. But I miss Mom. I cut slices in my thongs with nail clippers to keep track of the days, like I heard the hostages did on their walls. Is that what I am?

Maybe I should just run off fast while he's over there, down by the ring toss and the rabbit race where I might win that fuzzy white unicorn if I'm lucky. Past the caramel corn. Twenty dollars in my pocket. Just go off in the lights, back behind those trailers.

But he said they'd look for me everywhere. I'd have to go back and get all sick again.

Theresa felt the child shiver, shrink as if hiding inside herself, hiding her voice away where she couldn't hear it clearly. The man, beside her again, seems huge, touches her hair, hands her tickets. They climb in something like a boat, and up they go, sailing.

Then Theresa felt a sudden dizziness and she started to pull out of the scene. Her perspective shifted as if she were flying up a thousand feet above the fair, looking down at the child in the midway below. Simultaneously realizing this was the exact second that the child knew that something was wrong, terribly wrong, the precise moment that her life changed forever, spinning out of her hands like a dropped and broken thing.

Way down below, the speck of her getting on the Ferris wheel with the man who had promised he was her friend. All this time she had believed him, even though she felt the sad badness in him. She missed her mom. Dad. Mom. Dad.

Theresa didn't know why it felt so threatening, a little girl just climbing on a midway ride, but she wanted to scream down at her, *Don't go with him!* She called out to the girl in the picture in her mind, called out to her through the high blue summer air, higher now, black up here among the stars: *Get off! Get off and run like hell!*

Theresa blinked her eyes in the softly lit kitchen. She picked up a pink pen and her hand moved back to the drawing of the car, the square window, passenger side. A small round face appeared with open mouth and brown pageboy hair. Two open hands held up on either side of her face. At first, Theresa thought the girl's hands were reaching. Maybe waving. *Hello. Good-bye.*

The picture was nearly finished. She could feel the urgency leave her hand, the otherness in her mind fade. But then she picked up the blue pen and drew two perfectly symmetrical rows of tears dotting down the girl's cheeks. Her hands were not waving, thought Theresa. They were pressing against the window, pounding.

Theresa set the pen down, stood, and backed away from the table. She felt for the striped Guatemalan shawl from the hook behind the back door and wrapped it around her shoulders. At the sink, she drank tap water from a coffee mug, then hung the drawings on the refrigerator with round magnets, turned out the lights, and went back down the hall to her room. Deep breathing did not help her get back to sleep, and she lay awake in the rising light, suddenly remembering a time as a kid with her grandmother out at Jones Beach, watching the swing dancers and the big band in the band shell on a summer night in the salt wind. She'd turned and her grandmother was gone. Swarms of strange faces and the feeling that she was lost though she hadn't moved and knew just where she was.

She could hear rain dripping off the eaves, but not on the roof. It had been a cold summer so far—something about a volcano in the Philippines creating ash-dust in the atmosphere and El Niño, a shift in the jet stream. No global warming this year. Theresa turned over and pulled the covers up.

She knew she was waiting for the child's voice to come back. It didn't, and finally she slept.

IT WAS MUCH EASIER than he thought it would be. After looking in on her a few times, and familiarizing himself with the routine, he had simply gone to her room with a clipboard. Looking official was one way of being invisible, he'd found that out in the army. The Demerol had gone in easily. She was used to taking a hypodermic without any trouble and she was as quiet as a stone.

The halls were empty and dark, the service elevator dropped quickly with no stops. Then a short push to the dock that led out to the dumpsters. The metal door clicked shut behind them. It was raining, only a mist, gray and still. He pushed the cart over to the dumpster. He'd parked back here earlier. Now he backed his truck up to the dumpster, lifted the towels and sheets and her small body into the back of the camper, shut and locked the door, leaving the empty laundry cart there. He was sure that no one had seen him. It was just after 5:00 A.M.

He didn't feel safe until he got to the freeway and headed south, not sure where he was going. Funny, he'd thought it all through up until this point. He pulled a black garbage bag out from under his seat and lifted it to the passenger seat. Put his hand on the contents inside, just touching it. It had a good feeling, that much cash. Call it a present for all the birthdays he'd ever missed. Again he reached under the seat and felt for the .38, a memento from an old flame, something to remember her by. He hadn't needed to use it. He hadn't needed the 9-mm. Beretta stashed under the maps in the glove compartment either. That one he'd bought for himself, when he got out of the army years ago, and he preferred it to the .38. It held more rounds and that could be useful. You never knew.

He drove for an hour or so, until the traffic started to get thick, morning rush hour, then headed inland across Orange County and up into the foothills, vacant scrub woods high above the freeway din and the clatter of suburban houses under construction. As he rose up, following the winding road, he glanced behind him nervously in the rearview mirror, although he knew that no one was following him. The air hung over the city like a yellow liquid.

She'd be out for a couple of hours at least. Anyway, the door to the camper was locked, she couldn't get out, and he'd hear her when she came around. He slept for a while, sitting up in the cab, and woke after seven with a crick in his neck. When he checked on her in the back, she was still out. He covered her with a couple of towels. It had stopped raining.

He had come up here before to fish with an old man who'd been staying at the motel. The reservoir always looked strange to him, like a lake plunked down on the moon. No trees lined the shore, just brown hills rising straight up from the water and rocks. He went down to the edge and sat on one, wondering what to do next.

He had felt this way on his last day of service. He had felt this way on the last day of his marriage and he had felt this way anytime he left something and right at the beginning of the new thing that might save his life and make it brand new, a clean slate wiped as fresh as that single cottonwood over there and the ocean out beyond where everything started over as salt.

He had a chance here to do something right in his life. He threw stones into the water and watched the rings go out from them like zeros repeating themselves. They were in a new life now, one that had not existed before, and the world felt good. He wondered why it was so hard to sustain that freshness, why things became so contorted and entangled, but he didn't want to think about that now. He had saved her life, he knew that, and created a new one for her.

If he hadn't seen her mother coming out of the elevator the day before, he wouldn't have known the girl was there. Now, as he thought about it, it was odd. Definitely odd. As if he'd had a plan even back then, but it wasn't much of one. Just that his future had appeared in his mind like a straight road home. That clear.

Nothing had ever given him that sense of purpose before. Not school, not friends, not even drugs or booze. He could take or leave all that. And he'd never been in love with a particular woman. At least he didn't think so. They all seemed the same, sitting on bar stools, smoking. He hadn't the slightest idea what was in their heads.

But Tory was pure. The one person on the planet who had never judged him and seemed to know him inside out. That was pretty close to love, wasn't it?

The leaves in the cottonwood shivered in the dust of the sky. If he was to take really good care of her and do it right, he would need some kind of solid existence. It wasn't good for a kid to just float in the void. That's what he'd done and, yes, it had taught him some things, but he wouldn't call it a form of love.

So that was his first dilemma. To be safe they should stay invisible. But to really love a kid you had to sink down into a life, try to give her what she really needed, what she'd never been given. What he himself had always been denied.

He stood, stretched his legs, and walked back across the gravel parking lot to where he'd parked the truck beneath a scraggly pine. He opened the back and peered in at her. She was skinny, with bony knees, her elbows angled over her chest, mouth open. He could hear her ragged breath, her dark hair lopsided now, all messed up. Awake, she had brown bright eyes that looked down when she was shy or out of the corners, peeking to see. An elf on the sly. He liked her because she was quiet, like him, not a pest like most kids. She was a thinker and sometimes she seemed way off somewhere in her head in a fantasy land, humming a tune from a cartoon movie. Drifting in her own little world. He closed the door of the camper again and locked it.

He really had a chance here to make the perfect childhood. If he got to do his over again, what would he want? He would have to think about that. Maybe they would settle down eventually. But it would better if they kept moving. For now.

THERESA SAT AT A WROUGHT-IRON TABLE out in the small courtyard behind her house. The lieutenant's voice came through static over the cordless phone, and a vague country-and-western tune from some stray radio station hummed in the background.

"Was it a dream?" he asked.

"Not at all," she said.

"What's the difference?"

"In a dream, the world seems continuous. Solid. It's an alternative world that you absolutely believe in while it's happening. You're totally in it. But when I get a vision, or whatever you call it—God, I hate calling it that—I'm both wide awake and watching this inner movie. It's more like a memory, like scenes from the past flashing inside me, but it's not my past. It's simply not mine! Also, it came in spurts. Dreams don't spurt. Then there was the impulse—or, I should say, the command—to draw. When was the last time a dream ordered you around? That's when I went in deeply, when I was coloring and the picture was taking shape."

"It's not connected with some other reading you've done in the last few days?"

"Not that I'm aware of. Sometimes I get impressions or information for regular clients that I'm tuned to, but I can't place the source of this."

"Okay. Hold on a minute, Theresa. I'm going to call down to Missing Persons and see what's up. White female, nine to ten years old, wearing a blue dress, barefoot, brown pageboy haircut. Be right back."

Lieutenant Oliver Jardine put her on hold and she watched the morning light on the roses wet from the garden hose. Sun dried the puddles on the bricks. The lieutenant had called to confirm their dinner appointment for next Monday, following the Fourth of July weekend. He said he had a case he wanted to go over with her, get her take on. That was his excuse, anyway. But she enjoyed his company—and perhaps he could help her out with this.

"I'm back," said the lieutenant. "They have nothing on a missing child going by that description. No reported disappearances from any of the amusement parks, either. I don't know what to tell you. I'll keep my eyes open for any similarities with what's coming up here. Missing Persons said they'd be on the lookout, too."

"Thanks," Theresa said.

"It's bothering you, isn't it?" he asked. "How come?"

"Because it came from out of nowhere. Because it seemed so strong. Because it's a kid. Because it felt, I don't know, personal in some odd way."

"What do you mean?"

"Like it had something to do with me."

"Like how?" he asked.

She was silent for a moment, but couldn't answer.

"Keep it separate, Theresa," he advised. "Our work is like that. You've got to get involved, but you can't go down with it. Right?"

"Yeah," she said. "Thanks. Are you picking me up on Monday or am I meeting you there?"

"I'll pick you up. Say, what about the Simon Foundation? Are you working with anybody over there?"

Yes, she thought. *That's it.* "Oliver, thank you. I don't know why I didn't think of them. I'll call over there right away."

"Check it out. Sometimes they're working on cases that the police have given up on, or cases where the officials don't have enough to even open a case. It could be a case from another state. They've got that national data base of missing children."

The lieutenant hung up and Theresa went up the stairs of her studio to look through her files. Third drawer down, client files under "Volunteer Work/Benefits." The Simon Foundation for Missing Children was a private, nonprofit center for missing and exploited children. Two years ago the lieutenant had invited her to speak there on a panel with law-enforcement officials, to talk about how to make use of psychics in missing-persons cases, what kind of information was helpful, photographs, maps, clairaudience, clairvoyance, the different ways that psychics worked. Appropriate fees. How to watch out for charlatans and flakes. A few months later she'd done a workshop for the volunteer staff on how to work with psychics, and she had consulted with several families.

Ever since that homicide case nine years ago, the one in which she'd met and worked with Jardine and the Los Angeles Police Department, she had occasionally made herself available for a missing-persons case. She didn't particularly enjoy that kind of work and didn't go out of her way to do it. When it came up, though, she would offer her services free of charge. She wasn't sure why. She'd told her friend

Camille that it just didn't seem right to charge people for it. But Camille, also psychic, had known better. "You're just trying to do penance for Michael's death," she'd told Theresa.

Theresa had been quiet and had known Camille was right.

Theresa's normal clientele was in the area of what she called spiritual direction or life guidance—the inevitable questions about relationships, career choices, health, and money, and the wacky ones about other dimensions, interplanetary conversations with aliens, past lives as the Czar of Russia, and lucky numbers for the lottery.

And she'd had a bit of success, none of it financial. She'd tracked a runaway girl to her aunt's house in Boulder because she'd kept getting an image of an iron smoothing the side of a mountain. "The Flatirons," the girl's mother had said, snapping her fingers. "I'll bet anything that little stinker went to see my ex's sister, Pam." Sure enough, the girl had stolen money with her mother's ATM card and flown to Colorado to see Aunt Pam. But Theresa couldn't really take credit for finding the girl. She'd only gotten the image; the mother had figured out where the girl was.

Theresa flipped through the files for the families she'd consulted with at the foundation, but none seemed to fit with last night's vision. The bed, the money, the midway, the car—nothing seemed to coincide with any of her previous cases.

In her office she put in a call to Leslie Simon, the director of the agency, describing to her the images she had picked up, as well as the intensity and oddness with which they had come.

Leslie was quietly thoughtful. Finally she said, "No, I'm not familiar with a child of that description locally, Theresa. I'll feed it into our computers here, though, and I'll also put in a call to the National Center for Missing Children to see if they have anything that corresponds to what you've said. Why don't you make some color photocopies of the drawings you made and bring them over, if you have time? It's not much, though, is it? I mean, you don't really have anything that would help us find the supposed child, even if the child is real."

Theresa sighed when Leslie Simon said "real." Leslie was very down-to-earth and quite skeptical about Theresa's work, but Theresa also knew Leslie respected her. She actually appreciated Leslie for her doubts. After the call, she paged through the *L.A. Times*, looking for articles about missing children or abductions. The rest of the morning and afternoon was filled with client appointments: a real-estate agent perpetually anxious about her investments, a strange young man who'd had his second ecstatic religious experience in six months, and a woman who came once a year on the anniversary of her divorce to question whether or not it had been the right thing. As always, Theresa tried to use the imagery she got to lead the querents to some grounded sense of their own intuition for their lives. In fact, that was the thrust of her work as a psychic—not to read for others, but to empower them to read for themselves.

But at the end of the day she'd found herself losing it, irritated with the divorced woman. "Sarah, did you ever think that it might have been the right decision simply because you chose it? It's been what, six years? What if you declared that your decision to divorce was correct?"

Sarah had looked down at her hands. "You mean I'm second-guessing myself?"

"Something like that." Sarah looked scolded. Usually Theresa was gentler, but she couldn't help it. Aside from that, nothing interfered with the day's readings. All had come clearly with a sense of ease and fluidity.

At three she rode her bike down to the Venice Beach boardwalk and pedaled slowly along the bike path, the sea wind in her face, the Santa Monica Mountains in a haze to the north. She sat for a while in the lacy shade of a palm tree, watching Black men with beautiful muscles play basketball on the new court. A beach ball bounced toward her on the grass and she tossed it back to a small child in a tie-dyed T-shirt. The child's father caught the boy up in his arms and twirled him around, dreadlocks spinning out from his head. The child grabbed the man's amber beads, whooping, and nuzzled into his father's shoulder. Theresa thought of the image last night of the man lifting the girl, her arms around him. Not the touch of a father, she thought. Unless the father was a stranger.

A steady stream of people cruised the boardwalk in the bright sun, and after a time Theresa headed back south, sweating, toward Venice Pier, then rode a few blocks inland until she got to the bridge and the sidewalk along the canal that led to her tiny house. She'd bought the place three years ago through one of her clients who had told her that since she had become a Venice fixture she should live on the canal. He'd given her a great deal because it was falling down. It had taken her a while to make it livable, and now it was like a gingerbread doll-house from the front, white clapboard partially covered with ivy. Violet and magenta bougainvillea on either side of the front porch. A short white picket fence separated the front yard from the canal, though the fence up closer to the house was high and wooden, with a Japanese-style gate resembling the entrance to a small Zen temple. She didn't care that none of the elements went together. Osiris, her cat, lay across the sidewalk out by the canal, eyeing the lazy ducks, and she was not surprised to see her friend Camille slouched in one of the pink wicker chairs, a baseball cap pulled down over her eyes. Sarene, Camille's fifteen-year-old daughter, perched at the edge of the porch, dangling her feet. Their two bikes were leaning against the fence.

"It's about time!" called Sarene.

"We were just leaving you a note," Camille added.

"Robert wants you to come for dinner. He's trying out some new recipe for coconut shrimp for the café and he's going to have two versions, one heavy on the lime and one with red peppers, plantain on the side."

"And I just came along to remind you that my birthday's next week, and since you are my surrogate auntie, you have got to take me somewhere extremely wonderful."

"Such as?" Theresa asked.

"I thought we'd start with breakfast, then go shopping, maybe get a facial, then head over to the Orange County Fair, which opens on Thursday, and end up by seeing Bobby Brown in concert."

"Is that all?" Theresa smiled.

Camille and Theresa's friendship went back years, to when they had both studied with Elizabeth Brandon, a noted psychic. Camille had her own private practice now, as well as a call-in radio show, "Life Lines," in the Los Angeles area. She was a tall, elegant woman with fine black braids gathered together in a ponytail under her baseball cap. Her warm brown face eased into a smile. Seven gold hoop earrings gleamed on one ear. Over her biking shorts she wore a T-shirt that said ISLAND CAFE, the name of the restaurant her husband, Robert, owned with his cousin.

"We can't really stay," Camille went on. "We just rode over to bother you for a minute. Can we get a glass of water?"

As soon as they entered the kitchen, Sarene spotted the drawings on the refrigerator. Like her mother, Sarene had a dancer's body, long-limbed and graceful, which she put to good use all summer on a softball team. Her latest hairdo was a sleek beehive, coiled up around her head Supremes-style. It looked especially fashionable when she stepped up to bat. Sarene leaned in close to the drawings, squinting.

"These look old," she said.

"Old? What do you mean?" asked Theresa.

"Old-fashioned. That little Alice in Wonderland dress. That haircut straight out of Christopher Robin. The blue shoes are hip, though—what are they? Turquoise rhinestone high-tops? Look, Mom."

Camille filled her glass and came over to look at the drawings. "Puts me in mind of those patent-leather party shoes we had when we were coming up," Camille said. "Or did your mama only let you buy those brown Catholic-school oxfords that were so ugly you'd like to die? Is this you?"

Theresa ran water into a glass and handed it to Sarene. "Why do you think it's me?" asked Theresa.

"Don't know. That's what I picked up."

"What else do you pick up? Give me a take, Camille."

Camille stood back, crossed her arms, regarding the colorful strokes on the white pages. She waited several minutes, then spoke. "At first I thought it was you, but no, it isn't quite, is it? That little girl surely is lost, she's looking for home. There's money in the picture, but she doesn't have much herself and she can't get out of where she is. She's stuck. As far as past-life stuff, on a soul level, I'd say she's come to learn to move herself of her own accord. Be free of things and people that entrap and imprison her. See that little cage there? And to live in the real world. Get out of her illusions, learn to see through people to the rock-bottom truth of who they are." Camille pointed to the castle. "Fairy tale," she said. "And look at her in that car. She definitely wants out. Theresa, who is this supposed to be?"

Theresa filled her in on the drawings, the way they'd come last night and the child's voice, her attempts to locate the source of the drawings. "Did you ever do a reading that way, by drawing a picture?" Theresa asked.

"I knew one psychic who did automatic writing on a computer. She'd just take a deep breath, listen to the question, and start typing away. At the end of the session she'd print out the reading and give it to the client, easy as you please. But I have to say this is new. Only time I've heard of it before is in the remote-viewing experiments up at Stanford. Didn't they draw sometimes?" Camille filled a glass with tap water and drank it down. "Anyway, Theresa, the source of the drawings is in you. Close in to you."

"Well, I know that, Camille. I drew them."

"I mean that in order to find out who it is, you aren't going to get it from no newspaper or organization. It'll come to you. Just wait."

"Don't be so mystical, Camille."

"I can't be mystical around you, baby?"

"Especially around me." They both laughed.

"I just mean that in some way the connection is in closer than you think."

"Should I pursue it?" Theresa asked.

Camille adjusted the band of her baseball cap. "Do you have a choice?" Camille gave her a hug. "What are you doing over the Fourth of July, Resa?"

"Staying off the roads and the beach, away from the hordes," she answered. "I'll probably do some gardening."

"Hattie's making barbecue. You know you're always welcome."

"Tell your mom to pack up some chicken to bring back to me. And send her my love."

They set a time to talk next week about dinner with Robert, and Camille let the screen door bang quietly shut behind her, calling back, "Shrimp with red peppers and plantain."

"Lime," Theresa called back. "Tell him lime with peanuts."

Sarene turned back at the sidewalk along the canal. "You be thinking of something special for my big day, okay?"

Theresa held her thumb up. She stood alone in the sunny kitchen, staring at the drawings again. And yes, she thought, yes, I do have a choice. She no longer had to go into the vortex over any vision or voice, either. When images had come to her like this before, personal, imposing, uninvited, she'd gotten sucked into a course of events that had nearly killed her. It *had* killed Michael, her ex-husband. That doesn't have to happen again, she told herself. I don't need to get swept away.

And anyway, a lot of the vortex was caused by resistance and fear. A few years ago she might have run away from the compelling nature of these drawings. But now she knew, when it came this strong, there was something important to be experienced. Something to be learned. No point in running away. These things would only run after her. It was better to simply turn to them, open and receptive.

"Come on," Theresa whispered to the child's drawings. "Come on ahead. Come to mama."

MONDAY,
JULY 6

4

THE WOMAN CONNECTED to the images arrived three days later.

Theresa was preparing to meet her first client of the week when the phone rang. She almost answered it, then decided to let the answering machine screen the call. But she listened as she stepped out onto the patio, a woman's voice saying, "You don't know me, but I got your number from the Simon Foundation." Theresa stopped. The phone was next to the open window in the kitchen. "My name is Ellen Carlin, and my child is missing. I've been dealing with the police so far, and it's been very frustrating. Nothing much has turned up. Leslie Simon recommended I call you. If you could return my call at—"

Theresa ran back into the house. "Hello? This is Theresa Fortunato."

"I can't believe I'm getting through to you," said the woman. "This is the first good thing that's happened. They said it would take ages to get in to see you, that you're backed up in appointments for months, but if there's any chance that—"

Theresa interrupted the woman again. "I can see you this afternoon. Can you come at five? I'm over in Venice, just a few miles south of the foundation's office."

"Oh, thank you so much for fitting me in like this. I can't tell you what this means."

Theresa gave the woman directions to her house. "I'd like you to bring something that belongs to your daughter, something metal if possible, some article of clothing, or the shoes she left behind, the blue ones. A coin purse or a wallet, something she might have kept money in. A photograph would really help. Jewelry is especially good, too."

Ellen Carlin cleared her throat. There was a silence. "Excuse me," she said. "I don't think I mentioned it was a daughter."

Theresa sat down on the stool next to the phone. She shouldn't have jumped in so quickly. *Don't get ahead of yourself,* she thought. But knew she was right anyway.

Ellen Carlin continued. "But she is. My daughter. And she did leave her shoes behind, the blue ones, just like you said. There they were, sitting right in the closet. I have no idea why she didn't wear them. She took her doll with her. She just loves those stupid shoes. That's why I'm just certain she didn't run off. She wouldn't have run away barefoot. If she'd run off, she would have taken those goddamn shoes. They matched the dress that was missing from the closet, the one they think she was wearing."

"Yes," said Theresa. "She wasn't wearing shoes because she was carried out." Theresa remembered the bed in the drawing, the bed in the car and the wheels, around and around. "Wheeled out," she went on, feeling it strongly. "I'm getting 'wheeled.' Where was she when you last saw her that someone might have wheeled her or taken her out covered in some way, maybe with a blanket?"

Ellen Carlin hesitated. "That's just exactly what the security guard said. That she may have been taken out in a wheelchair or on a gurney. That someone might have made it look as though she were being transferred to a different hospital or even being prepared for surgery."

"Oh." Theresa breathed. "A hospital." She pictured the railings on the side of the bed in the first drawing. Not a crib, a hospital bed. A rolling hospital bed. Of course. *All the shots and the tests, all the pills . . .*

"I'm a little confused," said Ellen Carlin. "Did Leslie Simon already speak to you about my daughter?"

It was Theresa's turn to hesitate. The woman sounded scared suddenly, as if her privacy had been violated.

"I talked with Leslie on Friday morning. Did she tell you about the conversation I had with her?" Theresa asked.

"No. She just urged me to call you."

She realized that Leslie had not filled the woman in on the drawings, or the images that she'd picked up on. Leslie must have simply told Ellen to contact her, trusting Theresa to convey the information regarding the uninvited reading. Leslie's healthy skepticism at work. She would never have said to Ellen Carlin, "Please call this terrific psychic I know who had a vision of your kid's blue shoes while she was in a trance state the other night."

Slow down, Theresa told herself. *This woman is very vulnerable.*

Theresa was aware that her psychic abilities could seem invasive to people, even if they had asked for a reading. She would tell Ellen about the drawings when she arrived.

Ellen Carlin appeared at Theresa's door at exactly five and rang the bell. Theresa came around the brick walk at the side of the house and opened the high wooden gate. She asked Ellen to come this way, back through the patio to her studio.

Theresa's first impression of Ellen was of softness, roundness. She was of medium height, her face large and handsome, a strong, straight nose, wide mouth, and large blue eyes. She was moonlike and full of space. You could fall into that face and keep going. Her brown hair was straight and shiny, cut precisely in a chin-length pageboy like the girl's hair in the drawing. She wore dark berry-colored lip gloss but no eye makeup, her beauty understated and natural. Her gaze was direct, filled with grief and exhaustion, the delicate skin around her eyes slightly bruised from crying and lack of sleep.

Theresa judged her to be around thirty-seven or thirty-eight, shapely and slightly overweight in black bermuda shorts. Though her waist was narrow, her hips were large, like the women in Renaissance paintings. Her white blouse made her pale skin look even more washed out. The hand she extended to Theresa was graceful, long-fin-gered—good working hands, a mothering, womanly presence, used to appearing competent, organized, loving, now fragmented in agony. Ellen's hand trembled as Theresa grasped it. Her palm was cold. She wore a gold wedding band on her right ring finger, changed over from the left hand. *Could be her mother's?* thought Theresa. But no. Divorced, she intuited. But why still wear it? She'd moved it to the right hand because she couldn't bear to part entirely from the identity the ring brought her.

All this came to Theresa in a witnessing presence as if someone just off to her right were taking notes. Theresa stepped back and took in the second look at her, through the other eyes. Just briefly, keeping her eyes slightly out of focus. Black-yellow at the center, in her chest area. At the heart, black, yellow, held in and contained. The woman was holding in tremendous grief, coping in a rigid and methodical way. For just a moment a flash of animal face pushed out of the woman's features, then receded back into her softness. *Cat. Mothercat. Undomesticated, fanged. The ragged fur.*

"Thank you so much for seeing me today," said Ellen. "I need to say

I've never done anything remotely like this before and I'm very nervous. Especially after you knew so much when we spoke earlier, about Tory being a girl, about the shoes and all. I guess it made me hopeful and, at the same time, a little spooked."

"It's okay to be nervous. It can be a little disconcerting. I'm just glad you came." Theresa wanted to add, *I've been waiting for you,* but held her tongue.

Theresa locked the gate, then led Ellen Carlin down the sidewalk under the shade of a row of cypress trees alongside the fence. It was good to have a place to conduct her readings that was separate from where she lived. Out in back of the house, a carpenter friend of hers had converted a shed into a studio the size of a small two-story garage. Ellen followed her through the lavender and herb garden, across the little patio where the wrought-iron table and chairs were shaded by a trellis of ivy, through the clumps of white roses Theresa meticulously tended, and up the narrow wooden stairs to the studio.

The room where Theresa conducted her readings was enclosed on three sides by floor-to-ceiling windows. A ceiling fan circled slowly overhead. A white couch faced the back windows, and unmatched wicker chairs were gathered around a rough wood table. On the table were objects that Theresa considered, now, more conversation-starters than tools of her trade: a crystal ball; a leathery, worn deck of tarot cards placed on a purple silk bag; a glass dish of I Ching coins. A shallow box of pale sand and a tiny rake, seven smooth black stones set on the sand: a miniature Japanese rock garden. Clients could rake the sand into patterns if they felt agitated, or peer into the crystal ball, not to glimpse the future but to see the upside-down image of the present. Three white candles, unlit, in a silver candelabra, an heirloom passed down from Theresa's grandmother. The room smelled of jasmine, the day-old blossoms wilting in a glass vase by the window.

Ellen walked to the windows and gazed out over the jungle of odd terraces and second-story porches, telephone wires crosshatching the view. One perfect, glittering strip of ocean was visible between the Venice rooftops. Then she returned to the center of the room and settled onto the couch.

"Well, I'll go over the whole thing again." Ellen swallowed hard. "I've been over this with the nurses, the doctors, hospital security, the police . . ."

Theresa held up her hand as Ellen leaned back against the pillows. She felt it again, the cat body, furry, warm, pressing forward up and out of the woman, her energy large and wild, but not in a hurry.

Hungry. Theresa felt engulfed by it. She pushed her hand at the energy, palm up. *Back up,* she thought. *Back.*

The woman receded into herself.

"Let's just wait with what exactly happened, the events and so forth," Theresa suggested. "First I'd just like to get some initial images. The police, the detectives, will work the logical end of things, proceeding from concrete evidence, all of that. Where I can help is in the nonlogical realm. I'll just see what I pick up from your being here. Did you bring any of your daughter's things or a picture? And also, what did you say her name was?"

"Tory. Short for Victoria. Victoria Margaret DeLisi. That's her father's last name. We're divorced." As she spoke, Ellen reached into a canvas bag and pulled out the blue sneakers decorated with silver and pink swirls of glitter. She also gave Theresa a snapshot of the girl. Tory had dreamy, dark eyes, slightly downcast, not looking directly at the camera, and a lopsided smile, as if she'd been caught by surprise. Her teeth were too large for her rosebud mouth, new front teeth, Theresa thought, just grown in. They were crooked. Her bangs were cut straight above her eyebrows and she appeared to be peeking out from under them. Tory looked shy, funny, unformed.

Theresa sat in a wicker chair across from Ellen and reached for one of the shoes. "We can just be quiet now," she instructed. "A reading is basically a kind of listening. It's a way of hearing outside the bounds of what we think of as normal conversation."

Closing her eyes, Theresa pictured the shoe in her hands changing into a small square box tied with a gold ribbon. In her imagination, she let it transform: white tissue wrapping paper. Gift. The box became heavy and condensed. It quickly grew hot in her palms. She set the shoe back on the wooden table in front of the couch, her eyes still closed.

THIS WOMAN BRINGS A GIFT TO YOUR LIFE, said the Voice. THE GIFT HAS A COST. AS ALWAYS YOU HAVE A CHOICE WHETHER YOU WANT TO RECEIVE IT OR NOT.

The Voice came over her right shoulder, and from within. It had been with her a long time, soothing, low, sometimes quiet for months, then coming with very clear WORDS as if spelled out in CAPITAL LETTERS in the interior air of her thinking, right next to her thick black hair.

Nothing else came.

"Were these shoes a gift?" Theresa opened her eyes and looked at Ellen.

"Yes," said Ellen. "From Tory's father."

For a second, Theresa had a strange sensation, a kind of reciprocity in Ellen, a reaching toward Theresa, grasping. Not the usual passivity of a querent.

"Have we met before?" Theresa asked.

Ellen was silent, then said, "Well, I did hear you on the radio, once. A few months ago. That's why it felt all right to call you. It was some psychic call-in show a friend of mine was listening to in the car."

"That was 'Life Lines,' Camille Taylor's show on KESP. Now and then I'm her guest, she's a friend of mine. She mostly does past lives."

Ellen smiled. "Isn't that just L.A. for you?" Then she looked away. "I mean . . . well. I don't remember much from the show. Just that you sounded smart and like you had some common sense. And even though I don't believe in any of this, I suppose you made a strong impression, whatever you said."

"And you were surprised."

Ellen nodded. "My doctorate was in the sciences," she said. "Scientists are an awfully left-brained bunch of people, I'm afraid. We're always looking for proof."

"So are we," said Theresa. "We just have different methods. Let's go on."

Again, Theresa closed her eyes. She knew the gift image was more than just the fact that the shoes had been a gift to Tory. *What's in the box?* she asked internally.

Baby.

"Are you pregnant?" asked Theresa, eyes still closed.

"I certainly hope not."

"Does Tory have a baby sister?"

"No."

Weird, weird, thought Theresa. The baby shriveled up down to the bones, transformed into a small skeleton. A tiny coffin collapsed to white dust blowing away. She didn't like this and did not want to tell Ellen what she was seeing. Don't block, she told herself. Don't judge, just stay open.

Then she saw an image of herself in church, North End, Boston. *I am two or three. White lace dress, white shoes. Mother holding me by the votive candles. I burn my hand. Mom lost that baby. Miscarriage. Didn't hear about it until years later, Aunt Rose told me at Mom's wake. "Your mother was depressed after she lost that second baby, right after you." I never knew. Why didn't anyone ever say?*

Stop. Clear your mind, Theresa told herself. *Erase and clear.* She didn't like it when thoughts and images from her own life intruded on a reading. She'd been trained to separate the edges between the self and the other. Keep the channels open for the querent's pictures to come in. Not her own.

Theresa imagined a light surrounding her own body, emanating from her heart as if a wand were drawing a protective boundary around her. She continued drawing the line across the room to where Ellen Carlin sat, searching for the woman's heart. The light-line moved through the black-yellow but kept on going.

Here Theresa stopped. Her light had moved through the woman instead of connecting with her heart. She pulled her light back, her eyes still closed. Ellen was quiet on the couch. It was like backing up a car.

Again she moved through the area of yellow-black. What did the colors mean? Sulfur. Charcoal, dust, fog. Smoke. Colors like a cloud, but thinner. More like a fume, but no substance to it. She tried to remain there, hold, hold, let the picture blink on. What do you see?

But nothing. Theresa put her hand—this, too, in her imagination, her imaginal unconscious—into the area of yellow-black. Her arm disappeared. Nothing past here, she thought. Her heart leapt up, wings off a still branch. Breathe, hush.

Ellen was blocking her very strongly. Theresa didn't know if it was coming from Ellen, exactly, from her fear or from the intensity of her concern for her daughter. Maybe it was Theresa herself who was over-invested in the images she'd gotten in the drawings. Maybe it was the fact that she hadn't told Ellen about the drawings, it occurred to her now. Things withheld between them.

Theresa opened her eyes, shocked that Ellen was not seated on the couch at all. She was gone. Startled, Theresa turned to look behind her. Ellen stood in the corner of the room, pressed into the glass-walled corner framed by the view of the rooftops and the thin glimpse of the Pacific.

"Are you all right? What's going on?" asked Theresa.

"You tell me," said Ellen. "I'm very uncomfortable. I call you up for an appointment and before I tell you anything, you seem to have information about Tory that I've never mentioned. I'm all set to tell you everything I know about her disappearance and you don't even want to hear about it. Then you drift off into a trance and ask me totally unrelated questions about babies. Look, I told you I've never been to a psychic before, and if it weren't for Tory I never would. I've only come here because Leslie Simon encouraged me, but maybe I'd just better stick with the police."

Theresa pushed her chair back and motioned for Ellen to return to the couch. "I apologize," Theresa said. "Of course this is uncomfortable for you. Ellen, I'm used to working with people who are mentally prepared for a reading. They've chosen to see a psychic, they've chosen me and usually had to wait quite a while for an appointment. I wasn't taking your situation fully into account, and I didn't really explain my process to you. Forgive me. I didn't mean to be insensitive.

"When I do a reading, I do prefer to know nothing at all about the situation I'm reading for. At least at first. Then whatever comes to me—pictures, words, images, voices—it's pure. It's not clouded by the intellect. But I can completely understand why you'd rather review everything first. Let's do that. And to tell you the truth, I have something I need to disclose. The reason I knew about the blue shoes, about Tory being your daughter, was that I had a very strong vision—or dream, if you will—three days ago. And out of that I drew these pictures."

Ellen looked at the pictures as Theresa explained to her in detail about the initial voices she had heard, and the images that had followed, how she had contacted her police detective friend and then Leslie Simon at the Simon Foundation.

Ellen was nodding, and Theresa felt the trust building between them. "This is just the way Tory draws," said Ellen quietly. "They could be hers. It's uncanny. She's very artistic, always has been. Even at a very early age she could draw in perspective. She learned how to sketch like this, these wispy lines. But why would she come to you like this? Is that what you think she's doing?"

"I don't know," said Theresa. "It's rare for me to receive images out of nowhere like this. That's why I wanted to see you right away. This first drawing seems to be of the hospital room. At first I thought this bed was a crib, with the railings on it. There's this money floating away, that's why I wanted you to bring a purse or wallet if Tory had one. Here are the sparkly shoes."

"Who is this?" Ellen pointed to the smiling face of the woman with too many teeth.

"I don't know. It's a giant face outside the window."

Ellen sat back on the couch. Her hands were trembling as she grasped the picture. "You know what it is? It's a billboard for cigarettes. I sat by that window all last week, doing needlepoint while Tory slept. I remember thinking how ironic it was to have a sign like that right outside a hospital window. Salems, I think it was."

Theresa handed her the next drawing. "It's not in any of the pictures, but the man was described in words as 'strong man, muscle man.' Then, in this picture, there's this car with a bed in it and these images floating above her in the background—a ship, a cage with a little brown animal inside, a castle, and a Ferris wheel. And there's Tory at the window."

Ellen closed her eyes, shaking her head, a pained look on her face. "But what does it mean?"

"Does 'strong man, muscle man' mean anything to you?"

"Not really. Her father is somewhat muscular, but he's no weightlifter or anything. No one would ever describe him that way."

"How would you describe him?"

"Forty-two, five feet ten inches, black coarse hair, longish at the neck, graying a little. Medium weight, in good shape, a runner, biker, all of that. Brown eyes, Tory's got his eyes, Italian. He's very . . . He's handsome," she said.

Theresa took that in, held Ellen's words inside her for a moment. Nothing she said matched the visual or kinesthetic cues she'd gotten of Tory's abductor. "Is she close to her dad?"

Ellen nodded. "She loves him very much."

"Because I had the sensation in the initial scene that the man's touch was not that of a father. But not entirely unfamiliar, either. Any other men in your life who are close to Tory?"

"I'm not seeing anyone at the moment. I can't think of any men I know who I'd call 'muscle man.'"

The ceiling fan clicked overhead as Ellen studied the two drawings again. "It makes me think of Disneyland," Ellen said.

"Go on," said Theresa. "Good. What else?"

"Just the ship. There's that big pirate ship, Captain Hook's ship. Cinderella's castle. The cage could be from the jungle area. And the Ferris wheel? I'm not sure Disneyland has a Ferris wheel, but they do have rides."

"Has Tory been there?"

"No. But she's begged me to take her. We've lived here a year and I haven't gotten around to taking her yet."

Theresa took notes on a tablet. *Disneyland: Call Jardine, Leslie Simon.*

"Is that it?" Ellen asked.

"There was more," said Theresa, "but that was it for the drawings. After that I just went very deeply into a scene. It's like going into a dream, but I'm awake. It was definitely a midway or carnival of some kind. There was a man with a dragon tattoo. Does that sound familiar?"

Ellen said no.

"There was an Indian. And the words 'Superstition Mountain.'"

"Aren't there mountains by that name outside Phoenix?"

"Yes, I think you're right. And there was also the mention of eating fry bread and 'Texas Tacos.' So that gives us two other states to look into, and possibly a Native American, someone with a dragon tattoo. We can have the police check with Disneyland to see if they have any employees that fit that description."

"Or the whole native population of Arizona and Texas." Ellen looked dejected. "Well, at least it's something."

"The only other notes I have written down are 'time capsule' and 'white unicorn,'" said Theresa.

"Tory loves unicorns. She has a little collection of them in her room."

Ellen bit her lower lip as she studied the drawings one more time. She set them on the table. "Can I tell you about what happened now?"

"Absolutely," Theresa said.

"Tory was in the hospital for some tests. The Kettler Institute Children's Hospital, over in Westwood near the university complex. She's not been well for quite some time, she's had a history of medical complications and I like Kettler because it's small and there are so many specialists there. Tory's always been a delicate child. There have been all kinds of difficulties ranging from diabetes to respiratory problems, chronic coughing, fevers and night sweats, digestive disorders like ongoing diarrhea and vomiting, rashes that don't clear up, fatigue— you name it. She doesn't seem to gain weight, she reacts badly to a number of foods such as wheat and dairy products. Her constitution just isn't that strong, I guess. She picks things up. We've traveled a fair amount and the doctors have thought for some time that she may have gotten something in Asia or Africa, a viral infection complicated by parasites from the water. She's also allergic to a number of things, so we've done the whole dietary restriction thing, but they haven't been able to find a real treatment for her, and she just can't seem to pull out of it. It's been agonizing.

"Last week she spiked a high fever, one hundred and four over an eight-hour period. At one point it reached one hundred and six. She couldn't hold down any food or liquids and she was getting dehydrated. They suspected an *E. coli* infection—possibly from some bad meat from a fast-food place. Anyway, they stabilized her and got her holding liquids and ran the usual battery of godawful tests on her, and she seemed to be doing better. They were going to start her on a special diet so they could do some very refined allergy testing.

"I was with her all day on Thursday. Actually, I'd been with her pretty much the entire time. She wanted me there with her. She seemed in good spirits, the fever had gone down, and she was having her last meal of normal food—if you can call hospital food normal— before she would begin the new diet. For dessert she had cherry Jell-O. She loves that hospital food, can you believe it? I don't know why. She's been in hospitals so much. She likes the tray that swings over the bed and the way the beds go up and down with the push of a button."

Ellen stopped as if caught in her last memory of Tory, spoonful of Jell-O held to her small mouth.

"She even likes the hospital gowns," Ellen nearly whispered. She gazed out over the houses, then came to focus again on Theresa.

"So I was with her Thursday evening until eight-thirty or nine, just sitting with her until I was sure she was resting quietly. Doing my needlepoint. Then I went home. Just before six A.M., Friday morning— God, it seems like weeks ago now." Ellen stopped, swallowing hard, hesitating. "The head nurse called me," she went on, "and asked if I had come back in the night and taken Tory home. She was gone. Of course I said no. They called the police immediately. Hospital security was alerted and they began a floor-by-floor search. The grounds and parking area too, but . . . " Ellen lifted her empty hands. "Apparently she was abducted sometime during the night, probably between four and five-thirty A.M."

Four thirty-seven, Theresa thought, remembering the green glow of the clock beside her bed. The exact moment she had heard Tory's voice.

"I called Tory's father right away," Ellen continued. "He lives in Cambridge. Our divorce was not what you'd call amicable, but we usu- ally communicate well about Tory, and I knew he'd want to know right away. She spends some of the holidays and part of each summer with him. The police talked to him to see if there had been any violation of our visitation agreement, because Tory had just been out there with him. She got back about two weeks ago."

Ellen stopped her rush of words and seemed to hold her breath for a moment before going on. "I need to say that coming to you is just something I've decided to do by myself. I'm not telling Joe about it. I feel that I need to have one outlet, one source of information that is outside his knowledge and control. Can you understand that? I'd like my seeing you to be absolutely confidential."

Theresa nodded. "That's fine. And, by the way, I do have a contact with the LAPD and I might be able to get a handle on how the search for Tory is going if you'd like me to check into that for you."

"I would. I'd really appreciate that."

"What do the police think at this point?"

"As I said, they have very little. They're interviewing hospital personnel, parking-lot personnel. They found nothing in the room itself, no fingerprints or anything like that. No one noticed anything out of the ordinary. There's just nothing. Poof. Thin air. Gone. My little girl is gone."

"All right," said Theresa. "Are you comfortable trying the reading again?" Ellen nodded. "Now just relax, close your eyes if you want to, picture Tory the last time you saw her, or just let your mind wander. All I'm going to do is notice what images come up in my mind and write them down on this pad. Then we'll discuss those images and see where it takes us.

"Psychics read in many different ways. They use all kinds of methods—cards, tea leaves, smoke, dreams, tossing of sticks, coins, you name it. All of them are basically methods to evoke the intuitive process. My preference is for my client to sit quietly in an open state, in a kind of listening or receptivity that we share between us. We make the opening together, and in that opening I hear things, I see things. It is actually a lot like daydreaming."

Ellen seemed to relax. She uncrossed her legs and twisted the wedding band around on her finger.

Again, Theresa imagined drawing a line of light between the two of them, connecting them at the heart. Again she felt the yellow-black, a sort of amorphous color field, but no heart, no light. She kept moving through the center where she thought Ellen's energy should be. It wasn't there.

How else should I proceed? she asked inside. Just dark, dark behind her eyes. No image, no voice. Blank. Far under the quiet, Theresa felt her own anxiety rattling like a slow engine.

LATER, she heard. She opened her eyes and turned her head to the side, listening. Saw Ellen look at her oddly. Voices in her head. Theresa had been hospitalized years ago for the voices. They didn't fit into the realm of the logical world, she knew that. Fortunately, it no longer mattered to her whether she fit into that world or not.

So it might be better to read from Tory's belongings later, after the mother leaves? she thought.

YES.

"Okay," said Theresa, mostly to the Voice, but also to Ellen. "I'm sorry. I'm still having a difficult time getting a clear reading. What I'm getting is that it would be better to read later from Tory's things, whatever else you've brought with you. For some reason I can't read with you here. Sometimes the heaviness of emotion that a person brings with them blocks a reading. It interferes. Why don't you leave me your number and I'll contact you when I've been able to do this more successfully? I'll try again later tonight, and then I'll call you to let you know how it goes."

Ellen laughed, a dry, bitter spurt of a laugh. "All of a sudden I realized that I was hoping you'd actually contact Tory. As if you could just call her up on some kind of psychic telephone. Isn't that crazy? For all my scientific education, I had this wild hope that you'd just know where she was. Grasping at straws. Less than straws. Wind."

"If my previous contact with her was any indication, I'm sure there will be more information coming. It was a very strong connection," said Theresa.

"At least we have a few things to go on," said Ellen. "Thanks, Theresa. Thanks for trying it again."

Ellen picked up the drawings, but Theresa held her hand out for them.

"I'll need to keep these," said Theresa, "but I'll be happy to make copies for you."

Ellen nodded. She looked very tired. Whatever color she'd had in her pale skin was gone now. She jotted her address and phone number on the pad of paper that Theresa had set on the table, then stood, reaching into her canvas bag. She pushed the shoes across the table, as well as a small brass pillbox with the initials *VMD* inscribed on the lid. "I got this for her on a trip last summer," said Ellen. "She loved it. She kept it with her all the time after that."

She stood, picking up the bag, and walked toward the open door of the studio. Theresa followed her down the stairs, across the patio, and alongside the house in the shade of the cypresses. Then she unlatched the gate and held it open for Ellen.

Ellen turned as she left. "There's something else," she said. "As long as we're putting all our cards on the table. After you agreed to see me this morning, I did some research, checked out your references on file at the Simon Foundation. Leslie Simon gave me some newspaper clippings about a missing-person case you helped with a number of years ago. You did a reading for a family whose daughter had disappeared and then you found her body. After that you worked with the police on what turned out to be a series of related murders."

"Yes," said Theresa. "That was me. I had never done that kind of work before. I still feel that my strongest work is in the area of personal guidance, clearing out the past, opening the heart, spiritual direction, relationships, career, money. Your basic fortune-telling."

"You don't seem like your basic fortune-teller."

Both Ellen and Theresa smiled.

"Missing-persons work—yes, I've had some success with that. But sometimes I've gotten a series of images that don't lead to anything. I'll be honest with you about that. I don't claim some kind of fabulous success rate. Actually I think the success in it comes when the images I receive stir up something in the clients themselves. I spur them to make their own intuitive connections. If that makes any sense."

"Could you know if she was still alive?"

"I might get a strong feeling one way or another." Theresa stared past Ellen at the green water of the canal. "She's . . . I already feel that she's alive, Ellen. Because of the way the drawings came, the strength and vibrancy of the images. It's not a guarantee."

"It's something. Well, thanks," said Ellen, extending her hand. She put on her dark glasses and said, "I'll wait for your call." Her sandals clicked down the sidewalk along the canal toward Washington Avenue. As she passed, sleeping ducks woke up and slid off the hot grass into the water.

As she watched her go, Theresa experienced a dizziness. She leaned against the gate, closed her eyes, and took several deep breaths. It was not as if she were tipping or the world were spinning around her. It was the sensation of no gravity, of flying down feet-first through the air at a cold speed. Like a bullet flying through air. She opened her eyes as Ellen reached the sprawling bougainvillea that dangled over the sidewalk. Ellen ducked under it.

Then the scene in front of Theresa disintegrated into tiny dots of color that coalesced into a cat, a multitude of cats, extending back from where Ellen had just been, like repeated images in a dressing-room mirror. Just as quickly, the scene resumed its bright normality, Southern California, perfect late afternoon, post-holiday rush hour on a Monday in L.A., the ground fairly vibrating from the traffic all going home. Six o'clock.

Theresa shut the gate. As the latch clicked, she knew why she had not been able to read for Ellen Carlin, why she could not find her center, her heart-light, during the reading. She was sure there were many things that Ellen had not told her, and she was flooded with a certainty that Ellen had a very short time to live.

How long? she asked.

The cypresses moved overhead. Theresa stood locked in their shadows. Was there more?

Nothing. Wind in the flowers. *Grasping wind.*

She turned and walked back toward the patio. As she approached the end of the brick walk, she heard the Voice inside.

Spoken, quiet as a whisper in a library:

THREE DAYS.

THE DEAD MAN'S HOUSE looked tranquil and serene. Lieutenant Oliver Jardine pulled into the driveway behind the two patrol cars already parked there. Across the driveway a wooden gate stood open between two pillars. There was no fence. The gate was only for looks.

He stepped over the dry jacaranda pods and up the three steps to the Spanish Mission-style house, a nice, big, middle-class spread masquerading as something more elegant, like a miniature mansion. Tastefully ostentatious, thought the lieutenant, turning to look back over the well-manicured lawn, the palm trees, the oleander in blossom, the hibiscus.

When he'd been at the academy, and afterward, coming up as a street cop assigned first to the narcotics division and then to a sex crimes, abuse, and neglect unit, he'd gotten used to wrongful death occurring in garbage-littered alleys and abandoned buildings, in houses where feces were smeared on walls, on dark urban streets, 2:00 A.M., the red lights of squad cars dizzy across the black bricks of warehouses. It never failed to unnerve him to find homicide victims in calm and beautiful places, expensive houses and luxury hotels.

He always had to stop for a second before entering such a crime scene, clear his mind. What he would see would be incongruous. It would cut across the expectations he had, even after all this time, that murder was a messy, nasty thing, that the environment surrounding it ought to be snaky and low-down, with some element of filth. Your better houses and pretty yards could cloud his investigative eye. *Better Homes and Homicide,* he thought. *Metropolitan Murder.* Some magazine ought to do a piece on the interior decoration of the rich and violently dead. Maybe they already had. This victim wasn't all that rich by L.A. standards, but he was well off. His house sure beat Jardine's sparsely furnished house in West Hollywood. *Let's say this about the guy,* thought Jardine. *He had nice flowers.*

A uniformed officer pulled away the orange crime-scene tape that cordoned off the front door, nodded at Jardine, and let him in.

"The victim's sister is waiting out back on the patio, sir. She's the one found the body and called in."

"Tell her I'll be with her in a few minutes. Has anyone else been in the house?"

"Just my partner and me. He's back in the hall by the bathroom."

Jardine oriented himself to the layout of the house before going to look at the body. He let his eyes roam around the surface of the living room, not looking for anything in particular, just looking as she had taught him to do. Peripheral vision, watch the edges, don't concentrate. Just the opposite of all he had learned at the academy. There they'd told him to go slowly, scan the room with concentration, see everything, take everything in. Notice. Take notes.

Theresa had told him to forget all that. Not as if he were sleepwalking, but looking with the edges of his seeing. Field vision.

There was a clean spot in the fine dust at the center of the cherry dining room table. Jardine stepped back and glanced in the kitchen. The back door was open. A cheap glass vase of wilted red roses sat next to the sink, petals falling off one of them. Three roses, along with a spray of baby's breath and some ferns. They didn't fit the sophisticated interior of the house, all ivory leather and bookshelves. He'd never seen so many books.

The guy was a gardener or fussy enough to hire a landscaper. The tiled area out back by the small pool showed that the man had a special interest in plants. There were clumps of well-tended lilies and some topiaries neatly sculpted into globes on skinny trunks. A plum tree by the pool was cut in the shape of an overgrown bonsai. If he'd bought flowers himself, or had them delivered regularly to the house, they would have been something like bird of paradise, odd-colored irises, or some weird ginger. Someone must have given him the roses, brought them over. And he had been about to throw them away.

It stuck in Jardine's mind: *The man did not appreciate the roses.*

He didn't fully appreciate them. They were given to him by someone below his class. Not in his league.

Jardine went up and looked at them more closely. They'd never opened, really. They were the kind you could buy for two-fifty sitting in a white plastic pail at a superette. Kind you bought at the last minute, didn't make a special trip to a florist. Guy put them on the table in some old vase he had, then was getting ready to dump them.

The officer who had met him at the door was watching him. "His sister said that the back door was wide open when she got here," said the cop. "She thought it was unusual because her brother had asthma and liked to keep the air conditioning up high. And the body is down the hall, this way, sir." Jardine nodded at her, knew the cop thought he was strange. Come into a place and check out the cheap roses in the sink instead of going straight to the dead man. He was getting a rep, he knew it. He'd heard them talking in conference rooms downtown before he came in. *Spacehead. Looks like he's in a trance state sometimes. Thinks too goddamn much. Sometimes working a crime scene, you can't even talk in the same room. Tells everybody to shut up like you're in the third grade. Yeah, but he's good, man. You could learn something from him. Walks around with that little tape recorder, whispering cryptic messages to himself. Used to be a regular dude. Played pickup basketball with him on the league a few years back. Ever since that serial thing. Ah, don't talk to him about that. Do not even bring it up. He's touchy. He doesn't miss anything, though. Mr. Methodical. Gets stuff other people wouldn't even consider noticing. And don't mention that psychic unless you want a transfer to another department.*

Jardine glanced at the collection of postcards tacked to a bulletin board, then walked around the living room, the other cop eyeing him. Baby grand piano. On the bookshelves behind the piano, a bunch of those round plastic toys that had fake snow in them and little scenes, Mickey Mouse dressed as the Sorcerer's Apprentice and a more expensive one of Merlin the wizard, in a starred hat. They were spaced at odd intervals on several shelves: Statue of Liberty, Niagara Falls, Mount Rushmore. Some looked fancy; others were just tacky souvenirs from a trip taken back in the fifties. There was one of the Everglades, shaped like an orange. One looked like a miniature TV set: Hawaii. Inside were palm trees and a long boat. And snow.

For a moment he stood at the center of the room. *What do you see? What don't you see?* An oily fingerprint smudge on the edge of a big mirror. Glass of wine, half filled, on the table by the couch. Get the prints off the glass. Have the wine analyzed down at the lab.

Finally he proceeded down the hall, stopping to look in at a bedroom. The uniformed officer standing at the door moved out of the way, arms crossed over his chest. The bed was neatly made, smoothed over. But something not right, he thought. Neatly made but the spread uneven, dripping down over the carpet on the far side of the bed. And those big pillows on the floor by the closet were supposed to be on the bed, weren't they? This place was designed. One of those beds with so many pillows you couldn't find the mattress. Someone had made the bed who didn't really know how the bed was supposed to be made. Tucked the sleeping pillows in under the spread like June Cleaver would have made a bed, the oversized decorator pillows all left in a pile over there. The dresser tops were clean. Perfectly clean. Not so much as a pile of pennies left out.

On a wall over a small couch was an oil painting of a man with a beard. It was an old-fashioned portrait, 1800s, maybe, Civil War era, the guy posed with his hand on a pile of books. Jardine wondered if the painting was really a family portrait, or did some designer get it out of an antique shop to give the impression the dead man had fancy relatives? Came from stock. For some reason, Jardine thought, very clearly, *Check into that.*

He turned away from the painting. Come on, he thought. What—talk to the guy's interior decorator, where did he get the painting? He waited a minute and didn't exactly hear a response, but just felt the *yes,* the affirmative in his chest. A *no*—he felt that down in his gut, like he hadn't eaten in a while. A yes was like *yeah, way to go, check it out, why not?* A warm, open feeling spreading out to his rib cage. Listen more to your body, she'd told him. Most of the time it will know much more than your thoughts. If your body says one thing and your brain says another, go with the body. Right, he thought. That had gotten him in trouble more than once.

But he had wandered enough. It was time to look at the victim. Jardine already knew from the initial phone call the man was in his fifties, white, and floating in a tub of cold water, face up. Jardine went in.

"Could be a drowning," said the officer behind him. "No obvious sign of a struggle. The floor was dry. No apparent bruises or red marks on him. Maybe he took sleeping pills or something. Maybe he fell asleep in the tub or passed out. Stroke or heart attack. What do you think?"

"No bath mat," said Jardine. He nodded at a towel rack, the mat hung over it. He touched it. Also dry. The man was fairly tall, silver blond hair slightly receding, prominent, well-defined features, good looking when he didn't have his eyes open underwater and his mouth ajar. The corpse did not look surprised. There was a weird sense of ease in his face, as though he'd been totally relaxed in death. Kept himself in good shape, nice tan. His knees were drawn up a bit even in the Jacuzzi, he didn't really fit lying down. Sometimes people made the water too hot, stayed in too long, could pass out from that. But no. Put there. Placed in the tub, he was. Jardine was sure of that.

"Photographer on his way?" Jardine asked.

"Yes, sir."

"He didn't take a bath by himself," said Jardine.

"You think somebody got in there with him?"

"No, I mean I don't think he walked to the tub and climbed in himself."

"Why not?" the officer asked.

Jardine bent down close to the body and nodded toward the man's head, floating just under the surface, the tiny drops from the faucet falling into the water just above his face, rings of tiny waves rippling out from the fallen droplet. *Plink, plink, plink.*

"What's wrong with this picture?" said Jardine. "First, the bath mat was not put down. This man was very precise, clean dresser top, not even so much as a nickel sitting around. And where's the robe? Where are the towels? Besides, no one takes a bath that way, with their head up by the faucet. Especially not in a Jacuzzi, with the other side of the tub comfortably sloped like that for a backrest. Somebody carried him in here. Dragged him, maybe. Have the coroner's office check for skin abrasions on back and legs."

As Jardine stood and turned away from the tub, he saw that the criminal analyst, Jackson, had arrived from downtown and stood square in the doorway, hands in the pockets of the pleated trousers of an immaculate navy suit, jacket pulled back slightly, showing a white silk blouse and a tangle of pearls and gold chains. Jackson checked her watch. "How long has he been dead?" she asked.

"Last night sometime. Before midnight. Anyone from the coroner's office here yet?"

Sondra Jackson slid her large-framed dark glasses off and replaced them with a pair of round tortoiseshell frames she took from a black leather hip bag she wore over the waistband of her slacks. Once she'd told Jardine, "I can't carry a purse on the job, but neither do I have to dress like a man." "You cruise around in a squad car like you just came from Lord and Taylor," he'd told her. "Nordstrom's," she'd said.

At thirty, Sondra Jackson resembled a DA more than a homicide cop. She'd gone to Spellman, then Columbia, daughter of a public-school music teacher and a deaconess of the First Temple Baptist Church, loved to play bridge, and kept trying to get Jardine to take ballroom dancing with her and her husband.

"You'll meet people, Lieutenant. You tend to isolate yourself. If you spend too much time without a woman, it makes you strange. You know? And boring. You've got to lighten your life up a little."

Jackson looked now at Jardine through her tortoiseshell glasses, her large amber eyes with that silver gleam, shoulder-length black hair, neatly turned under, honey-mahogany skin, perfectly applied lipstick and gold earrings. Except for the black hip bag and the holster under the jacket, she looked as if she were a CEO for some East Coast marketing group.

"Tell me what we've got here, Oliver." There were three people in the world he allowed to call him Oliver, and they were all women: his mother, Sondra Jackson, and Theresa. "Give us a little of that gypsy blood, Lieutenant. It looks real clean."

Jardine explained about the man being the wrong way in the tub. "It had to be someone—or two—who could drag or carry him in there and lift him into the tub." Then, without thinking about it beforehand, he added, "And the way the sun is shining on the water in there? Look at it. Like a thin rainbow surface. A film of oil, you know? Forensics can sort it out, but I'd say it's massage oil. Not bath oil. I don't see any here. Have somebody check for sheets, towels in the laundry, any residue of oil on them. Did the guy have a massage therapist come to the house?"

Jackson pointed a manicured finger at him. Sculpted moon nails on her large regal hands, but no lacquer. "Chips," she'd told him once, "when you're loading your piece."

"That's good, Oliver. You're in quite a witchy frame of mind today. What else?"

"I want to make sure that there is a screen placed in the drain when they let the water out of the tub, in case any fibers or hairs or anything are in that water. The bottom of the mirror in the living room is smudged. See if that's some kind of oil, too. Otherwise, yeah, everything looks very clean. But they always forget something. Find out if the victim was using any Valium, lithium, sleeping pills, anything like that. Special care printing the contents of the medicine cabinet."

"Right," said Jackson. "Anything else?"

"Mickey Mouse," he muttered.

"What?"

"I don't know. Mickey Mouse. There's a bunch of those dome paperweights, those snow-filled things on the bookshelf by the piano. One of Mickey in Fantasia."

"I saw them. We used to call them 'shakies.' Snow domes," said Sondra. "But what about Mickey?"

"Don't know." He shrugged.

It was time to talk to the victim's sister, who had been waiting patiently out on the patio by the pool. Jardine led Jackson to the large glass doors and slid them open, and they stepped out into the early evening sun that still flooded the back of the house. The sister appeared to have fallen asleep on a chaise longue in a shady spot beside the pool. She lay still, with her hands folded over her chest.

"Looks pretty relaxed about the whole thing," Jackson observed.

"She called this in about two or three hours ago. She's probably exhausted."

But as they approached her, the sister sat up and waited for them without standing, her hands folded in her lap. Apparently she'd been awake after all, watching the green shadows take shape in the trees overhead. The woman stayed seated as Jardine pulled up two metal lawn chairs beside the chaise longue and introduced Sondra Jackson and himself as the detectives who would be working on the case.

"Mary Oslin," said the woman. "I'm Gerald's sister. I'm the one found him." Her voice sounded detached, barely audible. Every now and then she cleared her throat.

"He owns a very successful antique shop, Oslin's Antiques, just off Melrose Avenue. He also did quite a bit of collecting. He has a special interest in antique toys, some considered valuable, some he just collected for fun. He also handled selected pieces from the Far East, Oriental screens and Buddhas. He was very particular about what he would handle, very specific. That's the kind of person he was and that's why I knew something was very wrong when he wasn't in the store today. He was always in the store on Mondays, doing the books and writing at his computer. He writes for collectors' magazines, newsletters for different organizations he belongs to, and so forth."

As Mary spoke, Jardine observed something he'd seen often in people who'd just found out a person close to them had died unexpectedly: they spoke of the deceased in both the present and past tense, not yet fully able to think of them as gone.

"Well, he was supposed to meet one of his suppliers at the store, to buy some things from this man by the name of Wes Young. When Wes got there, at one o'clock, the store wasn't open and Wes just knew it wasn't like Gerald not to call if he was going to cancel. Then he looked in the front window and he could see perfectly well that Gerald's file drawers were all pulled open and the computer light was on. He could see the glow of the screen, he said. Gerald never left things like that. He was tidy, even fastidious. Gerald was a very careful man and a private man. He liked routine. Oh, he had his adventurous side—he belongs to a parachuting club, for instance. I always told him that scared me, and he'd say, 'Oh, Mary, that's the last way on earth I'm ever going to die.' And you see? He was right. He usually was. But in his day-to-day life he's—he was, that is—always very precise and organized." Her voice grew soft and she cleared her throat again.

"So Wes, he could see right off that Gerald's office looked messed up, so he tried him here at the house. When there was no answer here, and the answering machine was not even on, Wes called me. I help Gerald with the bookkeeping—that's what I do. I'm a CPA. I met Wes at a wine-and-cheese party Gerald gave last fall to celebrate twenty years of business at the store."

Mary Oslin took off her glasses and rubbed her eyes. They were not red. She looked slightly dazed, as if she had not yet really taken in the death of her brother, had not yet cried about it. She was big, like her brother, but not in good shape, plump, dressed in coral-colored knit slacks and a T-shirt covered with a painting of a swan. Different-colored rhinestones were set into the cotton. The gaudy outfit didn't seem at all to go with her pale, puffy face and short brown hair.

"So I drove in," Mary Oslin continued. "I live out in Pasadena. I came here rather than going to the store. I just had this inkling. I have a key, so I let myself in, found Gerald in there, and called the police right away." She lifted her hand. "No, wait a minute. First I tried lifting him out of the tub, before I called, but he was too heavy. Then I thought I'd better just leave everything. It hit me at first, he must have had a heart attack, but something told me different. The thing that bothered me the most was that the kitchen door was left open. Now Gerald always kept the house air-conditioned. He wouldn't have left that door wide open. That's a small thing, I know. But something wasn't right. That and what Wes said about the store."

"Ms. Oslin," said Sondra Jackson, leaning forward. Mary Oslin straightened herself in the chaise longue. "We can't classify your brother's death as a homicide quite yet, but we're going to investigate, for now, as if it is. It doesn't appear to be a burglary, at least not here at the house. There are no signs of a struggle. Was the security system activated when you unlocked the front door?"

Mary shook her head. "No, but that wasn't unusual. He didn't turn it on if he was home during the day. Only at night, with the motion detector bypassed."

"Do you know of any reason why anyone would want to kill your brother?" Jackson asked. "Any business dealings that weren't going well, personal relationships?"

"Gerald's a dyed-in-the-wool bachelor. He's gone with the same woman for going on fifteen years, Jane Wood. Jane and Gerald, Gerald and Jane. They were a perfect match. They led separate lives and neither of them wanted to marry or give up their own houses. I think they were pretty happy. They met when he took up skydiving. Later she went on to become a pilot. I can't think of anyone who'd ever want to hurt Gerald. He was an intense and intelligent man, somewhat consumed by his collecting and his skydiving and his other interests. He did get caught up in things, but they weren't troublesome things. Horticulture, he loved gardening. Genealogy. He enjoyed world travel. He was passionate about his interests, had a small group of friends, and me. I'd describe him as a generous person. He gives to charities. I do his books, like I said, and his finances have always been in good order. Both of us had a small amount of family money from our father and Gerald invested well over the years in addition to the store." Mary Oslin trailed off, staring into a bank of irises along the curved edge of the patio.

"What about the roses in the vase in the kitchen?" asked Jardine. "Had someone given him flowers?"

Mary looked up into the leaves overhead, as if the answer might be floating there. "I think he did say someone gave those to him. I remember seeing them right in the middle of the dining room table. Why do you ask?"

Jardine shrugged. "With his interest in flowers, obvious from the landscaping here, the roses just didn't seem like the type of arrangement he would buy himself."

"Why, you're absolutely right about that," she said. "But I have no idea who gave him those. It doesn't seem like Jane would have. I'll ask her."

"Did your brother have a birthday recently? Or did he and Jane celebrate some occasion?"

"His birthday was way back in March. He was fifty-four. I can't think of any occasions except the Fourth of July, but the roses were here for at least a week. I remember seeing them weekend before last. Maybe even before that."

"What about a will, Ms. Oslin?" Jardine asked.

"You'll have to check with Gerald's attorney about that. I can give you his number."

Jackson pressed on. "Tomorrow, when you've had a chance to regroup, we'd like to speak to you again. We'll need to get a list of regular clients, associates, the group of friends you spoke of. By then we'll have the results of the autopsy, the prints, and the forensic examination."

Now it was Jardine's turn to check his watch. Christ. He wasn't going to have time to go over to the antique store before meeting Theresa. He wasn't going to get down to Long Beach, either, to talk to the family of that boy who'd been missing for several months now. He'd scheduled that interview this morning before he'd gotten the call to come here, and he'd completely forgotten about it. Why had he been thinking of that family today anyway? Oh yes. That dream he'd had last night, he'd recorded it in his microcassette recorder first thing when he woke up.

Jackson and he both stood and in turn shook Mary Oslin's hand, offering their condolences. Mary Oslin gave them the keys to the house as well as to the antique store. Jardine checked inside the house, where photographers and the crime-scene team were now at work. The coroner's office had arrived, and Gerald Oslin was carried out on a rolling stretcher, respectfully covered and placed in the back of an ambulance waiting in the driveway. Neighbors stood around outside the gates, peering in and talking among themselves.

"So, to the store?" asked Jackson. "Or do you want to interview the neighbors?"

"Why don't you do the neighbors? I'll meet you at the store about nine."

"Come on, Lieutenant. I want to go home to my darling husband sometime tonight. It's his night to cook. I happen to find that very romantic. I'd like to get this done in the next hour or two. Let's go over to the store now."

"Can't. Got an important interview on another case."

"Which one?"

Jardine fumbled for an answer. Damn. He was slow at intuition and slower at lying. "Kid missing down in Long Beach, Billings family."

"Simon Foundation case?"

He nodded. "I promised. I could get to the store by eight."

Sondra Jackson unzipped her hip bag and changed her glasses from the tortoiseshell ones back to the moon-sized sunglasses. "I think this is more important." She said it in a singsong voice. "But you are my superior and my mentor, Oliver. Lieutenant. Sir." She threw him a dazzling smile. "Tell you what. I'll talk to a few of the neighbors now, and you meet me at the store right after your interview. If either of us sees anything we need to discuss, we'll get in touch. Call me on the pager."

"You're on," Jardine said.

"Are you sure you don't have a date?" asked Sondra, hands in the pockets of her trim blazer.

"Yeah, right," he said, rolling his eyes. "I have a date."

At least he didn't have to lie, he thought. It wasn't exactly a date. Not the way Sondra thought.

He'd been meeting fairly regularly with Theresa Fortunato for almost four years now. About once or twice a month they would meet for dinner and then go back to her studio for his class. Private class. Tutorial.

As he drove in evening traffic, he reached into the glove compartment for the microcassette recorder. He wanted to listen to the dream. It had been one of those dreams in which he really thought he was awake. Continuous reality, just as Theresa had said. He'd awakened drifting down from the top of a high-rise in his blue-striped pajamas. The descent was slow and the breeze billowed out the arms and legs of his pajamas as he sailed down to the pavement. Only the raucous buzz of the alarm clock stopped the dream-fall. He'd jerked awake, flung his hand at the snooze button, then sat at the edge of the bed, rubbing the bridge of his nose for a minute before grabbing the recorder and taping the dream.

He clicked it on, pressed rewind, then listened to his own sleepy voice. "July sixth, 1992, six-ten A.M. Pre-waking dream. I'm falling from a high-rise balcony. I'm sailing down on my back like I'm doing the backstroke through the air. My eyes are wide open and I'm looking in the windows of apartments as I fall past them. In one window a man with the misshapen muscles of a bodybuilder is kissing a thin woman in a housedress. Her hair is tied up in a little bun. In another, a boy is carrying a bucket of water to the edge of the balcony and jumping off to join me.

"The fall is taking an awfully long time. I hear a voice-over as if I am writing about this dream. I dip my pen into the black bottle of ink to record what the voice is dictating, but there's no ink. So I have to scratch the message onto the notebook, gouging the paper as I do so.

Meanwhile I'm still falling. Suddenly the scene switches. School is out and we are all running out onto the playground, climbing up on the jungle gym and hanging by our knees. Jousting for position and scrambling as high as we can go. I'm eight, maybe nine years old by the end of the fall. End of dream."

He clicked the tape off at a stoplight. He'd play it for Theresa, see what she made of it. *Ink spot. Incorporated. Pen and ink. Inkwell.*

Nothing was coming. It had been a long day, he was hungry. He started humming a tune, half whistling through his teeth. What was it? "Climb Every Mountain." Now that was a sappy tune. He hated it when some song he didn't even like was stuck in his mind. He snapped on the radio, flipped around until he found a semi-jazz easy-listening station. Damn, he thought. She'd even want to know that, the song. Okay. You listen to your dream on the tape and now you're humming "Climb Every Mountain." So what is that telling you?

Dream of falling. Falling and climbing. High places. What the hell?

Sometimes he cursed the day he had begun to study with Theresa Fortunato. At one time he had been a very thorough, commonsense, perceptive man who simply noticed things and paid careful attention. Why did a homicide detective, a successful one at that, undertake to study privately with a professional psychic, to learn techniques for opening up his intuition, for "watching the edges"? It made everything more complicated. Now, in addition to investigating the crime scene and interviewing people, he had to keep a fucking dream journal. Forensics be damned, he had to wonder why "Climb Every Mountain" was running through his head in the remnants of rush-hour traffic. And he had to think about her and see her and arrange special tutorial consultations with her and avoid taking goddamn ballroom dance classes with Sondra Jackson and her darling husband or getting fixed up with some cousin of hers named Portia because he wanted to see Theresa, but he wouldn't tell Jackson about that and most days he wouldn't even tell himself. He kept that interest well hidden from anyone, including Theresa. Especially Theresa.

He signaled the turnoff toward Venice, veering across two lanes of traffic because he hadn't been paying attention. Then thought, *Shit. She's bound to know anyway. She's psychic.*

But neither of them ever brought it up. Neither of them spoke of it.

6

Tory slept most of the weekend.

He had driven her out to the desert, stayed in a motel for truckers, watching TV and drinking while she slept in the next bed. Nothing whatsoever about her had appeared on the news out of L.A. That had surprised him, but he was relieved.

She woke up slightly a couple of times and he gave her water, but she wasn't hungry. He didn't think she'd remember anything about the place. He was still not clear about the plan. He kept thinking he should get as far away from California as possible, but there was something else he had to do first, and he wasn't sure what it was. Something he'd forgotten, some mistake he'd made, some obvious thing, if only he could think what it was.

On Sunday afternoon he had realized what it was and decided he had better take care of it. He'd backed up to the motel and carried everything out to the truck, including Tory curled up in a sleeping bag. Then he had headed back to the city, taken care of the situation, and driven out again. It was strange, the way he felt invisible. As if no one could see him at all. It seemed as if they could move through time and space unseen. He knew that wouldn't last, though.

They had stayed Sunday night at a KOA campground. He slept in the truck and Tory was still back in the locked camper, not making a sound. Finally, this morning, he'd decided to stop giving Tory the Demerol. It took her all day to come around. Toward dinnertime, he could hear her stirring around back there and he didn't want anyone at the campground to see her, so he took off, heading east further into the desert. After a few miles, he looked up in the rearview mirror, and there was her little face pressed to the back window of the cab. She started pounding on the glass and he exited at the next town, driving until he spotted a playground next to a school. It was empty, no kids there now. He parked and unlocked the camper, and she crawled to the door. She smelled of salt and damp cotton, her eyes puffy. The Demerol still hadn't all worn off. He was going to have to get a comb and some clean clothes and some other things for her. She sat beside him at the edge of the camper and yawned.

"You sure did sleep a long time, hon. You took a good nap."

"The shot made me sleep. Is it the next day or what?"

She was no dummy, that was one of the things he liked about her. He smoothed her dark hair back. "It's night, but the sun hasn't set yet."

"Oh. That was a long time."

Longer than you know, he thought.

"How are you feeling?"

"Woozy."

"Are you hungry?"

"Not too. But I'm really thirsty. Where are we? Where are we going?" she asked.

He looked up at the haze of the sky, the late light slanting golden against the mountains, then put his finger up as if feeling the wind. *Whichever way the next bird flies, that's where.*

"I have to pee." She stood, touching the truck once to get her balance, then walked over to a portable toilet at the edge of the playground. She tiptoed across the gravel barefoot, and nearly fell once.

Where were her shoes? Forgot them, he thought. Put her dress on, then right into the cart. No damn shoes. Hadn't even thought of them at all this whole time.

When she came out, she tiptoed over to the swing set and sat down on one, but didn't swing. He went over to her. "Want me to give you a push?"

She bent over and threw up, a thin line of brown liquid dribbling from her lips, then leaned against him, her arms around his waist. "I think I better go back to sleep again," she whispered.

He picked her up and carried her to the truck and she climbed in. After he'd straightened the sleeping bag and the towels, she burrowed down in her little nest, squinting at him out the camper door. She'd found her doll and was holding it next to her. At least he'd remembered that.

"Are we in California?" she asked.

"Almost to Arizona," he lied. "We're going to be meeting up with your mom, just as soon as she lets us know where."

"Why didn't she just come and get me? Why can't she meet us now?"

"She is real busy, hon. She knows I take good care of you. Right?"

Tory shut her eyes briefly, then spoke again. "How will we know where to meet her? We don't have a phone. You should get one of those car phones for your truck. My dad has one of those. They're awesome. You can talk right while you're whizzing down the road."

"We'll call her," he explained. "But we're supposed to wait a few days. So we're just going to kill some time. We'll do some fun things. Once you're feeling a little better. Would you like to go camping?"

"Mom wouldn't ever let me go to camp. I was too sick."

"Well, you're going to be getting a lot better now. You're going to be able to go camping any old time you feel like it. You wait and see how good you're going to feel."

"Are we going to that place in Mexico?"

"What place is that, hon?"

"I don't know. Some clinic with special treatments or something. I heard Mom talking about it on the phone to Grandma."

"That might be the place. We'll have to wait and see what your mom says."

"Can't I just call her and say hi?" she pleaded. "There are pay phones at gas stations."

He shook his head.

Again she closed her eyes. "I don't feel so good."

He tucked her feet under a towel. He was going to need a foam mattress back here. "We can't call her yet, Tory. She doesn't want the doctors to know where you are. They might make you go back. You don't want to go back there, do you?"

She appeared to fall off to sleep. Then, without opening her eyes, she asked, "Are we hiding?"

He thought for a moment. Then told her the truth. "Yes."

"My mom isn't supposed to hide me from my dad," she said. "There's a law about that. It's called a court order. My dad told me. Maybe I better call him."

He massaged her foot under the towel. "Maybe so," he said. "But for now you just get some sleep. I'll go find us a spot to camp for the night. And some ginger ale. You like ginger ale when your tummy hurts?"

But she was already sleeping.

In a Wal-Mart parking lot he opened the camper door and said her name, but she was definitely out. If he didn't waste any time in there, he could get what they needed before she woke again.

Pushing the shopping cart through the aisles, he picked out some clothes that looked about her size, a pair of sneakers, rubber thongs, comb, brush, toothbrush, shampoo, some sunscreen. From the sporting goods department, a second sleeping bag, a foam pad, and a flashlight. Circling back through the toys, a coloring book, crayons, a tablet, and he threw in a little jewelry set for good measure, a necklace and a bracelet of pink plastic stars.

At the checkout counter he suddenly felt nervous and started chatting to the cashier about his niece's birthday coming up and did this outfit look about right for a ten-year-old on the small side? The cashier seemed bored, and he cursed himself inwardly. Don't talk about her, you fuck, he told himself. You're practically giving the woman a description she can give the cops. He hurried out of the store with his bags and checked the camper, but Tory was still asleep. He had to get back out to the middle of nowhere so he could think.

He made one last stop before getting back on the highway. Filling the truck with gas, he wondered if he should get rid of the truck somehow and pick up something different. Inside the station, he bought a couple of Cokes and two cans of kerosene, and by the time he hit the road, he was talking to himself, window down and the hot desert air rushing in at him. "You left something back there, didn't you?" he muttered. "Something still isn't right back there, is it? But you can't think what it was, can you? You should have done like you said you were going to do. But no, you didn't do that, you didn't want to cause a fucking stir."

At least he had the cash, close to five grand, but with family life, that wasn't going to last long. He couldn't just drive her around in a truck the rest of her life. And he wasn't going to be able to just wing it with her, he was going to have to work it out in his mind so it made some kind of sense. She was too smart, she knew too much. She was a kid, yes, but she knew what was what. At least in some areas. In other areas she was blind. He'd seen her being blind. He couldn't understand it, but he'd witnessed her blindness with his own eyes.

He'd just have to make sure he didn't leave a trail. No past, he thought. It really doesn't exist. Erase it, get rid of it. It was pretty empty, all right. Not much back there anyway.

Except for what? he wondered. He had this dread feeling in him and he almost turned around then and there in the middle of the goddamn highway. What was it?

Her mother, that's what.

Ellen.

It flashed once in his mind, the face under the water, then he put it behind him. The first stars were popping out in the deep blue up ahead. He flicked the headlights on.

Full speed ahead, he thought. Into the perfect childhood.

7

"I JUST SAW A DEATH," Theresa told him.

She watched the lieutenant's eyes move over the menu. He was sneering. She knew he only tolerated this place and would be happier at a bar with a draft and a microwave pizza.

"Me too," he said. "Dead man floating in a bathtub. Got to go over yet tonight and check out the antique store he owned off Melrose. Whoever put the guy in the tub put him in the wrong way, head up by the faucet. People are so stupid when they kill someone. All the cover-up work they do, wiping off fingerprints, getting rid of dishes, clothing. Then some glaring thing like that. Or leaving a door open," he said, without looking up. "The pizza looks good. I don't know about goat cheese but what the hell. I hate goats. They're mean and dumb. What are you going to have?"

Theresa was staring at him, her mouth pursed, and he wasn't even looking up at her. When he finally did, he looked surprised. "What? Did I say something?" he asked.

"I said I saw a death, and all you can think about is pizza."

He set the menu down. "I forget," he said. "I see death every day. Sorry. What happened?"

He was focused on her now and listening. Furrowing his brow appropriately and leaning toward her.

She explained to him about Ellen Carlin's call and the odd visit they'd had. "And she brought me a snapshot of the little girl. Tory is her name." Theresa handed him the photograph Ellen had given her.

Jardine studied it, then gave it back. "This kid sure fits the description you gave a couple days ago. You say you looked into the future and saw her mother's death?"

"No. What I felt was the absence of her life. I realized that was why I couldn't read for her. She wasn't there. Her spirit had partially checked out. I got the feeling that at some level she's aware of this. Her soul knows, so she's—it's like she's split open, like a cubist painting."

"What details did you pick up regarding her death?" Jardine asked.

"There weren't any. I just knew. I have to try the reading again tonight. But it's such a dilemma if you get this kind of information. Should you communicate profoundly negative perceptions? Is it written in stone? If a person has a choice at soul level about their time of death—they might alter things to choose life, if they knew this image was strongly present. It could be a warning, you know, to drive more carefully or . . . I don't know. I don't know what to do with it."

Jardine stared at her, keeping eye contact as if trying to look past her eyes into her brain. Then he looked away. "I still can't get how you can see something future in the present. That's out of my league. I'm all for the time-space continuum, but I have to draw the line somewhere."

"They're not so separate," said Theresa. "Right this instant, possible futures are forming." She swirled a hand over her head. He swirled his, too, then clapped his hands.

"And I thought it was just a fly," he said.

The waitress appeared at their table, and Jardine ordered a large goat cheese and asparagus pizza.

"They only come in one size, sir," said the woman. She made a round shape with her hands.

"Then bring me some bread, too," he muttered. Theresa said she'd have the soup and some tea. There was a low humming in her, like a computer downloading from other sources, and she wanted to keep the meal light so she could read tonight. Then again, she'd rather forget the whole thing. Go listen to that World Beat band she heard was playing over in Hollywood. Who was she to tell some woman whose child had been abducted that she herself was going to be dead in three days? Forget it.

Over dinner the lieutenant told Theresa about his dream. He set his microcassette recorder on the edge of the table and replayed his telling of it.

"What do you make of it?" she asked him.

He shrugged. "I can't do the symbol thing. I mean, some Popeye wrestling maniac, a kid with a bucket, a dry inkwell . . ."

"Just try free-associating," Theresa said. "You said you'd planned on going to talk to this family about their kid. Can you make any connections with that?"

He took a pencil out of his suit-coat pocket and doodled on the check the waitress had just brought, sketching a fairy-tale well made of stones, the kind with the little roof and the handle to wind the pail down into the water far below. Then he threw the pencil down, flipped the check over, and reached for his wallet. "I can't do it, Theresa."

"You're just resisting."

He grinned. "You're right. I feel like an idiot, analyzing my fucking dreams. I should be seeing a shrink if I want to do this."

"I'm less expensive," she said.

"You call ten ninety-five for a small pizza thrifty?"

"It was *your* pizza." Theresa reached in her bag and put a ten down on the table for her soup. "Anyway," she said, turning the check over again to his sketch of the well, "it's all right there, as plain as day. You said dry inkwell, but you drew a water well. Kid with a bucket, a bucket and a well leads to what? Jack and Jill. Fell down and broke his crown. Two of the dream images connect up with the idea of wells. When you drew the picture, your imaginal unconscious provided you with this little drawing. You're intuitive when you don't even realize it."

Jardine grabbed the check away from her as if he didn't believe he had drawn it. "You're the one making the connection, not me. I never would have thought of that in a million years."

"But you did think of it, Oliver. You just didn't consciously interpret it. That's what we're trying to work on. Okay. Then you go from there. So why a well? When you go talk to the family, you ask them if there are any wells or cisterns or viaducts in the area where the kid might have gone to play. Maybe he fell in. And what about Popeye? You describe him to the mother, see if she knows anyone of that description."

Jardine sat back in his chair and took one last sip of coffee. "Oil," he said quietly. "You're brilliant, Theresa."

She looked up at him inquisitively. "What did I say?"

"Popeye. Olive Oyl. Oil well. The family lives in Long Beach. There are all those refineries and oil rigs down there, some that have been dried up for years. No one would think to look in those abandoned rigs. Especially if they were all fenced off." He looked at his watch. "How'd you like to drive down there with me? Help me find it? I need your help, Theresa."

She thought of the reading she'd have to do tonight. Doing this with Oliver would cloud that; she'd be tired.

"I can't tonight," she said. "Got to work."

"Yeah," said Jardine. "I've got to go over to that antique store anyway. Come on. Let's take a short walk first."

"Real short," she said.

On the way out of the restaurant, Jardine stopped at the pay phone by the parking lot and called the mother of the missing boy to reschedule his meeting for the following day.

When he had finished, Theresa suggested, "Maybe there was a particular well that all the neighborhood kids snuck into, places that kids know about that adults never think of going and never think kids would go either. Didn't you have a place like that when you were growing up?"

"Devil's Wood," he said. They got in his car and hooked up their seatbelts and he blasted the air conditioning on, a thick musty wind in her face. "My cousins and I would go there on bets when we visited our grandmother up by Eau Claire. There was a rumor that someone had once found the skeleton of a baby in a shoe box buried under some leaves. All we ever found in there of interest to us were used condoms."

"Pretty interesting," she smiled.

"We thought so. We saved them in a bucket in Bobbie Bersowski's garage."

The image flashed through her mind, an odd split-second picture of it: that baby shrunk down to bones, the tiny skeleton that had appeared in her reading for Ellen Carlin.

They drove south on Pacific toward Venice, and he pulled into a parking lot near the boardwalk. She looked over at Jardine's odd profile, the nose bent down—broken a few times, he'd told her—wiry reddish hair, receding, and thank God he didn't try combing individual hairs over his baldness in some futile attempt to cover it. He had good cheekbones, a square, strong jaw, and his eyes—she could glimpse them behind his sunglasses—were brown and intense, even a little sexy sometimes, sparkling with a consistently sarcastic view of things, a defense, she thought, against things that he was exposed to in his job, but it was deeper than that. Under all the teasing and the irony, there was actual love for all that he encountered in that world, and she didn't mean that in some blissed-out, unconditionally all-embracing way. No, somewhere way down inside, Jardine loved the black dark of homicide work. She knew he had little fear of the drop-dead chasms of people's bad sides, lies, murder, fraud, and abuse. It was a strange part of him that she liked to observe, knowing it mirrored some part of her. He glanced at her now, sensing her staring.

"What?" he asked.

"I end up doing the weirdest things with you," she said.

"Me?" he protested, laughing. "You've got to be kidding. You're the one who's weird. I can't believe I schedule an interview just because I dreamed about Popeye and Jack and Jill. What's so weird about taking a walk?"

The thick heat hit her as she got out of the car. They cut through the back of a booth selling African jewelry and headed south. The circus scene along the boardwalk never ceased to fascinate her. A man with Christ in flames tattooed on his back and up his neck twirled in circles on rollerblades as if dancing with a pigeon. A very dirty, obese woman sat on the grass wearing a "Do the Right Thing" T-shirt. At the last moment, Theresa saw she had a beard. An old man sat in a lawn chair at the edge of the boardwalk, shouting a speech to no one about the racism of the Los Angeles Police Department. She glanced over at Jardine, but couldn't see his eyes or expression beneath his mirrored sunglasses.

It was hard to believe she'd known Oliver Jardine nine years. She had called him after a family had come to her about their missing daughter. *Maybe that's what feels so strange tonight,* thought Theresa. *The similarity.* She'd called Jardine at the LAPD after she'd gotten a very clear picture of the body of the young woman who'd disappeared and a pretty good sense of where it was. Then she'd led Jardine exactly to the site. Working with him on the case, he'd almost gotten her killed. But he'd also saved her life. There'd been something between them after that, and they'd stayed in touch. He'd become protective, checking on her, making sure she was doing all right. Occasionally he would call her when he had cases where there wasn't much to go on, or strange disconnected facts that didn't add up to anything.

Theresa did it as a favor to him, even though police work bothered her. It was always disturbing and totally outside the realm of her everyday life. Maybe that's what she liked about Oliver, that side of him that could banter comfortably with some biker in a leather bar on Sunset or take her to places she would never have gone by herself, worlds she'd be afraid of, but for some reason was drawn to.

About four years ago, Jardine had asked her to go with him to a rental house where a suspect had been hiding for days under surveillance. The surveillance team had finally decided they were watching an empty house, and when they'd broken in, they'd found out they were right. Jardine had wanted her to "read" the house. He'd said it felt strange there, but he didn't know why.

He'd drawn his gun before they entered the place, then motioned for her to follow him in. The shabby house did seem permeated with a vague melancholy. Jardine kept saying it was as if the air in the house was talking to him, but he couldn't understand what it was saying.

"Don't laugh at me," he'd admonished. "If you tell a soul I said an empty house was talking to me, I'll—"

"You'll what?" she'd said. "Are you threatening me?"

"I'll make you go bowling," he'd said.

The space in that house had been easy to read. Some psychic imprints were very loud and large as if the information were written in BIG CAPITAL LETTERS FOR ANYONE TO SEE. When she had tuned inward, she'd gotten the name "Billy" and flashed on a man in black boots in a frayed easy chair in a corner. A tooth missing, scraggly beard, tattoo on the back of his right hand, outspread wings. Red, black. The picture was so clear she could have identified the man in a lineup.

So she'd encouraged Jardine to read the place himself, to see if he could pull up intuitive flashes, pictures, voices. It had been their first impromptu class. He'd done pretty well. Of course, he was damned intuitive at times, but he just didn't think he was. Theresa had a theory that he got a psychic flash first and then his cognitive side went back to look for the clues and information to back up what he already intuitively knew. She was just training him to pay attention in a clear way to what surfaced first.

She'd instructed him to go to the room where he felt the strongest pull or urge to be present. He'd gone to a back bedroom where a single mattress lay diagonally across the floor, an ashtray beside it. "What do you pick up on in here?" she'd asked.

He'd squinted around in the yellow light angling in through the ancient Venetian blinds. "Cigarettes," he'd said. "So the man smokes. I'll check the brand."

"No, that's logical," she'd said. "What's coming up that doesn't fit, that doesn't make any sense? You're getting stuff all the time that you just filter out because it doesn't fit. Close your eyes," she'd told him, "and just tell me what images pop into your mind. Don't think."

"Ah . . . numbers," he'd said. "Seven, eight, six. Yeah, it's like I can see them. And some pine trees. Okay, now I see red, red plaid. I see a red plaid shirt and . . . Right. Fishing." He'd seen completely different images and numbers from what she'd seen. He'd opened his eyes and grimaced. "Now what the fuck good is any of that? It's just me wanting to go fishing instead of doing this."

"Keep going," she'd encouraged. "Close your eyes and just let it flash, like a little private slide show."

He'd squinted his eyes shut, then started to laugh. "Oh shit . . . Let's get out of here, Theresa."

"What?" she'd asked. "What did you see?"

"You wouldn't want to know." He was still laughing.

"Come on, I tell you what I see."

"Okay," he'd challenged. "What did I see?"

She'd stood, hands on her hips, and swung her dark hair back over her shoulders. Then she'd blurred her eyes slightly out of focus and told him exactly what came into view. Breasts. "Great, big, beautiful female breasts. That's what you saw, didn't you? You're supposed to be practicing your intuition, you jerk, not having sexual fantasies."

"I couldn't help it! That's what I saw. You told me to trust what I saw. I saw a fantastic naked broad on a surfboard, sweating like crazy."

Theresa covered her face. "Are you even from this century, Oliver? Do people really say 'broad' anymore?"

They'd walked out of the damp house into the orange L.A. twilight, standing for a moment in the dirt yard.

"Hey," he'd said. "I just thought of something. Seriously. There's a sauna joint not far from here called Surf 'n' Sauna."

"Go for it," she'd said. "What else have you got to go on?"

He'd reported back the next day that he'd checked into the backgrounds of the women who worked at that sauna place. One of the masseuses lived on Pine Street. Number 687. When he saw the numbers written on a piece of paper taped to the wall next to the phone, he'd been stunned. Same numbers he'd seen in his mind in the rental house, only reversed. He took a chance and drove to the woman's house without calling first. The suspect they'd had under surveillance was there, wearing only torn jeans, drinking a beer, and watching the NBA playoffs with the sound turned off. When Jardine showed him his badge and said he was there to ask him a few questions, the suspect reached behind the couch and Jardine pulled his gun on him. He was only a kid, sixteen or seventeen.

But the kid wasn't going for a gun. He was only reaching for his shirt, which had fallen behind the couch. Red plaid. It turned out the kid gave Jardine information he needed to make an arrest that later led to a conviction. The man they convicted was named William Casey, but everyone, even the judge, had called him Billy. He had a tattoo on the back of his right hand, the Harley-Davidson wings insignia.

Jardine had celebrated by taking Theresa fishing up in the mountains above Palm Springs, where he'd asked her if she'd be willing to work with him on a regular basis on "that stuff."

"What stuff?" she'd asked.

He could hardly say the word. "You know. Hunches. Seeing stuff in my mind."

"You mean you want me to help you open up your psychic abilities?"

Jardine had stared off into the stream, watching the current divide over the smooth rocks. "I wouldn't exactly call it that."

"Oliver," she'd said. "I would."

They'd been working together ever since. And he did have moments of strong intuition, she thought, but he was stubborn. And though he'd started out hot that night, almost perfect, he was wrong a lot. He needed practice, although his left-brain, rational side was very clear and strong. She admired that.

They'd come to a crowd gathered on the Venice boardwalk and, peering through them, Theresa saw a man doing the limbo, holding a conga for balance as he went under the bar. The woman in front of Theresa had hair so pink she looked like one of those dogs you could win at the chance booth at a fair. She thought of Tory then, of that powerful image of her at a midway. But where, what midway? Disneyland? She didn't think they had a Gravitron at Disneyland, and they didn't have Texas Tacos.

She took Jardine's arm and motioned with her head. "Let's go. I've got to do that reading." He looked so out of place here, like a Secret Service bodyguard for a presidential candidate. They walked back to the car, past the leather-corset-and-handcuff shop, where a tape of Julio Iglesias was booming out a ballad of love and tenderness. One of the weightlifters from the open gym strode past them, still wearing his leather lifting belt.

"Oliver? You know that Popeye image in your dream? When I first started picking up on this little girl, one of the first things I got was 'strong man, muscle man.'"

"So? What's the connection?"

"I don't know."

"How can you make such brilliant connections about my dream, and not know if there is a connection between my Popeye and your strong man?"

"It's an art, not a science," she said. "And I'm fallible."

8

THE GLITTERY BLUE SNEAKERS were sitting on the table by the couch in Theresa's studio. Theresa dimmed the lights and pulled the white drapes across the windows, looking for a moment out over the neighborhood. She knew that black space past the last house was her strip of personal ocean view. Many years ago, when she'd first moved to Venice, she would walk down there at night alone, either brave or stupid. Many homeless people slept on the beach now, and, walking by them, she would wonder what good her services could possibly be for them. Avert her eyes, then look again: edge of the world in beauty, silver water, gulls, Santa Monica Mountains to the north in a haze. The flung-up remnants of human lives, full of whatever craziness they'd created. But she wouldn't live anywhere else in L.A.

Theresa returned to the couch and sat down. She picked up the shoes and held them. Closed her eyes. She repeated the child's name several times in her mind and waited for images to come.

Black trunk, closed with a gold lock. Pull up the lid, pieces of fabric, cloth, all different colors. Sewing needles. A package of them. White thread. Needle pressing into skin. Syringe.

Stop. That image was complete. Okay. Shots: we got that.

The pictures rose up in her mind. She didn't try to control them or make sense of them. Just let them rise. Quickly she jotted down what she saw on a tablet beside her on the couch.

Next: *white.*

White thread? she asked in her thinking.

White figure, angel white protector. Doctor. Doctor's coat, lab coat, figure turned away.

May I see your face? she asked.

The figure turned, growing large.

Ellen, smiling, reaching out her hands.

Tory? Theresa repeated. *Where are you?*

Silver, gleaming, curved like the nose of a plane. Inside a small room, hot.

Theresa felt herself sink down like a piece of gauze dropping toward the child. Again: *Tory? Where are you?*

Looking up, looking around. Don't know. Don't know where I am.

Where is this room? Theresa asked.

Small, cramped, hot. Blankets on a cot. I'm feeling a little better now. I want my mom.

Where is this room you are in, Tory? Do you know where you are?

Road flashing in front of her. Black highway, white broken lines.

What highway?

Green road sign. Picnic table. Get out in pine needle sun smell. Pee in the grass by a tree. Hungry. How far away is town? Find a telephone. Dial 911, I know how to do that. He says Mom will tell us where. When she says it's okay. Arizona? Home on the range. Maybe call Daddy. Long distance. I could call collect.

A car in the parking lot, kids in the backseat. They climb out, run down to the stream. The mom and dad get out, they look at me. I start walking over to them. Then he's there, he takes my hand. We walk back to the trailer. He's pulling me. Don't pull me, I'm coming. He tells me there's a phone up ahead, we'll call Mom. But sometimes Mom is funny. Sometimes no one's home or you can't talk to her. Right? I know. How about Dad? He's far away. Far away Daddy. I'm feeling better because I'm hungry now.

Theresa breathed in, waited as the internal word-sounds, images, and body sensations faded. She scribbled down her notes and impressions on a tablet. Trying to be exact. Green road sign. Arizona. Stream. Nothing at all about Texas.

Taking in a deep breath, she cleared her mind, went down again.

What does the car look like? she thought.

Flying a silver plane behind a black horse. I'm flying! Flying over a bumpy road through the mountains.

What kind of car is it?

Black, dusty, old.

What is the license plate number?

Silence.

What does the man look like? Show me the man.

There was no image, but a kinesthetic sensation of bulk, of largeness, hovering. Warmth. She could not get a picture of the man.

Sensation, then, of food, eating, filling. The feeling tone around the child was one of caution but safety. Odd, mixed-up feeling that the child knew she was being restrained and thought maybe she should run away. But she also felt safe.

It's safer here.

Safer than what? asked Theresa.

She listened for a while longer, but heard nothing.

*   *   *

Theresa set the shoes down on the table and picked up the pillbox. She
held them for a while, closing her eyes, but nothing more came. She
just felt a vague tenderness. Then she heard: *Truck.*

Theresa picked up the tablet and glanced over her notes. There
were places she couldn't read, odd lines in a writing not quite her own,
as if her hand had suddenly taken over. Then the writing resumed as
her own, recognizable, if messy.

She reached over and snapped on the small lamp next to the couch
and read through the notes again, more carefully. What could be
drawn from them? She had an uneasy feeling of not quite trusting the
images that had come up. But why? Was she just inventing them, were
they all too expected, the stereotyped images that one would imagine
in such a case? *Truck,* that was useful and exact. *Small cot or bed.*
Maybe it was a recreational vehicle of some kind or a camper on a
truck. Or stopping at a motel, small rooms.

Black horse; black, dusty, old. An older-model black truck. But
what was the silver about? A plane? They may have flown out of the
state. But no, they're driving. Moving around, stopping at roadsides.

The image of the mother that had first come was radiant and
angelic, all in white. A goddess-figure image. Both trust and fear of the
man. Theresa could not picture his face.

Some of that might be useful to the police. Arizona? That had come
as a question. But it was all so vague.

Theresa could try again later, perhaps first thing in the morning.
She would have to decide about Ellen Carlin, about whether or not to
tell her what she had seen earlier. Nothing had come up just now that
added to the perception she'd had that Ellen would die. And one had to
be very careful with such impressions.

No psychic she knew wanted to give out death information. People
often came begging for the future. Will my daughter's leukemia go into
remission? How will my husband's triple bypass surgery turn out?
What will come of this brain tumor? How long do I have? Should I
have a hysterectomy? Will chemotherapy be effective, or should I try
alternative therapies first?

Psychic intuitions were tricky; images came without any judgment
attached to them. In response to such a question, a psychic could have
an image of the person bathed in white light—but what did that really
mean? That the person was healed, or dying and in transition to
another level of existence?

And people wanted that, too—to speak with loved ones on "the

other side," communicate with them. What Theresa knew in such communications was this: how people were in life was how they were in
death. There wasn't any difference.

But this was the main thing to watch out for: an image of death
could be a sign of transformation, the death of a way of life. A sudden
change, even an awakening. Physical death was not always what was
meant. She'd heard of a psychic who saw the death of a child in a
woman's reading. But it wasn't her five-year-old son that the image
referred to. Quite soon afterward the woman became unexpectedly
pregnant and had a miscarriage.

Once, in her early years of reading, Theresa had seen the death of a
woman's husband in a car accident. After Theresa told her about it, the
woman tried to prevent her husband from driving for weeks, and he
thought she was crazy. Finally the woman gave up. A month later she got
a letter from her ex-husband's sister. She'd been divorced for seventeen
years, but still exchanged Christmas cards with her former sister-in-law
with whom she'd been close. In the note, she was informed that her ex-
husband had been killed in a car accident returning from a ski trip.

Theresa stood, turned off the lights in the studio, and locked up.
She paused out in the patio for a moment, looking at the roses in the
dark. She decided to hold off telling Ellen Carlin about any intuition of
her death. It didn't feel solid.

Theresa felt dissatisfied and had an incomplete feeling about the
reading, as if she'd been on an important phone call and had been put
on hold, listening endlessly to somebody else's choice of music.

OSLIN'S ANTIQUES WAS HALFWAY down a quiet street just off Melrose
Avenue. Jardine was there by 8:00 P.M. As he drove past, he noticed the
lights were on inside, though a sign in the window said Closed. He
parked down the block in front of a French restaurant where accordion
music drifted out under red awnings.

Through the front window of the store, he could see Sondra Jackson seated at a large desk at the back. As he rapped on the glass, she glanced up, peering through her glasses, then came forward to open the door. It rattled as she unlocked it. "You made it after all. What happened to your date?"

"Stood me up."

"You don't look peeved."

"Peeved? Sondra, have I ever, in the time you've known me, looked peeved? Exactly?"

Sondra Jackson put her hand to her chin, tilted her head as if deep in thought. "Many times, sir," she said, "many times. But not just this minute. You look fine, I'd say. Not like a stood-up gentleman caller."

He stepped into the store and Jackson pushed the door shut, relocking it.

Oslin's Antiques was a small store but classy, thought Jardine. The gold letters across the front door had read OPEN TO THE TRADE, BY APPOINTMENT ONLY. Oslin must have dealt mainly with professionals—designers, decorators, collectors—not the public. There were no price tags on anything. A statue of a gold angel stood in the front window flanked by two large ceramic Afghan hounds. Gilt mirrors and framed paintings hung over mahogany bureaus, armoires, sofas, and tables. The paintings looked to be of the same vintage as the one Jardine had seen in Oslin's bedroom. The right side of the store featured a number of crystal chandeliers over a long dining room table that was cluttered with vases, candelabras, and expensive looking bric-a-brac. As he passed a glass figure of a Buddha on an elephant, he unconsciously pulled his arms in as if he were a kid in a store, afraid of breaking something.

"There have already been several people here knocking on the glass, wondering why the store hasn't been open," said Jackson. "They all had appointments for this evening. All were regular customers, both buyers and sellers. They seemed genuinely upset to hear about Oslin's death. Shocked. I took their names down so we can talk to them later." She gestured toward the back of the store. "Fortunately, as his sister mentioned, Gerald Oslin was very organized. He's got an IBM 486, nice big system. I opened up a few of the documents—current customers are all cross-referenced by interest groups on a client data base—China, Korea, Japan, Thailand, Burma, France, England, buyers, sellers, figurines, lighting, toys, and so forth. Then he's got a large mailing list, contacts for any number of associations he belonged to, affiliations, clubs. If we want people to talk to, we don't have to look far. There are probably hundreds."

Jardine walked to the office area at the back of the store. Oslin's large glass-topped desk faced toward the front windows, the computer at an angle next to an antique leather blotter. Behind the desk, a mahogany credenza stood against the back wall. The wall held numerous framed photographs that appeared to be of personal significance, rather than of any artistic quality. Two comfortable chairs were arranged in front of the desk, presumably for customers.

The desk was neat, oddly so, empty even, just as Oslin's dresser top had been. But the black file cabinets to the right were a mess. Long drawers were pulled out and files were stacked in piles, papers scattered across the Oriental carpet. Ceiling-high shelves over the files were filled with old-fashioned toys, windup clowns and lions, train cars, metal cowboys and Indians. Each shelf held a different type of toy. The toys seemed incongruous with the refined furniture, and Jardine thought of the snow domes at Oslin's house. There were no snow domes here. The man liked to categorize and collect. He liked to find things, group them together.

Sondra Jackson sat down before the computer and brought up the directory for the mailing list. "Here we go," she said. Jardine looked over her shoulder, then glanced up at the numerous framed photographs on the wall behind the desk, black and white family photographs, some turn-of-the-century up through the World War II era, a few more recent. It struck Jardine again as it had at Oslin's house— the emphasis on the past and on family. Oslin obviously valued this part of his life, yet he'd had no children of his own. Above the credenza hung a framed studio portrait of Mary Oslin and her teenage daughter. A couple of wallet-sized school photos of the girl when she was younger were stuck in the edge of the frame.

Jardine walked over to the file cabinets. "Well, somebody was definitely looking for something," he muttered. "Whoever got in here must have had a key. What kind of security system is there?"

"Standard keypad system with a secret code. Must have known the code, too."

"Or else Oslin let him in. A lot of those file drawers are pulled out, but only one is dumped out."

Jardine bent to look through the files in a heap on the floor. Across the room from the file cabinets, he spotted an enlarged photo of a group of skydivers in a free fall, holding hands to form a star formation in the empty blue of the sky. It wasn't until then that he noticed that the ceiling of the office area was hung with a white silk parachute, neatly tied at the corners. He felt suddenly that he liked this man, Gerald Oslin, who had seemed at first to be somewhat tight-assed and controlled. Jardine liked this playful side of him, the toys and the parachute. He wasn't just a fusty-dusty neatness freak who liked old shit.

Jardine picked up Oslin's calendar from the corner of his desk, noting the names and times of appointments. "Get the numbers for all the people he saw last week and those he was supposed to see this week, including Wes Young."

"I'm pulling those names up now." Sondra's face was intent, and there was a green glow on her cheeks from the computer screen. He sat down on a chair in front of the desk and it creaked. The store smelled of lemons and the faint odor of good cigar smoke.

"Here's the genealogical work that his sister mentioned," said Sondra. "Here's the genealogical directory of names and first initials, then a subdirectory for each, family trees, ancestors. Did she say if it was a business or a hobby? We should ask her about that."

"That fits. He liked the past," said Jardine. He was more tired than he realized. He hadn't wanted to leave Theresa tonight, and he wondered what she was doing right now. He'd been distracted at dinner, thinking about Oslin. He hadn't listened to her when she talked about seeing a death. Why not? Because he didn't consider what she saw "real." He remembered when they were working on that serial murder case nine years ago, back when they'd first met. She had taken him to a ravine in Topanga Canyon because, she'd claimed, she had "seen" a body there. But when the two of them had searched the area, there was no body to be found, no evidence of any wrongdoing or violence at all. Until the next day, when local police discovered the body of a dead woman down in the tangled brush of the ravine. Theresa Fortunato had seen the woman's murder ahead of time. She'd predicted it. *I should have listened to her tonight,* he thought.

Maybe he should call her, stop by her house on the way home even though it was totally out of his way. It was getting so that their dinners only made him feel an edge of loneliness. When he'd turned fifty last year, he'd come to realize that the solitude he'd always been so comfortable with was now just emptiness, plain and simple. He supposed he'd been guarded all these years with women, dating them as if they were some foreign species with their panty hose drying on shower-stall railings, their cloth napkins and coffeepots. He wanted something from them like comfort. He realized last year during a brief affair with a bartender named Marsha that he never looked at the women he made love to. Marsha kept saying, "Open your eyes, open your eyes, look at me while you fuck me, it turns me on." He'd found it difficult to do. That looking was more intimate than sex.

He'd been accused by women of being numb, and he'd never realized what they'd meant. But it was true. He felt closer to dead strangers whose rooms he could enter, peer into, leaf through, and disturb. He could imagine Gerald Oslin's life. He thought *that* was knowing someone, getting the facts, nailing down the motivation, finding out why. And the dark pleasure of truth when he realized his theory was correct and went to confront the murderer. Calmly telling them, *Look, I know you killed the man and here's why. Now why don't you just make it easy on yourself and everybody and give me a statement?*

It was that moment that felt most intimate to him. When they broke out of their lying and the mean thrill of what they'd done and simply said, *Okay. I put a choke hold on him until he blacked out. Then I pressed a pillow down over his face until he stopped breathing. I put him in the bathtub so it would look like he passed out in there, drowned maybe.*

Why did you do it? Jardine would always ask.

There was something he knew about me, about my past, and I couldn't take the chance he'd tell anybody.

"Oliver?"

Jardine started in the chair. Sondra faced him in the circle of light from the bent-arm desk lamp.

"Were you sleeping?" she asked. "We can do this in the morning—or go for coffee if you want. Personally I'd just as soon head home. The ball game is probably about over anyway."

Jardine stood, rubbing his chin. "I wasn't sleeping really. Maybe I was. I was thinking." *Or not-thinking. Thoughts coming. Let them come. Receptive to them, that was different than thinking. That's what Theresa meant.*

From where he sat, Jardine scanned the family photos on the wall over Sondra's head. "I was thinking about how Oslin ended up in that tub. I'm thinking a choke hold—then he was smothered with one of those big pillows. I'm thinking Oslin knew something about this guy's past."

"Guy?"

He looked into Sondra's round eyes, magnified by her glasses.

"Yeah, male."

She took off her glasses. "What else?"

Jardine looked past her to the wall of family photographs.

"Let's ask his sister who all those people are," suggested Sondra, turning back to scan the wall.

Jardine stood and stepped back to eye them from a distance. Sondra came to stand beside him.

"Look," he said.

"What?"

"A space on the left where there used to be a picture. A blank spot." He walked up to the wall. "Yes. There's a small hole in the wall where a nail's been. See if you can find out what's missing there," he said. "What picture is missing."

Sondra made notes in a small, loose-leaf organizer, then glanced up at him, squinting one dark eye nearly closed. "It's just a good thing I'm your partner. Because you're strange, Oliver. You're strange."

"All I do is I get ideas," he said. "That's not strange." He walked over to the stack of file folders on the floor and began picking them up, riffling through them. "You're working a crime scene, a room, an office like this, you've got to approach it the same as you would an interview with a person. Spend time in the place, get to know it. Warm up to it. What are its tics and eccentricities? What do you see? What don't you see? You've got to be almost in a relationship with it."

This time Sondra lowered her glasses and peered over the top of them at Jardine as she sat down at the computer. "Now I know I have got to fix you up with Portia. Oliver, when you're starting to have relationships with a crime scene instead of with a woman . . . Wait a minute. Bingo," she said. "I was hoping to find something like this. He's got a data base for the entire contents of his filing system, both in the hard drive itself and in the file cabinets. I knew he was the organized type."

Suddenly Jardine turned and walked behind the desk to face the wall of photographs again. He examined the two wallet-sized photos that had been tucked into the edge of the portrait of Mary and her daughter. In one picture the girl was blond, curly haired, and pudgy. She looked just like Mary Oslin and was obviously a younger version of the girl sitting beside Mary in the portrait. The girl in the other school photo had dark hair, straight bangs, a pageboy cut. Jardine realized that this second photo was of a different child. This other child was not Mary's daughter.

Jardine took out his handkerchief, pulled the photograph from the edge of the frame, and studied it. He tried to remember the name of that little girl Theresa had talked about at dinner. The kid's snapshot, her haircut, an old-fashioned bob, Buster Brown shoes, Prince Valiant. The hair was the same, but he couldn't be sure until he saw the photographs side by side.

TUESDAY, JULY 7

10

IT WAS NEAR DAWN when Theresa woke in her room with that expectant feeling she'd had the other night. She sat up as the girl's voice surfaced inside her, saying "draw." She rose and quickly went to the kitchen. The felt-tipped pens were still there. She opened the tablet of drawing paper and watched her hand sketch over the page. Then the pressure of the pen was harder and she stopped watching the lines, just drew blindly and listened instead to the speaking that was loud inside her.

I don't remember a lot because I was sick. When I'm sick I have a feeling in my head like a fog and I sleep. I come up for air to see the sun and blue sky and it's like another world I want to live in. But then it just goes away and I can't find the world. Mom stays close to me. She tries to make me better. Maybe I am dying, she says. The doctors don't know.

Summers are the best, when I go back east to see Dad. I'm always nervous to go, but I'm better when I get there. He takes me to Martha's Vineyard to a green house. I lie down in the striped hammock and read Laura Ingalls Wilder. I rest and I remember my dad. I forget him in between even though he calls me up and writes me letters and sends me pictures. When I see him I'm so happy. Sometimes he comes to visit me in Los Angeles but when he comes sometimes I'm sick. So I don't remember a lot because of the fog.

I'm glad you're with me again even though I don't know who you are. I think I had you when I was little. Smaller than I am now. Maybe I was about four or five. I'm ten now and I can't remember having you around too much for a long time. Mom used to say I had an imaginary friend. I just call you Star. Little star in the black dream. I'm glad you're here to talk to and it feels like you're listening because everything is changing now. I want to remember. Sometimes I feel like I have different people in me. The sick one and the well one. The one that talks to you. And the one who doesn't know what to do.

When he came in the night and took me away I was glad. He said Mom had a plan for me to go someplace else because hospitals made me even sicker and she was going to sue the doctors and take everyone to court and blame somebody because no one knew how to make me better. She told me she's afraid that I got something bad from a sick person that's making me even sicker. That I might die from it. But she doesn't want me to have any more blood tests because it's none of their business.

Maybe I never will go home. To either home. Mom's or Dad's. I like it here in the trailer but it's kind of hot. Sometimes I'm sad and sometimes I don't really care where I go. It's hard to care about things in the fog.

When the voice stopped, Theresa looked down at the tablet. The drawing was nothing but a tornado shape spun over the paper in a tangle of coiled lines. She dated it anyway—Tuesday, July 7—and wrote "Tory" in the corner, turned the paper over, and wrote down a few key images from what she'd just heard, especially about the trailer. That was new.

This morning's *L.A. Times* sat next to the cat-food bowl on the floor by the back door and she retrieved it, spread it out on the counter by the sink, and paged through it carefully. There were pieces about damage from the quake, new fault lines running through the Mojave Desert, Hillary Clinton's speech, and the failure of the Bush administration to respond to the real needs of the Black community following the riots, but there was no mention of Tory or Ellen Carlin, the Kettler Institute Children's Hospital, or the Simon Foundation. She went back through the paper again as the thin dawn light rose in the room, but there was nothing in the newspaper about a missing child at all.

"DID I WAKE YOU?" Theresa asked.

"No," said Ellen. Her voice on the phone sounded low, as if she were standing right next to Theresa, leaning into her so close that Theresa wanted to step back. "I've been up for hours," Ellen continued. "I can't sleep. I wake up and instead of going crazy I just get up and read. I don't know what else to do."

"I was able to do the reading last night, or, rather, very early this morning," said Theresa. It was just after eight. Osiris brushed his fur against her bare legs as she opened the back door to let him out.

"Is there any news?" asked Ellen.

"I get images, associations, not news. But there were some things that came up and I'd like to see you this morning, if you have time."

"You didn't get any locations, any idea of who she might be with?" Ellen hesitated a moment, then asked, "Do you still get the feeling she might be alive?"

"Yes, that's my feeling. Can we get together?"

"How about eleven? I'm meeting with Tory's father and the police at nine-thirty. We could get together after that, here, at my house. Would you mind coming here?" Theresa checked her calendar. She'd only have to reschedule one appointment to free up the morning. Ellen gave Theresa directions to her house up Laurel Canyon. It's ironic, thought Theresa, the name of Ellen's street: Wonderland.

"It would be really good if I could meet with both you and your ex-husband," said Theresa.

"No." Ellen spoke emphatically. Then in a quieter voice, she added, "I told you, I want to keep this private. I mean about seeing you. I don't want this to be any weirder than it already is. What I mean is, my ex-husband will go crazy if he knows I'm seeing a psychic. And the police . . ."

"I think I mentioned that I do work with a police detective on occasion," said Theresa. "So it depends who you're talking to, what they think of psychics."

"Well, I know what Joe thinks. And I don't want him to know."

Right, thought Theresa. She didn't need to be psychic to know the two of them were still attached in some way. Hubby still pulling the strings, probably intimidating her, probably some East Coast big shot with a summer home on the Cape. For a second she wanted to join right in on Ellen's side, but there was something else going on. Ellen had that kind of victim stance that led to withholding of information, secret-keeping. The power play of weakness. So instead of supporting Ellen in this, Theresa suddenly shifted. "I can understand that, but why don't you talk to him about it? I can give your ex-husband the name of the detective I've worked with. He'd give me a good recommendation. It actually would be extremely useful if I were to meet with both parents."

Ellen was silent on the other end of the line. Then she just repeated, "No."

The sun blazed suddenly through the yellow-gray cloud cover as if it had burned a hole to shine through. *It'll be hot,* thought Theresa. Already her skin felt grimy. She decided to stop in at the Simon Foundation office before going to Ellen's.

As Theresa drove up on Pacific Avenue, she noticed that some part of her didn't really want to be doing this. She sat at a stoplight at the edge of Venice, where the neighborhood got nicer and became Santa Monica, and there was a kind of low-grade panic in her that was not related to coffee or L.A. traffic or being single or filing estimated taxes. It had to do with extending herself outside the sphere of her own life and the feeling of deep water that went with it. She felt it every time she took on this kind of client.

Searching for a missing person was desperate work with an element of tragedy in it. Her first impulse was always to go in and try to take over, get the right clues, put it all together fast. Solve the thing. But there was no solving anything in a situation like this. Not at the level where Theresa functioned best, the whole of a person's life, its meaning. The anxiety she felt sitting in morning traffic was about that—tolerating being close to a very intense level of emotional trauma and just letting it be. She couldn't take care of these people. No one could. And sometimes finding the missing person alive was only the beginning of a life that would never, ever, be the same.

For the police, the case was over when the missing person was found, the murderer or kidnapper located, the solid evidence compiled in order to make an arrest, the evidence needed for a conviction. But for Theresa the case did not have such closure. Even if the person was found, dead or alive, a terrible event had still occurred that would forever shape the rest of her clients' lives. Theresa's role was to indicate that level to them, to provide whatever direction she could toward the healing. Otherwise, whether the loved one was found or not, the querent would continue to carry unresolved fear, anger, and grief. It was always more than a search for clues. She envied the lieutenant his detachment and knew that her empathy was both her gift and her downfall.

The foundation office was in a modern, cement-gray building on Santa Monica Boulevard, the windows dark glass. Nearby were small medical clinics, a Taco Bell, and an auto-repair shop. A wash of cool air met Theresa as she stood by the elevator. People in business suits flowed through the atrium, their heels clicking on the tiled floor, and a fountain splashed somewhere in the blue light.

She'd first come here with Jardine two years ago last April. "Some of us are volunteering to speak on child protection laws and profiles of abductors," he'd told her. "Things people can do on their own if their child is missing, ways they can assist the police, how private foundations can support law enforcement efforts, preventive measures. Some of the work we do is to keep the Simon Foundation in the news, as well as to keep the issue up front for legislators. Tougher laws for sex offenders, more funding for battered women's shelters, better custody laws, and so on."

He'd asked Theresa to speak on the panel because people often asked if private detectives or the police ever worked with psychics. He thought Theresa's approach was interesting and grounded. Often it was a toss-up, he thought, whether she actually received information psychically, but her presence amplified everyone's awareness of the intuitive process.

She'd had several families come to her since that panel, but mostly she had gotten a very blank feeling. But once she kept getting an old car, rust and water. It was Jardine who had asked her if she could see any numbers or letters associated with the car. She kept saying New Mexico, but after a while that reading had clarified. "NMX," she'd said. "The first three letters of the license." They had run it through the state computer and tracked a number of vehicles, questioning all the owners of the vehicles for possible connections to the case. Finally they'd tracked down a car that had been in an accident, and was at a junkyard outside Stockton. The remains of a teenage girl were found in the trunk of the vehicle, which was tied shut with twine. The night watchman at the junkyard was eventually arrested after questioning.

In another case Theresa kept getting a dog, a big fish, and a mountain. She felt that the missing person was alive because the images came very quickly. When the missing person was dead, the images came slowly. They were thin but deliberate. She could add substance to them, amplify them, bring them in with a stronger frequency. In this case she sensed that the missing boy was alive, but the images she kept getting seemed disconnected and made no sense.

Eventually Theresa started picturing Elvis in her reading, and with that she decided to give up. This was ridiculous, she thought. She didn't even tell the mother about it. It was too embarrassing. But for a week she couldn't get the song "Hound Dog" out of her head, and finally she broke down and told Jardine about it during one of their dinner meetings. "Maybe the police should use a greyhound on this case," she'd suggested.

"Bloodhound, you mean," he'd said.

They'd both looked at each other. They'd tracked Greyhound bus depots in states where there were mountains, and it was so obvious it was like neon in Las Vegas. Big fish, mountain: Whitefish, Montana. They were trying to decide how to proceed—contact the Whitefish police department, leaflet the town—when the call came to the boy's mother. "I'm calling from a pay phone at a bus station," the kid had said. The boy had seen a show about missing children on TV on a Sunday evening, and had started asking his dad questions. He'd been with his father for four years, but his father, fearing the boy would tell a teacher or coach or baby-sitter the truth, had put him on a bus, given him a quarter, and told him to call his mother when he got to Whitefish. The boy had been surprised; his father had told him all along that his mother had died.

A squad car was dispatched to the bus station to pick the boy up. He was eight years old. He didn't remember his mother much, but said his old room looked kind of familiar and his mother smelled the same, just like Johnson's baby powder. He remembered his bedroom curtains with the trains on them and said he felt happy being home and liked the new toys his mother had bought for him, especially Nintendo.

But not all the other contacts Theresa had made through the Simon Foundation had been so clear. Often what came was a feeling tone of terror, dread, and confusion, or just a blankness as thick as fog on a dark road in the country. She was not always able to bring the images up to the surface. When that happened, she considered it a personal failure.

Sometimes she felt so much like a failure when it came to those families that she began to wonder, *Why bother?* After all, the clients who came to ask about love and children, mates and loneliness, money, career directions, buying houses, blocks and resistances of all kinds, those people went away deeply satisfied with their readings. They always felt elevated, directed, and awakened.

Why not just concentrate on those people? Why invite disappointment by trying to find people who were missing, often violently so? She hadn't come up with an answer. Maybe she was just stubborn.

In the elevator, Theresa studied her reflection in the polished glass walls. She wore her black curls clipped back, and a long black jumper with a white T-shirt underneath. Her arms were tan, her nails unpolished. She wore three silver bracelets on her left wrist, and silver hoop earrings. After all the publicity following her involvement in that case years ago, she'd given up dressing in white.

The foundation's office did not have a separate reception area, just a crowded front desk in a long room filled with desks. It looked like a small newspaper office or a campaign storefront for a local groundswell candidate. Clippings from magazines and newspapers were neatly displayed on several large bulletin boards. Grainy photographs, enlargements of school photos or snapshots, were framed around the room— smiling, gap-toothed kids, gleaming with innocence. "Erica Schol, at age four, missing since December 21, 1985," read one. "Tim and Carrie Wolfson, missing since April 5, 1990." "Roberta Machado, last seen in Austin, Texas, June 17, 1987." Some of the pictures were of children who had been located, some of them as many as seven or eight years later. *Found,* it was written beneath their pictures. *Returned.*

Looking at the photographs, Theresa had the disconcerting feeling that childhood was not a time in a person's life, but a country, a country under siege, from which certain individuals were taken too soon and never allowed to return. All people were exiled eventually, but whatever happened to them there marked them all their days. Children abducted were children stolen from childhood. Even if they got back, they were never fully citizens again. They knew what lay outside the borders. They watched the borders with the backs of their heads, and their dreams were threaded with black patches that spread over things they would not be asked by their own psyches ever to remember.

A large woman with tightly permed, clownlike hair came around a partition and asked if she could help Theresa.

"I'm here to see Leslie Simon. I called earlier this morning." She handed the woman a business card.

The woman picked up the phone, then nodded back over her shoulder. "Ms. Simon's office is straight back."

"I know which one it is."

Theresa wound through the maze of desks, most of them empty. There were only a few full-time staff members at the Simon Foundation for Missing Children. The rest were volunteers, many of whom came in the early days, weeks, and months following a child's disappearance, slowly dropping away if the child was not found or until new evidence surfaced.

Leslie Simon was waiting at the open door to her office. "Theresa," she said. "It's good to see you. You don't come to see us enough." She closed the door behind them and motioned for Theresa to sit down. Her office stood in contrast to the front room, more plush, but tastefully so, not overdone. A floral-print couch faced several easy chairs, and a wooden rocking chair. Her desk was at the far end of the room, the files on the desk neatly stacked. Order and comfort. That was the picture Leslie Simon presented personally as well. She was not tall, wore her gray-brown hair pulled back in a chignon, very little makeup except for a bright lipstick. Her features were plain, her brown eyes wide-set and kind. She held half-frame reading glasses in her hand and wore a gray suit, the skirt stylishly short, but her legs were thick and she wore flats that her feet looked squished into.

"I hear good things about you, Theresa. People still ask me often about hiring a psychic. I think they're wishing for magic. It gives them the feeling that they're satisfying something, covering all the fronts. But then there are your successes, of course."

Theresa nodded. *Satisfying something. Even when she found nothing.* "I need to talk to you about Tory Carlin," she said.

"DeLisi," Leslie corrected her. "Carlin is Tory's mother's maiden name. She went back to that name after her divorce. So she did contact you? As soon as she got hold of us, I thought of that conversation we had last week. The things you mentioned were so similar to Tory DeLisi, especially the physical description and the color of her dress, that it almost scared me. I wasn't sure Ellen would contact you, though." Leslie sat across from Theresa in a wing-backed chair.

"She did. I'm meeting with her for the second time this morning, and I just felt the need to get some more information. Ellen filled me in some, made quite a point of it, actually. I don't know if you remember, but I usually prefer to do my initial work reading with a client without knowing the so-called facts."

Leslie nodded. "I remember your saying that. But in a missing persons case, at some point you review the entire situation, don't you?"

"It depends. In this instance I would like to. There certainly hasn't been much publicity. I didn't see anything at all in the paper. Why do some abductions get so much news coverage, while others get little or none? Was this in the paper—or did I just miss it?"

Leslie sighed. "It hasn't been in the news media yet, not in the paper or on TV. Unfortunately, cases where a custody abduction is suspected are given much less press, or none at all. It's like domestic violence—if it's within the family, there's a dirty-laundry rule. The thinking goes, 'If it was her own father who snatched her, it's not newsworthy.' Also, I'll admit that Ellen has attempted to keep this very low-key. Some parents push for all the publicity they can get. She hasn't seemed to want that."

Theresa couldn't help glancing over at the photographs of Leslie's own children on the bookshelf behind the desk. Her daughter had been the victim of a custody abduction years ago. Leslie's ex-husband, an international businessman, had taken the child out of the country and the girl was eventually located years later in a small town in Denmark. Leslie got her back when the girl was fourteen. Ages seven to fourteen, a whole childhood, a whole country gone. Gone from Leslie's life as well. Now her daughter was in her twenties, studying political science up at Berkeley, Theresa had heard, and she had an interest in law focusing on the needs of families and children.

Leslie had started the foundation as a way to make her own search for her child a nonprofit organization and to pass on to others what she was learning about missing children. When she'd first started her search, the whole subject was a hidden issue.

"So Tory's father is suspected of having something to do with this?" Theresa asked.

"He has an alibi for the actual time of the abduction. He was in Boston at the time, but there's got to be at least some question about his role simply because there was a very heated custody battle over Tory—and she'd recently returned from a visit with him. Just after she came home, she became ill and was hospitalized. Her father—his name is Joseph DeLisi—has recently filed for an appeal of the decision that awarded custody of Tory to Ellen. He claims that the child exhibits psychosomatic symptoms while living with Ellen. She has been in poor health, it seems, most of her life. Of course, I haven't seen the actual medical records yet, just what Ellen has told me."

"What's the official view? Do the police see this as a custody abduction?"

"I don't believe it's been classified either way. To tell you the truth, the police are being pretty closemouthed about it. I don't think they're coming up with much. Another factor is this." Leslie leaned back in the salmon-colored chair. Though it was early in the day, a look of fatigue passed over her. "Tory had a history of running away. I gather that Ellen is a devoted mother, but she's quite strict with Tory. The girl just turned ten. I know you don't have kids, but maybe you're close to some. You can't control them like they're robots."

"You think Ellen did that?"

Leslie shrugged. "My perception of Ellen is that control could very likely be an issue. It came up in the custody struggle. Ellen mentioned it to me herself. I haven't seen any of the court documents yet, but I did speak with Mr. DeLisi. There are always two points of view, often conflicting, when you're dealing with custody issues."

"Is that why Ellen doesn't want publicity? She sure wants to keep my involvement private."

"That's part of it. Beyond that, at this point, I can't say."

Leslie's eyes widened at Theresa. Beseeching. "Perhaps your friend Lieutenant Jardine could get the police information on this for you, Theresa."

Theresa stood and walked over to the fake fireplace. A glass vase of silk flowers stood on the mantel. "Leslie, has Ellen Carlin requested some sort of confidentiality regarding Tory? I just need to be clear. This conversation all seems a bit veiled, if you don't mind my saying so. You've been so much more generous with information on other cases I've consulted on."

Behind Theresa, Leslie stood and went to her desk, where she straightened papers. Finally she sighed and sat down. "The privacy issue . . . it does get sticky. People come in, they're under stress, they want you to help them, they're frantic and vulnerable. Then, particularly with children who've been fought over in custody battles, you start finding out things. On both sides.

"There was a woman, for instance, in another state, a psychiatrist. She claimed her ex-husband had sexually abused both their daughter and son on visitations. She couldn't get a court order to restrict the ex-husband's visitations on the basis of the evidence they had, so she kidnapped her own children and went into hiding for several years. Eventually she was found, arrested, and convicted. The judge awarded custody to the father. The jury thought there was proof that the woman was fabricating the sexual abuse stories. But who's to tell? The jury, I guess. As for me, I deal with people fresh in their anguish over a missing child. I tend to take them all at face value, I believe in them all, it's true. I guess it's because I was once in their shoes."

Theresa was quiet. She knew that Leslie was going to tell her more.

Leslie sighed. "What I'm trying to say is that there are definitely some questions about the whole situation. It's not so simple as a wonderful close family, a stranger abduction. It feels sticky. That's my feeling, but until I get more substantial background information, my hands are a bit tied. Tory could have run on her own, is what I'm saying. And if that's the case, if she's seen as a runaway, the resources for finding her become much less available. From the standpoint of the police as well as the media."

"But why would Ellen be resistant to publicity in any case, whether Tory is a runaway or has been abducted?"

"I think Ellen is resistant because she fears that her mothering will be scrutinized, as apparently it was in the custody case. That's why she moved to California from the East Coast last year, to get away from all of that. Apparently her ex-husband was ruthless in trying to get Tory from her." Leslie made some notes on a pad of yellow legal paper. "So are you going to work with her?" Leslie asked.

"I already am," said Theresa. "I'm picking up on that same resistance you're speaking of, and an equally strong and very authentic longing for her kid. Resistance and longing is exactly the quality. And because of that, the reading I did with Ellen was very odd, something like a writer's block. A psychic block. But only when I read for Ellen. When I read from Tory's belongings, something different happens."

"How is it different?"

Theresa hesitated. No matter how supportive or open to her work people appeared to be, Theresa was never quite sure how much to tell them. "I get Tory directly. She's channeling to me, or through me, speaking directly."

Leslie stood abruptly, slipped her hands in her suit jacket pockets. "And?"

Theresa continued. "I don't know where she is. I have some images, a description of a vehicle, a possible direction. My sense is that the girl is alive. And because of *my* client confidentiality, I need to go over this stuff with Ellen first. I need her permission to communicate my findings to you and to the police. I didn't even tell her I was coming here to talk with you."

Leslie shook her head, not sure she understood. "You say the girl is talking to you psychically?"

"She's drawing and writing and seeing through me. I hear her thinking. My sense is that she is even somewhat aware that she is doing this. She senses that there is a communication involved. Someone listening."

"Well." Leslie crossed the room. "You know, I did hire two psychics when I was searching for my daughter, and I never felt that either of them had much to offer. Anyway, nothing came of whatever they did offer. I know you and Lieutenant Jardine have been able to work together in a useful way. And my commitment is to doing whatever I can to find Tory DeLisi. I must say I don't know what to think of some of the things you've told me, but I do want your help. I don't have to be a believer, do I?"

Theresa smiled. "Thanks, Leslie."

"And I hope that when you get Ellen's okay, you'll share your information, in whatever form, with us at the foundation."

"I certainly will," said Theresa. "And in the meantime I'd recommend a background search on both parents. Especially the court documents on the custody suit and Tory's medical records."

"I think the police are taking care of that. Thanks, Theresa." Leslie opened the door for her.

Theresa turned back and said, "Another area to look into would be anything regarding money. Money left to her by a grandparent, for instance, that would be awarded to a custodial parent in the event of the child's death. Trusts, inheritances, that sort of thing."

"I understand." Leslie held out her hand again to Theresa, and she shook it. As she left the Simon Foundation, Theresa had the fragrance of roses in her mind and a picture of a green gate, opening.

"'CAUSE OF DEATH: suffocation. Time of death: Sunday, July fifth, nine to nine-thirty P.M.'" Jardine read aloud from the medical examiner's report on Gerald Oslin in a muttering breath, almost as if he were reading to himself. Sondra Jackson stared past him through the venetian blinds, a clipboard open on her lap. She jotted down notes as he continued.

"It was not a drowning, no water deep in the lungs. Had probably been in the water about seventeen hours. No indication of any drugs, medications of any kind in the bloodstream. Small amount of alcohol. No indication of sexual intercourse. No abrasions on lower back or backs of legs . . . "

Jardine broke off. "I asked them to check for that specifically, to look for signs that somebody dragged him across the bathroom tiles. So whoever moved him had to have been pretty good-sized. They carried him. Oslin wasn't a small man. Could have been more than one person." Jardine stopped to think it through. "Okay. Let's say he applies a choke hold—not choking Oslin, but causing him to pass out. Like a wrestler."

Jackson added, "What about a Shiatsu pressure point? Or some kind of martial-arts move? There are places on the body that you just press on or strike and the person blacks out."

"Right. So he's smothered after he's already out cold. That's why there's not much sign of a struggle."

He stopped for a moment, then went on. "Residue of lotion on the skin, but it was not any kind of massage oil. Possibly a muscle cream such as Deep Heat, something containing camphor." Jardine leaned back in his desk chair and his head rattled the blinds behind him. He trailed off, trying to think, but no thoughts came, so he watched the thin line of a cobweb dangle off one end of the fluorescent light. He liked getting the medical examiner's report, the specific information of death that the body revealed, a message the dead had left for him. Read it and weep, he thought. But it didn't make him sad, not really. Maybe it was the scientific language, the official-looking sheet the findings were written on. He didn't think of himself as a cold person, but maybe he was.

When he looked up, he knew he'd been dreaming again, mind wandering to nothing. Sondra Jackson twirled her pen in her fingers, staring at him. "Well, you were right about the cause of death. You said it wasn't a drowning. It could have been any number of things, electrocution, heart attack, stroke, overdose. You said suffocation. How did you know?" Sondra asked.

Jardine thought about it for a minute. Was that an intuition, that daydream conversation in his head last night, almost falling asleep in the chair in Oslin's office?

"Well, I knew last night he did not get into that tub by himself, that he was likely moved in there. There were no obvious signs of struggle in either the bedroom or the bathroom—so that means he was probably unconscious or already dead. I guessed dead."

"But why wouldn't you have guessed that he had passed out in the tub and then drowned? That would've been the first thing I'd have thought."

He shrugged. Had it been just an educated guess, then? And what was the difference between that and an intuitive flash? "I figured even a person who was drunk or high would get in the bathtub the way he always did, leaning back against the slope of the tub with his feet by the faucet. It's habit. It's logical."

"So who killed him, Mr. Wizard?" Jackson prompted.

"A massage therapist, a personal trainer, somebody knowledgeable in esoteric Asian medicine, somebody he would have let give him a rubdown, work on a sore shoulder. Somebody Oslin would have let right into his home, no problem."

"What's the motivation?"

"Something in his office files, right? But the damnedest thing is that I want to say it was all because of those roses."

"What roses?"

"The cheap-ass wilted roses by the sink in Oslin's kitchen."

"That doesn't sound particularly logical," Jackson offered.

No, he thought, it didn't. But then he changed his mind. "It's backwards logic. The roses didn't fit. They were out of place, given his taste in horticulture. I look for things that seem odd, and the roses seemed odd, but I have no idea what the connection is. And last night when I stepped back and looked at the wall and saw that space where a picture was missing—sometimes evidence is in what you *don't* see. As in, 'What's wrong with this picture?' "

"Too bad evidence that's missing isn't admissible in a court of law, Oliver."

"Then there's the girl, his having that picture of her." He had tried to reach Theresa about that this morning, but she'd already had her answering machine on.

"Did Rukheyser say it's the same girl?" Jackson asked.

Jardine glanced at his watch. "Don't know yet. He's not due back until eleven. If it's the same kid, it's going to get complicated."

Jackson glanced down at her notes. "I think I'll go back to the store and get into those files. See if I can pinpoint what's missing by cross-referencing the data base with the filing cabinets' contents."

Jardine nodded. "I'd like you to interview a few more of Oslin's neighbors first. I'm going to talk with Mary Oslin again. She's meeting me at the store. I'll come back here to meet with Rukheyser and then I'm going to try to see Oslin's girlfriend. She flew back in this morning from Hawaii. Why don't we meet up at the store later."

When Jardine arrived at the antique store, he could see Mary Oslin sitting in an upholstered chair near the front window. She was staring in an empty way at a display of Buddha figurines. The Closed sign near the door faced outward, and Mary Oslin rose to open the door for him.

Immediately he noticed that since he'd seen her yesterday afternoon, she'd had the time and the privacy in which to fall apart. Her fleshy face was blotchy and red from crying. She hadn't bothered with lipstick. She was dressed in bright yellow pants and a floral-print shirt, but the outfit seemed incongruous with the grief in her expression.

"Come in, Lieutenant Jardine." Mary Oslin turned and walked to the back of the store, gracefully lowering her fleshy frame into a chair that faced Oslin's desk. "I took the day off work." She sighed a full, long breath. "My mother's flying down from Oregon this afternoon. I still can't believe any of this. It didn't hit me yesterday at all. I thought I was just in a bad dream or something." She folded her thick fingers in her lap. Jardine sat down beside her in a matching chair.

As Jardine reviewed the medical examiner's report with her, she frowned as if she were very angry with the findings and disagreed completely with the official report and the way it had been conducted, as well as with the entire Los Angeles Police Department. But he knew that she was deeply angry about her brother's unnecessary death.

"And that open back door—your brother may have had the door open or been out in the backyard when someone entered. Or he could have let them in the front door, and the back door might have been left open as the person or persons exited. Because of these things, and because there was nothing to indicate a typical burglary, we are assuming, for now, that this could have been someone he knew and trusted. It may have been a person he had some kind of physical relationship with. Not necessarily sexual, but we can't preclude that either. The traces of a camphor-type lotion suggest the possibility of a massage. There were no listings in his home address book for massage therapists specifically, but he might have listed them simply by name. Did he ever mention going to one, having one come to his house?"

Jardine handed her Oslin's pocket-size address book and she paged through it, shaking her head.

"Let me see his Rolodex," she said, and Jardine reached across the glass desk and handed it to her. After flipping through the cards, she went to the computer and turned it on. "With Ger, the best thing is to look for a data base. He loved data bases, they fit his mind, the organizing and cross-referencing of everything."

Jardine stood behind her as she opened up the directory and did a text search, typing in MASSAGE. Several names came up: Hands On Massage, Philip Brown; Tom Vang, Certified Licensed Massage Therapist and Sports Massage Practitioner; Sandy Spohn, Massage Therapist, Pacific Fitness Center. All three were located in the Santa Monica area.

"This ought to help," said Mary Oslin. "Ger was very active. He swam, played racquetball, worked out with all that Nautilus stuff. He tried running, but complained about his knees. I think he saw some kind of naturopath or chiropractor occasionally. Let's see."

Again she followed the procedure for text search in the address directory, coming up with names of two chiropractors and a number of doctors, one a naturopath. Mary Oslin printed out the names and addresses of all of them for Jardine.

"It would be in character for Ger to have seen any of these people. He was health-conscious, especially with the asthma and all. But I can't see any of them coming to his house. That seems weird. And even if a massage therapist did come to the house, why would they kill him if nothing was stolen? What would the motivation be? You're suggesting some kind of affair, maybe?"

"It's just a line of inquiry. And it could be that something was stolen. We haven't ruled that out. It just didn't look like your typical burglary where they go through drawers, trash the place, take the television, stereo, and so on." Jardine paused a moment before asking the next question. "Did your brother ever have relationships with men?"

"If he did, I sure didn't know about it. Like I said, he'd been with Jane for years, monogamous as far as I know. No, if he had some kind of secret life, that's what it was—secret."

Jardine picked up Gerald Oslin's calendar, examining it for scheduled appointments with any of the names on the computer printout. He did not find any.

"Why men?" asked Mary. "What makes you think that?"

"Just that he was probably carried to the tub, so that means it was someone pretty strong."

Jardine explained his theory to her, the one he and Sondra had gone over this morning. Mary listened quietly, looking down and slightly to the side, not sure she wanted to hear all this. After he finished she was silent for a time.

Mary pushed the chair back from the computer and sighed. "He was always taking vitamins, all that health-fiend stuff. He wanted to live a long time and he thought he would. Homeopathic remedies, Chinese herbal formulas. I think he even saw an acupuncturist once, but he didn't like the needles."

"Could you check to see if the acupuncturist is on the computer? Do you know where he got the herbal formulas?"

Once again Mary scanned the directory, shaking her head. "Nothing under acupuncture or herbs, and under 'China, Chinese,' there are just listings for Oriental rugs, screens, and so on. Items for the store here."

"Let me have a list of his contacts in that area," Jardine requested. He stood and went behind the desk to the wall of photographs. He pointed to the portrait of Mary and her daughter. "Is this your daughter?" he asked.

She nodded. "Hannah. She's twenty-five now and has a daughter who's three. I'm a grandmother. I raised her on my own. I was married briefly in my twenties."

Jardine handed her the other girl's school photo. "Do you recognize her?"

She regarded it, then said no.

"I found this picture last night, wedged right in here next to your daughter's school photo."

"I've never seen her before. I suppose it could be the child of one of his clients or friends, someone I'm not familiar with. But it isn't someone I'm aware of."

"A lot of family photographs. Your brother seemed a bit obsessed with the past. It was almost a theme for his life, wouldn't you say? Collecting old books, antiques, toys, the portraits in his home. Was the one in his bedroom a family member? An ancestor?"

"Great-grandfather on our father's side. Bankrupt lumber baron." Mary reached over beside her for a pack of cigarettes. "I'm going to smoke for two weeks," she announced. "Then I'm quitting again." She snapped a lighter and inhaled.

"Yes, the past was Gerald's theme." Mary Oslin smiled briefly. "I never thought of it that way. When Mom moved out of the big house after Dad died, Gerald wanted all those paintings and photographs and the big furniture. I go for the modern stuff myself. But Gerald, he was always looking for some kind of identity in the past, as if that would give him substance. I wouldn't say he was stuck in the past. I wouldn't call it an obsession, but an interest. He lived for the present. You could see it in his skydiving and his travels. And he never seemed to want to marry or have children of his own. Never seemed to have an interest in leaving a legacy behind. I think maybe all that interest in the past, as you call it, took the place of having his own family. That was how he created a sense of family."

Mary drew in hard on the skinny cigarette, and tapped it in a glass ashtray.

"Gerald's interest in genealogies—we found a directory of files on the hard drive. Was that a sideline?" Jardine asked.

"Oh, that. Yes, he was really getting into that. It was a hobby at first, but then he started to charge for it. And you know, now that I think of it—his interest in the past—it's funny because Gerald and I were both adopted. We didn't find out until after our dad died. Mom finally told us. Said she'd always wanted to, but Dad had made her promise she never would. It was all so secretive back then. See, Gerald had done our family tree. He was so into his roots, you know—the Dutch side and the German and the Welsh. And here comes Mom finally saying, 'Honey, I hate to tell you this, but none of that is actually your background.' I think she wanted to free him up to find out who he really was. He'd been searching all that time and thought he had it nailed down, but that wasn't him at all. Well, that sent him off on an altogether new tangent. Looking for his birth mother and then doing her genealogy. Funny—I think he was more interested in the research than in actually meeting her."

"So he did find her?"

"I guess it wasn't all that hard. Mom told us what agency she'd used, and they helped him. His birth mother was a teacher, retired, never married. She'd had an affair and gotten pregnant. This was in the thirties. She took a sabbatical and traveled for a year. That's what she told all her family and friends. But actually she came down here to L.A. and had Gerald. Our parents, our adoptive folks, lived down here then and got us both through an agency here in L.A. But the weird part of it all was this genealogy thing. Gerald's birth mother—her name was Miss Betty Tucker—that was what Gerald always called her, Miss Betty Tucker—she told him something and made him promise he'd never tell a soul. Another deep family secret. And he didn't tell, but I came across the records once when I was looking for some financial information on the hard drive."

"And what was that?"

"Gerald's real father—his birth father—and Miss Betty Tucker had the same family tree. They were first cousins." Mary eyed the collection of photographs. "There she is, Miss Betty Tucker. I thought he had at least one picture of her." She stood and pointed to a small framed picture of a smiling young woman with a pearl necklace.

Jardine asked Mary Oslin to retrieve the files for the family trees of Miss Betty Tucker and her cousin and print them out. He stood behind her as she typed in the commands.

"Could any of that possibly have to do with Gerald getting killed?" Mary Oslin asked.

"It could," said Jardine. "Maybe somebody else got hold of that information and was threatening him with it. Or maybe he was going to tell somebody."

"But why would it matter?" Mary pulled the papers out of the printer and gave them to Jardine.

"Is Miss Tucker still around?" he asked.

"She died about two years ago."

"What about her family, her cousin, Gerald's father?"

"I wouldn't know. I never even met Miss Betty Tucker, I just heard about her. But it seems farfetched that someone would kill Ger for a reason like that. It was all so long ago."

Jardine made a note in his small notepad. "Well, one reason could be money, inheritances, that sort of thing. Insurance policies. Did Gerald receive any money from her will?"

Mary had become pensive again. "I have no idea. He never mentioned it."

"What about you?" asked Jardine. "Did you ever look up your birth mother? Did Gerald do a genealogy for you?"

"You know, I could care less about all that. My adoptive family *is* my family. I live in the present, not the past. I don't consider bloodline my true identity. It's who you are in here." She touched her chest with a manicured nail. "That's who a person is. It's how you live your life."

Jardine showed her the pinpoint hole in the wall where a picture had once hung. He asked her if she knew what had been there. She stared at the wall for a moment, then said, "I do. There was a picture of Gerald in his navy uniform. I wonder what happened to it."

Jardine made some notes about their conversation, and Mary crossed the store. She sat down again in the chair by the window. For the first time he noticed that she was pretty. Her features were plain but fine. Anyway, it wasn't so much in her face as the way she moved,

like a dancer under a layer of flesh. He bet she was warm and generous in bed.

He slapped his notebook shut. It was definitely getting to be too
long since he'd been with a woman. He thought of looking up Marsha,
the bartender, again, trying harder to pay attention to her. He'd look
her straight in the eye while she moaned *yes, yes.* First Theresa and
now Mary Oslin, sister of the homicide victim he was investigating.
You lonely, horny goddamn sonofabitch, he thought.

"Here's Wes," said Mary, rising to unlock the door for a large, red-faced
man with unruly blond hair that resembled a thatched roof. He clam-
bered in, set down his briefcase, and gave Mary Oslin a big hug. With
that she began to cry, sobbing silently against Wes Young's shirt. He
let her cry for a minute, then comforted her and gave her his handkerchief.

Jardine introduced himself, and Wes Young plunked himself down
in one of the delicate antique chairs. He seemed a giant in a shop of
miniatures, and it made Jardine nervous to watch him wend his way
through the figurines and vases. He had to be at least six-four. Young
told Jardine how he had come to the store for his appointment with
Oslin, peered in and seen the mess in the back, and called Mary at
once.

"It's hard to take in," said Wes, glancing around the store. He had
an odd voice; it sounded like the radio announcer advertising agricul-
tural products that Jardine remembered from his Wisconsin childhood.

"What is it that you sold to Mr. Oslin or purchased from him?"
asked Jardine.

"I'm the Buddha man. Occasionally I have some carpets, antique
chests, painted screens, but mostly it's these fellas." Wes Young rose
quickly and grabbed a small ceramic figure from the table. He turned
to Mary. "Remember how Gerald would tease me, saying I was the
least likely Zen student he could imagine?" He turned back to Jardine.
"I read Gary Snyder back in college and I was stationed in the Philippines in the service. Just got interested in things Far Eastern and set
up my life so I could do a lot of traveling."

Jardine handed him the list of health practitioners he had printed
out, and asked him if he recognized any of the names. Wes pointed to
Tom Vang. "I gave him that name."

"Does he sell any herbal formulas, Chinese potions or medications?"

"Tom Vang? I don't think he actually sells them, but he'll recommend things if you ask him. You can get that kind of stuff at any good health-food store. I don't know if Gerald took any supplements or not. We mainly talked business."

Jardine glanced at his watch. If he wanted to catch Rukheyser, he had better head back downtown. He gave his card to Wes Young. "Call me if you think of anything pertaining to the questions I've asked you."

He thanked both of them for their time, and all three of them left the store together. As he unlocked his car, Jardine turned back to look at them. Wes Young was leaning down to give Mary Oslin a kiss.

HE ASKED TORY TO WAIT QUIETLY while he finished up with the paperwork.

"She can come in with us, no problem," the salesman said. "She's quiet enough."

"I think she'd rather just play out in the trailer. She thinks it's her own personal dollhouse."

He followed the salesman into the small office, the front door open, and sat opposite the desk. The parking lot outside was filled with Great Deals!, Fabulous Buys!, and Drive Me Homes! Tattered plastic streamers hung limply from a wire stretched over the used cars, not blowing in the wind because there wasn't any wind.

"You're really going to enjoy that little honey. And your wife is going to appreciate that kitchen in there, it is totally functional."

"We're not actually married yet," he said. He'd been going on about his "other half," nervous again and talking too much. "We haven't gotten around to setting the date quite yet."

"Well, when you do, why, you can honeymoon in your trailer out there and save yourselves quite a bundle. Now just give me your John Hancock right where I've put all those red x's and we'll be all set."

He counted out the cash in the amount they'd agreed on, signed

at all the x's and handed the salesman the registration for the
camper truck. The salesman said he'd be right back with the keys.
He was glad he'd gotten rid of the Pinto, paying that old man in a bar
last week, two hundred bucks and the Pinto for his raggedy camper
truck. But this was going to be sweet, just like the salesman promised.

Only 80,000 Miles! was scrawled on the front window of the pickup
in white paint. Glancing out the door, he saw Tory sitting in the trailer
at the dinette table that folded down into a bed easy as pie.

Much better, he thought. Better than taking a chance checking in
and out of a lot of motels. He wished he did have a girlfriend, it
occurred to him suddenly. It would look a lot more normal, more like a
natural family, and he wouldn't feel that he had to justify why he had
this little girl with him. He surely had never thought he'd want to
remarry, but it might be good for Tory. He'd have to keep his eyes open
for someone. It might even be real nice, he thought. The three of them,
on the road, camping in the trailer, sitting around, playing cribbage
and eating whatever the woman cooked.

It was late morning by the time they found a campground. He
unhooked the trailer from the hitch, and they settled into the place.

"We're going to need some dishes," Tory said. "Maybe we could
even get a little TV. There's a plug right there. This is so cool. I never
ever thought I'd get to do anything like this."

"You like it?"

"I love it. Mom is going to love it, too. After she gets used to it."
Tory went over to where he was sitting at the dinette bench.

"I told you Doc was going to take good care of you."

"Thanks, Doc." Tory put her arms around him and gave him a hug.
He closed his eyes for a second. She made him happy, but for some reason he also felt sad. God damn it. No one had ever bought him a trailer
when he was ten. Well, he could have it all now. By giving it to her.

"So," he said. "If you could have the most fun of any kid in Amer-
ica, what would you do? Like, say, if you were in charge of inventing
the best childhood, what would it be?"

Tory slid in across from him and looked out the tiny window over
his head. "Well, first thing, I'd have my mom and dad love each other.
I'd live with both of them again at Dad's summer house and we'd live
there all the time, all year long, and I'd take gymnastics and have a
blue and white leotard that was kind of shiny and we'd have horses of

our very own to ride, a black and white spotted one for me and I'd name her Dancer and—"

"Now that's all a fantasy, Tory," Doc interrupted.

Her face changed suddenly, the brightness in her eyes flattening. "I thought that's what you said."

"It's okay to have a fantasy," he said, "but it should be something you can actually do. You know your mom and dad aren't getting back together. But it would be possible to live with both a mom and a dad, it just wouldn't have to be Ellen and your dad, right?"

She picked at her fingernail. "I guess so," she said. "Like when Mom almost got married again, but it didn't last very long."

"Know what I'd do if I could make the best childhood?"

"What?"

"I'd do something totally fun every single day."

"Like what?"

"First day, I'd go to a baseball game and eat hot dogs and drink beer and—"

"You can't drink beer if you're a kid!" Tory laughed and pointed at him.

"Okay then, lemonade, okay? Next day, I'd go . . . "

"To the zoo," she suggested.

"Yeah," he said, "the zoo. Now you got it. You could think of something like that for every single day of the rest of your life, you know?"

"If you had lots of money," said Tory.

He nodded. She was right about that. He'd spent more than he'd wanted to on the truck and trailer, and they were going to have to get dishes, like she said, and a TV would be a good idea. Family life was going to cost something, that was for sure. They were going to need some more cash, more than he ever thought.

Tory yawned and leaned back against the trailer wall. "I'm sleepy again," she said.

"Why don't you lie down in your own little bedroom and take a nice nap?" said Doc.

She scooted out of the bench and in two steps was in the tiny trailer's one bedroom, the door swinging quietly shut with a metallic click.

"Wake me up when it's fun time," she said from behind the door.

"I will," he called.

Outside the trailer, he sat in the pine shade at a weathered picnic table. He remembered the only vacation he'd ever taken with his parents. They had rented a one-bedroom cabin at a resort by a swamp.

The linoleum crackled underfoot and a giant space heater took up the whole kitchen. There was no living room. The lake was so full of algae he couldn't swim in it. Every night his parents got drunk and fought, while he tried to hide from the mosquitoes under a scratchy white sheet. He could still remember the cowboy lampshade over the bed. About three days into the week, his mother drove him back to town and dropped him off at her sister's. She didn't come back to get him until it was almost time for school to start. He didn't want to go back home, but he had no choice. He was only about seven or eight then.

A poor childhood was shit. He should have gotten more money. He didn't know why he didn't plan ahead more. Now he was going to have to go back there again even though he didn't want to and it would be stupid. He thought about that for a while and decided it would be too dangerous. There was an alternative, though. He checked his keys, even though he knew he had it on the ring.

And when he stopped to think about it, Ellen should be giving him more for his trouble, a whole lot more than she ever had, considering what he was doing for Tory. A whole lot more.

THERESA TURNED UP Laurel Canyon toward Lookout Mountain and then onto Wonderland. She passed a small brick school nestled in the trees. Kids romped on swings and a jungle gym behind a chain-link fence. She missed the driveway to Ellen's house and had to back up to it, then parked in the driveway under a bay laurel. For some reason she was taken aback at the sight of Tory's bike leaning against one of the trees. She realized that she had Tory placed firmly in her imagination as a disembodied voice. *Watch that*, she said. Taking a deep breath, she got out of her car.

Ellen Carlin's house was white stucco, Tudor-style, English country, with a white picket fence around it and a tower with a pointed roof. It looked out of place in the wooded canyon, straight out of a fairy tale. Here was a candy house where everything would always be wonderful in Wonderland. But the trees loomed, the dark forest was here, and they had wandered in. They had all wandered in, much too far.

Ellen answered the door wearing a blue cotton kimono. She didn't seem the type to have met the police in her robe. Her hair was disheveled, and the skin around her eyes had that glossy, yellowed swelling from crying, although she appeared composed now.

"Come in." Ellen held the door open for Theresa. The house was decorated in a claustrophobic yellow and blue chintz, a perfect match for the cheerful exterior. It was tastefully decorated, but it made Theresa cringe. She hated rooms like this and was relieved, somehow, that the flower arrangement on the piano across the room was wilted, the orange daylilies shriveled. She was even oddly relieved that Ellen looked so broken—she'd seemed so detached yesterday. Her appearance today was more congruent with what she must be going through.

"Why don't we sit over here?" Ellen gestured to the table littered with books and papers, pulled a tissue out of her robe pocket, and blew her nose as she sat down. She wiped at her eyes. "I finally lost it. This morning, talking to the police again, and my ex-husband. I mean, I knew it was weird, the way I was acting. I couldn't cry, everyone kept asking me how are you doing, how are you doing? I just kept saying fine, fine, I was all business. Holding up well. Tory was going to turn up any minute. That was certain, as long as I just stayed calm. I thought it was like losing my keys or locking myself out of my car. It was just going to be taken care of by the proper authorities, and all would be well." Her words fell out in a tumble. Now she stopped, her voice a small moan at the end of her breath. "I think it took Joe being here. I could just finally let go with him here. Isn't that strange? After all we've been through."

"It makes sense. He is Tory's father, after all."

"We were both blaming the other, and in some way that made each of us feel safe. If it was Joe that took her, then at least I'd know she was safe, you know? He wouldn't hurt her. I'd know she wasn't with some stranger, some maniac. I'd know she was alive. So I was going about the whole thing as if it was just another part of our ancient custody battle. But seeing him today, I knew he couldn't have anything to do with it. He couldn't sit there and lie like that about her. I'd know it. I'd just know." For the first time Ellen looked directly at Theresa. "So." She paused. "You were able to do a reading. What did you come up with?"

"First, I brought you these." Theresa gave Ellen a large mailing envelope with color Xerox copies of the drawings she'd made—Tory's drawings, Theresa's hand. Then she handed Ellen the scribbled drawing she'd made only a few hours before, with her notes written on the back of it.

"Specifically, I got a black truck, an older model. They may be pulling a trailer of some kind or they may be in an RV, because I got a picture of a bed or cot in the vehicle. They may be in or heading toward Arizona or Texas. They may have flown somewhere because I kept getting an image of silver. I thought maybe it was a plane, but the images were definitely of stopping by roadsides, so I'm not sure about that. It could be that they flew somewhere and are now driving. I also got the sensation that Tory is with someone she feels safe with. Someone she's even fond of. Someone she knows. I feel she hasn't been physically hurt. She's feeling, in fact, better." Theresa stopped, watching Ellen's face.

"The car stuff and driving around, that all seems very general." Ellen sniffed. "I could have guessed any of that." She looked down at the tornado scribbles on the paper Theresa had brought. "Someone she knows? Where do you get that? A man?"

"Yes, a man. I can't see him. I can't get a description. There is a familiarity in how she relates to him. She is not terrified, there is not that feeling. In the second part of the reading, I didn't get images or pictures so much as her voice, almost like I'm listening in on her thinking. The man indicated to Tory that he was taking her to you, Ellen. That you had made plans for her to leave the hospital with this man and that he was taking her to you. I got that you were opposed to any further medical tests for Tory and were, perhaps, considering legal action against the doctors or the hospital. And again she said something about feeling foggy. 'In the fog' was the phrase."

Ellen wet her lips with her tongue and looked washed out and, suddenly, angry. She set the drawing down and raised her eyes to Theresa's. "Well, that's preposterous." She turned and looked out the window. "But there is some truth in what you've seen. The part about legal action. I have been looking into that. I did say something to Tory about it, more in frustration than anything else. You know the way you mutter things under your breath? It was like, 'Why can't they make you well? What is the matter with them? I can't stand you having one more diagnostic test that doesn't lead to anything, I'm going to take them all to court.' I have said that sort of thing to Tory, I know I have. I shouldn't say things like that in front of her. As if she wasn't under enough stress."

"Ellen, I have to ask you this directly. *Did* you have anything to do with arranging Tory's disappearance? Perhaps with the thought of protecting her somehow?" She wanted to say more, but left it at that.

Theresa watched Ellen's eyes closely—she could tell a lot from doing that, but not what people thought. Jardine had taught her that people lying were actually more likely to maintain direct eye contact than were people telling the truth. But Ellen's eyes darted back and forth, scanning Theresa's face, the room, the green view from the window.

"No, of course I didn't," Ellen nearly whispered. "If I had done that, why would I be looking for her? I'd know where she was."

"You'd do it if you wanted people to think that someone else had taken her, or if you had arranged for someone to take her."

Ellen stood. "Then why would I hire you and demand absolute confidentiality? I'd want to advertise any effort I made to find her, in that case. I'd make a huge fucking deal out of it in all the newspapers and blame my ex-husband." Angry tears came up as she spoke. "I am being victimized by this entire process. The hospital, the police, Joe, now even you. I can't believe you are accusing me of—"

"Wait a minute." Theresa stood now, too, in front of Ellen. "I am not accusing you. I am trying to work with you. What I get in a reading can be a way into a process of deeper questioning. If something doesn't sound right, we explore from there. I'm telling you exactly what came from the reading and I want to be absolutely clear if you had anything to do with it. If you say no, we go from there."

Ellen looked at her with vivid rage. When she spoke, her voice was very controlled. "No, I did not arrange for the abduction of my own child, thank you very much."

"Then perhaps what is coming up is that Tory was *told* that. That is what she *believes*."

Ellen stared past Theresa, her arms locked across her chest. "You're talking as though you had a conversation with her!"

"In a sense I did, Ellen. That's how the reading came. As if she were talking to me."

"Then you still think she's alive."

"Yes, I've told you that."

"Well, that's something. That's something anyway." Ellen picked up a pack of cigarettes from the table in front of the couch, took one out and lit it, visibly relaxing as she sucked the smoke deep down with her breath and exhaled. She sat on the couch and crossed her legs.

She held up one palm. "I'm sorry, Theresa. I apologize for the way I'm acting. I'm a mess. I'm falling apart. I'm losing it. It's seeing Joe.

It's everything. So. Someone could have told Tory they were taking her to me, to make her safe from the hospital in some way? That makes sense. She might have put all that together with my blaming the doctors and the hospital. I can see how she would have that idea. I do blame the hospital. The whole medical profession. I've been in despair over her health for ages."

"What sort of diagnostic tests were you opposed to her having?"

Ellen blinked at her, hesitating. "HIV testing."

"Has Tory had blood transfusions?"

"Yes, she did receive blood during an appendectomy several years ago." Ellen looked down at her hands and swallowed. Her shoulders dropped and she suddenly looked exhausted. In a quiet voice she added, "It was when we were traveling in Ghana." She looked up at Theresa. "It wasn't on her hospital records here in the States. And when the doctors found that out, well, you know . . . AIDS is rampant in Africa. The likelihood of her having received blood with the HIV virus is pretty high."

"But why would you oppose the testing—after all that you've gone through to find out the cause of her illnesses?"

"I'm not opposed to the test. I'm opposed to having the test done at the hospital."

"Why?"

"Because it would be part of her medical record, her school record, and so on. And I just don't think that sort of thing is anyone's business. And there is still tremendous discrimination against HIV-positive people, not to mention the difficulties with the insurance companies. I wanted anonymous testing for her, but in order to do that I would have to remove her from the hospital and take her to a city health clinic. I argued with the doctors about it. Tory was aware of that, we spoke about it in her presence."

That could be the reason Ellen wanted to avoid publicity about Tory, thought Theresa. She walked back to the table and picked up her notes. "The other thing that came up in the reading was this business about the fog. Had Tory been receiving any medications that might make her feel sleepy, hazy? Was she sedated?"

"When she was younger she was on Ritalin for a while. She used to say it made her feel foggy."

"She was considered hyperactive?"

"There were problems in school, attention, that sort of thing. But we took her off it. It just seemed to contribute to the weight loss and her heart would race. She was a lot easier to handle, though."

"She's a difficult child?"

Ellen laughed. "It's not that she's difficult. It's that my whole life has been difficult. A horrible divorce, losing everything. Putting it back together. The debt, being alone. All of it. Yes, she's difficult at times. She's very bright, intuitive, precocious, and she has a mind of her own."

"Leslie Simon mentioned that Tory had a history of running away."

The glance Ellen threw Theresa was full of mistrust. "You talked this over with Leslie Simon? But I wanted our meetings to be confidential, Theresa."

"I didn't tell her anything that came up in the readings, Ellen. And after all, Leslie was the one who sent you to me. I've worked with her for several years at the foundation. I need to be able to discuss my findings with her."

Ellen sighed. "All right," she said quietly. "But I'd hardly say Tory had a history of running away. She ran off a few times. Mostly right after visitations with her father. It's very difficult, passing children back and forth between parents. All the bitterness they soak up. She's had trouble readjusting, and she has run off now and then—but never for longer than a day. Once she was gone for a day and then she came back."

"And did you contact the police at that time?"

"Of course I did."

Theresa put her notes down. "In the reading, there was a series of images about Martha's Vineyard, a green house, reading in a striped hammock. And having an imaginary friend to talk to. One she called 'Star.'"

Ellen exhaled, then stubbed the cigarette out in a large brass bowl. "That's absolutely uncanny. That's our house on Cape Cod. Joe's house, I should say. I lost custody of that, too, of course."

Theresa thought it odd, but fitting somehow, that Ellen used the word *custody* in speaking of the house.

Ellen continued. "I think that the Cape house ought to be checked, don't you think so? It should be checked immediately, it now occurs to me."

"In the reading, that image came in the form of a memory, a pleasant memory, not a place where she is at the present time."

"How can you tell?" Ellen asked.

"I guess I'd call it the tone of the imagery and of her voice," said Theresa. "I know that sounds vague. The images that are closer to the present have a more urgent quality. More fear, usually. In Tory's case, the images that I associated with the present seemed highly charged with fear when I first got those drawings of someone taking her from the hospital. The pictures I got last night just seemed clear. A clear, quiet voice."

Ellen was imperceptibly shaking her head. She said very quietly, "I don't know if I can do this."

Theresa was silent. *Just let her finish.*

"I don't think I can talk to you about Tory like this. As if she really were communicating with you. Through you. I don't know if I can afford to invest that much hope in this. I don't know if I can stand for all this to be true."

"I understand."

Theresa didn't know if she could stand it either. But for a different reason. Throughout the time they'd been speaking, she'd been aware of Ellen's anxious physical presence. She had not gone into her, had not read her, entered her, but she was aware, in a very physical sense, that nothing had changed. That slightly beyond where they stood in present time, there was not-Ellen.

Ellen approached Theresa, her hands in the pockets of her kimono. "Thank you for coming over, Theresa. I apologize again for yelling." Her eyes reddened with tears. "I can't help it, I am angry. I'm taking it out on you, the police, Joe." She swallowed the tears back, trying to regain control. "I'm just trying to do everything I can, and at the same time I'm not sure that anything I'm doing is right. I feel so helpless."

"Do you want me to continue?" asked Theresa.

"Oh, absolutely. Absolutely. What else will you do?"

Theresa paused for a moment. Tell her. Tell her what you're getting for her, she thought. She looked at Ellen, pale skin and swollen eyes. Her child was missing, her ex-husband had just flown in from the East Coast. Maybe it was the amplification of emotion Theresa was picking up. She didn't know. Suddenly she felt that she couldn't speak of it, that it was an invasion somehow. She hadn't been asked to read for Ellen specifically, but for Tory. If she did, she might be able to get a more accurate reading, clarify her sense of this before telling her some awful thing that could be stupid and mistaken.

"I could do a reading for *you*, Ellen, and we could see what comes up," Theresa offered.

"I guess we could."

"Would you like to arrange a time to do that?"

Ellen looked exhausted. "Maybe tomorrow. Let me think about it."

Theresa nodded. This was right. This was the better way to go than blurting out, "And by the way, I don't think you have a future."

"By the way," said Ellen, "I did tell Sergeant Rukheyser about Disneyland. I didn't tell him where I got the idea she might have gone there. He said he'd make sure that their security department has a description of her." She paused. "Is there anything more you need in order to read for Tory? I could show you her room . . . " Ellen gestured down a hall that led off from the living room.

"That would be good," said Theresa.

Theresa followed Ellen to Tory's room and stood just inside the door. The furniture was modern, white laminated. Matching pieces lined the walls, a dresser with an attached desk and several bookshelves. A trundle bed. Green and coral—chintz again—curtains and comforter, sheets and pillowcases. Even the fabric for the desk chair matched. Books were lined up neatly on the shelves, toys immaculately sorted into white plastic stacking boxes. Her collection of unicorn figurines was lined up on a shelf. Nothing was out of place. Certainly it was a child's room, but it didn't feel emotionally inhabited. It looked and felt designed. It was pretty, but impersonal.

"She's a very neat child," said Theresa.

Ellen nodded. "She likes her things arranged."

"Is she obsessive about it?"

"A little."

Suddenly it came to Theresa, the word *generic*. This was a generic child's room. It could be a display in an upscale furniture store. It was no-child's room. Again that feeling of absence.

Then she saw the one area that seemed not to fit the store-bought room, the dresser. A snapshot was tucked in the edge of the mirror. Theresa went to it and slipped it out. It was a picture of Tory with her father. She was sitting on his shoulders, her hair swept back, grinning widely with her mouth closed, that lopsided smile of hers. She was hanging on to the bearded edge of her father's face. His dark hair, too, was windblown and he was wearing a gray sweatshirt and baggy khaki pants. He reached up with his hands and held on to Tory's wrists as she clung to him. She had her legs wrapped around his shoulders. They stood in sea grass in the sand, the ocean beyond.

Ellen came up beside her and looked over Theresa's shoulder at the snapshot. "That's Joe. They're right down the beach from the Cape house."

"The divorce was pretty rough?"

Ellen snorted a laugh. "You ever been divorced?"

"Years ago," said Theresa.

"It's a form of death, isn't it?" Ellen asked.

"So it was bitter?"

"It was the custody thing that killed me."

"Was there any particular reason why you didn't want to share custody with Joe?"

"I didn't mind the idea of *sharing*. He didn't want me to have her at all."

"Why not?"

"He claimed I was mentally incompetent. Mentally ill, I should say. I was hospitalized at one point for exhaustion when Tory was an infant. He used anything he could get his hands on to keep her from me." She turned to face Theresa and grinned. "But it didn't work. I hired an excellent lawyer. So she summers with him. But I'm telling you, divorce is a prison sentence for kids. That's the source of all her problems—the fact that he left me. That he broke the family. Now her life is stretched across the country like a rubber band. I don't know if she really knows where home is."

Theresa thanked Ellen for her time and checked her watch. It was nearly noon. She had client appointments scheduled for this afternoon, and she wanted to check in with Jardine, to see what he'd been able to find out about Tory DeLisi, but she didn't know if she'd have time before late afternoon. She had to get hold of Camille, too.

She glanced around Tory's bedroom one last time, trying to read it for a moment, not just see it, but it was very blank here. For a moment her eyes rested on the dresser top neatly arranged with cologne bottles, a jewelry box, a snow dome of the Golden Gate Bridge and one with a carousel horse inside. She picked it up and shook it, watching the specks of snow flutter around it. It isn't a horse, she thought. It's a unicorn. Then Theresa looked again at the snapshot, staring at it for so long that finally Ellen held out her hand to take it away from her. Even as Ellen replaced the picture on the edge of the mirror, Theresa kept her eyes on Tory's father. It was as though he were peering ahead at her into the future and the white ocean sun.

15

LIEUTENANT OLIVER JARDINE stepped into his office briefly to drop off the file of materials from Oslin's computer. He wanted to call Theresa, to check in with her about the girl's photo, but he didn't want to miss catching Rukheyser. The day was getting away from him. And he'd made that appointment to meet with the Billings family down in Long Beach about their boy, Royce. As he headed out the door, the phone rang. He should have known better, but he was still surprised to hear Theresa's hello.

"I was just now at this very moment thinking about you," he said.

"It's my internal paging service," Theresa said. "I hear this ringing in my ears, pick it up, and find out who wants me to call them. It was you."

"You're serious, aren't you?"

"I'm serious, Oliver."

Jardine filled her in about the picture.

"Are you sure it's Tory?" she asked.

"No. But I'm checking downstairs with Missing Persons in about two minutes. You say her name is Tory?"

"Victoria DeLisi, nickname Tory. Oliver, I definitely want to see that picture. And I'd like to get as complete a review of her case as I can, as soon as I can."

"You're starting to sound like a cop," he said.

"I am not a cop."

"I know. I said you sounded like one. You didn't used to want to know anything about a case. You said the less you knew the better, it kept your readings pure."

"I've been hanging around with you too long, then. Now I want the facts, Oliver. Good old cognitive, concrete facts."

"Is there some reason for this sudden veering toward the left brain?"

Theresa hesitated. "I was just with the mother. I don't trust her. I don't have any reason, exactly, and I'm trying to make allowances for her being under an enormous amount of stress, but . . . " She stopped in midsentence. "I get a double message from her. Like when someone both loves you and hates you? Ellen Carlin wants me to read for her desperately. She sincerely wants me to find her daughter. But she also wants me to keep the hell out. She's terrified of what I might see. I'm thinking I should talk to the police."

"I am the police," said Jardine.

"You know what I mean. Officially."

"You're going all out for this, aren't you?"

"I have to," she told him. "I've got this little girl out there calling me."

"Theresa, if you ever talk to Rukheyser down in Missing Persons, don't say shit like that, okay?"

"I'll try," said Theresa. "When can I see the picture? Do you have time to swing by here this afternoon?"

Jardine looked at his watch. "I have to go down to Long Beach and then back up to Marina Del Rey, so I could swing by in about an hour on my way down."

"See if you can find out what's going on with this little girl, Oliver. What's the undertow, what's in the background."

Jardine needed something from the machine, some rotgut coffee with insect-poison non-dairy creamer, so he stopped on his way down the hall, sipping the steaming sludge from the paper cup several times as he took the stairs down to Rukheyser's office.

As Jardine neared the door, he heard a sharp voice that he did not recognize. "I want you to get a list of every boyfriend, lover, and fiancé she's had in the last five years and I want you to interview every god-damn one of them. And, no, I do not consider that an unreasonable request at all."

Jardine stepped up to the open door. "I'm sorry to interrupt here, Sergeant, but I've got something that may pertain to one of your cases. May I come in?" He entered the office before Rukheyser could refuse, and turned to nod at a tall, bearded man in an expensive-looking gray suit, standing against the wall with his arms folded. Jardine tossed Tory's photo down on Rukheyser's desk.

"Is this one of yours?" he asked.

Rukheyser snapped up the picture and handed it immediately to the angry man. "Where did you get this?" Rukheyser asked.

The man said, "That's my daughter's school picture from last year. Third grade."

Rukheyser pushed his chair back. He was a serious, hawk-nosed cop in his midthirties, too thin, too tall, and too blond. He was so pale he made Jardine nervous, his honey-white hair and oval forehead extending high over his long face. He had gray-blue eyes, as small as dots, that were made to seem even smaller behind thick frameless glasses that faded into his face. Often he frowned. Rukheyser was also something of a smartass, but he played the tenor saxophone part-time in a little group. Jardine had gone to hear him a few times on a weeknight at a supper club no one had ever heard of. He wasn't bad. Jardine wondered if he didn't memorize the riffs he did on the improvisational parts. They sounded the same every time he heard them. But he played them with energy, bending low over his horn so you couldn't see his face. All in all, Rukheyser was a joyless fucker, Jardine thought, but not stupid.

"Some introductions are in order here," said Rukheyser. "Lieutenant Oliver Jardine, Homicide. Dr. Joseph DeLisi, father of Tory DeLisi, the girl in the picture. Dr. DeLisi is a mathematics professor at MIT," he said. "We were just reviewing what little progress we've made here. What about this picture, Lieutenant?"

"I got a homicide I'm working on. Found the picture yesterday at the man's place of business, an antique store."

"No shit," said Rukheyser.

DeLisi sat down in a metal chair and put his head in his hands for a moment, then looked up and let out a long breath. "But Tory is not the homicide, is that correct?"

Jardine said, "Not that we know of."

"When he said you were from Homicide, I thought . . . "

"No, Doctor. Not at all." He dove right into interviewing DeLisi, even though he knew Rukheyser might not like it. "Did your ex-wife buy antiques, do any business with an Oslin Antiques over off Melrose?"

"I have no idea, you'll have to ask her."

"Skydiving? Ever have a family tree drawn up?"

DeLisi lifted his hands. "Not me. Again, you'll have to check with Ellen, although I'm positive she's never jumped out of a plane."

"What about old toys, collector kind of stuff? Antique toys?"

"She bought folk art now and then." DeLisi stuffed his hands in his pockets. "You're saying a man was murdered and he had Tory's picture? What does that mean?"

"We don't know," said Jardine.

Joseph DeLisi had a certain presence, a direct gaze that didn't falter, an odd stillness about him, as if he were sizing everything up in a very conscious way, but it wasn't adding up. He was good looking, with a well-defined, rugged, but off-center face. The beard was close. Unruly eyebrows arched over his black-dark eyes and he had a kind of brainy, befuddled look, nodding slightly as he took it all in. Looked to be in his forties, his dark hair longish, not particularly well cut, going gray. At least he had hair to go gray, thought Jardine. He'd been noticing that lately as his own disappeared, leaving a freckled, vulnerable skull.

DeLisi's thick nose looked as if it had been broken once or twice. Jardine didn't usually like good-looking men with some kind of pretty in their eyes that women went for, but he was willing to make an exception for DeLisi because his nose was fucked up. He must have some kind of street side to him, played kick-the-can in an East Coast working-class neighborhood as a kid, before he went on to win a football scholarship to some Ivy League school.

Rukheyser said, "We haven't circulated any photographs of the child publicly, Jardine. How did you know she was one of our cases?"

"Through someone who works with the Simon Foundation."

Jardine turned to DeLisi. "Your ex-wife has consulted a psychic, Theresa Fortunato. She's someone I've worked with here before. She's very reputable."

Rukheyser's eyes narrowed behind the thick lenses. "You got some kind of access to information we don't have, Lieutenant? The Simon Foundation hasn't told us about any psychic. You're not talking about that one you worked with on that serial killer in 'eighty-three or 'eighty-four?"

"Yeah, same one. August 1983." Jardine wished he hadn't mentioned Theresa. It had just floated out. He'd have to watch his mouth. Mind floating, mouth floating. If he hung around Theresa too much, pretty soon he'd start channeling and then he'd be canned and he could start his own call-in show on cable TV. *Psychic Cop Channels Celebrities from Atlantis. Tune in next week for ancient weight-loss formula from Egypt. Tales of Long Lost Loves Reunited from Past Lives. The audience could vote for the most likely candidate from behind a screen on late-night TV. It would probably go in this town. At least a pilot,* he thought.

"Is this psychic part of the foundation's staff?" DeLisi asked.

"No, but they refer clients to her sometimes. If their people want a psychic, the foundation has a few they recommend. Fortunato comes highly recommended because she's worked with the department."

"Fortunato. Good Italian name," said DeLisi. "Could you give me her number? She's here in L.A.?"

Jardine scribbled Theresa's number on one of Rukheyser's pink message slips and handed it to DeLisi.

"Dr. DeLisi," said Rukheyser, "our department down here doesn't condone the use of psychics in police work. Up in Homicide, they make their own decisions."

"Is there some problem if I at least talk with her? I deserve to have all the available information regarding my daughter, I don't care where it comes from."

"I don't think that the kind of things a psychic comes up with can exactly be called information," said Rukheyser. "But do what you want."

"Is there a private phone I could use for a few minutes?" DeLisi asked. Rukheyser told him to use the one next door, and DeLisi excused himself.

"So you and Jackson are covering this?" Rukheyser asked. "What's the connection with this Oslin?"

Jardine shrugged. "So far, the picture itself is the only connection. I talked to Oslin's sister; she's never seen the kid before. What do you have here, a custody abduction?"

Rukheyser opened a file on his desk. "How did you guess? I'll be straight with you. I got two parents, divorced three years, who each, at some point, snatched the kid for periods of time, a few weeks or longer. I'm waiting for a FedEx of the complete court records coming in from Boston, supposed to be here by now. Well-educated people, both Ph.D.s, professor types, very intelligent, sophisticated. You don't know people at a glance, am I right?" He put a finger on the file, ran it down the edge of the page, then looked up at Jardine and went on.

"Example. The mother takes the kid to Africa to a village in Ghana for two months. The kid has poor health to begin with, she only brings the kid back home after she has some kind of kidney failure following an appendectomy. The following year, Dr. DeLisi takes the kid to California to visit his mother, the kid's grandmother, and fails to return her at the scheduled time. Rents a beach house up near Mendocino where the grandmother and girl spend the summer without the kid's mother knowing where they are. The wife hires a detective to find them.

"You know? People don't give a fuck about the kid in my opinion, they do things like this. Hey, it's just an opinion. People have their reasons. I'm not even saying these people in particular. I'm saying anybody who keeps a child from the other parent. What does that do to a kid? People are crazy. Tell me, Lieutenant, why are we in a business that deals mostly with crazy people?"

"To serve humanity," Jardine said flatly.

"Yeah, right. I almost forgot." Rukheyser took off his glasses and rubbed his face with both hands.

Jardine asked, "Are there allegations of sexual abuse?"

"Not that I'm aware of. The court records will tell us that. But I've got to proceed here with the likelihood of some kind of custody abduction, and I can't come down on either side of it yet. DeLisi's the one eventually lost the bid for sole custody. He's initiated a legal proceeding to try to get his daughter back, and now the kid ups and disappears, you know what I'm saying? We got very little from the hospital where she was taken. We're interviewing hospital personnel, family, neighbors, friends, teachers, et cetera. The abduction was real clean. We got motivation in the family up the wazoo, but exactly zero actual leads."

"What about the mother? What can you tell me about her?"

"DeLisi was husband number two. We're looking for number one, another doctor, a medical one, a skin specialist. Acquaintances describe her as a devoted mother, intellectual, likes opera, classical music, belongs to a book club. Bit of a martyr, overworked single mother with two creepy ex-husbands, maybe a woman-who-loved-too-much type, always married men who didn't love her enough. Doesn't socialize much outside of the current man she's involved with. Most social contacts seem to be with the husband's or current boyfriend's social group. Apparently she entertains beautifully. You hear that a few times. Very fine cook."

"And there's nothing that indicates a stranger abduction?" asked Jardine.

Rukheyser shook his head. "Most stranger abductions happen outside, where kids are playing. An abduction right out of a hospital or a school is a pretty risky thing. Someone actually seeing you take a kid out past the nurses' station. How many kids walk out of a hospital in the middle of the night? Of course, it could have been an employee. Kid could have been hidden in a food service cart, taken on a freight elevator. So that's the other line of questioning—nurses, food staff, janitorial, all of that."

"And so far?"

Rukheyser raised empty palms. "Like I said. Zip. No witnesses. Last check by the nurses was at four A.M. They checked on her again at the next round—five-thirty A.M.—and she was gone. No fingerprints except for family and personnel you would expect to be in the room, nurses and so on."

Rukheyser handed Tory's photograph back to Jardine.

Rukheyser's office door squeaked as DeLisi pushed it open. He sat down and crossed his legs. "Theresa Fortunato didn't answer. I left a message on her machine saying I'd like to speak to her as soon as possible."

"She's probably with a client. I'm going over there right now," said Jardine. "If you'd like, you can come along."

"Thank you. It's a relief to be getting some cooperation from someone here." He glared at Rukheyser. "Sergeant, I would certainly appreciate a similar attitude from you. A child's life is at stake here. This is not only a missing child, but a child who requires medical care, who was taken from a hospital, for Christ's sake. I realize that we have not had much of a chance to discuss the situation—I only arrived here last night—and that you have had several days to discuss all this with my ex-wife. Let me say, frankly, that she does not hold me in particularly high regard, nor I her. Not uncommon in divorces. However, before you jump to conclusions regarding my character, I suggest you examine the court records regarding Tory's custody.

"Your concerns about the so-called snatching of Tory are blown completely out of proportion. First of all, both my ex-wife and I had Tory with us for extended periods before we were legally separated. As far as the law is concerned, we were two parents taking our child on a trip or vacation without the other spouse. That is not kidnapping. It was not a custody violation, because no custody had been awarded.

"During the summer that Tory was living with my mother in northern California, Ellen was in a residential treatment program for prescription drug abuse. She was addicted to an antidepressant called Xanax, as well as Percodan and Ritalin. The prescription for Ritalin was for Tory, but her mother took the pills. Ellen didn't remember where Tory was, because she was totally out of it. Then she claimed that I was hiding her.

"So let us keep the record straight, Sergeant. I'm not suggesting that you overlook anything regarding custody issues between Ellen and myself, but please do not let that distract you from other possible avenues of inquiry that may lead to finding my little girl. Do I make myself clear?"

Rukheyser cleared his throat. "Dr. DeLisi, I'm assuming you were standing outside the door listening in on my conversation with Lieutenant Jardine here."

"Correct. You have issues with me, talk to me about them directly."

"We will schedule an in-depth interview with you once we have received the court records, Mr. DeLisi," said Rukheyser. He stood, as if to intimidate DeLisi, but DeLisi stood too. DeLisi was taller.

"Doctor," DeLisi said. "*Doctor* DeLisi."

Rukheyser shot his eyes at Jardine.

"Shall we go?" asked the lieutenant.

"I'll try to follow you in my car," said DeLisi as they left Rukheyser's office.

They were silent in the elevator. Jardine had noticed that DeLisi had at least two ways of speaking, two different modes of syntax, the Italian *buon giorno* street talk with its assertive rhythms, and the professor quasi-attorney addressing the opposition during a deposition. He was probably a department chair, used to being a big fish in a swanky academic pond. His good old broken nose couldn't compensate for his ivory-tower ego, Jardine thought.

The elevator doors slid open and DeLisi said quietly, "You might assume I'd be the last person who would want to talk to a psychic, but what I've always liked about mathematics is that if you follow the logic all the way out as far as you can, it is ultimately very mysterious. It was Einstein who said, 'Imagination is more important than knowledge.' Besides, I'll do whatever it takes to find my girl."

OSIRIS LEAPT UP on the patio table. Theresa was stroking his long white fur when she heard the doorbell from inside the house. The cat padded ahead of her as she followed the shaded sidewalk. For some reason she stopped halfway to the gate, where she knew Jardine would be waiting on the other side. Stood there in the shadows, her senses suddenly heightened: wind chimes, pungent cedar scent, humid breeze. A motorcycle roared down Washington Avenue. In the distance, someone practicing steel drums, starting and stopping. Birds. There was that prescient feeling, not the déjà vu of time repeating itself, but that of a moment about to occur, one that would change everything.

From within, the words came, welling up in her: TWO DAYS.

Theresa realized she was standing near the same spot where she had heard that Voice the previous afternoon.

Should I tell Ellen? she asked in her mind.

There was no answer. She was going to have to do a reading specifically for that question, to confront her own resistance to knowing and her vague doubts.

Theresa opened the gate and the lieutenant greeted her, then introduced the man standing beside him. "Theresa, this is Tory's father, Dr. Joseph DeLisi. He's a professor of mathematics at MIT."

Don't I know you from somewhere? she thought, shaking his hand. Then: *Oh God, not that tired line. Very original, Theresa.* He was as Ellen had described him, not the windblown, bearded daddy from the snapshot in Tory's bedroom, but more refined and every bit as intense as his ex-wife. His astonishing dark eyes seemed so familiar to her that it was like being with an older cousin back home, North End, Boston, Sunday dinner, her parents and aunts and uncles hollering over the clams, the pasta, the green bottles of Chianti. Finally she turned and led them back to the patio.

"Lieutenant, can I speak with you a moment?" she asked. DeLisi sat in one of the wrought-iron chairs and Theresa stepped back alongside the house with Jardine. "Why didn't you let me know you were bringing him?"

"What's the problem? I thought you'd be dying to see him. You said you wanted to know everything about the case."

"The mother wants my seeing her to remain confidential."

"Well, Dr. DeLisi and Sergeant Rukheyser are aware of your working with the foundation and meeting with the mom."

She narrowed her eyes at him. "Did you tell them, Oliver?"

He paused, then nodded with a shrug.

"Okay. Well, he's here now. The truth is I do want to meet with him." Theresa followed Jardine back to the patio and sat at the table. DeLisi had gone over to examine her roses. He'd left a folder filled with photographs of Tory open on the table, and as she thumbed through the pictures, she kept glancing from the girl's bright eyes and elfin features to the father's thicker bones and broad nose, his strong Roman profile and unruly eyebrows. Occasionally he rubbed his beard along the chin line while he was thinking. Tory looked very much like Ellen, but she had her father's eyes.

"I understand Ellen has met with you already," said DeLisi, "and I just wanted to know if you'd . . . found anything that will help us. I thought you might want to see pictures of Tory."

"Thanks," she said. "But I need to say first that I feel somewhat awkward here because, quite frankly, Ellen requested confidentiality regarding any readings I did for her. Specifically, she did not want you to know that she was consulting with me."

"That figures."

"My client relationship with her is similar to that of a lawyer or a therapist—but not legally. There's no licensing for psychics in the State of California, no psychic bar exam or oath. It's just a professional boundary issue. But now you already know about me, and obviously the police know." Theresa sighed, thumbing through the photographs again: Tory at a birthday party, in a sailboat, at a dance recital, sitting at a piano. Tory gap-toothed, still gangly. Dressed up for Easter in a yellow coat, holding a basket. White gloves.

Jardine handed her a school photo of Tory, protected in a Ziploc bag.

"So you found this at that man's store." Theresa thought for a moment of the holes she'd felt in Ellen, her mistrust of her. And the urgency of Tory's images, the child's voice in Theresa's mind.

She addressed Dr. DeLisi. "I need to stay clear with Ellen about all this, but I have to say that my first allegiance is actually to your daughter. I did not initially read for Tory at Ellen's request, but . . . " She paused, not wanting to explain that she'd begun receiving images before she'd even talked with Ellen. "My services are really a benefit for the Simon Foundation for Missing Children."

"Can you help me?" Dr. DeLisi asked. He stood with his arms crossed, shirt sleeves pushed up, revealing muscular forearms and big hands.

"I think so." She asked them to wait a few minutes while she brought the coffee she'd already made out from the kitchen. When she returned to the table, she gave the pictures back to DeLisi and sat down next to Jardine, smoothing out folds in the lap of her dress. The silver bracelets jangled on her wrist. The sea wind rustled the bougainvillea. She caught DeLisi glancing down her shoulders and arms to the curve of her breast under the silk. He looked openly at her for a moment, not trying to hide his gaze, looking down at the patio bricks and back up at her knees and legs and gold thongs, the ones Jardine called, teasingly, her "goddess shoes." Jardine cleared his throat and DeLisi joined them at the table.

"Tell me about your daughter," said Theresa. "Free flow, whatever comes to mind."

"Tory's strong-willed in a quiet way," DeLisi began. "Not feisty, exactly, but determined. At the same time, she's vulnerable, tender. Like those young gymnasts you see getting ready for the Olympics. She can be totally focused on something, as if she's in a trance. She lives up in her head a lot, a bit of an introvert, only child. And sometimes, I'll admit, she's what you might call a little needy. You know? Clingy, hungry. And while she can seem shy, she's also very open, she latches on to people. She'll pick a person and make them special, a ballet teacher, an older kid in the neighborhood, a baby-sitter. Idealize them. Get attached. You know what I'm saying?" DeLisi looked from Jardine to Theresa.

"Be sure to let Rukheyser know of anyone like that in Tory's life," said Jardine.

"Do you feel she's overly trusting of people?" Theresa asked.

DeLisi considered it, nodding. "Someone could easily warm up to her, get her to trust them."

DeLisi sipped his coffee, pushed it away, covered his mouth for a moment with one hand, thinking. "She's brainy, you know? Likes word-find puzzles and crosswords, makes up riddles, reads everything, memorizes things . . . names of endangered species of birds, facts about the weather."

When he stopped, Theresa paused for a moment. It was different, this interviewing. Usually she would tell the querent all this herself, not get the information from him. There was a humming in her, just behind her right shoulder, as if answers were waiting in line to be heard, biding their time. *Just wait,* she thought.

"What about the divorce?" she asked. "How did Tory deal with all that?"

"She was five at the time. I know it affected her some. But it was the custody thing that was the most stressful for her." DeLisi folded his large hands, bent forward over the glass-topped table. "It's her mother. I don't want to bad-mouth Ellen—I know it always sounds bitter. The hostile, noncustodial father." He glanced over at Jardine, addressing him. "You heard Sergeant Rukheyser, his opinion of me obviously formed by what Ellen has told him. I've gotten used to being portrayed by her in a bad light. Ellen is paranoid about me, hateful even." He stopped, gathering his thoughts.

"My daughter is everything to me. It's not been good, us being on opposite ends of the country. I've been making plans to move out here, leaving MIT so I can be closer to her without this back-and-forth thing. Tory was happy about the idea and Ellen's been upset, claiming I'm

harassing her, following her around the country after she moved all
the way out here to get away from me, to start a new life.

"I still honestly feel I should have sole custody. Ellen is a wonderful mother—but I say 'wonderful' as a pejorative. I've always felt that
she smothers Tory. She promotes what is an overly close bond between
them. She dresses Tory like her. Ellen takes tennis lessons, Tory's got
to take them. Ellen plays classical music, Tory's got to practice two
hours a day. They learn the same songs. Bartók, Erik Satie. Ellen gets
her hair cut, Tory gets the same cut. Ellen decorates her room in rose
chintz, Tory's in green chintz. Some people think it's cute. I don't.

"Another thing: Ellen has a hard time sleeping alone. Tory is ten
and she still sleeps with her mother. How would it look if she was
sleeping with *me* at that age? Everyone would say it was incest. Even
with no sex, no touching at all, it would be what they call emotional
incest. And what about the men Ellen gets involved with? Where does
Tory sleep when they're over? Ellen uses Tory to fill some kind of
emptiness in herself, and that, in a nutshell, was the issue in our former marriage. I had a wife in love with her daughter, a child disappearing into her mother.

"Well, I've let go to an extent. I've had to. What Ellen does on her
own with Tory, it's her business. What can I do? It's tricky because
Ellen makes it all look so *wonderful*." DeLisi opened his hands. "On
the outside, anyway."

Finally, Jardine spoke. "Have you mentioned this aspect of Ellen's
boyfriends to Rukheyser?"

"There hasn't been time. I met with the sergeant for the first time
this morning over at Ellen's. When you came in, that was our first conversation without Ellen present, with the exception of some phone
calls over the weekend. I think he's too focused on me as the major
bad-ass in a supposed custody-abduction scenario. He should be focusing on Ellen. I did tell him my gut feeling is that Ellen arranged for
Tory to be taken out of the hospital, for her to be kept somewhere, and
have it look like she's been abducted and blame me for it."

"But if your ex-wife has an overdeveloped sense of dependency on
Tory," said Jardine, "would she actually arrange to be away from her?"

"Ellen is a very intelligent and manipulative woman," said DeLisi.
"And she has a very facile imagination—I mean, what she imagines,
she lives as if it were true. I wouldn't put it past her to have created
this whole thing and to be totally believing, in some part of herself, that
it's so. All caught up in an imagined drama that Tory's been kidnapped.
Only, in another part of herself, she knows exactly where Tory is and

has plans to join her later, maybe out of the country. She's done that before. It wouldn't surprise me at all if, in two or three days or a week or a month, Ellen completely disappeared as well and it will be almost as if she and Tory had both died. That would be her scenario: to 'die' and to start a new life somewhere and to believe it, absolutely, utterly!"

"What about your relationships since the divorce, Dr. DeLisi?" asked Theresa. "Have you remarried, are there women who might have become attached to Tory, or she to them?"

"I've dated, yes, and there have been a few women I've seen on a more serious basis, but when Tory comes to stay with me, I make sure that it's just the two of us. I have her with me so infrequently that I want to make the most of our time together. I know it's more difficult for the custodial parent to pursue relationships. But don't get me wrong. It's not that I am opposed to Ellen having men stay with her, but in light of her habit of sleeping with Tory . . . I do worry about all that."

Up close, and with Oliver sitting right there, Theresa tried to look nonchalant. For some reason she felt embarrassed about her strong attraction to DeLisi. She didn't want Jardine to pick up on it and to give her a hard time. At the same time she sensed a darkness in him behind his obvious love for his girl and his concern for her safety. He did not seem as anguished as Ellen, as emotionally overwrought, but men were more often like that. They responded to tragedy by going numb or becoming enraged or highly analytical; some women did, too. Ultimately that sort of person took much longer to work through his or her grief. Maybe what she sensed in him was his hostility toward Ellen. More than hostility—yes, it was rage, knotted tightly. She flashed on a tangle of ropes that began to move, uncoiling and hissing as they slithered down in him, farther down where they could hide in damp places, under the stones.

She checked herself. *Dark, tangled men; just your type, Theresa. You always go for that intensity and drama. Which ones were poisonous? What were their markings?*

Jardine asked DeLisi, "But you also kidnapped Tory at one point, didn't you? Hid her from your ex-wife."

DeLisi straightened. "As I said to Rukheyser this morning, Tory visiting her grandmother for the summer is hardly kidnapping. Ellen was extremely unbalanced that summer, and she still is, in my opinion. She was whacked out on drugs and in treatment, and it wasn't the first time she was hospitalized for so-called exhaustion. She knew damn well Tory was with my mother in northern California."

"But did she know exactly where they were?" asked Theresa.

"Not every minute. They were traveling around. Eventually they rented a cabin in Mendocino. Ellen hired a detective to find out where Tory was. You know how the guy found her? He called me and *asked* me where Tory was and I told him. Ellen wouldn't speak to me directly at that point; she could have called and asked me herself. You see how these things get slanted?"

DeLisi stood and walked over to the roses, fingered one that was very open, as white and ragged as a full-blast peony, then shoved his hands in his pockets. "Theresa, in these readings or intuitions you've had about Tory, did you pick up on anything close to what I'm saying? About Ellen? Does any of this fit?"

Theresa thought about Ellen's "death," the strange hole or absence she felt in the woman. "Yes," she said. "There are echoes. What's helpful is your description of Tory and all these pictures. I've been getting strong impressions, and what you're telling me, along with the visual images of her, might help me get something more concrete." Osiris walked by under the table, then wandered toward Joe DeLisi, brushing past his leg.

"I asked Ellen if I could try a reading with the two of you present, but she was opposed to it."

"That doesn't surprise me."

She went on. "I'd like to try to talk her into it again. And I'd like to feel free to disclose any information I get to both of you. I feel boxed in. I'll get back to you after I've checked in with her."

DeLisi rolled down his shirtsleeves and buttoned them at the wrist. "I suppose if she doesn't agree, I can always hire my own psychic. After meeting with Rukheyser, I'm strongly considering hiring a private detective anyway." DeLisi opened his fist, looked at his palm, closing his hand slowly, curling the fingers in. "I just want to know everything I can. It's the not knowing that's killing me. My daughter has been missing now for five days and I've got to find her. What's going on is sick. And it's been sick for a very long time."

Five days, Theresa thought. And he came into town only last night. If it were my kid, I'd have been on a plane to L.A. the second I heard she was gone. Why didn't he come sooner? Maybe they did this a lot, accusing and tugging and not telling the other where Tory was. But Theresa could understand why he might think Ellen herself had taken Tory out of the hospital. She'd certainly revealed a motivation, if not an intent, to do so.

Theresa glanced at Jardine to see if he would ask any more questions, but he was staring deeply into the bottom of his coffee cup. For a moment she wondered if there were stray grounds down there he was reading, and she leaned toward him to peer into the cup. There was nothing but a half inch of cold coffee, and Jardine looked up at her oddly.

Theresa walked Jardine and DeLisi down the brick walk next to the ivy-covered fence. DeLisi slipped his suit jacket on. Theresa pictured him taking the jacket back off, unbuttoning his white shirt, and stepping close to her, pressing his chest against the silk of her dress. She couldn't tell whether it was a glimpse of the future or her own desire. She felt flushed and began to look away, but exactly at that moment, Joe DeLisi looked back at her. He smiled and shook his head.

"Fortunato," he said. "That's a perfect name for a psychic."

"I took my grandmother's maiden name a number of years ago. My father's name was Lamberto. I grew up in Boston, you know."

"No kidding, where?"

"North End."

"I can't believe this," he said. "That's right where I grew up. Lamberto's. Your family owned that little grocery right down from my school."

She felt herself blush again, as if he knew the most intimate things about her, all that she'd come to California years ago to forget about and escape.

"This is unbelievable," he repeated. "I used to go over to Lamberto's on my bike, get sausages and lamb chops for my mother."

She pictured herself standing in her father's store after school, wiping the glass cases with a clean, damp towel. Smell of fresh meat, refrigeration, blood. Her plaid school uniform.

"I probably came in after school," DeLisi went on, "and you were standing there helping your father. I was probably wearing a letter jacket, trying to look cool, and you were probably what, ten, twelve?"

Jardine came up behind Theresa. "I've got to get going. Maybe you could show Dr. DeLisi your high school yearbook sometime."

Theresa cut her eyes at Jardine. Joe DeLisi smiled, shook her hand, and thanked her, then walked out ahead into the sunlight toward the narrow sidewalk along the canal.

"Excuse me, Lieutenant," Theresa said quietly. "You got a problem with my talking to the girl's father? Italians from the old neighborhood stick together, discuss the old days, eh? *Capiche?*"

Jardine widened his eyes at her. "Okay, I'm protective, the guy's looking all over you. I notice these things."

"Oliver, I didn't know you cared."

"Since when would I care? I'm not the caring type. Just remember, you don't know anything about this guy. You're too trusting, Theresa." He looked north up the green canal, the ducks asleep on the bank and the white wooden bridge arching over the water. "Look," he said, "I've got a lot more on all of this from downtown, and the doctor is not some 'Father Knows Best,' but I've got to focus on this Oslin thing. I'll call you later and fill you in."

Standing at the open gate, Theresa realized she'd learned much more about Tory from her father than from anything Ellen had said. Ellen spoke of the events of the abduction, but not much about Tory herself.

DeLisi returned from the canal sidewalk, crossed the front yard, and handed Theresa a business card, "Westwood Plaza Hotel" scribbled on the back. "Here's where I'm staying. Call me when you've checked with Ellen." He walked back out to the canal and headed toward Washington Avenue, disappearing under the low-hanging bougainvillea that nearly blocked the sidewalk.

Suddenly Theresa turned to Jardine and spoke as if dictating from a source just over her shoulder. Her voice was louder than usual.

"That dream you had yesterday? Jack and Jill? That boy's mother, Mrs. Billings, you ask if her son had any friends named Jack you could talk to. You got that?"

"What about Jill?" asked Jardine.

"Jack," she said. "Jackie. Talk to Jackie. See what Jackie has to say."

Jardine had taken out his small loose-leaf tablet and was hurriedly writing down what she said. "How do you do that?" he asked. "That other voice?"

"What voice? It's just my voice." But she shuddered once, hearing it herself in the bones of her skull. The North End, Italian voice with the hard *t*'s, the in-your-face cadence, voice from home, the voice of her mother yelling down the back stairs from the apartment above the store, "Tell that girl to quit daydreaming and get up here to help me with these potatoes. How many times I got to ask for some simple chores to get done around here?"

Jardine hesitated beside her a moment, then reached out and touched her bare arm. Theresa shivered, as if coming back to herself.

"You're going down to Long Beach now?" she asked.

"I should work on this Oslin homicide. I shouldn't even be here with you now."

"Oliver?" she asked, distracted in the sunlight, looking down the sidewalk where DeLisi had gone. "DeLisi knew his wife was going to die. Did you notice that? He predicted it."

"Ex-wife," Jardine corrected, "*is* going to die."

"You're getting it too?" She grabbed his elbow.

"No, I'm correcting your past tense. You said 'was going to die' like it had already happened."

"Is . . . was . . . What's the difference, Oliver? From where I stand, time is different."

"I don't know about you," said Jardine, "but I'm standing here on the sidewalk in Venice Beach, California, on Tuesday, July seventh, 1992, at one-twenty-seven in the afternoon."

"Time isn't just on a watch," she whispered. "Einstein brought that to our attention."

Jardine looked at her strangely. Just before the bougainvillea, he turned back toward her, squinting into the midday sun. "Don't be so open, Theresa," he called.

"I know, I know." She waved him on.

But she was going into that place where she didn't know. Green light filtered down through a tree. Shadows flew on the sidewalk like birds, flying into shapes of letters from an ancient language she couldn't decipher. She could almost be afraid of going into those letters, down into the writing of them moving across the hot cement, but she wasn't. She noticed the fear as a place she could stop or be stopped, but she chose to move past it, leaving the fear where it was, trembling and whispering, its familiar admonitions calling after her.

THERE WAS GOING TO BE TROUBLE, Jardine thought. He slammed the car door and turned the air conditioner on in the enclosed heat. There was something going on with Theresa that made him uncomfortable, and it was more than Joe DeLisi. She was mercurial and sometimes he didn't know her.

He pulled out onto Washington, heading for the freeway. Damn it, he did feel protective. She didn't need to be up to her neck in somebody's ugly custody war, with a lost kid stretched between two hatreds. He'd blown it utterly by taking DeLisi over there in the first place. But she was a professional, she knew what she was doing. In fact, he thought, she'd been pretty goddamn sly. She'd interviewed DeLisi. Done a quite passable job of conducting an investigative interview—telling him she had client boundaries she'd have to check out. Gotten everything she'd wanted and given him nothing. Handled it fine.

What is it, then, Oliver? he asked himself, picturing Theresa in her sun dress and gold sandals, her black tangles pulled back and tied up with a strip of lace off an old curtain or something, the early gray streaking her temples. The way she'd looked at DeLisi, stared at him over in the shade by the fence. It was almost embarrassing, like listening in on an intimate conversation between them that hadn't even taken place yet. DeLisi was hitting on her in the silent undercurrent between them, and then Jardine realized what was really getting him. DeLisi had acted all right, on the up and up, straight ahead. What man in his right mind wouldn't admire Theresa's odd, intense beauty? It was Theresa he'd picked up on, it was *her* desire. She'd turned it on like some sonic female message radiating out in concentric circles, an emanation like perfume, floral and heady, something he'd obviously, *obviously, dickhead,* never felt her radiating in his direction.

Jardine looked in the mirror at his bulbous sunburned nose, and his wiry reddish hair receding over his shiny forehead. And was suddenly furious with himself for entertaining any protective guardian-angel thoughts about Theresa at all. They were colleagues, they were friends, she was his teacher, for God's sake. *Get real, Oliver.*

But still, cruising fast through midday traffic, heading south to Long Beach through the acrid July day, he thought, *I should warn Theresa about DeLisi. Not just about the custody stuff. Guy like that, good-looking, smart, accomplished, out-of-town, you know he isn't unattached.* Jardine couldn't tell whether it was an intuition or whether he was just pissed. Stuff it, he told himself.

The disappearance of Royce Billings was not his case. Officially it was none of his business and was under the jurisdiction of the Orange County Sheriff's Department. But they considered the case dead in the water, and there was no active investigation under way, so the family had gone to the Simon Foundation. Sometimes Jardine wondered what he was doing, crossing over into working with these families. Marsha had given him shit about that, too: *You're a workaholic. You trying to get into heaven or what? Not only is your cop work too heavy, you got to take on volunteer work. Very convenient way to never be available, Ol. Then you wonder why you're lonely. Someday you'll drop dead all by yourself, reviewing your impressive case load.*

A private detective friend of his who worked with missing-person cases had started consulting with him. His friend had been hired full-time by the foundation, though he no longer worked there, and he'd asked Jardine to go over his files with him on a regular basis. Sure, Jardine saw it as volunteer work. Maybe he did want to go to heaven. But really it was the hopefulness in the work, however slight, that drew him. With a homicide, somebody was cold dead and he was looking for a murderer. Here he had a chance to find someone who might still be alive. There were kids actually located, many of them taken by noncustodial parents. It was a relief to find someone alive and be able to bring them home.

Occasionally some case caught his eye and he'd get more involved. This one had, and he wasn't sure why. Royce Billings had been ten when he'd disappeared. The family was working class, Dad a laid-off oil refinery worker and Mom a home-care nurse. After Royce had vanished, the neighborhood had rallied around the family, putting up posters, even gathering a sizable reward for any information that might lead to finding the boy. He'd been out with a group of friends playing near a canal when he had disappeared. No one had seen him go, but it was assumed that it was a stranger abduction. Jardine had gone back a number of times to help the local police interview Royce's friends. He'd always had a gut feeling that there was something the kids knew that they weren't telling. It was like picking up on shame, something hidden.

Four months had passed now. Maybe there were details somebody could remember now, something they couldn't get out of their minds.

The Billings family lived in a grid of cheap stucco houses with carports. Some of the houses were nicely maintained, but the neighborhood had an abandoned feeling to it. A cactus grew on either side of the Billingses' front steps. Jardine walked past a car under a tarp and saw Mr. Billings out in the carport patching the underside of a small sailboat. He said he'd finally gotten work again and things were looking better. If only it wasn't for Royce. Did they have some new lead? Jardine didn't want to tell him it wasn't a lead but a dream. Mrs. Billings joined them shortly, wearing her white nurse's uniform but not the hat. The TV was on inside the house, the sound of empty laughter rippling through their somber conversation.

"Did the kids ever play in the oil wells in the area?" Jardine asked the parents.

Mrs. Billings said, "There's a lot of them around."

"What about any dry wells, wells not pumping currently?"

She shrugged, shook her head. "They're all up and down the coast. I wouldn't have put it past them."

"Did Royce have any friends named Jack? Jackie?"

Mrs. Billings swept some cobwebs off the mildewed canvas of the sailboat. "There's Jackie Rebek, right, honey? Down the street."

"Could you give me his address?" asked Jardine.

"She. Jackie's a she. Tommy Rebek's little sister. She's about seven. Tommy is Royce's best friend. You talked to both Tommy and Jackie before."

"Is he the chubby kid with the funny teeth?"

"That's him. And Jackie's the little skinny one with the big eyes."

"I don't remember her."

"She's pretty shy. I can take you over there if you want."

"That's okay. I'd like to use your phone for a minute first, if that's all right." Mrs. Billings rinsed the last dishes in the sink as Jardine left a message for Sondra Jackson on her pager, and another on Jane Wood's answering machine. He wanted to stop off to question Oslin's girlfriend on his way back.

Jardine followed Mrs. Billings out onto the driveway, where she pointed to a house kitty-corner across the street. Jardine thanked her and crossed over to the Rebek house. Tommy answered the door, standing behind the screen, holding a fistful of baseball cards. He didn't smile. Jardine reminded him who he was. "We're just making some rounds, talking again to a few more people. I'd like to talk to Jackie."

"Jackie?" Tommy repeated. "She's in her room, I think. I'll get her."

He could hear them talking down the hall, and then Jackie came out. She was thin and small, with scraggly blond hair and long bangs. Jardine vaguely remembered her. She wore an oversized Beauty and the Beast sweatshirt, purple leggings, and scruffy pink sneakers that looked too big for her. The laces were untied. She sat down on the couch and stared at "Darkwing Duck" on the TV. Tommy finally unlocked the door and let Jardine in.

The boy stepped outside and Jardine heard the thump of a basketball on the driveway. He sat down on the chair across from Jackie.

"Do you remember when I came and talked to you after Royce was first gone?" he asked.

Jackie nodded.

"We didn't get a chance to talk much, though, did we? Do you have any idea what Royce and Tommy and all the big boys were doing the day Royce disappeared? Do you know anything special, Jackie, that might help us find Royce? Things you've heard Tommy and his friends say that maybe they forgot to tell us?"

She shifted in her seat next to him on the couch, and fiddled with a bracelet made of pastel hearts.

"I believe in God," she said.

"I do, too," he said.

"And Jesus."

"I'm not so sure about him."

"My mom started taking me to church after no one could find Royce. Dad's kind of mad about it. Tommy won't go. Dad says Mom's getting all religious on him. I learned that God knows everything and He knows where Royce is and people should love each other and be kind to each other."

"Do you know where Royce is?" Jardine asked the girl.

She sat very still, then nodded. "Me *and* God know. And I don't know if it's better to love Tommy or Royce or God or my mom or my dad. I don't want to get my brother in trouble. If Tommy goes to jail, Mom will kill me. For sure, my dad will. He'll kill both of us."

"It's usually best just to tell the truth, Jackie. You feel a lot better. And when they say God knows stuff, I think that's what they mean. That there is truth and it ought to come out. It's best for everybody."

"Will I have to go to jail?" she asked. "For telling?"

"No," he said. "You're too young for jail. So is Tommy, no matter what happened."

"Okay. I think Tommy might kill me, though. But he doesn't know I know. Not really."

"Where is Royce Billings?" Jardine asked.

"He fell down in a hole. A big giant hole. They were all climbing way high and messing around and Royce fell down in a crack. He landed somewhere far down and he never came out. Maybe he hit his head real hard or something. Or fell in and got stuck. All the other boys ran off. They were scared they'd get in trouble and have to go to jail. No one told. I wonder if Royce is still there. I heard Tommy talking one night and the big boys went back and looked to see if they could find him. I don't know if they found him, but I have a bad feeling. I feel bad if he's stuck somewhere waiting for someone to pull him out.

"And ever since I've been going to church with my mom, at night I have bad dreams about Royce. I knew someone should tell. I guess it was me. It wasn't their fault. No one pushed him in the hole. He jumped all by himself. It was a dare. But no one told. That wasn't a good idea, was it? I thought if they had it on 'Unsolved Mysteries,' I'd call in and tell and not say my name. But instead you came. So I'm telling you."

"Where is the hole, Jackie? The crack?"

She shrugged her birdlike shoulders. "I'm not sure."

"You're not sure or you don't know?"

"I don't really know."

"Was it an oil well or a drainage ditch or a sewer pipe? A construction site where a building was being put up?"

Jackie Rebek shook her head. "That's kind of why I didn't tell. I knew the boys knew where, but I didn't want to tell on them."

"You did good, Jackie," said Jardine. "Tommy can tell us where it is."

But Tommy had disappeared. He was nowhere in the house, and Jackie rode her bike up and down the street calling for him and checking at houses of his other friends.

Jardine called the sheriff's department, and a squad car was waiting out front when Mr. Rebek arrived home from his shift. He was a huge, barrel-chested man with a mean face and bags under his eyes. He clutched a black lunch pail in his massive hand. Jardine understood immediately why Tommy would never have told where Royce was.

Mrs. Rebek arrived home shortly afterward, her arms full of grocery bags. Jardine told them what Jackie had said, and the sheriff questioned the Rebeks about where Tommy might have gone.

Jardine asked several times, "What about a well? A cistern, a viaduct, a ditch? An oil well, a water well? Something to do with oil and wells, anything . . . "

Mr. Rebek had said very little, but at last he mumbled something.

"What was that?" asked Jardine.

"I was just saying, over at the refinery where me and Billings both work, there's this place between a couple of the structures. Everyone hates to have to get up there to repair anything on them ladders. There's like a big crevice down there, and a piece of machinery cranking up and down and everybody always calls it 'the well.' 'The well to hell.' Guys'll come home and say to their old lady, 'I went to hell and back today.' I said that before to you, didn't I, Patty?"

"Did your son know about that place?"

"Yeah, he did. I took him over there to the refinery one day and showed him around. Took the whole Cub Scout den. They were getting a career badge or something."

"And was Royce in that Cub Scout den?" asked Jardine.

"Yes, sir, he was."

Mrs. Rebek started crying. "I think I know where Tommy is," she sobbed. "He hid there once before when Stan was going to punish him for something. Even cut himself a little air hole," she explained. Her face was streaming with tears and she made no attempt to wipe them away. Mr. Rebek cast a stern look at her and she snapped at him, her voice shuddering. "A mother knows things about her children a father never will, Stan. You're so goddamn hard on the boy, he's probably scared to death to tell what he knows. And I'm here to tell you Tom will not be punished for this. He's scared, is all. You lay a hand on that boy and I will call these officers right back to the house in two seconds flat."

Rebek slumped down on the front steps and pulled Jackie onto his lap. The sheriff and Jardine exchanged glances and followed Mrs. Rebek to the alley, where Tommy was found crouched in a large plastic trash can. Though he was big, he fit right down in there. The air hole he'd cut was wedge-shaped, like the holes kids cut in the tops of jack-o'-lantern pumpkins so the candle won't go out.

They drove in a pack of squad cars over to the wasteland of oil refineries, giant structures of metal coughing fire into the blackened sky just a few miles from the ocean. Tommy seemed shrunken in size next to his father. He cringed in his presence as if anticipating a blow, but Mr. Rebek had become oddly gentle and sad. He sat in the squad car with his arm around his fat son.

Tommy and Mr. Rebek led an Orange County sheriff's deputy up a zigzag of metal stairs and ladders, climbing four or five stories up the dragon. The rest of them followed their progress from the parking lot far below. Near the very top of the huge structure, Tommy climbed out on a pipe and pointed down. From where he stood, Jardine could see the deputy trying to peer down into the crevice. The deputy looked back at them in the parking lot below, then down again into the canyon of machinery. He called to Tommy to climb back across the thick pipe.

Jardine turned and walked back to the squad cars parked in the refinery lot. He didn't want to climb up and see the body himself, didn't need to. Mrs. Rebek sat in a squad car, holding Jackie on her lap. Jardine went over to them. "You did the right thing, Jackie," he told her.

"Are the Billingses going to press charges against Tom?" Mrs. Rebek asked.

"It sounds like it was an accident. The kids should've told, is all. The sheriff can let you know what's going to happen next."

Jardine strolled away from the squads, watching a refinery nearby spew black-orange flames into the brown air. Trucks charged through the lot, engines spitting. The sheriff came over to Jardine and shook his hand. "Thanks, Lieutenant. What led you to talk to this little girl again, anyway? We didn't spend a lot of time interviewing the younger kids, but they sure do know what's happening, don't they?"

"It was just a hunch," said Jardine. "Just a hunch."

He drove north in gridlock traffic to Marina Del Rey, wondering what dreams knew.

THERESA ATE A QUICK LUNCH of fruit, cheese, and crackers while standing up at the kitchen counter. She was relieved that she had two readings scheduled for the afternoon. The old, easy, available hearts of her regulars. Was she only telling them what they already knew? They nodded, said *yes, yes that's exactly how it was with my family growing up.* They would ask a question directly, or they'd write it down on a piece of paper, fold it, and hand it to Theresa, and she would just hold it, listening to the answer of the unspoken question appearing in her mind, in her quiet breathing. This was an old-fashioned way of reading, called Billets. She could do the same thing with a photograph in a sealed envelope.

Years ago she had read mostly with tarot cards, occasionally consulting the I Ching or rune stones. She'd had a collection of cards from all over the world, drawing from various cultures: Incas and Aztecs, medieval patriarchy, feminist witches, Huichol shamans, Native American medicine cards, Jungian archetypes, and Celtic and Gypsy packs. She had loved the paraphernalia of readings, and had always lit incense and spread the cards out on a square of silk to protect the energy of each deck. If the room had felt messy with someone's leftover problems, she would burn sage between clients, the way a doctor might unroll clean paper on the examining table and stick the thermometer in alcohol.

She still burned sage now and then, but the cards, stones, sticks, and coins had fallen away. Gradually, over time, she had noticed that the reading actually began in her before the cards were even laid out. She had taken to beginning the reading while her client was still shuffling the deck, and once she had given an entire hour's consultation while the man sat holding the unshuffled deck in his hand. It had been a reading of depth and accuracy, and the man had felt opened, challenged, and enhanced. At the end of the session he had asked Theresa what he'd been supposed to do with the cards. "We didn't need them, did we?" he'd said, handing the deck back to her.

After that she'd put all the cards away, as well as the incense, candles, and anything else that had served as a vehicle for the readings. Had they merely been props, devices? she wondered. But no. They were in her now, an internalized language of symbols, and she could read the way a gifted chef would cook, knowing precisely which herb to throw in, how much salt, and when to drain the fat away. She went on intuition now, but intuition trained and practiced over years. The only vehicle now was the mind itself, fluid, singing, speaking psyche, which, in her, for reasons she didn't altogether understand, was like an open door. She stepped through that door into another person, listened inside the person, and then spoke. Recently, though, she'd eased up a bit, leaving some of her old tools out on the table in her studio.

Her second client of the afternoon was a man named Don who came every year around his birthday and was, this year, thinking about remarrying. Going in, she saw the man's hands untying a knot, then saw him climbing into a boat and beginning to row strongly out into the center of a beautiful lake. At first she "thought" that the untying of the knot meant *don't marry, there will be a breakup,* but she waited and the words came up from under her conscious thinking. "This decision to marry is going to be very freeing," she told him. "You're unraveling your hold, your control on your single life—but it's not a leash or a restraint. It has been a way that you've stayed close to home, to the shore of yourself, to what you know of yourself.

"Now, with this loosening, this letting go into marriage—you're climbing right in. There's no holding back. You are wholehearted and the very act of loving is propelling you. It's a movement toward your deepest self, your center. This loving the other, this risk and movement, is taking you to a deeper, more fluid, and very beautiful place.

"You'll have to be aware that your loving," Theresa continued, "your pulling into it, muscling it—leaves her room. Don't pressure her. She's subtler than you are, Don—so let her be still a lot. She'll settle, like the surface of a lake you've rowed across. Go to the center of the lake and wait patiently for the surface to calm. She'll teach you receptivity and openness. You'll teach her will and movement. Anyway—make the decision and leave her time to catch up to you. She'll seem hesitant and holding back for a while. But you're ready—and there is so much beauty in it. I don't sense any blocks. Right now you're untying your identity from where you've had it tethered. You're rearranging yourself toward this deeper movement. It's good."

That was when it started, in that space after Don's reading when Theresa was very open. Normally, the connection with the client would gently close and she would open her eyes, as if waking from a nap in which she was not really asleep, but listening.

Tory came into that open space. *She is looking out a window. Pressed to the glass, a crack there, she can see out.* Theresa heard Don shift restlessly on the sofa, uncomfortable with the long silence.

"Excuse me," she told Don. "I'm not quite done yet. Let me just take a few moments . . . "

Theresa let herself go in farther. A swing set and the ache of longing, as if the swing set were unattainable for some reason. *Can't get there.* Prevented from it, from the pleasure of it. A road, then driving. Another playground. This time Tory gets out, runs across the grass to the swing, leaps on, pumping high, higher. It is night now, late. No one else is there. Except the man standing behind her, watching. Tory is singing. She sings right into Theresa's head.

Star light, star bright, first star I see tonight . . .

She hums the rest, stares up at one star not the brightest but look how it glows and blinks.

I got my wish already: to stop here. Funny to be at a playground in the black. Wish I may wish I might, have the wish I wish tonight, dark park, car park, Whitney Park, Lark, Hark, Hark the herald angels sing. I wish I had one to fly me home. I want to go home, but then again I don't. I don't know where I want to live, I don't want to have to pick, or hurt someone. Don't want to be hurt either. Doc is nice, he's nice to me, he doesn't yell, he doesn't hurt. I don't know what to do, though, I don't know what to do. I miss my mom. Glad that I'm gone. This is my song. I wish there was a special star I could talk to. There she is. I feel her listening.

"What does Doc look like, Tory?" Theresa had not meant to, but she had spoken the question out loud.

She pressed Record on the tape recorder beside her and spoke in a softer, lighter voice, singing, *"He's real nice, he's kind of chubby and big, kind of like the Incredible Hulk on 'All-Star Wrestling.' His hands are soft to hold. He wears those funny old glasses made of round wires and he's a little bit bald. But not too old, not too old. A round, funny nose. He looks like a younger Santa without white hair and no beard. He's a giant elf. I didn't remember his name at first, but now I do. But Doc's not his real name."*

"What is his real name?" Theresa asked, in her own voice.

Blank silence.

"Come back," Theresa whispered. "Tory? Is he one of your doctors? What is his last name?"

Empty sound, inner-ear hum, no words. Only the image of the park, night, teeter-totters, angled shadows from a streetlight.

"Tory, when did you know Doc before?"

You know. When I was so sick that time.

"Where are you, Tory?"

Theresa dropped down into the black dream, where she was in the story as if it were happening right now. She could feel the swing slow down, the rhythmic flying ease.

The child looks back at the figure at the edge of the playground, waiting in the shadows for her to finish. She calls out, "Where are we, anyway, Doc? Is this Arizona?"

He starts toward her. She isn't afraid, she trusts him. Almost. But there's the catch right there in her breastbone as he approaches.

"We're almost there," he says.

"Where is here?" she asks.

"I told you we have to wait until they're ready for you. We got to wait a few more days."

Look at him, Tory, let me see his face.

Theresa felt her inner looking strain in the darkness. The man stepped into the light and she saw him, a kind, round face, soft, the way the child had described it. She studied it, tracing the details in her mind, wishing she could draw it now as she was looking, but she did not feel the urgency in her hand. The image was only visual, not kinesthetic. Clairvoyant, not clairsentient.

"Thank you," Theresa whispered out loud.

The child said, "You're welcome." She stopped swinging altogether.

"Who are you talking to?" asked Doc.

The child hopped off the swing. "Her," she said, pointing. "That star right up there."

Theresa opened her eyes and grabbed her notebook, furiously scribbling notes, a description of the man, the name "Doc," what the child had said and the name of the place where she was: *Whitney Park.* She did not know of any city park by that name, but there must be hundreds, even thousands, of small playgrounds and community centers in the L.A. area, much less between L.A. and Arizona. She tried to draw the face she had seen, sketch it, calling inwardly for Tory's hand to draw through hers, but it wasn't there. All she got was a doodle of a muscle man with John Lennon glasses and a round nose. She couldn't seem to get Tory to draw. That sketch artist Jardine had at the department, maybe she could work with her again. *Good,* she wrote on the bottom of the drawing. *Good work, Tory!* as if she were a teacher grading a paper.

When she looked up, Don was peering at her suspiciously, bewildered. "What was all that?" he asked.

Theresa turned the notebook over on the coffee table. "It had nothing to do with you. I'm sorry. I know it seems strange. Sometimes information comes through in a reading for another person. It bleeds through."

"How can you tell it wasn't about me?" asked Don.

"It was a very particular voice," said Theresa. "Several voices, actually. Everyone has a sound to their thinking, so I know when it shifts. Same as when different people talk out loud. Even if you can't see them, if you only hear them, like on the phone, you still know their voice."

Don looked at his watch, then took out his checkbook. He looked embarrassed as he said, "Theresa, you went over by almost a half hour."

"Was it that long? Don, I'm sorry."

"I just don't feel comfortable paying for that time if it wasn't even about me."

Theresa placed her hand over Don's checkbook. "This one's on me," she said. "There's no charge."

Theresa had not been able to reach Ellen Carlin all afternoon. She'd left several messages, saying it was urgent. She wanted to meet with

Joe DeLisi as soon as possible, but she didn't want to do it behind Ellen's back. Jardine was also out, and she didn't feel right about calling Rukheyser with the name of the park unless Ellen knew about it first.

This was disconcerting, to engage in a conversation with someone not present, to be speaking both voices. She was not a channel, receiving voices from other realms. No Venusians, angels, or soon-to-be-reincarnated beings had ever come through her with noble thoughts and advice for the earth-plane, and though she knew some fairly reputable channels, she'd always had her doubts about them. It just wasn't her style.

But Tory had spoken to Theresa internally and out loud, as if she were speaking to an imaginary friend, as if in prayer to a star. The two voices were right there on the tape. Their connection was uncanny and telepathic. Theresa wished she hadn't told anyone about it, Ellen, Leslie, even Oliver. No one but another psychic would understand. From now on she would relay what she thought of as "the information" to Ellen, but not how she received it. Finally she felt so restless with what the reading had given her that she decided to go over to the Island Café for a real lunch. Camille was often there in the afternoon.

Theresa drove to the Island Café, just over the edge of Venice Beach, in Santa Monica. It felt good to be outside, the steamy air damp on her skin. It made her black hair curl wildly, and she took the clasp out of her hair and shook it back over her shoulders. She parked in front of the café, then pushed open the green-framed glass door into the cool stillness.

The café walls were painted a green so pale it was almost white, and the ceiling was crisscrossed with lattice painted an airy pink. Primitive paintings from Haiti and Jamaica lined the walls, and on the back wall, near the kitchen, hung a collection of baskets. White Christmas-tree lights had been wound through the lattice. Even though it was afternoon, the tiny lights glowed overhead. It was a small, elegant space, perfumed with the scents of cilantro, cardamom, and strong coffee.

Camille and Robert were seated at a table near the back. They looked up as she came in. "Hey, hey!" called Robert. "Resa! Where you been hiding yourself? My plaintain specialty came and went without your taste buds' approval, and I've already moved on to red snapper and fresh peas with mint."

"That'll do," she said. "When do I start?"

Theresa gave Robert a hug and sat down next to Camille. Camille leaned forward in a wicker chair, going over the books. She wore a brown and black African cloth wrapped high around her hair, and a blue dress with gold threads shot through the fabric. Her usual regal self. Robert went back into the kitchen, calling for his cousin, the chef. "Bobby, my man, can I get a sampler platter?" The sound system kicked in softly, Jimmy Cliff, the slow reggae calming Theresa, bringing her back to a sense of what she thought of as her real life.

Camille set down the calculator and leveled her almond eyes at Theresa, eyes so dark the iris and pupil seemed a single well, black as space, and they shone from deep down with a glimmer of silver. "My friend, I'm getting old," she said in a low voice.

"You don't look old, Camille. You're ageless."

"It's mothering that's made me old. I had Sarene when I was twenty-three, and now I could be a grandmother at thirty-eight."

"Sarene is pregnant?" Theresa gasped.

"No, thank God, but I found birth-control pills in her purse. She is messing around and she even admitted it!"

"Well, at least she's using her head."

"What head? The girl is fifteen. She's going out with a young man who is twenty-one, and you know the child does not look fifteen, she doesn't act fifteen, all savvy, Ms. Hip-hop, lady be good tonight in my beehive hairdo, but, Resa, that child's brain is fifteen. You know what I'm saying? She doesn't have a head, she has hormones. She's saturated with them." Camille sighed.

"Well, did you talk to her?"

"We sat up till all hours. She's a good kid, it's not that. She's got the safe-sex thing down, at least she says so, it's just that I don't want her to go and be a fool. I was fool enough when I had her. I handled it, you know, but still I got to fret and fuss about it, don't I? Otherwise I'm not doing my job."

Theresa twirled the salt shaker, shook a few grains into her palm, and rubbed them around with her finger. It was strange to think of Camille being a grandmother. Why, Theresa still hadn't even resolved whether she wanted any children at all, not that she had a potential father in mind.

Her own mother had been harried, either quietly suffering with her saint-eyes rolled heavenward to the Madonna, or screaming at the five girls lined up in the hallway with lace doilies bobby-pinned to their hair that if they were late for mass again she'd show them a thing or two and then they'd be sorry, mark her words, God as her witness.

It was all those years of taking care of the four younger ones that had dampened her maternal urges. The neighbors had even called Theresa mamasina, "little mama," never free to take off for the playground or stay overnight at a friend's house. She didn't even get to earn money baby-sitting, she did it all the time without pay, even when her parents were home. And her mother hadn't appreciated it. Her mother had always been unhappy in such a way that it was her accomplishment. Her career. Theresa had always feared the horrid inner workings of family life, at least what she remembered of it, those crowded rooms in cold Boston winters, all five girls in one bedroom, until Theresa fashioned herself a cot in the back hallway, strung a curtain over her newly claimed space, put a red light bulb in there and posters of the Beatles and Donovan and Laura Nyro.

"Camille?" Theresa asked. "Does being a mother bring out the worst in a woman? My family—I think they scared me out of having a kid. But I adore Sarene, I do like kids . . . "

"It brings out the deepest," said Camille. "The deepest and the strongest of all you got, good, bad, and everything in between. I always said if God meant parents to be calm and patient and steady, She wouldn't have made children so wild in the first place. Kids kick up everything in your face for you to look at about yourself. You know that from all the readings you've done. What's up? You got something on your mind under that question?"

Camille went to the table by the kitchen, poured a cup of coffee, heavy with cream, and brought it to Theresa.

Theresa explained about Tory DeLisi and her parents, the strain she perceived in both of them. She left out her minor crush on Joe DeLisi. She knew better than to mess with a client. "I guess the thing I'm having the most trouble with is the death imagery. It isn't even really a picture or image, exactly. It is a sensation of profound emptiness and absence, like the woman is being erased. Like something written in invisible ink, fading right off the page. And I don't know whether to tell her. I can't get a clear direction."

"Did you ask?"

Theresa tilted her head, questioning in the silence.

"For clear direction?" Camille continued.

"Not exactly."

"Well, then ask. Ask exactly. Clear the whole space out. Clear out mama and daddy and daughter, and wash the whole space with light and then smooth it over with velvet blackness and ask for a clear direction. It's like trying to pay the bills when you haven't opened your mail for two weeks and you don't even know how much you got in your checkbook. Sounds like you got intense voices competing for air space, and the question of whether to tell the woman or not is something about you, about what you're up to, rather than about her. Not is it right for her to know, but is it right for you to tell."

Theresa nodded. That made sense. She needed to read for herself about this. "I've just never felt like telling people the bad stuff. Illness, abandonment, bankruptcy, death, breakdowns . . . "

"It wouldn't come up in the reading if they weren't ready to hear it, you know that. All that material is just life, life talking to us, trying to get our attention."

The coffee tasted of hazelnut, warm and smooth in her mouth. "I do feel I have to wait for clarity," said Theresa.

"Clarity," Camille mused. "Now I heard she moved out to Montana somewhere because she couldn't take the smog."

Robert strode out of the kitchen with a plate held high, Sarene behind him with a black apron on, tight jeans and a black T-shirt, plum-colored lipstick, carrying a wineglass filled with juice.

"A little something courtesy of the Island," Robert pronounced, pointing out the sampling of delicacies on the plate before her, black beans and rice, green-chili corn bread, red snapper, pineapple compote, jerk chicken, and spicy beef. The juice was guava and sparkling water. "Let me know what you think," he said.

Theresa tugged at Sarene's apron. "What's this?"

"I'm helping out three afternoons a week till school starts. I get monster tips, too. I am good." She grinned.

Camille rolled her eyes.

"I haven't forgotten about your birthday expedition," said Theresa. "How about this Friday?"

"Friday would be great!"

Sarene came up behind Camille and put her arms around her mother, held her, resting her cheek against Camille's head cloth.

Camille leaned back into Sarene's embrace and said, "This is my baby, blooming into a woman right before my eyes. Magical danger."

"Mo-ther!" Sarene scoffed. "Just the magic, not the danger!" She winked at Theresa. "Isn't she just so dramatic?"

Theresa could almost physically feel the love between them, rich and complex, full of humor and power and tenderness. It hadn't been easy for Camille, long years on her own with Sarene, before she'd hooked up with Robert. She had made something good that put families like Tory's to shame. She wondered why it was that some people's lives were so infected and full of fear.

Camille walked Theresa out to her car. "Why don't you come on my next show? I think the subject of abandonment and the search for lost children, both actual kids and that feeling of a lost child within that so many people have, would be a good topic. And you could get the word out about this little girl."

"But the show is on Friday. I just promised Sarene—"

"The show starts at two. Take her on Friday night."

Theresa agreed; she'd be at the station early to prepare for the program.

On the drive to the Simon Foundation, Theresa felt angry at Ellen. By compartmentalizing the investigation, by keeping everyone separate, Ellen was actually hindering efforts to find her daughter. Theresa found herself planning ahead to contact Joe DeLisi at his hotel to talk with him more about Tory, more about Ellen, even if Ellen didn't want her to. His presence was making Tory more real to her, bringing her voice in more clearly. *I want to see him again,* she thought. *It's been so long since I felt that way about a man.*

She checked herself. *Red flag. Client boundaries.* Then clearly the thought came: NOT NOW, it said over her right shoulder.

"What are you," she asked out loud. "Some Jiminy Cricket goody-goody conscience or something?"

NOT NOW, the Voice repeated.

"Okay, okay," she muttered. "So it's not appropriate."

She drove north on Pacific Avenue, stopping at a light. Sitting there watching the wind in a palm tree, she thought, *Screw appropriate.*

She waited, but no countering Voice rose from the emptiness.

She parked at a meter next to Lincoln Park just off Wilshire Boulevard. The afternoon light was thin and green. Coming down the line of parking meters, checking them for change, was a homeless man, talking to himself. He was barefoot and wore baggy corduroy trousers, no shirt. The skin of his chest was as leathery as that of an old sailor, his hair matted into dusty blond dreadlocks, though he was white. She watched him, wary of getting out of her car, wondering if that was how she would end up, off the deep end, rattling on about voices of missing children speaking to her and she knew just where they were, moving around the country, taken from their homes, full of longing for mother and father, hungry for love. For a moment she felt a wave of panic.

The homeless man was standing by her car now, checking the nearest meter for coins. Her windows were rolled down and he was muttering to her, bending into the car.

"Blah blah blah blah blah!" he whispered.

She started her car up and pulled out onto Lincoln to find another place to park. *I don't have to put up with this shit,* she thought, then felt a wave of compassion for the man, and even, briefly, reverence. She couldn't help laughing. Even after all her years of intuitive work, doubts still ambushed her. But now she could hear them and banish them.

She parked again a few blocks away, but still had to walk by the park on her way to the Simon Foundation. She didn't see the blah-blah man, but spotted a woman asleep on a pink shower curtain near an azalea bush. As Theresa approached, the woman's eyes flew open and she flipped over, turning away toward the shadows.

Theresa didn't have to look any further for Ellen Carlin. As she pushed through the glass door into the office, Ellen looked up from her conversation with another woman. Ellen was dressed in dark green linen pants and a patterned blouse, a jacket draped over one arm. She'd pulled herself together since this morning's meeting and was more as she'd appeared when Theresa had met her the previous afternoon.

Theresa stepped toward Ellen. "I have more," she said. She wanted to say, *Tory contacted me again and I even spoke with her,* but she restrained herself. "Is there a place where we can talk alone, Ellen?"

"How about Leslie Simon's office? She's expected back shortly."

Ellen checked with the receptionist, and Theresa followed her to Leslie's office. Ellen leaned against the desk. "What did you come up with?" she asked.

"First I need to clear some things with you. I met with your exhusband this afternoon."

Ellen straightened. "But that is expressly against my wishes, Theresa. You know that."

"Let me explain," said Theresa. "My colleague, Lieutenant Jardine of the LAPD, brought your ex-husband to my house this afternoon unannounced. Lieutenant Jardine knew I was working on this; you did give me your okay to discuss the case with him. He thought I'd want to meet with Dr. DeLisi. Lieutenant Jardine was not aware of our confidentiality agreement—which I did tell your ex-husband about immediately."

"So now Joe knows." Ellen looked disturbed.

"He only knows that you have consulted with me. I didn't tell him anything at all about the content of our sessions." Theresa waited a moment. "Look, Ellen. I'm going to be very frank with you. I have, for some reason unknown to me, a deep and intense connection with your daughter, a psychic connection. She began to come to me before you ever called me. I feel hampered in being able to be effective because you want to keep me separate from other avenues of investigation. I'd like to be able to talk freely with Leslie Simon, I'd like the police to be able to work with me up front. I'd like to be able to talk with your ex-husband and to try a reading with the two of you present. Why not open it up, Ellen, and pull out all the stops? For Tory's sake."

"He's got to control everything," Ellen hissed. "He's got to have his hands on every aspect of this. I wanted someone I could consult with confidentially, and I can see it is not you. I can't even trust you! I don't feel I can work with you anymore, not now. Now that you've met with Joe, it feels contaminated."

"I assure you I didn't give him any information regarding our sessions or any of our conversations, Ellen. That's why I'm here. I wanted to check with you first. I'd like to review with you some of the things I got from a reading I did this afternoon. Does the name or nickname 'Doc' mean anything to you?"

Ellen shook her head.

"Could you provide Leslie with a list of all the doctors that have seen Tory?"

Ellen paced across the room. "There are probably a hundred. I'm sure they'd all be in her medical records."

"I got the name of a park, a playground where she stopped. It was night. I got the name 'Whitney Park.'"

Ellen spun suddenly to face Theresa, and lowered herself slowly into one of the wing chairs that faced Leslie's fake fireplace, then spoke quietly and firmly. "I will give these fragments to the police. And if I want any further consultation, I will call you. But until then, consider yourself free of any professional association with me. I consider all the information you've gotten so far to be strictly confidential between you and me. If you speak to anyone else regarding the contents of our sessions together, including the things you have just told me, Theresa, I will take legal action."

Theresa looked straight at Ellen and thought, *Fat chance, lady. I didn't sign any contract with you, and I'm under no obligation to keep my information from anyone. Got that?* She sent the thought boring straight back into Ellen's pupils and Ellen looked away.

What Theresa said out loud was "I feel that I'm getting some-where, Ellen. Don't cut me off. What if Tory comes to me again?"

"Just tell her to come home," Ellen said sadly. She stood and gazed out the office window over the parking lot. "I'd prefer it if you'd just leave Tory alone."

"It's Tory that's coming to me, not me to her."

"You're off the wall. That's not the way this works. You're the psy-chic. She's just a child."

"She's a psychic child."

"Stay away from her! You scare me. You really do. Stay away from her—in your, your—whatever it is that you do. Your mind."

"There's something else you should know, Ellen," Theresa per-sisted. "I didn't tell you before, because I didn't know what to make of it. But it came to me very strongly and repeatedly. I couldn't get a clear interpretation and I still can't. But if this is to be our final meeting, I feel obliged to tell you."

"And what's that?"

Theresa stopped, not sure what to say. "I feel that you're in danger in the next few days." She couldn't bring herself to tell Ellen she'd seen her death. It was not totally clear. "Just be careful, please."

Ellen looked shocked, then began to laugh. "Oh, this is choice. This is some kind of harassment, isn't it? I suppose Joe put you up to threatening me. I've a mind to sue your ass. Can you sue a psychic for malpractice?"

Theresa pressed on. "It's a feeling of your being absent. You've dis-appeared in some part of your being. Either you're going to disappear physically—by going away, by leaving—or you're in danger of . . . I don't know what. I'm sorry. I don't usually give this information out to a client."

"But you just felt you had to support me in my hour of need, is that it? Why, thank you," Ellen said sarcastically. "Thank you so much. I should have hired a bodyguard instead of a psychic. Or perhaps Joe paid you to tell me that. He likes to try to drive me crazy, but you can tell him that shit doesn't work anymore. I'm free of him."

With that, Ellen stopped and stared at Theresa with an odd look. Her mouth quivered and then she said, "I would like to go away, I can tell you that. That would be a great plan. I'd like to go somewhere and go to sleep and wake up when this is all over. Maybe that's what you're picking up on." Ellen cleared her throat. "I know I'm on the edge. I didn't mean to fly off the handle again. I'm under a terrible strain here, Theresa."

Theresa watched as Ellen flipped into different parts of herself, first angry and defensive, then fearful, vulnerable, and tender. She looked lightheaded, and sagged against the wall as if she were going to faint. Theresa helped her back to the chair. Ellen bent over and put her head down on her knees.

"Ellen, are you seeing a doctor yourself, a therapist, someone who could support you through this?"

Ellen shook her head. "I can't believe what you just told me."

"I'm afraid for you, and I want you to be careful."

"Should I tell the police?"

"Yes, or I can, if you want."

Ellen sat up, rubbing her temples with her fingers. "I just can't take that in right now. It's too much. It's too much for me to talk to you or to have anything to do with you. Please, Theresa. Please—leave me alone. I do better when I don't see you. Maybe I'm just afraid of you."

Theresa picked up her purse from Leslie Simon's desk and opened the door just as Leslie Simon was coming in.

"Theresa!" Leslie called out. "Good, we can all meet together at last. Ellen tells me—"

"That I'm fired," said Theresa. She brushed past Leslie with a feeling of tremendous relief. She didn't really want any further dealings with Ellen Carlin, either. If Tory came to her again, psychically, she'd just tell Jardine. He could relay the information to either Rukheyser or the foundation. In some way she hoped Tory *would* leave her alone. But Theresa knew that she wouldn't.

"ARE WE HAVING FUN?" Doc asked.

Tory's face was turned to the window. She seemed tired and had hardly spoken since she'd gotten up from that nap in the trailer. He couldn't tell whether she was sulking or sick, and that worried him. He wasn't sure what her treatment had been in the hospital, or even what was wrong with her this time. She didn't seem to have an appetite, didn't have a fever. She just sat holding that doll.

He parked the car, opened the passenger door, and took her hand as they walked toward the ship. "Do you know where we are?" he asked.

Finally she brightened a little. "It's huge," she said. "It looks so little inside the snow dome. Is it true all ships are named for girls?"

After Doc paid for the tickets, they climbed up a series of steps and crossed the walkway onto the *Queen Mary*. The ship was docked in Long Beach harbor and maintained as a tourist site. The circumference of the ship was a wide wooden deck. Big white lifeboats with blue canvas covers hung over the deck at intervals. Tory ran her hand along the smooth railings and leaned over the edge, watching a pelican out by a white buoy. Out in the harbor, a tiny island was covered with gulls. She tried out a deck chair, reclining on the chaise longue, staring at the afternoon sky.

The inside of the ship resembled a luxury hotel. Mahogany walls lined the giant ballroom. Art deco chandeliers glistened overhead. Portraits of kings and queens and movie stars who'd sailed on the ship hung on the deck walls. Tory asked to use the restroom and he waited outside the door for a long time, checking his watch. *Damn it, where is she? Is she sick?* he wondered.

He stepped toward an older woman who was heading for the bathroom and asked her to check on the little girl inside. When the woman looked at him suspiciously, he blurted out, "I'm a friend of her mother. I'm taking care of her." He even went so far as to show the woman an old ID from a job he'd had a year ago, his name printed right across the top. He felt sick himself at how stupid he was. *Next time just hire a plane, have your name in skywriting all over L.A., why don't you?*

Tory came out a few minutes later, her face pale and her shoulders rounded over as if she were aging into a tiny old woman.

Doc bent down to her, brushing her hair out of her eyes. "You okay? You had me worried there."

"I don't feel good," she whispered. "I want to go back to the trailer."

The old woman bustled out of the restroom, looking back over her shoulder at them as she hurried out toward the deck.

"Did that gray-haired lady talk to you in the bathroom?" he asked.

"She asked me if I knew you and what your job was. I told her I did and that it was none of her business 'cause I'm not supposed to talk to strangers."

Doc smiled. "Good girl," he said. Picking Tory up in his arms, he headed the long way around the ship and down a level. As they neared the walkway that exited the ship, a security guard appeared with a two-way radio in his hand.

Doc slowed down. She'd fallen asleep on his shoulder like a baby, her arms wrapped around him. The security guard looked past Doc at the families strolling the ship with their children. The guard must not have seen anyone who looked as though he had a child who didn't belong to him, thought Doc, stroking Tory's hair.

THE EARLY-RUSH-HOUR TRAFFIC had let up some, but Jardine was late anyway. He drove slowly, switching lanes for no other reason than to keep busy. He listened to an oldies station and felt old. He never thought he'd see the day when "Layla" would bring him down. But it wasn't "Layla," it was Royce Billings and Tory DeLisi. Royce had been found, Tory was still out there, and Oslin had had her school picture in his office. He had no idea why the man would have that picture. Somehow he had known her and had put her picture in a place of importance, along with those of his sister and his niece.

Jardine found himself bothered by the afternoon with the Billings and Rebek families. It wasn't the resolution of the case; he felt good about that, as good as one could feel when he closed on a death. It was the way he went back there, because of that dream, because of Theresa going from a well to Jack and Jill, from Popeye to oil. Was any of that in the dream itself, or was it just Theresa doing her psychic work on his dream material? He didn't see any intuitive work on his part, not really. And even when he thought about the dream itself, all of it had a rational explanation, none of it was particularly intuitive. He had talked to Jackie before, even if she hadn't stood out in his mind at the time. And he had known that Mr. Billings worked at an oil refinery, so it figured that oil might come into a dream. Was a dream just a way, then, of highlighting thoughts to your conscious mind, using the language of pictures? A sort of data base that could scan for items useful to you? But he knew that nothing in the dream would have been useful unless he'd had that conversation with Theresa about it. Then he remembered something she'd said many times about her readings for people—that she saw her role as "indicating the intuitive direction" to the person, activating the person's own intuitive processes by giving her attention and energy to it. Maybe that explained it.

Don't think, she often said. But he couldn't help it. He liked thinking. Thinking made a lot of sense. Intuiting did not.

Jardine was hungry, but he didn't have time to stop off at Burger King. He arrived at Jane Wood's Marina Del Rey condominium half an hour late, and found a scribbled note taped to her mailbox in the foyer, with a map showing him where he could find her down at the marina.

Ten minutes later he located her sailboat, moored along a dock crowded with other large craft. The name, neatly lettered in blue and gold on the back of the sloop, sounded like one she and Gerald Oslin had chosen together from their skydiving experience: *Free Fall.* Jane Wood sat in the back of the boat on a padded bench, holding a wine cooler and staring out over the water. Jardine leaned down and introduced himself, handing her a business card. Jane Wood stood quickly. She spoke in an agitated way, all in a rush, though she'd looked calm enough a few seconds earlier.

"Oh, you're here, good. I hate waiting. I can't believe any of this is happening. I can't believe it. I keep wanting to go over to the store and just walk back to his desk and Gerry'll be sitting there at his computer the way he always was and it'll all be okay. But it isn't, is it? Going to be okay. I mean, it's definitely not okay and it never will be." She looked down at the card, and it seemed to focus her. When she let out a sigh, her voice carried with it the wind of grief and denial. She gazed out at the late daylight shimmering on the water and dropped her hands. "Oh God," she whispered. "Now it's real."

She motioned for Jardine to step down into the boat, and covered her mouth with her hand as if to stop herself from crying. From the wheelhouse she fetched a box of Kleenex. Jardine leaned in the cabin door as Jane wiped her eyes. The inside of the cabin was paneled in dark wood, outfitted with shiny brass fittings. A sword was mounted above a small door at the back of the cabin. The sword looked like an antique, and the whole place had Oslin's touch, classy and well tended. A row of framed diplomas had been mounted above the sword. The diplomas had Chinese or Japanese writing on them and "Jane Wood" was penned in neat calligraphy on each of the degrees, leading up to that of black belt, second degree.

Jane Wood was tall. She wore black nylon running shorts and a Sierra Club T-shirt, and she was barefoot. Her thighs were muscular, her hands large, and she moved with the grace of an athlete, comfortable in her body. Her long brown hair was held back with a tortoise-shell clip, bangs wisping her forehead in the slight breeze. At first glance she looked plain, yet attractive, with a look of natural health and no pretense. She stretched out again on the padded bench, her long legs extended in front of her and crossed at the ankles. Jardine took his suit jacket off and sat down across from her.

"Mary called and told me about Gerry last night." Jane Wood stopped and swallowed, holding back tears. "I was in Honolulu. I'm a pilot for a small private company. She tracked me down through the company's answering service. I just got back around noon. Haven't slept or eaten since Mary called. I haven't even had a chance to go see Gerry at the funeral home. Mary's coming to get me in a bit, and we're all going together, me and Mary and Gerry's mom. I don't know if I could sleep if I tried. Lieutenant"—she glanced down at the card—"Jardine, I'm telling you, I can't think of a single reason anyone would ever kill Gerry. All I can think of is the store. Those antique people and those rare-book people are eccentric. They're fanatics sometimes, but they always seemed pretty harmless to me. Not violent types. And he was never in any kind of trouble. Mary said you thought it could be a burglary, even though nothing valuable was taken from the store."

"That's right," he agreed. "It looks like someone might have been after something in the files."

Jardine was surprised at how young she looked, thirty-five or an extremely youthful forty. That would have made Oslin perhaps fifteen years her senior, and Mary had said they'd been together almost fifteen years. "My associate, Ms. Jackson, is going over the store inventory and records as we speak. There was a photograph missing from the wall. Mary said that it was one of Mr. Oslin when he served in the navy. Do you remember it?"

"Yes. It was one of his favorite pictures of himself."

"Would he have given it away? Or can you think of anyone who might have taken it?"

"I can't see him giving it away, no. Why would anyone take a picture like that? There are lots more valuable things in the store to steal."

"It might indicate that it was someone who knew him, or that he gave it to someone close to him." Jardine watched as Jane's eyes moved over the floor of the boat, as if searching for a small dropped thing.

"I don't know," she shrugged. "I can't help you with that. I know I don't have it."

A fat seagull wobbled along the dock, looking for something to eat. "Lieutenant," Jane Wood said softly, "I need to know exactly what happened to Gerry. Mary's been so vague. I don't think she can talk about it."

Jardine cleared his throat. This was the place where people wanted the details of the death. Over his years of interviewing people close to homicides, he had found that it was wise to give them as much as they wanted of the facts. It kept the investigation grounded. There was nothing to protect. He told her what he knew and what he didn't know, then added, "Nothing seemed out of place, with the exception of the back door left open, the roses by the sink, and a couple of large bed pillows stacked on the floor. Everything else was immaculate. Did you give him the roses?" he asked.

She shook her head continuously as she answered. "No, but I remember seeing them. He kept them for a long time, even after they wilted. I did think, 'What's with these roses?' When he cut his own flowers from the garden, he'd replace them every few days. I don't know where he got them. Are you thinking they were a gift from someone?" She paused. "I wonder who. And what was the occasion?"

"Had he celebrated anything recently?"

"The last thing he celebrated that I know of was Mother's Day. He sent his mom a gift certificate to a spa."

"And the neatness of the house, that was in keeping with Mr. Oslin's character?" Jardine asked.

"That was Ger. He drove me nuts sometimes. I can even tell you right where those pillows were—leaning against the wall between the long dresser and the closet, right?"

"That's correct. And the bed was made with the smaller sleeping pillows tucked under the spread. You know what I mean?"

She winced, put her hand to her forehead, looked as though she were about to cry, took a breath. "The bed was made up with only the small pillows? The big ones were left on the floor?" she whispered. "Then it had to be someone else besides Ger who made that bed. Shit. God damn you, Ger."

She pulled her legs up to her chest, head down on her knees for a moment, her body curled up tight. "He was screwing around," she said, shaking her head in disbelief.

"Was this something that had happened before?"

"Not as far as I know. We broke up once about a year ago—only for about seven or eight weeks. He dated a few other people then, but I don't know who any of them were. He was the one who reconciled our relationship. I never knew him to sneak around behind my back with other women."

"What about men?" Jardine asked.

Jane Wood looked blank-faced at him. Finally she said, "Absolutely not." She stood and walked to the wheelhouse, standing in the doorway, taking a swig from the wine cooler. "Not unless he had some hidden life I knew absolutely nothing about."

"Did you ever sense that he did?" He watched her as she pondered the question. Jane Wood thought it through, as if she were scanning inside for some truth about her longtime lover that was beyond her grasp.

"Well, it wasn't exactly a secret-life kind of thing, but a while back, when his father died, in 'eighty-eight I think, Ger found out he was adopted and he tracked down his birth mother. They were in touch for a couple years and then she died. I never met her. I don't know if that qualifies as a secret life."

"Are you aware that his birth mother—Miss Betty Tucker—conceived Gerald with her first cousin?"

Again, blank-faced. Blinking. "Old Miss Tucker and her *cousin?*" Jane asked. "Her cousin was Ger's biological father?"

Jardine nodded.

"Son of a bitch. No, he never told me. How did you find out?"

"Mary came across it in Mr. Oslin's genealogical files in the computer hard drive."

"It does make some weird kind of sense," Jane said. "I mean, doesn't that lead to weird genetic stuff sometimes? Pregnancy between family members, incest?"

"Go on," Jardine prompted her.

"See, one thing Ger and I always agreed on was that neither of us wanted kids. We didn't even want to get married. We were committed to each other—at least I thought we were. But a year or so ago, out of the blue he got it in his head he wanted a kid. It was a belated midlife crisis. I think he finally regretted not having had a family. And, I mean, Ger was like a big kid in some ways. You saw his house—all the toys and kids' books. But I wasn't ready and I knew I'd never be ready. Don't get me wrong, I like kids—other people's kids. I'm close to my nieces and nephews. I just never wanted any of my own. So we couldn't agree. That's when he broke it off with me.

"Just when I was about to give in—on the condition he'd do most of the work, hire a live-in nanny, the whole shot—all of a sudden he drops the whole idea. Comes back to me, says he's completely resolved he doesn't want to have a baby after all. And he never brought it up again. Maybe that was when he found out about his real father. Maybe he was afraid something would go wrong with the child if he had one. Something passed on in the genes."

"Did he ever mention any congenital illnesses he was afraid of developing?"

Jane Wood said no.

Jardine made a mental note to ask the medical examiner to run DNA tests on Oslin, to look for indications of genetic diseases—Huntington's, perhaps, or schizophrenia.

"Aside from the breakup, was there anything unusual in Gerry's behavior in the last year? Any hints he might have been having an affair, involved in secret activities, anything like that?"

Jane Wood stared at an amber ring on her hand.

"The only thing I can think of is that he went to Las Vegas a couple of times, which didn't seem like one of his top ten vacation spots. I think he went maybe three or four times. And he did seem a lot moodier. He was generally pretty even-tempered, but he did seem melancholy now and then, a little preoccupied, like he had something on his mind." Jane was quiet for a while. Then, under her breath, she said, "Damn. You know, it did cross my mind once he might be seeing someone. Maybe even in Las Vegas. I totally dismissed it on a conscious level, though, like I didn't want to know about it. And once, straightening up around the kitchen after dinner, I found an opened phone bill on the counter with a bunch of long-distance calls to Vegas."

Have Jackson check phone bills, Jardine jotted down.

"Did you ever ask him about it, or make a note of the number?" he asked.

"He said he'd gone out there to an antiques convention and was developing a contact there. Told me I was paranoid and jealous, and I agreed. But down here"—she pointed to her flat stomach—"I had this sneaky feeling he was lying. But, Lieutenant, you have to understand that it was so unlike Ger that I just had to brush it away. He was such a straight arrow."

She closed her eyes for a moment. "Okay. Okay, there was one other thing. Once I stopped over at his house unannounced. It was night, about nine or so. I think I'd been at volleyball practice, I play on a team. And Ger comes to the door and says I can't come in, he's meeting with a genealogy client. He practically pushes me away, backs me down the sidewalk.

"Well, I did something totally unlike me. I parked my car around the corner and walked back toward his house and sat down under a tree across the street and I waited, like I didn't believe him at all and I was goddamn well going to see who the hell came out of there. How could I have forgotten this! It was last fall, October, maybe. Finally this man comes out. It's dark, but he looks about my age. Maybe a little older, hair kind of thinning on top but long in the back, brownish, a bit heavy, husky, wearing jeans and a light sweatshirt. So he gets into a car and leaves.

"I felt relieved. If it had been a woman, maybe I would have been jealous, but . . . " Jane Wood stopped, picked at a tiny hangnail.

"Well, I went right up to the house and knocked, and Ger was so pissed. Told me he felt invaded, and I apologized. Autonomy was important to both of us, and I was acting strange. I knew it but I couldn't help it. I *felt* strange.

"He asked me to stay and have a glass of wine. When he went out to the kitchen, I spotted this guy's genealogy chart on the coffee table and knew Ger was telling the truth, that the guy really was a client. But, Lieutenant, it was like my body kept telling me, 'There's a lie here,' but my head thought, 'Don't be an idiot. Ger's on the up-and-up.' "

"Can you think of anything else about the man by way of a physical description?" Jardine asked. "Anything about his car, anything else Gerry might have mentioned about him? The name on the file?"

Jane Wood thought for a while, then said, "The car was black, kind of dirty, a beater. A Pinto or something. Older. I can't remember anything about the name."

"If the name pops into your mind, let me know, will you?" Jardine looked over the notes he'd taken. Jane Wood looked exhausted by the conversation.

"Just a couple more questions, Ms. Wood. You're involved in the martial arts?"

"Yes, for about ten years."

"One of my possible scenarios is that Mr. Oslin might have had a massage therapist come to the house, he might have consulted with someone knowledgeable in Shiatsu massage, Chinese medicine, acupuncture, that sort of thing. Someone who might have gotten him to lie down on the bed, not for sex, but for some kind of treatment. The pretense of a treatment. A person who might have known ways to make someone pass out, by pressing on the carotid artery, perhaps, when he was either sleeping or very relaxed."

Jane shuddered as if she could see the scene in front of her. "And then smothered him with one of the big pillows and put him in the tub to make it look like he just died in there."

"Are there certain holds or moves in the martial arts that could do that?"

"Oh yes," she said. "You have to be really careful in sparring. Some of the advanced moves can be lethal."

"What is the name of the school where you practice?"

"Pacific Karate Association."

"And can you think of anyone there that Mr. Oslin might have had come to his home for a body-work session, or anyone with whom he did not get along?"

Jane set the empty wine cooler bottle on a ledge beside her. "He knew some of my friends there, but no one there would have any reason to kill him. And I didn't know him to hire people like that to come to his home. I do know a number of people who are involved in body work, though, all different types, massage, Rosen Bodywork, Alexander Technique, Rolfing. I also know practitioners who do use Chinese herbs, a naturopath that Ger might have seen. I'll draw up a list of names, people you can talk to."

"What about Wes Young?"

"Wes?"

"Isn't he interested in the Far East?"

"Not martial arts, that's for sure. He sits. He's a Zen student. In a haphazard way. Although I heard he did study at a monastery in Japan years ago. Wes might well know of other people who are alternative healers."

"He and Mary are a couple?"

"They've been together about a year." Jane stood and stretched, turning away from Jardine to the harbor and the rows of sailboats and pleasure cruisers. "Is Wes a suspect?" she asked quietly.

"So far we do not have a suspect or a clear motivation. There is one possible lead." Jardine rose, feeling the slight shift of the boat beneath him. He pulled Tory DeLisi's school photograph out of his notebook and handed it to Jane. "Do you recognize this little girl?"

Jane Wood examined the picture. "She looks vaguely familiar, but I can't say I know her. Who is she?"

"She's missing. Apparently abducted from the Kettler Institute Children's Hospital on Friday. This particular photograph of her was found in Mr. Oslin's office. It was stuck in the edge of a portrait of Mary and her daughter. Did Gerry ever mention anything about this picture or the girl? Her name is Tory DeLisi. She's ten years old."

Again Jane Wood shook her head.

"Did he ever mention an Ellen Carlin, the girl's mother?"

Again, no.

Jardine pocketed the picture, saying, "I'm trying to find out why Mr. Oslin had a picture of a little girl who was abducted two days before he was killed. What the connection is, if any."

Suddenly Jane Wood began to cry, a loud, singsong sobbing with long breaths that shook her chest. Tears washed down the clear skin of her face. When she was able to speak, her voice quavered. "I feel like I've lost my Gerry twice in one day. He's dead. And maybe I never knew him in the first place. Never knew him at all."

Jardine waited until she had cried for a few minutes. He got a paper towel from the cabin and handed it to her. "I'd like to arrange for you to meet with a sketch artist at our office downtown. The description of that man you saw coming out of Oslin's bears some similarity to another description we've gotten. I'll have someone call you about it."

Jane Wood sniffed. Jardine stepped up to the dock and thanked her for her help, and as he stepped off the dock, he saw Mary Oslin pulling in to a parking spot. Good, he thought. Jane shouldn't be left alone.

"Lieutenant," Jane called from behind him. "Martin. The name on the chart that Ger was doing for that guy. I don't even know why I thought of it. And I don't know if it was a first or last name."

"Let me know if you think of anything else." Yes, he thought. He'd have Sondra run that name through all the genealogy clients on Oslin's computer.

Jardine removed the tape on Oslin's door that had sealed the crime scene. He let himself in with the key and disarmed the security system by punching in the secret code on the keypad. Find out who, besides Mary, had access to the codes, he thought, and where Oslin kept a record of the codes written down. Often people kept them in their wallets.

The house was cold inside, the air conditioner going strong. A grayish purple dust from the lab technicians had been left on the surfaces of the furniture. The petals from the cheap roses had mostly fallen off, and the stems hung limply over the edge of the glass vase.

He stood at the center of the kitchen as if he were the police cameraman videotaping the crime scene, quadrant by quadrant. East, south, north, west, facing in each direction, taking in every detail. The back door was closed now, and there was a bulletin board on the wall behind the door. Postcards were displayed in neat rows, along with calendars for the skydiving club and a film series. He pulled the tacks out of a few of the postcards and read the messages scrawled from friends vacationing in Tucson, Verona, London, a motel down in Long Beach, Seaside Villa.

Long Beach . . . He flashed on his afternoon there, a subdued Mr. Rebek with his arm around his son. Connection? he asked himself. The connection was two missing children and Long Beach. Whether it was coincidence, he did not know. He turned over the postcard.

"Think I found perfect house. Thanks for all your help. See you next week." The card was unsigned, postmarked June 16, 1992. Jardine replaced the postcard on the bulletin board.

He'd brought with him the file of material that Jackson had printed out last night from Oslin's computer, a copy of several of the genealogical searches, as well as lists of valuables from Oslin's various personal collections: folk toys, subdivided into robots, soldiers, and trains. Children's books in series: Oz books, the Hardy Boys, and some Jardine had never heard of, *Baseball Joe and the World Series, Baseball Joe and the Silver Stars,* and a series with some character named Chip Hilton. There were two pages of snow domes.

He turned the corner into the living room and reviewed the list of domes, where they were from, plastic or glass, estimated date of manufacture, where he'd purchased them, flea markets, antique stores, collectors, garage sales. Oslin had been meticulous in his recordkeeping. Jardine was glad Jackson had gone back to the store to print out more of the computer files. She was probably there now; he should call her.

Jardine crossed the room to the bookshelf and stood before the arrangement of domes. There was one shelf of domes commemorating cities: Chicago, New York, New Orleans, Colorado Springs, St. Louis. The next shelf down were all cartoon characters, many of them Disney figures, but not all of them: Jiminy Cricket, Donald Duck, Snow White, Pluto, Daffy Duck, Rocky and Bullwinkle. And there was Mickey in his Merlin cap dancing with a broomstick, and one with a bearded wizard, stars on his robe.

It was an odd collection, Jardine thought. In fact, most of them looked pretty tacky, like any cheap souvenir you might pick up at an airport or curio shop. Come to think of it, Oslin had left out all the

Santas and snowmen he'd have thought would be staples in any dome collection. Which left him with the third shelf.

These appeared to be from tourist attractions: several World's Fairs, including the Chicago World's Fair of 1933, CENTURY OF PROGRESS lettered in gold on the base of the dome and a miniature replica of the Trylon and Perisphere from the New York World's Fair of 1939. He had snow domes from Niagara Falls, the Grand Canyon, Hawaii, the Everglades, Mount Rushmore, the Empire State Building and the Statue of Liberty, Chinatown, Old Faithful, and Big Ben. An American flag. The *Titanic* by an iceberg, half sunk.

The lower shelf displayed animal domes: a deer from Yosemite, a bear from Yellowstone, a buffalo from the Black Hills, a polar bear next to an igloo, a snake from Wall Drug Store, and, moving into what appeared to be the fantasy section, three dragons and a leprechaun. There was even a dome from Graceland, for God's sake, with Elvis dressed like an angel in white, standing in the drifty snow by his Tennessee mansion. Jardine wondered how Elvis had gotten down by the dragons and the leprechaun.

And there were the spaces, uneven gaps in the way they were displayed. He'd noticed the snow domes, yes, but had no context for guessing what the spaces between them might mean. Now that he was getting to know Oslin and his habits, he knew that didn't fit. Oslin was a controlled type. He would have lined them up perfectly in a neat row, each so many inches apart. He knew the lab technicians would not have moved them around. They were unusually careful to leave things the way they found them.

Jardine went back to the computer printout and read through it again, comparing it to the collection on the shelves. There were supposed to be thirty-seven of them, and he only counted thirty. Seven were missing. Consulting the whole list again, he checked off the ones that remained and circled the missing ones: the Golden Gate Bridge, the *Queen Mary,* Sleeping Beauty's Castle at Disneyland, Zoo monkey, Angelfish from the Bahamas, Saguaro cactuses from Arizona, and a carousel unicorn. Jardine had a hard time picturing the angelfish one. Who would put a tropical fish in a snowstorm, or a cactus for that matter?

Maybe Oslin had sold some of them. Maybe they were in his office collection or on display somewhere else, loaned out to a museum. Could be.

Or stolen, Jardine thought.

Suddenly he turned and strode down the hall to Oslin's bedroom.

First he opened the closet door and stared down at the neat lines of shoes, clothes arranged by categories. He pulled out the dresser drawers again and leafed through the stacks of shirts back from the dry cleaner. Even the undershirts had been pressed.

There was a small wooden box of trinkets in the top drawer of the bureau, the kind of box people threw their nail clippers into, pennies, matchbooks, and ticket stubs. Jardine riffled through the contents, lifted a small locket out. The chain was tangled in a button that read JERRY BROWN FOR PRESIDENT. The locket itself was not expensive; it was engraved with a floral design and the letter *L*. He clicked it open. Inside was a tiny black and white portrait, possibly a high school graduation picture, of a girl with dark hair in a poofed-out helmet shape and bangs down to her thick eyeliner, looking serious in a round-necked sweater and a strand of fake pearls, circa late fifties.

He studied it more closely, then slipped the locket into the Ziploc bag with Tory's picture and headed down the hallway, through the living room, and out the front door. He was humming as he armed the security system, locked the house, and applied a fresh strip of tape to the door to reseal the crime scene. By the time he was in his car he'd reached the chorus and was singing out loud, the Righteous Brothers, slow dance, feel of a girl's back in a stiff lace dress, homecoming, don't squash the corsage, carnations because you were too chintzy to get a gardenia, "You've Lost That Lovin' Feeling" coming from the PA system. *Gone, gone, gone.*

He stuck the key in the ignition.

"Wait a minute," he said out loud. "I never went to the homecoming dance." He'd asked Sheila Bryerson, but she'd turned him down and he'd never asked another girl to a dance during all of high school, though he had been asked to the Silver Belle Ball at the private Catholic girls' school across town. His cousin had fixed him up with her roommate.

He took the locket out of the plastic bag and clicked it open, staring at the young woman's face. Was it Mary Oslin in high school?

At a pay phone in a Taco Bell, Jardine stood, listening to the repeating ring at Oslin's store. No answer. He dialed Sondra Jackson's pager number and indicated that she should call his pager, then hung up and went back to his soft chicken tacos and Diet Pepsi. He ought to go over to the store anyway, he thought. She might still be there, just not picking up.

He stepped up to the phone again and dialed Jackson's home number. Her husband answered. No, she wasn't back yet, said she had a lot of computer work to do. A call to the downtown office yielded similar results.

Damn. He should have checked in with her while he was at Oslin's. Now he wouldn't know what she'd come up with until tomorrow.

Maybe it was indigestion. He got in the car, fumbled in the glove compartment for the Tums, and pulled out into dinner-hour traffic. It had been a wearisome day. He could keep on going and be home at his mostly empty house in West Hollywood in no time, but he veered over to Melrose Avenue instead. He could just stop at Oslin's store on his way home and see if Sondra was there.

Maybe it was something back at Jane Wood's that had set him thinking something was wrong. That sword above the cabin house door. That big saber, gleaming there in that sunlit sailboat.

Swords, he thought. That was it. But that had been the other case he'd worked on with Theresa, years ago. And the swords had been those tiny plastic ones used in cocktails.

As he neared the store, he was first aware of the stream of thick smoke spewing up over the neighborhood. Then the sirens, two fire trucks bleating past him, lights strobing.

He pulled over with a feeling of dread and parked at a slight angle to the sidewalk. Three fire trucks were parked at the center of the small side street, the hoses dousing the building through the smashed front windows. Oslin's store resembled a gaping, blackened mouth. A stream of water flattened the flames, leaving charred, wet skeletons of furniture and broken glass.

Jardine broke through the small crowd, grabbed a fireman who was standing by the truck, and displayed his badge. "Was there a woman in there? Did somebody call this in?" He was shouting.

"We responded to a security system smoke alarm, sir. We believe there is no one in the building."

"Are you absolutely sure?"

"Do you have reason to believe there was someone in there, sir?" the fireman asked.

Just then the pager beeped once. Jardine yanked it off his belt, reading the words as they scrolled up: *Where are you anyway? Dancing I hope. Call ASAP. Sondra.*

Through the broken window he could see that much of the furniture had collapsed into wet piles, and that the computer on the desk had actually melted. Even the metal file cabinets were blackened. The chandeliers made an odd clinking sound, the prisms caked with smoke, rattling in the spray off the hoses. A gray tower rose from the ruined building.

THE RED LIGHT on her answering machine was blinking when Theresa got home. The house seemed too quiet and she was lonely. She thought of taking a stroll along the boardwalk at dusk, followed by a hot bath. Early to bed. Tomorrow she would return to her normal day of client readings and preparation for the seminar in empowering intuition that she and Camille would be teaching in August.

But underneath, she felt an unexpected sense of loss. She was sorry she'd had to break off communication with Ellen, but she trusted that it was right. For a moment she wondered if Tory hadn't just run away from her mother after all. She wouldn't blame her.

Theresa rewound the answering-machine tape, slipping her silver bracelets off and stacking them on the counter. There were several calls from clients wanting appointments, several new referrals, and one from the lieutenant. His message sounded tense and mysterious. "Jardine here, four o'clock. We found the kid in Long Beach. His remains, that is. You did it again, Theresa. I'll call you later with the details."

A high tone bleeped between calls, and then Joe DeLisi's voice. Her pulse jumped when she heard him. He wanted her to call. "Is there any chance you could meet with me this evening, possibly for dinner?" He repeated his name and number at the hotel where he could be reached. She dialed the number immediately and asked for room 406. It barely rang when he picked it up, answering brusquely, "DeLisi."

They made arrangements quickly, with no small talk. He'd pick her up in an hour and they'd go to a place nearby. Theresa showered and combed out her wet hair, letting the tangles drop onto her bare shoulders. She tried a saffron-colored sundress and sisal sandals that wrapped at her ankles. She couldn't remember when she had so wanted to spend time with a man, and it made her nervous. Joe DeLisi was vulnerable and in crisis. She was a consulting professional who'd just been fired by his ex-wife.

After a small glass of Chardonnay, she decided to change into jeans and a beige tunic with mother-of-pearl buttons. The dress was too provocative. *There. Disgustingly appropriate,* she thought.

He arrived ten minutes early and was wearing practically the same outfit she had on, jeans, white shirt, no tie. She suggested they walk up to the sidewalk café along the boardwalk. It was a warm evening, still light. They started out along the canal, then down to the water, heading up along the boardwalk crowded with summer-night strollers and greedy pigeons. The air from the ocean was cool, and a mackerel-scale layer of clouds drifted over the Santa Monica Mountains. Theresa knew, though, that the air was bad no matter how sweet the breeze. The last time she had flown into L.A., she could barely see downtown. The smog was sunk in over the huge valley, a green cloud, and only the blue-tipped ridge of the mountains to the south could be seen.

They wandered slowly toward the café, and Theresa explained to Joe DeLisi that as of this afternoon she no longer worked for Ellen, that, in spite of Ellen's threats, her commitment was to make any images, insights, or information she might get regarding Tory available to anyone who wanted them. She would ask Lieutenant Jardine to act as a liaison. She would not withhold her perceptions from anyone. She just couldn't work that way.

She filled DeLisi in on how Tory had first come to her last week, and told him she wouldn't be surprised by further spontaneous communications. When they got to the café, he took a few minutes to write down, on the back of a paper place mat, some of the things she'd said, and he looked over the drawings that had come through Theresa. Then he clicked the top back on the pen and sipped his wine.

"This reference in your reading to medical testing is interesting," he said. "I want to follow up on that. Tory's always been very susceptible to disease and infections, but no doctor has ever mentioned the HIV virus as a possibility. Ellen and I have never discussed it, either. The police should check with all the public health clinics. Even if she was having Tory tested anonymously, someone at the clinic might recognize them in a picture." He gazed out toward the ocean, past a woman seated at a card table at the edge of the boardwalk. PALM READ-

INGS, read a sign dangling from her table. "Your competition," Joe DeLisi said. He smiled at Theresa thinly, as if, under any other circumstances, he might possibly be happy.

"I don't do palms," Theresa said.

"What do you do?"

She shrugged. "I just listen. I'm an antenna."

He watched her over the small candle that flickered in a jar on the red and white checked tablecloth, and then he went on. "Even as an infant, Tory was sickly. She had four apneic episodes where she stopped breathing. The first time it happened, she was three months old. Ellen went in to check on her because she hadn't gotten up from her nap. That was not unusual—Ellen was always hovering, going in to check on the baby repetitively. When she picked Tory up, she was all gray and limp and not breathing. I'll never forget grabbing her out of Ellen's hands, Ellen standing there screaming my name. The way Tory flopped around, her head all lopped to the side. I told Ellen to call an ambulance and I did mouth-to-mouth. She was so tiny I could put my whole mouth over her mouth and nose at the same time. And she came back, she hadn't been gone long. She breathed, she just started up again. Got all pink and warm in my hands, like she did the night she was born."

Joe DeLisi refocused his eyes. He'd been deeply in memory, reliving the instant.

"There were three more apneic episodes by the time she was eighteen months old—once when we were out at the Cape and twice when Tory was hospitalized for other reasons. But it was inexplicable. They could never find a cause for it. It was as if she were a SIDS baby who kept lucking out. A little cat with nine lives. I even called her 'kitten' for a while. I'd forgotten about that.

"That's when Ellen started devoting herself completely to Tory. She'd been in graduate school, in a doctoral program. She dropped out, never went back to finish her Ph.D. She refused to get sitters. Had to take Tory with her all the time.

"Being in a field related to medicine, although on the research end of things, she became extremely impatient with the lack of a clear diagnosis. At the same time, there were ways that I thought she was irresponsible about Tory's health. She refused to take Tory to Mayo, for instance, and have a complete workup done on her. And she loved to travel. She'd take Tory with her. Off they'd go for two or three weeks to Costa Rica or India. A month in Bali, two months in Africa. Ellen would lie about the length of the trips. She'd say she was only going for one or two weeks, then she'd call to say she was having such a good time, she was going to stay on. Sometimes I'd join them. Sometimes I would go wherever they were just to bring them home.

"Often when they were away, that's when Tory would get sick. They'd be in places where the water was bad and the hygiene terrible. She picked up gastrointestinal viruses, weird bacteria, parasites. She even had hepatitis. Ellen and I fought bitterly about all this. I maintained that she was endangering Tory, pulling her away from home and her routine and, yes, me. Finally I started refusing to let Tory go on trips. We'd argue. Ellen would leave in the middle of the night, and of course she'd take Tory with her. And then Tory would get sick again, reacting to the stress. She was never seen continually by one physician, either. Always a string of doctors in Third World clinics, wherever Ellen happened to land."

"What about people who were concerned for Tory?" asked Theresa. "Aside from the two of you? Is there anyone who might want to see her cared for by a particular doctor or in a particular way—something that perhaps Ellen or you might have vetoed?"

Joe DeLisi thought for a moment. "Ellen wanted to take Tory down to Mexico for some kind of special treatment. I said no. I thought of it as just one more excuse for a trip."

"Could Ellen have enlisted someone to take Tory down to Mexico?"

"It's very possible," said Joe. He made another note on the place mat. "I'll mention that to Rukheyser."

"Did you ever get any counseling?"

"Ellen had tons of therapy. She was a therapy junkie, but she skipped around a lot. A Jungian here, a women's group there. I also demanded that we get counseling together. I was seeing a therapist, I had Tory assessed, and we all went briefly into a family treatment kind of thing. They thought that Tory seemed psychologically okay, except that she had a tremendous fantasy life.

"She had three imaginary friends and she said one of them was a star. It was like a fairy or an angel to her. Then she started getting interested in religion, though neither Ellen nor I am particularly religious. She loved to visit churches and cathedrals on our travels. She was curious about icons and miracles and crucifixes. I always thought she would've fit right in with those kids who saw the Virgin Mary in the clouds in Medjugorje—that pilgrimage spot in Bosnia.

"But that started to seem unhealthy to me, too, so I started taking her to mass just so there'd be something actual in her spirituality. Something to fulfill whatever craving she seemed to have for the divine, for ceremony and ritual.

"The therapist who said Tory had an overdeveloped imagination suggested that she could possibly have been imagining these different illnesses, that they could be psychosomatic. He brought up the point that the body can respond as if it were sick under certain circumstances, and that Tory's illnesses actually achieved a predictable outcome: a crisis, lots of attention from her mother. And I would come to get them, so we'd be reunited as a family. And in the first few years, Tory's illnesses did tend to bring Ellen and me back together. For one thing, if Tory was hospitalized, Ellen didn't have the excuse of sleeping with her. So she would come back to our bed with me, instead of sleeping with Tory night after night."

Joe DeLisi sighed. He had hardly eaten anything, and he ordered a second glass of wine. Theresa stared for a while at the candle in a glass on the table between them, the flame bent by the sea breeze.

They finished the meal in silence and ordered coffee. Finally Joe spoke again. "I'm glad you're going to stay with this, and I'm even glad that Ellen fired you. I would definitely like to hear anything that comes to you. If it would help to do a reading with me, or whatever it is that you do, or if any other of Tory's possessions or photographs would help, please, Theresa—anything I can do."

"I'm very willing," said Theresa. She watched his face, the sadness in it, and something just under that, something fierce, competitive. What did Oliver know about him? she wondered.

As she agreed to continue with DeLisi, she found herself disappointed. If she worked with him in this way, it meant that she certainly couldn't extend herself toward him on a personal level. It was not strange that the men she felt the most connected with were those who came to her as clients. They had no resistance whatsoever to her psychic abilities—the way her mind worked, her images, her intuitive leaps and sideways drifts. The men she met in other contexts were usually threatened by all that, and ultimately backed away. They experienced her as invasive, somehow, and the relationship was always out of balance. She'd tried working that out, tried to stop that part of her when she was not at work. Shut it down. Or to let that part of her in and ask, even demand, that the man acknowledge that it was simply who she was, to see her psychic ability as a gift, not a problem.

But it was a problem. Even her eye contact, she knew, was too intense for some men. The relationship would progress better if she made contact through her body, her sexuality, keeping her mind and her eyes out of it, averted, silent. But she couldn't love fully like that, and she was always withholding. Eventually she would feel resentful that she could not be fully present, that they didn't want her, they wanted who they thought she might be. She'd never found the right balance, though oddly she had found it with Oliver. But then Oliver and she were not lovers, they were friends, and that was different. She knew that at times he wanted more from her than friendship, that he kept it in the background, and that he would never bring himself to speak it. And neither would she. She didn't want to mess things up with him. She could count on him, and there was some way she actually depended on him emotionally. He offered her balance, humor, and ongoing, steady male companionship. But she wanted more, much more, with a man. This silent bond she felt with Joe was something she craved. It was as if they were conversing in another language, were totally fluent in it, and at ease. He had darkness in him, yes, complexity. She liked that.

They walked back to her house along the boardwalk in the fading light. "I could read for you tonight if you're up for it," she offered.

Joe DeLisi agreed.

They entered the side gate and she locked it behind her. Across the patio where Osiris sat in the center of the wrought-iron table. Up the studio stairs. She unlocked the door and turned on the track lighting, but kept it dim. The glitter of Venice shone around them through the large glass windows.

Joe sat on the couch. "What do you want me to do?" he asked.

"Just hold Tory in your thoughts," Theresa instructed.

She took the wicker rocking chair opposite him, closing her eyes. Immediately she got the image of a fish swimming down. Goldfish, the large orange ones seen in Japanese garden pools. As she followed it down, a small white fish receded out of sight into the murk of the water.

The image clicked off. She wanted something less metaphoric, something more direct. *Tory,* she asked, internally, *where are you?* The image of the fish returned. Theresa shivered, moved in close to Tory, then all the way inside her, looking out through her eyes, her mind.

"A man fishing, he's sideways."

Theresa turned on the tape player next to her to record what she was saying. She began speaking in a childlike voice. *"I'm by the water, I can't get up. Can't wake up. I'm lying down on the grass, it's cold."*

Where are you? Theresa asked internally.

"I'm trying to talk, I'm trying to yell at Doc, but it's coming out all funny like words are stuck to my teeth and my face is frozen."

Don't talk to Doc, Theresa thought. *Talk to me. Just notice what's around you. Look very closely at what's around you. Remember Hansel and Gretel in the fairy tale? When their father took them deep into the forest, how they dropped the little stones to find their way back?*

Theresa saw the view ahead of her like a video race-car game, zooming through the imagery, 3-D: a huge, long, green bridge, tall smokestacks all around, fire coming out of them. Another bridge, four tan smokestacks in a row. Skyscrapers, one curved like a mirror. Rocks along the water, piles of them jutting out into the water. Boats.

Then, quickly, just a flash under the scene, the queen of hearts, a playing card. A madonna in the clouds, blue-draped mother-queen, star-woman angel over her.

Theresa wanted to stop, to write down the images, but it was still coming, and fast. She had to ride it through, stay with it, remember.

Then, in the child voice, she whispered, *"I'll throw her in the bushes. And next time I'll write something down. I'll write things down and leave notes behind like stones."*

Theresa waited for a moment, repeating Tory's name several more times, but the voice and images faded. All that was left was her own inner voice asking Tory to return.

Theresa opened her eyes and told Joe about the images she'd seen, the bridges, fire, the curving mirror of a downtown building. She almost forgot the powerful female images, the goddess figures: angel, star, woman, mother, madonna, Mary, Queen.

"Where could it be?" he asked. "Did any of that seem familiar to you?"

"Theresa stood and crossed to the window, looking out over the lights of the houses. *Queen,* she thought.

She turned suddenly. *"Queen Mary.* That's it, Joe. I think there's even a glass building in downtown Long Beach that's curved like a mirror. The *Queen Mary* is in Long Beach harbor. She's down by the water where the smaller boats are moored near the *Queen Mary.* There's a marina down there. We should call Rukheyser. They can send a patrol car a lot quicker than we could get there. They can alert the Long Beach police."

Joe dialed Rukheyser's number and waited. Rukheyser was out, but Joe spoke to another detective. Yes, the officer said. We'll check on it. We'll alert someone down there right away.

Joe DeLisi hung up. "How long would it take us to get down to Long Beach?" he asked.

"Probably about thirty minutes if there's no traffic."

"I want to go. Will you take me?"

Theresa grabbed a jacket from the coat rack by the door, turned out the lights in the studio, and followed Joe out along the canal to his car. He drove and she gave him directions.

"The scene was sideways as I read," Theresa said, "and it was difficult bringing it through. It was that fog feeling. I think she's being sedated some of the time, off and on. It's something she's familiar with, I've gotten that body sensation before. I believe she was lying on a blanket on her side and she couldn't get up. There was a feeling of falling or sinking in her."

Theresa was relieved at Joe's silence as they drove south on the San Diego Freeway. She needed to shift into another kind of listening and watching. As they passed the exits into Torrance, she felt a heightening of her watchfulness, a sort of hypervigilance as if she heard a faint sound in the distance and was craning to hear more clearly. The listening and the watching were the same, no difference between the aural and visual cues.

"Exit here," she said as they approached the Harbor Freeway. "I want to take this route down to Long Beach, even though it's not the most direct way."

Joe complied and they sped south until they reached Ocean Boulevard. Theresa was disconcerted; she'd never been down this way before. In the distance, orange flames from the oil refineries lit the dusty night. "Here," she said curtly. "Turn here."

And there it was, the green bridge arching before them, the one she had seen in her inner sight. VINCENT THOMAS BRIDGE, a sign read. The naval shipyard sprawled below them. Within minutes they were crossing the second bridge, coming to downtown Long Beach. Just before they reached the downtown exit, Theresa whispered, "Here, take a right." She had no cognitive sense of exactly where she was headed. This was not the exit to downtown or the *Queen Mary* itself, but she felt sure this was where they should be. She pointed to the right again, and Joe pulled into a parking lot next to a canal. Gray rock, jetties jutted out into the harbor. LONG BEACH CATALINA LANDING, a sign read. Another said, GOLDEN SHORE. She wasn't sure this was it. Wasn't there a marina closer to where the *Queen Mary* was docked? They'd taken the wrong exit.

But it felt strong, a magnet, and she told DeLisi to pull over and park. Theresa got out. The wind off the water was strong, she smelled smoke in the air. Joe began to say something, but she motioned for him to be quiet. She put her hands out a slight distance from her body, and slowly turned around in a dancer's pirouette, feeling the space around her for some clue to Tory's location.

For an instant, in her chest, she experienced a surge of well-being, something like love, but she didn't know who it was for. Relief and longing with an ache that everyone always went away and no one remained, that the earth was some speck of blue floundering in perfect orbit at the edge of a vast darkness smeared with light. That emptiness had a meaning that could never be grasped.

She began stepping slowly, as if she were on a balance beam, as if any quick movement in her body would make the connection to Tory go away. She felt Tory close, a trace left in the air. *Are you here?* she asked inside.

Nothing. In the distance, a boat horn. A car rumbled over the bridge nearby, headlights streaking the darkness. She walked toward the water and stopped. At her feet she found a stone, and placed it at that spot on the metal railing.

Quickly she glanced to her right, a grassy area on the other side of a pickup truck, next to the parking lot. In her chest she felt a gulping, a gasping for air. She closed her eyes, asserting her sense of balance. *Slow,* she thought, *slow it down.* In the past, when the body sensations had become intense, she had struggled against them, tried to make sense of them, experiencing them as something wrong. She'd found over time that if she stayed with her breath, let her body relax, stand still in it, the intensity would pass and she could follow her body to what she needed to see. She did that now. Her body was led.

She had stepped back slightly from the physical. The body had its own wisdom that all her thinking could never rationally comprehend. She placed her thinking slightly behind her, witnessing. As she walked steadily toward the truck, the sensation became thinner, higher, like a musical note clarifying, then spreading into a high, humming chord.

There in the grass, a small square in the lawn. Near the cement sidewalk, the grass was matted down, as if a picnic had taken place only a short time before. Joe came to stand beside her.

"She was lying right here on a blanket," said Theresa. Joe bent down to run his hands over the grass, searching for clues. "No." She stopped him. "Don't touch anything. Let the police do it."

"Wherever the fuck they are," he muttered. "We called them about an hour ago, and they still aren't here."

"They might already have driven by the site and, not seeing anyone, continued on."

"They should be here searching the entire area." He was shouting.

"They will now," she said.

He stood, looking around him. "Tory!" he cried out. It startled her to hear the loud anguish in his voice. She spun around and touched his arm. Didn't he know he would frighten her away, not her, not the real her, but what was left of her here, something of her like a fragrance, a memory, a shadow of light? She didn't know what it was she could feel in such a place, or why. Joe DeLisi yelled his daughter's name again into the wind.

"Stop it," she demanded. "She's not here. I'm trying to listen."

He was breathing hard, a dry rasping in his chest. His face was contorted. He bent over in the grass, staring at the place where the grass was matted, but not touching it. Finally he asked, "But she was here? You can tell that? She was here only a short while ago? Is that what you're thinking?"

"I'm not thinking," Theresa said. "And I need you to shut up, Joe. Right now."

She faced the wind, cocking her head to one side. Cars, traffic, rustling bushes along the road. Her own heartbeat. But it was gone. Whatever connection she'd had was gone now, evaporated.

"Damn," she whispered. *Come back. Come back to me.*

She tried to bring the image of Tory lying here on the grass back into the screen of her imagination, the view the girl had of the bridge, sideways, the view of those bushes.

Theresa walked toward them, without thinking, and knelt down. She placed her hands under the leaves, along the damp ground, and pulled out a torn sheet of newspaper, a crunched-up paper cup. She reached in again, and her hand closed around the tiny, cold limb of a doll.

It was mud-streaked and naked, about ten inches long, with vinyl hair and eyes that wouldn't shut, painted on. A puckered rosebud mouth.

Theresa turned back toward Joe. He was still crouched in the grass behind her. She held the doll out to him and he stood, then ran toward her.

"That's Tory's doll!" He held the doll in his hands, staring into its blank face as if it could speak.

She heard me, thought Theresa. Heard me tell her to leave something, like Gretel's scattered stones. She wanted to leave a note, but she didn't have paper. She left her doll.

Simultaneously, over that realization, came the Voice, loud and big in her head:

NOW SHE KNOWS SHE IS MISSING.
SHE DIDN'T KNOW THAT BEFORE.
SHE TRUSTED DOC.
NOW SHE DOES NOT.

Theresa waited, in case something else came up from the dark well. She had closed her eyes without realizing it. When she opened them, a patrol car had stopped on the road above them, the police finally arriving, red and blue lights spinning a pattern over the shrubbery.

A patrol officer approached them, and Joe thrust the doll out at him. "She was here!" Joe DeLisi yelled. "My daughter was here. If you'd come when we called, you might have found her. She might still have been here!"

The patrolman scratched under his eye, squinting around him.

"That the missing kid's doll?"

Theresa nodded. She pointed to the grass. "She was lying here, where the grass is matted down. You'll want to search the whole area."

The patrolman looked past them around the grounds of the park along the landing, the black harbor water, the shadows cast by the parking-lot lights.

"We'd better see if we can get a boat in here too, and some divers. Probably not until morning, though."

When she looked over at Joe, he was rigid with fury, the doll trembling in his hands.

WEDNESDAY, JULY 8

SHE IS IN A ROOM, it is baroque. Red velvet brocade wallpaper, gilt-edged mirror, alabaster sculpture of a woman's head on the bureau, a canopy bed hung with heavy tapestry draperies. She turns to the child behind her, sitting on the bed.

"I'm going to look," Theresa says. "I have to see what's happening."

The child begs her not to look. Pulls at her long silk shirt. The clothes are beautiful, but old-fashioned. Turn of the century. Theresa approaches the mirror and takes it down from the wall. Behind it is a hole drilled in the wall. She can hear them arguing, the parents, father raging, mother almost silent, but every now and then there is a hissing filled with loathing and hatred.

Theresa turns back to the child. There are two of them now. Herself as a child, and Tory. The two girls are holding each other, burying their faces in each other's hair.

Theresa draws near the wall and positions her eye in front of the hole. On the other side, her father turns, notices Theresa's eye peeking through. He sticks a needle through the hole into her right eye.

Theresa turns back to the children, holding her eye in pain. She touches the needle, pulls it out.

The children are gone.

In their place, Ellen lies naked on the bed. She is blue, granite cold. A syringe lies next to her upturned palm.

Theresa woke with a start, eyes instantly open. She felt the bed beside her. Empty. Covers flat. She rose quickly and showered, letting the hot spray wash the dream away, memory fragments of last night surfacing, the doll, the black water of the canal, Joe DeLisi across from her at dinner.

After they had driven back from Long Beach, he had walked her to her house along the canal and there had been an odd moment, full of the charge of desire between them. They both knew it was out of place. Impulsively she'd given him a hug, just friendly, but they had lingered, holding each other, and she'd let her body ease against him briefly. That was all, but it had left her aching where she'd been contentedly asleep for nearly a year.

Oh God, she thought, turning off the shower. *Why is it always troublesome?*

The phone rang as she finished getting dressed, and it was Joe. He wanted to see her early, to give her more of Tory's things. She told him to meet her at the sidewalk café by the bookstore in an hour. That would leave her time for a walk on Venice Beach. She needed the waves and the wind to clear her mind.

Theresa took off her shoes when she got to the beach, and walked, following the edge of the surf where each wave dissolved into sand. She thought about Tory growing up saturated in the hostile atmosphere between her parents. Both Ellen and Joe could flip in an instant between an intelligent concern for Tory and extreme anger, reactiveness, even rage. Theresa knew about that from her own family. As a child, she'd learned to send herself into imagination in order to escape what was happening around her. Now she knew what it was called: *dissociation*. She could go so far into her imagination, it was like a trance state, a form of self-hypnosis. The present moment would seem to completely disappear. She'd be unconscious of what was happening, sitting at the dinner table, dreaming of a desert island or a pirate ship. In school, she'd be startled awake by the nuns rapping on her desk with a ruler, demanding the answer to the question about the capital of Louisiana. She'd never heard the question, she'd been gone, floating.

When she was growing up, her younger sisters would come to her bed. They slept together in the same room, in two double beds. They'd nestle near her, afraid of the screaming in the kitchen down the hall, glass breaking, her mother hissing. Theresa could never make out the words, just the snake of her breath. Crash of furniture, kitchen chairs flying across the linoleum, flung by witches and bad kings, thrown by her parents, those giants with two mouths apiece. Her sisters huddled beneath the covers, and Theresa was supposed to protect them, save them. But who would save her? There was nowhere to go. Nowhere safe.

Many years ago she had realized that she thought of her father as two entirely separate people. As an adolescent, she would help out afternoons in her father's grocery store downstairs from their apartment in the North End of Boston. He'd play opera on the radio, his charming tenor wafting above the shelves of olive oil, boxes of pasta, and tins of fish, while Theresa waited on Mrs. Landazuri. Her father was handsome, smiling in his white apron. This was the father she knew consciously, the one she loved, this father who called her "Beautiful," who teased the boys who came into the store. They'd better not talk to Theresa, he'd say, or he'd wring their necks like chickens, he'd chop them into bits like ground beef.

It was only as an adult, looking back, that she understood that he began his drinking during those afternoons down in the store. Mornings he was hung over, morose, repentant for last night's fight with her mother. He went to early mass in his black hat to kneel before the Virgin, but by afternoon, when Theresa came down to help, he was lightly drunk, gregarious. She thought *that* was love, that was her true father. At the same time she also knew, in a far less conscious place, not to trust him because at night he'd change into the ugly giant again, the one who beat her mother.

There were stretches of time—maybe he was on the wagon—when he was someone in the middle of those two fathers. They would drive on a rare Sunday after mass out to Long Island. Daddy, in brown plaid swimming trunks, buried his feet in the sand, Mother crocheting in the shade of an umbrella, never wearing a swimsuit, her dress pulled up over heavy thighs. She was irritated and withdrawn. Her legs had become as thick as logs at the ankles, black hair coiled at the back of her neck. She was old at thirty-three.

Riding home, with the girls stuffed in the hot backseat of the Pontiac, he'd turn with his outstretched hand as if to slap them. Theresa would cower, then move to protect the younger girls. Her mother pretended to be sleeping.

So, even when he wasn't drinking, he was angry, probably craving the booze so badly he could have screamed, did scream. Wanting only to be away from the close, crammed-in apartment of women, down to Luci's Bar on the corner, to Friday-night Gillette boxing on TV, back to his lovely brown burning Scotch.

Theresa had learned early to scan a room, sensitive to the slightest shift in mood, the subtlest tone of voice that might indicate anger, violence. Intuitives were often created that way. What was going on in the brittle psychic air of the family was fearful and unresolved, but it was never spoken of, never explained. She'd developed emotional feelers that seemed to extend out from her belly, a sense of messages coming to her through the air: *What just happened in the silence around me? Why do I feel as though I am about to be killed when all they're doing is sitting there watching TV?*

She was not aware of any of this as a child. An overdeveloped sense of reading the atmosphere around her had first been a way to survive. Only later had she developed it as a gift: highly focused intuition, hypersensitivity to others, a fluid sense of self that could almost seem to merge with another, and imagination so vivid she could walk into her images like a waking dream. No wonder she had learned to leave her own life and enter another's story. No wonder she was triggered to do so, even empowered to do so, by fear.

And though Theresa had never met Tory, she knew that the girl was like her. She only hoped Tory would survive and that her gifts would come to heal her.

Theresa and Joe sat facing each other at the sidewalk café. He had brought a grocery bag full of items that belonged to Tory: troll dolls, Barbie clothes, hairbrush, toy boat, Etch-A-Sketch. One of those plastic domes enclosing a tiny world, swirling with snow. Inside it, a bright tropical fish. An angelfish. *Bahamas,* lettered across the front. Instead of snowflakes, though, the dome was filled with flakes of multicolored glitter.

"Tory likes these things, doesn't she?" Theresa asked, holding the dome. "There was one from San Francisco in her room at Ellen's. And a unicorn."

Joe took the dome from her and shook it. The glitter went crazy.

He also brought several pictures Tory had drawn. Theresa examined them. They looked very much like the ones that had come through her hand: quick, sketchy motion, original, not typical little-girl pictures. The faces in these particular drawings were quite expressive, not just round circles with dots for eyes and saucer grins. She wondered if it might be possible to invoke a drawing, for Tory to draw, through Theresa's hand, the face of Doc.

When Theresa looked up, she spotted Jardine heading toward

them along the boardwalk. He was wearing a navy suit, though it was already hot, a brown portfolio in one hand. He waved when he saw her, and then, as he noticed she was with someone, a man, his expression changed slightly, very slightly, but she saw it. *Oliver,* she thought, *please don't say anything asshole-ish.*

As he approached the railing that separated the café from the boardwalk, Jardine recognized Joe DeLisi and he looked disconcerted for a moment as he greeted them, glancing at Theresa with just a hint of admonition, a hairline slit of the eyes, but she got it and spoke to it.

"Joe called me this morning from his hotel room because he wanted to show me these." She thrust Tory's drawings at Jardine and narrowed her eyes back. *Stay out of this,* she sent. "Ellen fired me, by the way," she added. "I think she got scared."

Jardine was captivated by the girl's drawings. "You really captured Tory's style in those drawings you did, Theresa."

It captured me, she thought.

He handed the pictures back, came around through the entrance to the café, and pulled up a chair at the end of their table. He flagged the waiter and ordered coffee.

DeLisi spoke. "Lieutenant, there was a possible sighting of Tory last night."

"I know," Jardine interrupted. "I just came from a meeting with Rukheyser downtown. He filled me in. The lab confirmed your daughter's fingerprints were on the doll. They've got some other prints off it, too, including both yours and Ellen's, of course. They're continuing their search of the landing area this morning. So far nothing has turned up in the channel."

"Well, that's something," said DeLisi.

Theresa gestured toward the toys and personal items that Joe had taken from the bag and set on the red and white tablecloth. "Dr. DeLisi brought some of Tory's favorite things from home. He thought I might be able to get a reading from—"

Jardine reached across the table so suddenly that he knocked a glass of water onto the floor, where it shattered. Everyone in the café turned to look.

"This is Tory's?" Jardine pointed to the angelfish dome.

DeLisi nodded.

"When did she get it?" Jardine asked.

"Recently, I'd say. Sometime this last year. She brought it out with her when she came to see me in June. Why?"

"Gerald Oslin collected these things." Jardine filled them in on some of the details of the Oslin investigation. "I was hoping to find more of these at the store. He had shelves of toy collections there, too. But it all went up in smoke, literally. There was a fire at the store last night. The place is demolished."

Theresa picked up Tory's hairbrush. "Someone is trying to hide their connection to her."

"You mean Oslin's connection to her, don't you?" Jardine asked.

"Oslin was a link, somehow. He must have been."

"You're thinking Oslin gave this dome to Tory?" asked Joe.

Jardine unfolded a piece of paper, setting it on the table where they could all look at it. It listed the contents of Oslin's collection.

Theresa looked over Jardine's arm at the ones he'd circled. "Items five and eighteen," she said. "I saw them in Tory's bedroom at Ellen's home— I was just telling Joe about them, wasn't I? The Golden Gate Bridge and the unicorn."

Jardine stared at them. "Good, Theresa. Good eye."

"I'll call and have my housekeepers check Tory's room, both in Cambridge and on Martha's Vineyard, for any more of these. Can I get a copy of this list? Have you searched Ellen's home for any more of these?"

"We will now," said Jardine. "I'd like to search Ms. Carlin's house for any and all possible connections between Oslin and Tory. I've got to get a warrant first."

"But Oslin is dead," said DeLisi. "He can't possibly have taken Tory."

"There are a couple of things to consider," said Jardine. "He might have known who did take her. He might have had information about the abduction, overheard someone planning it. A link, as Theresa suggested. Also, his murder followed Tory's abduction by two days. She disappeared on Friday, Oslin was killed on Sunday. So he could actually have abducted her. Or aided someone else in doing so."

DeLisi rose suddenly. "I'd better go over all this with Rukheyser. Theresa, Lieutenant." He nodded at them both. "Can I call you later?" he asked Theresa.

"Call me," she said. DeLisi left the café and entered the stream of early-morning runners along the boardwalk. Theresa turned to Jardine. "Do you need this dome right away?"

"I want to check it for prints, Theresa. Then I'll see if I can release it to you."

You'll see? He'd never pulled that on her before, that holding back. *Yeah, right?* she thought. *He used you as bait when he was investigat-*

ing Bonnie Humphrey's murder nine years ago. Controlling son-of-a-bitch, she beamed at him.

"Do that," she said, "because I may be able to pick up on someone besides Tory off it. Oslin, for instance. I also think it would be good if I met with a sketch artist. I'm getting a better picture of the man Tory is with."

"Great," he muttered. "I'll get you downtown with Oslin's girl-friend. She has a description of a possible suspect, too, a client of Oslin's."

She watched him examining his list again, not looking up at her. Finally she leaned across the table toward him. "Oliver," she sang, "I'm not fucking Dr. DeLisi, okay?"

"What?" he exclaimed. "Did I say anything?"

"Not out loud." She scowled.

"Hey, it's none of my business. I come down to the café, I know you often come here first thing in the morning, and here you are with DeLisi. What am I supposed to think?" He sipped his coffee. "I do know when I'm in some kind of sexual crossfire. That doesn't take intuition, teacher." The waiter refilled their coffee cups, and Jardine emptied two packets of sugar into his. "Anyway, there are some things about DeLisi you should know."

"All right," she said. "I'll admit there's a certain attraction. And I think he needs a connection. He's all alone in this. I'm not going to do anything inappropriate or stupid."

"Don't egg him on, Theresa."

"I'm not!"

"Look at how you're dressed!"

She was wearing a black T-shirt tucked into midnight-blue silk shorts, belted at the waist. Black sandals, silver pendant. Her hair was loose, and she'd dabbed jasmine oil on her throat before meeting Joe here. So what if she looked good at eight in the morning?

"You look like a fucking goddess," Jardine said under his breath.

Theresa smiled. "Why, thank you, Oliver. What a nice thing to say."

"Besides," he said, "don't you want the dirt on this guy before you go into a frenzied mating ritual?"

"Back off, Oliver," she said in a singsong voice.

He pushed his chair away from the table.

Theresa closed her eyes briefly. "Go ahead, Oliver. Let's hear the incriminating evidence."

"Rukheyser received the divorce decree and custody documents, as well as information from the Massachusetts court services' investigation on both parents' backgrounds. He showed them to us at this morning's meeting.

"Ellen Carlin got a restraining order against her then-estranged husband, Dr. Joseph DeLisi, after she claimed he shoved her down the basement stairs. She suffered a broken arm. He claimed his wife fell while intoxicated. Ellen also claimed he made threatening statements to her on a number of occasions, and he left a significant one on her answering machine. And I quote: 'Keep pushing me, Ellen, and you won't live to see her go to kindergarten.' Unquote."

Great, thought Theresa. *Hell of a good catch.*

"He was also involved in an interdepartmental scandal at the institution where he taught before he was at MIT, in which he was accused of designing a software system for concealing misappropriated funds within the medical school of a major university."

"Was he ever indicted?"

"No, but it didn't add to his résumé."

"Still, he got the job at MIT."

"Apparently he's quite good at what he does. He must be, or he would have been indicted as well as convicted. Another thing. Universities are not the only ones to have benefited from his talents. There are suspicions, never proved, that he may have tipped off some less-than-bona-fide companies on the how-to's of invading competitors' software."

"If he weren't Italian, you wouldn't be questioning the bona fides of his clientele. And what does the investigation say about our lovely Ellen?" she asked.

"She doesn't look too good either. She was in treatment at Smithers in New York for prescription drug abuse, just as DeLisi said she was. Xanax and Percodan, but also Ritalin and Valium."

"Ritalin? Ellen told me Tory was on Ritalin for attention disorder problems in school."

"Well, Mommy liked it, too."

"Does the report say she ever used needles?" Theresa remembered this morning's dream fragment, Ellen blue in the bed, a syringe beside her.

"The report only mentioned pills. And in spite of Dr. DeLisi's protests, there is a documented history of parental abduction. It strongly points to DeLisi being involved in Tory's disappearance in some way, and it could be that his mother is involved, as she was previously. Rukheyser's people are going out to Palm Springs to talk to DeLisi's mother today, and I want to drive out there this afternoon to interview her regarding any possible connections she may have had with Oslin."

Theresa stared at a flock of gulls swooping around a garbage barrel.

Jardine continued. "Then there are Tory's medical records. Theresa, Tory is a very sick girl."

"Joe filled me in on a lot of that last night."

"The doctors at Kettler Hospital suspect some kind of systemic allergy or immune deficiency disorder."

Theresa told Jardine about her conversation yesterday with Ellen, her resistance to HIV testing, the surgery in Ghana.

"DeLisi asked the doctors at Kettler to back him in his custody appeal," said Jardine, "and their records show there may have been negligence on Ellen's part. Okay, so the kid is in there for observation and a diagnosis leading to a recommendation for future custody of Tory. A timely disappearance. Either parent had motivation to nab her, the way I see it."

Theresa folded her napkin on the table, taking all this in. "Can I go along with you to meet with Joe's mother?" she asked.

Jardine closed his portfolio. He seemed reserved, almost secretive, she noted. Definitely holding back.

"Theresa, I think we should take a look at each of our roles in this. It feels . . . what do they call it? Entangled. You're doing work for the Simon Foundation, but basically at this point you're working with DeLisi. At the same time, I'm investigating a murder in which DeLisi and his ex are possible suspects for murder."

"Abduction—I can see that, but murder? How?" she cried.

"That's what I'm saying. Look how upset you are. You're attached not only to DeLisi but to Tory. I need objectivity. I'd like to be able to talk with you about all this, Theresa, but we need to keep our roles straight."

She looked at his eyes, his round, sunburned nose.

"Let's consult with each other," he said. "But I cannot have you in on my investigation itself."

"Is this coming from downtown?" she asked.

"No, it's coming from me."

"But, Oliver, what about the Catalina landing, the doll, my getting the dome from Joe this morning? I'm contributing valuable information. I'm getting you connections you'd never have otherwise."

"Of course you are. You don't even know the half of it. I haven't had a chance to tell you about Royce Billings."

He told her of his conversation with Jackie, of watching from the parking lot as Tommy Rebek led the sheriff up the refinery scaffolding.

"See?" she said. "You need me, Oliver. God damn it."

He stood and picked up the bill, waving her hand away as she reached for her bag. "I'm not saying I don't, it's just that it's too sticky to have you along with me as I'm doing my work. What if I asked to sit in on all your readings? Take it easy, Theresa. You don't usually get this involved in your clients' lives, do you?"

"Never," she said.

"Then why now?"

Theresa didn't know. She remembered the image she'd had when she'd first read for Ellen. Of a baby shrunken to bone. *Whose baby?* She had no idea what that even meant. She reached for the paper bag holding Tory's things, but Jardine reached into it first, removing Tory's hairbrush.

"I'll take this," he said. "The lab will be getting back to us about some hair samples we took from Oslin's house."

"So glad I could be of use to you, Lieutenant," Theresa muttered as she walked past him out of the café.

"I TOLD YOU," Tory cried. "I can't find her. I lost her. I must have dropped her somewhere." She slouched down in the bench at the dinette table in the trailer. When Doc glared at her, she dropped her eyes to the side and down, sinking against the tinny wall. He'd seen her do that around her mother, as if she were turning off the lights inside herself, dimming everything.

He looked out at the RVs in a line along the marina. He could see the *Queen Mary* from there, its black base and white tip, the red and black smokestacks and oval portholes. Somehow he'd thought it would be more fun. He realized that he'd had that illusion about a number of things in his life.

Tory looked so sad, he told her, "Okay, okay, we'll get you a new one. We'll drive over to a Kmart, you tell me exactly what kind of doll you want, and I'll go in and get you one."

He closed up the trailer and checked the hitch on the truck. Because she begged, he let her sit up in the truck instead of riding back in the trailer all by herself. But pulling out of Long Beach Marina, past the Catalina landing where they'd gone fishing last night, he saw the cop cars, four or five of them, in the parking lot, and a big power boat out in the water, a police boat, the coast guard maybe. Voices over a bullhorn—he couldn't make out what they were saying. What were they doing? He didn't want to slow down and look, but he could tell, as he wheeled past, that they were dragging the channel.

He brought her into the Kmart with him to pick out the doll, and that cheered her up. If they were going to be together, he couldn't keep her locked in the trailer. They'd have to get used to being seen. He'd explained to her why they had to pretend, and he thought she understood.

When they got to the zoo, he said, "Fun time," and Tory hopped out of the truck with the doll in her arms.

"Leave the doll in the car," he commanded.

She threw her sulk-glance his way, but placed the doll carefully on the front seat and shut the door. No more dropping evidence all over the city. He didn't say that to her, but it was best to leave everything in the car.

The Santa Ana Zoo was nearly empty on a Wednesday morning, but Doc could feel the roar of the traffic from the freeway nearby. This was a good choice, safer than the *Queen Mary*. No security guards and snoopy grandmothers. Inside the zoo, a molting peacock displayed his tail feathers under a stand of bamboo. The birds in the outdoor cages looked stressed out. So did the llamas and ostriches wandering around aimlessly on the bare dirt.

Tory wanted an elephant ride when she saw the sign that said RIDES THIS WAY! But there were no rides, not today. The elephants were sick, the groundskeeper told them as he jabbed at litter with a sharp pole. A llama screeched as they passed, sounding like an injured bird.

But still, it was peaceful here, thought Doc, and he was glad he'd come. He nodded politely to an overweight but nice-looking woman pushing a sleeping child in a stroller. There were probably a lot of sin-

gle mothers who wouldn't mind hooking up with a man like him and a
girl like Tory. He worked, he'd pay his own way. He didn't know why it
felt good in these places, the zoo and, yesterday, the ship. They were
places a family would go to. Maybe that's all he was looking for, a place
to walk with his little girl at the zoo on a summer morning.

Tory had run over to look at the monkeys. The female was groom-
ing the smallest one. It had pointed black hair and Tory said that it
looked like Pee Wee Herman. Older monkeys chased one another and
rolled wildly in the dirt near the mother. The largest male reached out
and cuffed them when they got too close to her.

"They're a family," said Doc. "Aren't they cute?"

Tory put her fingers through the wire-mesh fence and peered in at
them. A train whistle sounded in the distance.

"But they're prisoners," Tory said quietly.

As LIEUTENANT OLIVER JARDINE pulled up in front of Oslin's store, he
saw that the front windows had already been boarded up. A film of
black soot arched over each window and up the brick walls. Charred
shreds of an awning flapped in the morning breeze. Though the sidewalk had been swept, tiny shards of glass still sparkled on the cement.
On one side of a tree that protruded from the sidewalk, the leaves had
been singed off.

He got out of the car, and joined the conversation Sondra Jackson
was completing with the arson investigator and a woman from Oslin's
insurance agency. Jackson wrote notes rapidly on a clipboard, then
turned to Jardine. He suggested coffee, and they walked two blocks to
a small French restaurant. It had just opened for the morning. They
were the only customers.

They sat in a small courtyard with a lattice roof and scraggly-look-
ing vines that needed water. Jardine took two sugar cubes from a
white bowl on the table and dropped them into his coffee.

"It was arson," Jackson said. "No question about it. It appears that the store was entered with a key—no break-in—just as his residence was. Again, the security system had been disarmed with the secret code. I checked with their central office in Houston; the system was entered and disarmed at nine-twenty-four P.M.; the smoke alarm was triggered at ten-oh-seven.

"The store had been doused with kerosene and the place was torched. They concentrated on the office area. The burning in the rest of the store was erratic, indicating that the kerosene had been splashed around, but the desk and file areas had been drenched. The computer was a complete meltdown, and the file and desk drawer contents were burned to ash. Whoever did this obviously intended to destroy records. Merchandise was not the focus."

"Damn," Jardine muttered. "How much of that material in the hard drive did you get printed?"

Jackson grinned. "Not to worry. Yesterday afternoon I backed everything up to tape. He had a tape backup system, and I'm having all files on the hard drive printed out."

"You're a genius, Jackson."

"I can't guarantee it will duplicate what was in those files, but at least we didn't lose everything." She sipped her coffee and wiped away a cobweb on the glass candle holder. In the background the waiter had put on a tape of French rock and roll.

Jackson went on. "It was very clear to the arson investigators that the person who set the fire made no effort to make it look natural, so it does not look like it was an insurance scam. The insurance was adequate at best, which would appear to confirm that. There is the question of whether the heirs to Oslin's estate would stand to gain financially by receiving a single insurance benefit, but the insurance investigator said that in this case, because of the valuable nature of the antiques, they probably could have gotten more by selling off the inventory.

"Also I have some financial information. I spoke with Mary Oslin this morning. She's preparing the books for me to review. Oslin was doing good business, especially considering the recession. She estimated his net worth in the area of a million and a half plus. Again it is hard to say, because of the antiques. Because of this focus on destroying all of his records, I feel strongly that the motivation for the murder has to do with the store and financial issues. I don't know what the tie-in to this missing child could be, Lieutenant, but I think it would be best for me to concentrate on the financial investigation. A potential buyer or collector may be involved, there could have been some kind of deal in progress, and someone may have wanted to destroy evidence of that. Another angle—maybe Oslin was dealing in illegal properties. There was a case in the Midwest a few years ago where an old woman died, and when they cleaned out her house it was chock-full of rare books stolen from libraries, museums, and rare-book collections all over the world. Well?" she asked. "What do you think?"

"What about the will?" Jardine asked.

"Right. I've arranged to meet with Oslin's lawyer this afternoon. Mary is named as executor. She has not seen the will, but her understanding of her brother's wishes is that a substantial portion of the estate would go to his girlfriend, Jane Wood. She was not aware if she or her daughter had been named as beneficiaries, but she assumed that they had."

Jardine popped a sugar cube into his mouth. "Well, well. That brings Jane Wood right up there in terms of motivation, doesn't it? You know, when I questioned her, I concentrated on whether or not he might have been seeing someone else. Now I think it would be wise to find out if *she* is. Also, I've arranged for Jane Wood to meet with a sketch artist today." He told Sondra of the similarity between the genealogy client Jane had described and some of the details that Theresa had provided from her readings.

Jardine finished his coffee and they walked back to the store. The arson and insurance investigators were still there, and Jardine peeked in the open front door to look at the charred interior. The wall with the family pictures on it had been substantially burned. So had the shelves of toys. He couldn't help feeling that though the records may have been a focus, the financial records may not have been the object of destruction. It was something else, he thought. When they saw the contents of the hard drive, they'd have a better idea of what someone might have wanted to hide.

"What's the plan for today, then?" Jackson asked. "Concentrate on the financial, Oslin's clients, and Jane Wood?"

Jardine hesitated, watching the investigators in the store walk through the skeletons of furniture. "I'm going to stay on this connection to the kid," he said finally. "We have several concrete links to Oslin—the school picture and the snow domes. I told the lab to see if any hairs from Oslin's house matched those of Tory's from the hairbrush."

As he took one last look at the store, he noticed that the parachute hung over the desk area had also burned away. "You stay with the financial, Sondra. And draw up a comprehensive list of all these alternative health-care professionals Oslin may have consulted with. We need to start talking to them. Let me know what you find out about the will and who were the beneficiaries of the business insurance policies, too."

He reached into his pocket and handed Sondra Jackson the locket he'd found in Oslin's dresser drawer. She held the locket in her open palm, then clicked it open. "Do you think that's Mary Oslin?" he asked.

"Looks like her, kind of. Twenty years and seventy-five pounds ago." She snapped the clasp shut and returned it to Jardine. "But if it was Mary, wouldn't the locket have an *M* engraved on it instead of an *L*?"

Jardine fingered the engraved design, an *L* laced into the gold with filigreed flowers and vines. Why hadn't he noticed that? "Maybe it's a family piece passed down. I'll ask Mary and see if the picture is of her."

Jardine drove out to Palm Springs with the car windows up and the air conditioner blasting against the white noon.

Joseph DeLisi's mother, Carmen, answered the door wearing garden gloves and a wide-brimmed straw hat, her face creased with a desert tan, but her features refined, sharp, even pixielike. Jardine guessed she was in her early sixties, but her black hair showed no trace of gray and was cut very short, accenting her good bones and large dark eyes.

Carmen DeLisi let Jardine in, removed her straw hat and gloves, and sat in a chair opposite Jardine. She was barefoot. She asked to see Jardine's badge and wrote the badge number down on the business card he had handed her.

Then Jardine filled her in on Oslin's murder, the fire, finding Tory's photo in his office, and the connection between the snow domes in Tory's belongings and the ones missing from Oslin's collection. He held out the angelfish dome, and she examined it without touching it.

"I've never seen it." She paused. "You'll have to excuse me," she said, clearing her throat. "I finished meeting with Sergeant Rukheyser not two hours ago and I'm quite worn out, I realize. Now you come with more information, things he never even mentioned. Murder, school pictures . . . " Carmen DeLisi crossed her legs.

"There is a connection between the cases, but we have two separate divisions investigating. I appreciate your taking the time to talk to both of us."

She nodded. "I'll do anything to help find Tory."

"Mrs. DeLisi, have you ever visited Oslin's antique store, or purchased or collected antiques or folk-art toys?"

"No," she said flatly.

"What about genealogy? Have you ever hired anyone to do genealogical research on your family?"

"No, but my sister did. Years ago, back in Boston. She used some service in Manhattan. I do have the booklet they put together. Would that help?"

"Yes," said Jardine. "It might. I'd like to see it."

Jardine questioned her further for any areas of connection that she or Joe or Tory or Ellen might have had to Gerald Oslin.

The answers were negative. He left his questions regarding her role in keeping Tory away from her mother that summer in Mendocino until the end of the interview. "Mrs. DeLisi, I'm sure that Sergeant Rukheyser already asked you about your role in harboring Tory during the custody dispute between your son and Ellen Carlin."

"Rather extensively, I'm afraid. But I'll be happy to tell you every single thing I told the sergeant. First of all, there was no custody violation because they were still officially married and Ellen was unable to care for Tory. Joe called me to help with her, and we both decided a summer in the woods, near the ocean, would be good for her. We took her out of Boston. When Ellen got out of treatment, Joe did not tell her where Tory and I were staying until a month or so later. We both feared that Ellen would leave the country with Tory."

"Your son claims that Ellen had been told where Tory was."

Carmen DeLisi folded her hands in her lap. "I'm sure he told her eventually, Lieutenant, but to be perfectly honest with you, there was a period of time when his decision was that it was for the best if Ellen didn't know. I supported him in that. I don't think it was illegal, but maybe it wasn't wise. We were all in a lot of pain. Ellen was . . . " She hesitated. "She was out of control.

"I am convinced that Ellen Carlin is a manipulative, devious, sick woman who should not have custody or even access to her daughter," said Mrs. DeLisi. "I consider her toxic to the child. She's a cruel woman who is very good at appearing to be otherwise if any authority figures are present—social workers, for instance, therapists, lawyers, doctors, or judges. And police. Unfortunately, Tory adores her. Ellen is her mother. Children often can't see what's in front of their eyes. They can't afford to. It would put their deepest bonds at risk."

Jardine said, "Tory was in Kettler Hospital for allergy testing and to look into immune deficiency disorders, including HIV."

"I'm telling you, what Tory suffered from was an allergic reaction to her own mother."

Jardine stared into Mrs. DeLisi's harsh, clear eyes. Something she said rang true beyond what he could fully understand.

Jardine pressed on, asking Mrs. DeLisi to comment on Tory's health problems. She repeated much of what he'd already learned, but when asked if she thought the bond between Tory and Ellen was overly dependent, Mrs. DeLisi leaned forward in her chair. "Yes, but as a mother I do have some sympathy. I know why Ellen was so protective. I can't hold it all against her. It's just that she goes so far to isolate the girl. You knew she lost a child to SIDS when she was married to her first husband?"

Jardine glanced up. "No, I didn't."

"No one talks of it. They all walk on eggshells around Ellen, as if anyone mentioned it she'd fall right apart. I found out from Ellen's mother one night when she'd had one too many. That whole family loves to discuss illnesses. She ran down every medical problem Ellen had ever had, from fertility testing to impacted wisdom teeth. Then she let slip about the baby Ellen lost. Ellen had a hard time conceiving when she was married to Joe, and she had a few miscarriages. So I can understand why she hovers over Tory so. I don't approve of it, mind you, but I understand it. And I gather that when Ellen was a baby, she was sick a lot, too. Good thing her father was a pharmacist.

"Ellen's mother often took care of Tory when she was an infant— once for four months. Can you imagine? And then Ellen would come and take Tory away as her companion on a nice little trip. They'd both return ill, and Ellen would take to her bed. It was ridiculous. I don't know how Joe lasted in that marriage as long as he did. But Ellen is very clever, very charming, and very pretty. Can turn on that charm in a second and look very together. The perfect mother, spending every moment at Tory's bedside at the hospital, then collapsing herself from fatigue once Tory stabilized.

"Now if you were smart, you'd check out Ginny Carlin, Ellen's mother. She was very attached to Tory ever since she cared for her as an infant. I'm not saying Ginny would ever harm Tory. She might want to protect Tory from Ellen. I gave Sergeant Rukheyser her number down in Huntington Beach. I can't believe Joe hasn't told the police to go look there. He gets so involved in thinking Ellen's hiding Tory from him, he can't think of anything else."

Jardine asked her for Ginny Carlin's address and phone number. She scribbled it on a scrap of paper. As she gave it to him, she looked up sadly. "I went to mass this morning," she said, "praying for that child."

Jardine thanked her and rose to go.

"There's another person I feel you people should question," Mrs. DeLisi added as she showed him to the door. "I just thought of him. Ellen was engaged briefly last year to a doctor. It's no coincidence, this fixation with doctors. I don't know how she ended up with my son, a mathematician. One husband and one fiancé, both were doctors, and her own father a pharmacist. That classifies as a fixation, wouldn't you say?

"The man's name was Park. Dr. Whitney Park. He's in cosmetic surgery in Beverly Hills. But what horrified me was this: Quite soon after they were engaged, Ellen checked into some swanky spa for a week and Dr. Park took Tory to his vacation home in Baja. Alone!"

Mrs. DeLisi put her hand to her mouth. "Holy Mother," she whispered. "That's where you should look for Tory. He took her down there all by himself. For an entire week, can you imagine? A strange man that Ellen had only known in a whirlwind courtship for maybe two months. Now isn't that highly irregular? Why didn't Ellen ask Joe to come out and take Tory for the week? Or her own mother? Or me?"

"How did you find out about this?" asked Jardine.

Mrs. DeLisi began to shake, her eyes blurring with tears. She walked weakly back to her chair and sat down. "Tory told me." Mrs. DeLisi's voice creaked. "She said she had the most wonderful time and that she felt as clear as the sky. That it was the first time she could remember taking a trip when she didn't get sick. 'I didn't go into the fog, Grandma,' she told me. 'I felt just as clear as the big blue sky.' "

"Are you going to be all right, Mrs. DeLisi?"

For the first time Mrs. DeLisi looked her age. "Not until my granddaughter is found."

On the drive back to Los Angeles, Jardine's mind whirled with questions and possible scenarios. No one knew how Oslin knew Tory. Why not? Did he have some kind of secret connection to her? Oslin had dug into his birth parents, their backgrounds. What if Tory was actually a relative from Oslin's biological family? Jardine wanted to get a look at that genealogy chart of Miss Tucker's. He hoped to God it was on that backup tape. What if Tory was the child of someone Oslin had done a family tree for? What if something about Tory's background was secret, paternity for example, and Oslin had threatened to tell?

Maybe he was going to testify on behalf of one of the parents in the custody appeal.

Jardine trailed off, shaking his head. He tried to let go of holding on to any one track of thought. Step back, witness, let them all flow through. Stop trying to control the thinking, Theresa had told him. Step into the matrix, the field, and let the thoughts arise. Witness from back there. What came up?

The thought seemed irrational, but insistent: *Tory is somehow related to Oslin. But how?*

Her picture was in with family pictures. A child no one knew about. What if Ellen and Oslin had been lovers, years ago, while she was married to Joe DeLisi? If she'd had trouble conceiving, perhaps it had been her husband's fault. She might have sought out someone to impregnate her, a lover, a sperm donor, a one-night stand.

Her world travels, Asia, Africa. Oslin loved to travel, collections and artifacts from all over the world, especially the Far East. A liaison in a foreign country? Jardine thought of those pictures of Oslin on the wall in his office. He wished he could look at those old pictures again. A younger Oslin bore a striking similarity to Joe DeLisi, if it weren't for the beard.

Jardine fumbled on the seat next to him for his microcassette recorder. He clicked it on and spoke. "Gerald Oslin wanted a child. Then he changed his mind. Whose child was Tory?" he asked. "Gerald Oslin might have had a concern about having a child due to medical complications in his family history. Tory DeLisi has a history of unexplained illnesses."

Jardine drummed on the steering wheel, staring at the glittering line of cars snaking along the freeway at twenty miles per hour.

"Who are Tory's real parents?" he asked aloud into the recorder. "Who did not want Oslin to have access to Tory? Who wanted Oslin out of the way? What did he know about Tory that no one else knew?"

When he got back to L.A., Jardine stopped at a SuperAmerica and looked up Dr. Whitney Park's address and phone number in the telephone directory. His office was not in Beverly Hills. He practiced in a medical complex near the UCLA medical center and not far from the Kettler Institute Children's Hospital. Jardine drove there without making an appointment, parked the car, locked it, walked into a cool green glass building, and rose in the elevator to the seventh floor.

Jardine showed the receptionist his badge and asked to speak with the doctor as soon as possible, hoping he was not in surgery. Most doctors did their surgery in the morning. It was now late afternoon.

The receptionist spoke quietly on the phone for a moment, then looked up from reading *People* magazine. She was a very beautiful woman with a thin, perfectly formed nose and full, round lips. She resembled a drawing of a human being. A design statement. "The doctor will see you in his office at the end of the hall, Lieutenant," she said. She buzzed the door open.

Dr. Whitney Park stood behind his desk as Jardine entered. The doctor came around to shake the lieutenant's hand and gestured for him to take a seat.

"What can I do for you?" the doctor asked. He was a tall, burly man with dark salt-and-pepper hair and a mustache. He was slightly overweight, but classically handsome, midforties. His nose was perfect, too, but Jardine didn't bother hating him for it. The doctor folded his hands on the desk. A plate-glass window behind him was covered by a sheer silver gray shade. With the light behind him, Park's face was slightly in shadow.

"I'm investigating the murder of Gerald Oslin, an antique dealer here in Los Angeles," said Jardine.

"I saw it in the paper. Wasn't his store firebombed last night?"

"Not bombed. But it burned."

"That's a shame," said Dr. Park.

"I'm also looking into the disappearance of a child, an abduction that may be tied to Oslin's murder."

"Tory," the doctor said quietly. "I'm glad you came to see me. Ever since I heard she was missing, I've been thinking of contacting the police."

"How did you know she was missing, Doctor? It has not, as yet, been in the media."

"I do rounds at Kettler and know many of the doctors there."

"Why *didn't* you call the police?" asked Jardine.

"I didn't have any actual information about her disappearance. I just wanted to be of some kind of help." He paused. "I dated her mother for a while. As you must know or you wouldn't be here."

"Weren't you engaged?"

"For several months. Very intense woman, Ellen. Taught me something, though. I'm definitely on a hiatus from whirlwind courtships, I can tell you that."

He opened a desk drawer and pulled out a photograph of himself with Ellen, Tory, and two very attractive young women. "The older girls are my two daughters, home from college on Thanksgiving break when I was seeing Ellen last fall. Happy, blended family-to-be, right? Hah!" he snorted.

"Ellen showed up like the absolute woman of my dreams. I met her through a physician friend of mine. She was beautiful, stylish, intelligent, savvy, warm—very dynamic. We weren't together a month before we were talking marriage. I liked Tory very much. I'd missed out on my own kids' day-to-day upbringing. Their mother and I were divorced when my girls were very young, and I only had them eight weeks each summer and one holiday break. I knew it was too fast, but I'd put off commitment for years. I was ready to plunge. And it was a plunge."

"What happened?" asked Jardine.

"I got to know her. Once we were really intimate, it turned out that she had a very neurotic and grasping element to her personality. I felt subsumed. Love for her was playacting. It was Ellen starring in the romance of her life—for the third time. Slowly I came to see her real personality emerge, especially around Tory."

"Was she abusive?"

"I never saw any indication of that. But emotionally . . . she manipulated Tory, smothering her with affection. And soon she was doing that to me with a very clinging, saccharine quality, but underneath there was anger. If you didn't love her the way she wanted, she was furious. She wouldn't go into therapy, said she'd done all that. I had to break it off, and it was tough. In spite of everything, I had gotten very attached. I was in love with her."

Whitney Park was quiet. Then he said, "Poor kid. As if she hasn't been through enough. Tory's going to have a lot to sort out in her life, with Ellen as a mother, but she's a strong little girl, determined, very sweet. A sensitive kid and quite artistic. Are there any leads in this abduction? Do they suspect Tory's father?"

"We're investigating a number of angles. Dr. Park, in November of last year you took Tory with you on a trip to Baja. You own property down there."

"Yes. It was when I was just beginning to be concerned about Ellen's stability. I thought a week at a spa would help her, and I offered to take care of Tory for the week. We were engaged by then, and it was my effort to establish a closer bond with Tory as a future stepfather."

"Where exactly is the property you own down there?"

He flipped a Rolodex and read out the address and phone number of a property management company that rented out the condominium.

"We had a great time," he went on. "My girls were supposed to come down too, but opted at the last minute for a week in Vail instead. Tory seemed to warm up to me—maybe a little too quickly. She was into the fantasy of her mother remarrying, of a mom-stepdad-child circle. Wanted to call me 'Daddy.' I told her she had a father. She said, 'Yeah, but I call him Dad. I can call you Daddy.' I said no, it didn't feel right. I suggested she just call me Whit. But she started teasing me, calling me Señor. I called her Señorita. That was it, really. We swam, went on boat rides, touristed around. I felt good about the trip, but when I got back, things soon started to sour with Ellen."

"Did it ever occur to you that taking your fiancée's daughter away, alone with you on a trip, might look inappropriate?"

Park huffed. "That's preposterous. Ellen thinks I molested the kid or something? Is that what she's claiming?"

"Would you be willing to have us search your home here in L.A. and your Baja property?"

He took out a file from a desk drawer and tossed it on the desk. "I own property in Mexico, Southern California, and up in Idaho in Sun Valley. You can check with my lawyer to make sure it's a complete listing. Go ahead, search anything I own." He crossed his arms.

Park slouched in his chair and glanced at his watch. "I have patients waiting," he said. "Could we continue this conversation at another time? Listen, I know I sound upset about the implications of traveling alone with Tory. Look, I'm not an idiot, I was aware when my girls canceled out that it might look funny. But we went on ahead as if we were family. What can I say? Did Ellen suggest I had any part in this?"

"Actually it was her grandmother, Mrs. DeLisi, who suggested we question you."

Jardine hesitated, then asked, "Did Ellen ever mention Gerald Oslin? Were they ever involved?"

Park frowned, shook his head. "I don't know of any connection between Ellen and this Oslin. Though we were engaged, I didn't know Ellen. She was multifaceted. Too multifaceted for me."

"One more thing, Doctor. With your medical background, you were in a position to observe Tory's health over a period of time. Any thoughts about that? You know she was in the hospital when she was reported missing."

"I was well aware of her history of health complications. I encouraged Ellen to look at the immune system. In fact, I referred her to several specialists—a psychiatrist whose focus is biochemical and metabolism disorders and an allergist whose specialty is candida, a fungus in the body. People who've taken a lot of antibiotics can lose the natural balance of bacteria in the body and develop mysterious allergies that affect the entire system. Some people develop quite toxic reactions to wheat, MSG, fermented products like cider, vinegar, molds, yeast, and so on."

Dr. Park checked his watch. "I really should be getting back to my patients." He showed Jardine to the door.

Halfway down the hall, Jardine turned back to Dr. Park. "So you see patients at Kettler?"

Dr. Park looked past him to the nurse waiting at the far end of the hall. "I work with children in facial reconstruction caused by birth defects and following accidents. By the way, the allergist I referred Tory to is Dr. Nagai. N-A-G-A-I. We golf together. That's how I found out that Tory was missing."

At the end of the hall, the nurse held the door open. Jardine glanced back down the apricot-carpeted hallway. Whitney Park still stood with his arms crossed like a sentinel, waiting for him to go.

THERESA SAT CROSS-LEGGED on the floor of her studio, the things from the bag Joe had brought to the café scattered around her. Snapshots, a kazoo, a tube of sunscreen. Barrettes and hair clips. She picked up each item and held it in her hand, waiting for images to rise up, feeling as scattered and disconnected as the objects strewn around her.

Finally she stopped her hungry grasping for an image. *You're trying too hard,* she told herself. *Just breathe. Nothing comes when you're like this. Just surrender.*

She sat quietly then, in a posture of meditation, hands curled in her lap. For a while, dreamlike fragments flitted through the inner field of her vision. She decided not to tape-record or write, just observe. Stay receptive. After a while the dislocated images slowed, and she focused in on a physical sensation. Pressure on the back of her head.

The sensation was gentle, a hand petting her hair. Pictures danced through: the blue sneakers, medicine bottles, syringes with long needles. Sharp pricks on her skin, inserted into her inner thigh, her buttocks. A stinging of pinpoints radiating over her legs, rash of thorns, itching and burning.

Heat flamed through her like sudden fever.

Hand stroking back of hair. Pressure now. Hard.

I remember, came Tory's voice.

"What?" Theresa asked. "What do you remember?"

Silence. Pressure.

Suddenly Theresa exploded into a fit of coughing, almost gagging. She jerked out of the trance state, ran to the sink, and gulped a glass of water down. She steadied herself.

"No fear," she said out loud. "Take it easy." Years ago, on the rare occasions when her readings began to take the form of actual kinesthetic body sensations of the querent, she would also simultaneously experience the intensity of their emotions and memories. She had little sense of boundary with what she was reading. She would go too far into it, merge with and become it. It was exhausting, even dangerous.

Now she had learned to read from a more witnessing presence, even if the symptoms and sensations of the body were the form of the reading. But she needed to ground herself.

She returned to her meditation, imagining herself sitting inside a huge redwood tree, not just a hole in the tree, but as if she had gone inside the tree itself. She felt its roots extending deep into the earth for hundreds of years, unshakable. Surviving time past all human concerns. The trunk, gigantic and steady around her, towering skyward, ascending toward light, reaching both up to receive and down to root, surrounding her with its ancient and woody strength.

She opened her eyes and was drawn to a Polaroid photo of Tory taken by the ocean, coming out of the water, gap-toothed grin.

Very clearly and slowly Theresa returned to the scene of the Long Beach landing, the flattened grass, the black water of the harbor. The word "sea" floated up in her mind, then a small flame flickering, a tiny candle. *Sea. Book. Sea Book?* Jim Morrison, the candelabra her grandmother had left her. Theresa opened her eyes, reached for the matches on the table beside her. "Come on, baby, light my fire," she sang quietly, striking the match, lighting each of the three candles in the silver candelabra.

Sally sells sea shells by the seaside.

Seashore, she corrected herself.

Seaside, came the word.

Seaside? Seabook? What are you getting at?

DON'T BEG, she heard. OPEN.

Again she sat down on the floor, picking up the objects one by one, putting some back in the brown bag, except for the barrettes, two purple, two yellow. She set them in pairs by the matches.

Matching, she thought.

Matchbook. Seaside.

She stood then, went immediately to the phone, and called Lieutenant Jardine. He wasn't in. "Damn," she whispered. She left a message on his pager, but he'd said he was going to be out, seeing about the fire and interviewing people. Joe was probably meeting with Rukheyser, she thought, and she didn't want to deal with Rukheyser directly. She had to talk to someone. Now. Quickly she dialed the number at the foundation and asked to speak with Leslie Simon immediately, even if she was in a meeting. It was urgent.

"Leslie, this is Theresa. I got a word that might indicate a place where Tory could be. I don't know what to make of it, but it felt big."

"Dr. DeLisi is sitting right here," said Leslie. "Do you want to talk to him?"

"Put him on." She explained about the reading she'd been doing.

"What is the word?" Joe asked

" 'Seaside.' On a matchbook. Have Rukheyser check with the people who searched the landing area to see if they found a matchbook with the word 'Seaside' on it. It could be a restaurant, a resort, a café, a town, somewhere Tory stopped to eat. It came very slowly and very clearly. It feels important."

"Got it," he said. "I'll call both Rukheyser and the police in Long Beach."

"Joe, I'd like to read the hospital room where Tory was abducted. Can you arrange that?"

"I don't know," he said. "Maybe Leslie can set it up." He covered the phone for a moment, conversing with Leslie. "We're going to call Tory's physician over there. I'll call you back as soon as I hear something."

While she waited for his return call, she picked up a fine-point pen and began sketching on a drawing pad, Tory's hand inside hers, black lines across the page. For a moment she thought it would stop, go away. She wanted to hold on, but told herself, *Don't think, don't try.*

An eye appeared on the page. An eye inside a star.

"Yes, Tory. Tell me," Theresa whispered.

Wispy but authoritative lines scratched over the paper. A set of eyes, a nose, thin lips, a wide forehead, balding hair, longish in back, then five-pointed stars surrounding the face, pen digging hard into the page.

She sketched a tiny moon beside the man's face. Then an *X*, crossing the moon out. Redrawing it on his earlobe. *Earring. Pierced ear. Moon shape.* "Yes," Theresa whispered. "Good girl. What else?" It wasn't like a drawing a sketch artist would produce. It was a child's drawing, but it was clear and well defined.

She waited for more, hand hovering over the page, until she heard the phone ring.

Theresa met Joe DeLisi in front of Kettler Hospital. It was located in Westwood, not far from the UCLA medical complex. As he approached, she remembered all that Jardine had told her about this man. She didn't feel as open to him as she had before, but it didn't matter. This was about Tory, not Joe DeLisi, and what went on between him and his ex-wife, and in his dubious business dealings, was none of her business unless it would help find the girl. Mutual character-bashing was part of many divorces and this one was no exception.

She'd stopped at a copy shop on the way over and run photocopies of the drawing of the man's face. Joe DeLisi took one from her, nodding. "This is incredible, Theresa. It's like one of her portraits, like she was right there coloring. I'll get them to the foundation and Rukheyser right away." They crossed the brick plaza, and Joe ushered her through the glass doors and across the marble floors to the elevators.

"Dr. Nagai said this is a highly unusual request," he told her. "The room is currently occupied by a patient, but she said the patient is scheduled for pre-op X rays and will be out of the room for a while. I had to promise we wouldn't touch anything, and a hospital orderly or a nurse will be present." Joe glanced at Theresa, then added, "Also, Dr. Nagai said not to tell anyone you're conducting a psychic reading. Just say you're with the Simon Foundation and there won't be a problem."

The elevator stopped at the third floor. Joe walked slightly ahead of Theresa to the nurses' station. He spoke with the head nurse, then motioned for Theresa to follow them.

But she was already there, ahead of him in the room, waiting for herself. Or that's how it felt, arriving at the open door of this room she'd seen so clearly in Tory's drawings. The nurse told her to go in. As Theresa shifted into field vision, she felt slightly lightheaded, but not dizzy. She opened to the periphery so that she saw not just the things themselves, but the air, the space, the relationship between the room and the things in it, saw from higher up, just above her head, and also from her heart.

Theresa put a finger to her lips, indicating to Joe to be quiet. The nurse stood behind them, arms folded. Theresa walked to the center of the room, rotating slowly around next to the bed, facing each direction. As she faced the windows, she looked out across the street at the large billboard. It wasn't an advertisement for Salems; it was for Benson & Hedges. A huge laughing woman with a wide, toothy smile.

She could pick up on the current occupant of the room. There had been several of them, in fact, since Tory, layers of voices, smells. Images washed through her quickly in a blur.

Slow. Focus, she told herself.

She sat at the edge of the bed and put her hand on the sheet.

Again the sensation of heat came up, pricking on her thighs and buttocks. Tory's voice, from far away. Theresa could hardly hear it. She closed her eyes, went down within herself. *Go ahead, Tory,* she thought.

Don't want them anymore. No.

Anger around her, fear.

Slapping a hand away. Sting on her cheek.

Syringe scuttering across the floor.

Soothing touch on her cheek.

You're not my doctor.

No more.

Crying, heaving in her chest. *Can't—*

breathe can't

get my breath can't

get away

No

more No

more No

Hand on her hair, sick feeling. *Don't*

touch me there, my hair no.

Slapping the hand away,

the hand soft press,

slap away.

Theresa felt suddenly icy, like a fever that turns to a cold sweat.

Then a sudden jolt, as if electricity had shot through her and she had shifted into another point of view. This was not Tory. She dropped farther down into it, knowing who it was, familiar tone.

Crying in the distance, down the hall.

Infant hungry cry.

Wail hungry belly.

Hand on the back of the little head, stroking.

Who's there?

Baby's face against the pillow, pressing it flat,

soft blanket, comfort warm.

Can't breathe.

Can't cough it up out air in

Breathe   I can't

Breathe   I can't

Breathe   Hand pressing her face down

in the pillows.

Stroking petting loving

softly, her back.

Mommy's right here.

All better. Sleep now.

Black silence, cold as space.

Under the black water.

Down, down where it all stops

feeling bad where I'm safe in the

black dream.

Scream raking the silence.

And then Theresa flew out, eyes open, heart thudding in her chest. Still sitting at the edge of the hospital bed, she reached out to touch the pillow to steady herself. A small Asian woman in a white lab coat stood beside Joe in the doorway. The nurse was gone. The echo of the scream collapsed inside Theresa like the sound of a siren streaming away in the distance. But the voice was still there, not Tory's but Ellen's.

My baby, my baby, my darling darling

baby.

My dead baby.

Help me.

Help me save my

baby.

Theresa rode out the voice-wave and brought herself back fully to the room. She held up her hand to Joe. *Don't approach.* They didn't know that in order to read from that depth, it was as if she had slid outside her physical body. She didn't want them near, she needed to pull back in.

"I'd like some water, Joe," Theresa whispered.

He fetched a paper cup from the bathroom, filled it, and handed it to her. The cold water brought her all the way back.

"Are you Tory's doctor?" Theresa asked.

"Yes, I'm Dr. Nagai," the woman said.

"Did you ever have any reason to believe that Ellen Carlin was deliberately making Tory sick—giving her injections of some kind in the thigh and buttocks, administering substances that would induce fever or even a light coma? That would cause vomiting and diarrhea?" Then, to Joe: "Did you ever suspect that Ellen was purposely suffocating Tory in the crib, causing those apneic episodes by pressing her head down into the pillow? Then screaming immediately for help so that Tory would be saved either by you or by paramedics, ambulances called to the house?"

Theresa looked from Joe DeLisi to Dr. Nagai.

The doctor straightened her black wire-frame glasses.

"Oh my." Dr. Nagai's high voice was both lilting and strained. "Oh my God."

THERE WAS A SMALL WAITING ROOM down the hall with a round table and chairs, a sofa, a microwave oven, a coffee machine, magazines, and a wooden box filled with bright plastic blocks, cars, and dilapidated children's books. Hazy light filtered through the smoked-glass windows. The room smelled of antiseptic.

Dr. Nagai had asked them to wait. She wanted to get Tory's records as well as her own notes from her office on another floor. She also wanted to see if a colleague, a psychiatrist named Robert Silver, could meet with them as well.

Joe was very quiet. He stood at the window, staring out at the traffic crisscrossing below them, sipping black coffee from a paper cup. Finally, still facing the windows, he spoke to Theresa.

"I feel like my life is one of those M. C. Escher prints where you think all the stairs are going up, but it's an optical illusion designed to trick the eye. All the stairs are upside down and the whole world is reversed."

He was silent again, then added, "It never occurred to me— never—that Tory's illnesses could be *physically* caused by Ellen. I thought Ellen was making Tory *emotionally* sick. Because the doctors could never get a clear diagnosis, I really came to believe that Tory's illnesses were physically unfounded, invented by her as a way to get love, nurturing, and attention. And encouragement, even somehow praise, from Ellen."

Dr. Nagai and Dr. Silver came into the room then, and Dr. Nagai gently shut the door, motioning for them all to take seats. She introduced Dr. Silver, a short man with dark hair and a full beard. He looked young, still in his early thirties. He immediately spoke to Theresa. "What you're suggesting has very serious implications. Very serious indeed. Now, on what basis have you arrived at the conclusions you mentioned to Dr. Nagai? She said you're with this agency for missing children?"

Theresa explained her relationship to the Simon Foundation and her profession. She saw him inwardly dismiss her right then and there—even glance over at Nagai as if to say, *What the hell did you get me into?*

Theresa went on, explaining that she was working on a masters in Consciousness Psychology, that she had been associated with several graduate departments at Berkeley through the work of Dr. Franklin Brandon, and had even once been consulted by the federal government regarding the possible uses of psychic ability in conjunction with virtual-reality systems. In addition, she numbered among her clients many professional people, and was not some *National Enquirer* fortune-teller psychic, but a consultant and teacher of intuitive processes.

In spite of Dr. Silver's obvious skepticism, she went on to explain to all three of them how it was that she had read for both Tory and Ellen over the past few days. She concluded by relaying the sensations, images, and voices she had picked up just now in the room where Tory had been staying. "Toward the end of the reading, I felt a shift. What I picked up on was Ellen at the emotional moment years ago, but still present in Ellen, when her first child died. When she killed her."

Joe looked away from her out the window, and the two doctors glanced down at their notes uncomfortably. *They think I'm crazy,* thought Theresa. *I don't care.* "I'm suggesting that Ellen may have suffocated her baby. This is what I saw, intuitively: Tory was receiving injections of some kind in her inner thighs and buttocks. That she had acquiesced in being given these shots, thinking, actually believing, that they were part of a prescribed treatment for her, the way people give insulin at home.

"But in the reading, I felt Tory is now at a place where she has been resisting these injections, that she is profoundly and probably unconsciously angry at her mother, and beginning to refuse her mother's 'treatments.' She kept saying, 'You aren't my doctor.' With that came this repeated sensation that I've had throughout the time I've worked with Tory—intuitively, of course—of pressure on the back of her head, followed by an inability to breathe. At first I took it as a metaphor; it was Tory's resistance, pushing and pulling against her mother. Her mother symbolically smothering her.

"From there, I was aware of dropping to a much deeper place and to a different—well, call it a vibration. I was no longer 'in' Tory, reading from her point of view. I was in Ellen. I've read for her before, so I knew it was her, her 'tone,' if you will. I felt her pushing a baby's head into a pillow to stop the baby's crying, to stop the resistance, so to speak. It was at the exact moment when Ellen realized she had killed her baby and simultaneously she also did not know she'd done it. It was like a split in herself—a doer and a watcher. She immediately split off from her knowing that she herself had done this, and began screaming for someone to help her save her baby. But it was too late . . . "

Theresa stopped. Silver and Nagai had both been taking notes. Silver pushed his chair back along the tiled floor.

"I apologize for sounding"—he shrugged—"for not taking you seriously, Ms. Fortunato. Let me just say I'm a terrible skeptic of things occult, New Age, to begin with. Second, as a psychiatrist, I deal every day with people who hear voices and see visions and merge into other personalities, and we treat those people quite effectively with a number of medications. But for the time being I'm going to accept your 'intuitions' as those of any person who is close to the child, empathetic with her, and offering some very perceptive insights into the family's dynamic." Dr. Silver seemed to have forgotten that Theresa had never met Tory. He continued.

"What you've described is a very rare form of mental illness called

Munchausen Syndrome by Proxy. It is a serious form of child abuse that is easily overlooked and difficult to diagnose. The term is applied to people who fabricate or induce symptoms in another person, causing that person to be regarded as ill. When it goes on for some time, without being found out, there is a tendency for the person who is being abused actually to participate in the lie, even to aid in the creation of their own illness."

Dr. Silver cleared his throat. "One of the reasons that it is so difficult to diagnose is that mothers who have this disorder—and it is almost always mothers—will appear to many people, particularly to hospital personnel, including doctors, as very fine mothers, ideal mothers, caring and deeply concerned. They are the ones who stay at the child's bedside, follow every detail of their treatments and presenting symptoms. They often become quite close with the nursing staff and seem deeply bonded with their child.

"In fact, there is a symbiotic bond between these mothers and children, one that is very unhealthy. The mother sees the child as an extension of herself, even of her own body, and in making the child sick and then seeking treatment, she is essentially, at an unconscious level, seeking to overcome her own sense of being sick. One report on the syndrome suggested that a mother was bleeding through her child's kidneys.

"They do quite unbelievable things to their children. They induce gastrointestinal disorders by administering laxatives and various substances. A case has been documented in which seizures were induced in a two-month-old boy after his mother injected him with insulin. Eventually he was blinded. They inject bacteria into the child, causing infectious responses such as fever, dehydration, and any number of other problems. The injected bacteria have often been found to be from the mother's own urine or feces. When they introduce the foreign material with needles, it often produces a mysterious rash on the skin surface. There is a whole range of symptoms that are difficult to diagnose—bizarre neurologic symptoms, recurrent diarrhea, drowsiness, behavioral withdrawal, ataxia, unconscious states, electrolyte abnormalities, and so on.

"And yes, your perception of apneic episodes as a result of smothering is not uncommon in patients with Munchausen Syndrome by Proxy. The child who has repeated episodes is often diagnosed as having cardiac arrythmia. Some psychiatrists estimate that as many as ten to fifteen percent of SIDS babies are actually child homicides, either deliberate or neglectful.

"These moms often use drugs themselves, prescription and nonprescription. They've been known to give their children everything from antidepressants to chloral hydrate, even large amounts of salt. They are often familiar with the medical field; they're nurses, technicians, and so on. They thrive in a hospital setting. They are suddenly the center of attention, they feel in control in the highly scheduled environment, steadily timed meals, a clean, orderly environment. And in that setting they are perceived as valuable, good mothers, very good indeed."

Joe DeLisi leaned forward in his chair, covering his face with his hands, resting his elbows on the table. "I can't believe this. I can't believe this. This is monstrous. Hideous. What would make her do it?"

Silver continued. "The patients are usually what we call permeable—people with a plastic ego, no clear sense of self. They are enmeshed with their children and cannot get their needs met for themselves, so there is an attempt to get their needs met through the child. They usually have deep, unresolved loss and grief from childhood, and in trying to repeat a fantasy of 'getting well,' they are attempting what we call 'mastery of loss.' The mind believes it can overcome the unconscious childhood trauma by reenacting it in the present time, repeating it so as to attempt to overcome it.

"They often had a very rejecting parent and are extremely ambivalent in relationships, alternating between idealization and hostility. And this is exactly how they see the hospital staff, as both saviors and failures. There are patients who gain a sense of satisfaction from fooling the doctors, and they disdain the medical profession. They want to feel superior. There's an attitude of 'I can't believe they can't see this.' Then they are both proud of their abilities and angry at the doctors. They achieve a sense of revenge and control over the object who rejects them."

"Why was this never diagnosed in Ellen?" Joe's loud voice echoed in the clinical room. "She had tons of therapy, she was in treatment programs, she was hospitalized for psychiatric evaluation, and all they ever said was that she suffered from exhaustion."

"It was not diagnosed for the same reasons that you did not see it, Dr. DeLisi. Medical and nursing staff are very reluctant to accept that a mother could be so cruelly deceitful and so skilled at it. There is also the difficulty doctors and nurses have in accepting that, inadvertently, their very treatments for the children may have been part of the abuse—even to the point of having done unnecessary surgery and invasive procedures. And the very protectiveness these mothers demonstrate seems incongruent with what most people think of as child abuse, much less an actual manifestation of abuse.

"But there are things to watch for. We often sense in these people something we don't like. While they seem warm, bonding, caring, we experience a sense of recoil from them. There is a feeling on a subjective level of being uneasy around them. You feel as though you are being intrusive. They have poor eye contact. They speak in a mechanical way about their child's symptoms, they are minutely knowledgeable about the medical history, the repeated illnesses.

"And it can be difficult to prove. At one hospital where a father—this was an aberration from the usual pattern—was suffocating his child by holding his hand over his infant's face, then calling out for help—a hidden video camera was installed to catch him in the act. The medical staff have to amass substantial evidence in order to confront the patient and to have it stand up legally, so that the child can be removed from that person's care. There are ethical issues regarding privacy."

"Did you suspect any of this between Ellen and Tory?" DeLisi asked. Dr. Silver was silent, and Dr. Nagai looked out the window. "I'll be honest with you," said Silver. "No."

DeLisi stood, angrily shoving his chair back from the table, stuffing his hands in his pockets.

"I would hope that we would have seen it eventually, had Tory remained in the hospital. I must point out that we have no actual *evidence* of Ellen Carlin having Munchausen Syndrome by Proxy, beyond the intuitive perceptions of Ms. Fortunato here. We are going to have to go over our records and Tory's medical history very, very carefully. These are serious accusations, especially the suggestion that Ellen's SIDS baby was, indeed, a homicide."

Silver turned to Theresa. "If we were to accept your perceptions as fact, what we would have is this. Ellen may have been using her second daughter, Tory, on a deeply unconscious level, in an attempt to bring her first baby back to life. By making Tory sick, Ellen could then try to save her, thus portraying herself as the healer, the nurturer, the loving mother. This would allow her to act out that part of herself in an idealized form. It is a form of repetition compulsion.

"Now, Dr. Nagai is one of the top immunologists in the country. She did begin to suspect, after a number of tests on Tory, that the child was having allergic reactions to some foreign substances." Dr. Silver gestured for Dr. Nagai to explain.

"Yes," said the soft-spoken doctor. "Tory was being kept on a very strict diet in order to isolate the substance causing the reaction. I am somewhat familiar with Munchausen Syndrome and other somatoform disorders, people artificially creating illnesses in their own bodies— hysterical conversions of the type Freud wrote about, hypochondria. The body and mind are not separate from each other, and there is a continuum from actual physical illness to this sort of conscious—or unconscious—deception. But I am far less familiar with the mental illness as a form of child abuse. I was focused on the allergy testing. Ellen came to me to discuss Tory's restrictive diet, to ask me some questions—and it was that night that Tory disappeared."

Joe interrupted. He'd been standing by the window, arms crossed, alternating waves of grief, disbelief, and anguish washing over his dark features.

"Do you think Ellen was on to you, Dr. Nagai?"

Dr. Nagai paused. "No," she said, "because I was not really 'on to her.' I did not suspect Ellen of any involvement in Tory's illnesses, with the exception of the emotional aspect of their relationship. But I *was* pressing for additional tests and I had suggested that Tory be isolated from all visitors, including her mother, for a period of time. Dr. Silver and I wanted to observe Tory's psychological reaction to being separated from Ellen. Would her anxiety level and her symptoms seem amplified by the separation or would she seem less anxious, less sick, without her mother there? We discussed Ellen and Tory's bond as overly enmeshed, but we were focusing on possible anxiety-related disorders, such as depression, bipolar depression, and her brain biochemistry."

"And did you tell the police when Tory disappeared?" asked DeLisi.

"Yes. And I told them that I was planning to isolate Tory for a time. And, based on that, Sergeant Rukheyser, I believe, assumed one of two things: either that Tory left the hospital of her own accord to avoid being cut off from her mother, or that Ms. Carlin removed Tory or had her removed to avoid the separation. But, as I said, it never occurred to me—until Ms. Fortunato spoke of it so directly and so vividly—that it might be Ellen herself who was introducing a foreign substance."

"Will you be able to tell from Tory's medical records what Ellen was doing to her?" Joe asked.

"As Dr. Silver said, we'll have to go over the records again with this new information, with this new context in mind," said Dr. Nagai.

"Ellen was trained as a geneticist," said Joe. "She could have had access to a lot of weird biological substances."

Dr. Nagai turned her coffee cup in her small hands. "Well, the police should be notified immediately. We will cooperate in any way we can with this inquiry."

Joe DeLisi reached behind him for the telephone on the table by the couch. He jabbed at the buttons with his finger. When he got Rukheyser on the line, he said in a calm voice that chilled Theresa, "Sergeant Rukheyser, this is Joseph DeLisi. I'm over at the hospital with Tory's doctor and a psychiatrist. I believe there is enough evidence to bring charges of child abuse, kidnapping, and murder against my ex-wife."

THERESA WAS OVERWHELMINGLY relieved to see Jardine hurry out of the elevator on the third floor. She'd stepped out of the conference room into the hall just as he and Rukheyser emerged. She assumed it was Rukheyser who stalked toward her, then brushed quickly past her; they'd never met. Jardine came to her side.

"I'm trying to convince Rukheyser to put you on the case as a paid consultant," he said. "What you came up with here is brilliant, Theresa."

"I don't want to be on the case in any official capacity. I'd feel hemmed in. I'm doing this strictly as a benefit for the foundation."

Following introductions, Theresa briefly summarized her findings, and the doctors reviewed Tory's medical records for Rukheyser in light of Theresa's "intuitions." They kept calling it her "hunch," her "feeling." She wanted to scream through their left-brained, overeducated, analytical minds: *This is information, not feelings.*

Yes, they agreed, Tory DeLisi did present symptoms that could suggest Munchausen Syndrome by Proxy: the repeated apneic episodes, incidents of respiratory arrest, plummeting body temperature, curious patterns of rashes and welts, gastrointestinal distress, dehydration. And, yes, medical evaluations over the years had determined that such symptoms were caused by viral and bacterial infections picked up in foreign countries, or by food poisoning, parasites, allergic reactions, and immune deficiencies, and were logical explanations for Tory's varied problems. The fact that she had seen so many different doctors and no one had a complete record on her added to the difficulty in perceiving her mother's mental illness as the real cause, if indeed that could be substantiated. The doctors both stressed the need to verify that hypothesis, both in the actual medical records and through psychiatric evaluation of Ellen.

Silver and Rukheyser were engaged in a long discussion about whether Theresa's "hunch" could be used as a basis for further investigation when Jardine broke in.

"Look, Rukheyser," he snapped, "it doesn't really matter what you think of her method. If I'm on a case where the wife says she's had dreams that her husband is screwing a blonde who drives a blue car, I check it out—see if there's any congruence with what we think of as 'real life.'

"The point is to see if we can get evidence admissible in court that Ellen Carlin was doing this, not whether the seed of the realization was intuitive or rational. Hell, if Dr. Nagai here had had time to proceed further with her methods, she probably would have caught Ellen injecting something, and Ellen could have been placed under surveillance right here at the hospital. The kid would never have been taken out of here. Let's not waste time arguing about means. Let's get to the end, finding the kid."

Rukheyser drummed his fingers on a file folder in a silence following Jardine's outburst. He then turned to the doctors and to DeLisi. "This case is complicated by a homicide that appears to be connected to the child's disappearance. It's a challenge to try to keep the two cases separate, yet in communication. And each division does have its own preferred methods of investigation."

Silver interjected, "I'm not accustomed to consulting with psychics myself, although Ms. Fortunato here does have impressive credentials."

Joe added loudly, "And she's the only one of you making any goddamn sense!"

Theresa rose and put her hands at the edge of the table. "Excuse me. I feel that my work here is completed for now. I want to emphasize that I am here as a consultant to the Simon Foundation, not to Dr.

DeLisi, not to Ms. Carlin, not to the hospital, and not to the Los Angeles Police Department. Lieutenant," she said to Jardine, "I'd like to speak with you when you're done. I'll wait for you in the coffee shop in the lobby."

"Theresa," Joe said, reaching over and putting his hand on hers. "Thanks."

The tuna sandwich on wheat bread with a colorless tomato slice and soggy lettuce did not interest her. Theresa pushed it aside and waited for Jardine in the coffee shop, writing down her impressions from the reading of the hospital room in the notebook she'd brought with her. Finally, Jardine joined her. He slipped his suit jacket off and slid into the booth seat across from her.

"I got them calmed down. Frankly, Theresa, everybody's threatened that you came up with this linchpin, because they all blew seeing something really big. They've all got to act right now like it's somehow their idea—so let 'em. Fuck 'em. Did you have prior knowledge Ellen had a SIDS baby? Did she tell you about that?"

Theresa remembered one of the early images she'd gotten while reading for Ellen, the baby skeleton dried to ash. "I didn't know about it," she said, "not exactly. But some of the images I got make more sense now."

Jardine filled her in on his findings with Sondra Jackson, and on Mrs. DeLisi's assessment of Ellen. "And I also had a very interesting interview with Ellen's former fiancé, Whitney Park."

"Wait a minute." Theresa cried. "What did you say his name was?"

Jardine repeated the name, and Theresa leaned her face into her hands. "Oliver, the last time I read for Ellen, I got that name, 'Whitney Park.' I told Ellen it was probably a park or a playground where the abductor had stopped with Tory. It was right after that that she fired me."

Jardine stared at her, tapping his fork against the plate. "Look, Theresa, from now on I want a complete written report of everything you get pertaining to either of these cases, as well as copies of any tapes you record of readings. You're getting significant details, and you don't even know what they are!"

She motioned for him to lower his voice. She wondered what else she might have gotten that she hadn't paid attention to, and vowed to go over all her notes when she got home.

"Is it starting to come together?" she asked.

"Yes, but we still don't know where the kid is, or who killed Oslin. I feel stopped somewhere. Up against a wall."

"What's the wall?" Theresa asked.

"How Oslin knew Tory. He must have. He had her school photo. She had his snow domes."

He paused, staring at the tuna sandwich.

"Go ahead," she said. "I lost my appetite."

"If Oslin knew Ellen, he could have been on to this syndrome thing. Maybe she knew he was going to report her. Maybe she wanted him quiet."

Jardine gulped down the sandwich, glanced at his watch.

"Rukheyser wants to go over to talk to Ellen at her home. He called and she's there now. I want to go over there, too, but I'm waiting on a search warrant. I want to get those other domes you remember seeing in Tory's bedroom and see what else might turn up in the kid's toys. I'm also waiting on some lab findings I put a rush on."

He opened a file folder and slid a photocopy of a drawing across the booth. "Meanwhile, Oslin's girlfriend met with our sketch artist downtown this morning and they came up with this. I gave copies to Rukheyser and he's going to have all hospital personnel take a look at it and see if anyone recognizes a person that looks like this."

The resemblance to the man in her readings and in the drawing that she'd gotten this afternoon was uncanny. She'd grown accustomed to Tory's drawings; this one was professional, adult. Theresa examined the eyes for a few minutes. Suddenly she reached across the booth and grabbed Jardine's wrist. "I can't believe I almost forgot to tell you this. There's been so much going on. Another thing I got when I read from that stuff in the bag was the word 'Seaside,' on a matchbook. I told Joe to check with the Long Beach police to see if they found a matchbook like that when they searched the area."

"There could be a thousand places in California with the name 'Seaside,'" Jardine said. "But damn, it does ring a bell." As he finished the last of the tuna sandwich, his pager beeped. He took it off his belt and looked at the message scrolling on the tiny screen. "Lab calling. I'll be right back."

He excused himself, and Theresa watched out the window as people streamed through the hospital lobby. When Joe DeLisi went by, head down and in a hurry, she started to get up to go after him, but thought better of it. He had enough on his mind.

After a few minutes, Jardine returned hurriedly to the table. "Listen to this, Theresa. The lab matched Tory's hair from her brush to a strand found on one of Oslin's pillows. There were also fibers found in Oslin's bathroom that match fibers on the doll you found, some kind of synthetic carpet fibers. This evidence clearly places Tory at Oslin's home at some point. That warrant should come through fast now."

"Will they arrest Ellen?"

"They've got to make sure they've got probable cause. It may take a couple of days to get all Tory's records together. Maybe they'll hold her, I don't know."

Theresa paid for the tuna sandwich, even though Jardine had eaten it. "My treat," she said. "I bet it beat the asparagus pizza."

As they were leaving the hospital, Jardine's pager beeped again. "It's Jackson calling about some financial stuff," he said. "Can you wait a minute while I check in with her?"

Theresa sat on the edge of a cement planter at the center of the plaza. Some pigeons flapped near a small fountain. The afternoon sunshine warmed her and she was glad the dampness had blown away, but she felt edgy and tired. The readings had taken a lot out of her; she could use a nap. And there was more coming. She could feel it in the background, as if she knew she'd had a dream last night but couldn't quite remember what it was. *Don't push for it,* she thought. *Let it come on its own.*

Jardine returned, striding toward her across the plaza, smoothing back his wiry hair. He was out of breath as he spoke.

"Sondra is at Oslin's home, she's there looking through financial records. She's at the kitchen phone, so I ask her to check the bulletin board behind the back door, tell me what she sees. A schedule for his health club and a skydiving meeting, and postcards, all kinds of them, from Miami, London, Carmel. And get this: one of the postcards is from the Seaside Villa, a motel in Long Beach. I remembered seeing it there. I ask her to read the card to me. It says, 'Thanks for everything. I found the perfect house.' And it's signed 'Doc.' Sondra looked up the address in Long Beach and I'm going down there now. Why don't you come with me?"

"I thought you didn't want me along on your investigations."

He looked away, then back at her.

"Okay, so I'm a hothead. I didn't mean it. I was being a territorial asshole."

You were jealous, she thought.

"I don't know," she said. "I'm pretty worn out."

"Come on, Theresa. You're the one who got the name 'Seaside.' And if you hadn't gotten the name 'Doc,' the postcard wouldn't have meant anything to us anyway. Follow it up with me." When she hesitated, he added, "For Tory."

Inside Theresa's ears was the sound, not of ringing, but of breathing or wind, like the inside of a seashell.

Rukheyser hurried over to them, cutting diagonally across the plaza, his black briefcase swinging at his side. "Evidently Ellen Carlin has split," he snapped. "I called over to her house so we could get her in to talk with the doctors. The cleaning lady reported that Carlin left an hour ago with a suitcase. An airport cab picked her up. Ellen prepaid the cleaning lady and told her to lock the house when she left. She didn't say where she was going."

"Which cab company? They'll know what airline she went to," said Jardine.

"We're checking that now, and we're putting an all-points bulletin out for her. But I don't want her picked up. We don't have enough to book her at this point, and if we can spot her, I want to place her under surveillance. I want her followed. The odds are that she'll take us straight to her daughter."

"THERESA?" JARDINE ASKED, but she had fallen asleep, head leaning against the window. The sun on her black hair made it look glossy and red. He turned off the radio, reviewing what Jackson had told him on the phone about Oslin's will. After paying taxes, debts to the estate, and a few bequests to individuals, employees, and charities, the residue of the will was to be divided between Jane Wood, Mary Oslin, Mary's daughter, Hannah, and Oslin's mother. Jane was to get fifty percent, with the other three dividing the remaining fifty percent. Jackson was still looking into the insurance policies.

After driving south through downtown Long Beach, Jardine slowed to read the names of the motels along the beach on either side of the highway.

The Seaside Villa was a somewhat run-down motel with house-keeping units, just south of Long Beach. It stood back from the highway behind a row of ancient palms. Washed-out leaves sprouted at the top of the palms whose trunks were bearded with dried brown leaves. As Jardine pulled up in front of the pink stucco office, Theresa woke up and followed him into the office. A bell jangled as they opened the door, and a fat dachshund sat up on a chair.

A pointy-faced man in his fifties came out from a back room behind the office counter. The evening news droned from a television out of sight. "What can I do for you folks?" His voice was loud and jolly. His dog barked. He looks just like his dog, Jardine thought.

Jardine opened the wallet displaying his shield and, at the same time, pulled out Tory's photo. "We're looking for this girl. Her name is Tory DeLisi. She's thought to be traveling with a man called Doc. This might have been in the past week, but he also may have stayed here prior to that, registered back in mid-June. He sent a postcard from here to a man named Gerald Oslin, postmarked June thirteenth."

Jardine placed Theresa's sketch of Doc on the counter in front of the man. "A possible description of the man—short, muscular, bulky, receding hairline, but longish in the back, maybe a ponytail. He could have a pierced ear, with a tiny moon earring. Driving a black car, a Pinto, or a truck, possibly with a camper."

"Let me get my glasses," said the jolly man. "Donna? It's the police, looking for some man and a little girl."

Donna came from around the corner, wearing tight jeans with rosebuds down the side, and a pink T-shirt. She seemed to match the outside of the motel. She was bony, and had a dry, creased face. Her hair was tucked up under a red kerchief. She lit a long Benson & Hedges and was consumed in a puff of smoke. She sniffed, then inhaled again. Jardine repeated the description.

"Well, what about 10B, around back? But the girl in 10B looks to me younger'n ten. And her hair isn't this dark. She's got the prettiest red hair you ever seen. They been here almost a week now." She flipped through the registration cards in a file card box. "Registered under Simmons. Craig Simmons, plus child, it says here. Texas license plate."

Jardine jotted the name and license number down. "Are they here now?"

Donna shrugged. "We can go out back and see. He asked for a back unit because it's quieter. We got the highway out front here, with them trucks going by all night. And we put up that little playground back there too, so it was perfect. I think he mentioned he was looking for work in the area and the wife was coming up later with the boy."

Donna grabbed a ring of keys from behind the desk. "Lee, watch the office, will ya, hon?"

Lee was flipping through the cards. "Simmons. He ain't bulky. He's kind of scrawny. And his name ain't Doc."

"Still . . . " Donna emphasized, "it might be him under an assumable name."

"You mean an assumable mortgage," said Lee.

"Well, I wouldn't know nothing about the man's mortgage payments, Lee."

Donna led them down a cracked sidewalk, along a scraggly petunia bed. She rapped three times on 10B, then unlocked the door, and pushed it open.

The room was disheveled, clothes strewn around and wet towels draped over the back of a chair.

"Not here, I guess," said Donna. "You know, it's near supper time. They might be down at Burger King, about half a mile south. The little girl liked that playground too. They have one with a slide that looks like a hamburger."

"Do you recall the child's name?"

Donna frowned. "Sis? Sissy? I once heard him call her 'li'l sister.' 'Come on, li'l sister, time to get out of that pool, now, hear?'"

"Maybe he dyed her hair red," said Theresa.

They returned to the car, turned left and drove the short distance to the Burger King. Jardine went in and ordered a Coke, scanning the faces of the families seated at the tables.

"I'm going to check out the play area," Theresa said.

Jardine followed her in a few minutes.

There she was, Little Sister, with short-cropped strawberry blond hair, skinny knees under baggy cutoffs, wearing a Ninja Turtles T-shirt. Tennis shoes and no socks.

"It's not her." Theresa shook her head. "She's too young."

After a few minutes they drove back to the Seaside Villa. Lee emerged from the back room again at the sound of the bell, and the dachshund barked on cue.

"Lee," Jardine said, "I'd like to look through the registration cards for the month of June and the first week of July."

"That'd be just fine, Lieutenant, but I went through 'em already and I didn't spot no doctors."

"Thanks for looking. It might just be a nickname."

Theresa sat down on the chair where the dachshund had been. Jardine watched her close her eyes and become still, as if she were napping again. He knew she wasn't.

He thumbed slowly through the cards—looking not only for doctors, but for any names with the sound of "Doc" in them. Dockniak, Dochert, Dockman. There were none. He noted the names of any men registered alone. There had been seventeen men registered in single units in June and July. Probably truckers and salesmen. He wouldn't have had to be alone, he thought. But Theresa hadn't picked up on a woman.

Jardine snapped the lid of the box down as Donna poked her head out from the back room. She wore yellow cleaning gloves and still smoked a freshly lit cigarette. "Were they eating out at Burger King?"

"Yes, but it wasn't the right people. Just like you said, the girl was too young."

"And you didn't find anything you were looking for in that box?"

"I wrote down a few names. I'd like to get a photocopy of all the guests back to June first."

"Lee, did you have a look in the weeklies? That's the housekeeping units, the ones with the little kitchenettes. Right there in the blue recipe box."

Lee shoved the box toward him and Jardine once again flipped back to the beginning of June, examining each card, then going back through May, until he came to one that stopped him. The name on the registration card was Whitney Park. The address given was a post-office box in Portland, Oregon. The car was a 1982 Pinto, California license plate number MPX 337. Jardine stepped toward Theresa and she sat up and read it.

"What about this one, Lee?" asked Jardine. "Can you recall anything about him?"

Lee focused on the card. "Mr. Park," he said, handing the card to Donna.

"Whitney Park is a doctor in Westwood," said Jardine.

Donna peered at the card, drew deeply on the cigarette, and hacked out a cough.

"Yes sir, 3A in the housekeeping units," said Donna. "Come to think of it, he did look something like that child's drawing you showed us. Kind of big, football-player type of fellow, midthirties, I'd say. Quiet. Very neat, if I remember. Now that you mention it, he did have an earring. Yup. Don't think it was a moon, just a gold hoop. He did not have a child with him, though. Loner type.

"Only thing odd I remember about him—when I'd clean his room, he had white shoes. He had two pairs of white shoes. Not sneakers, mind you. But that would make sense if he was a doctor. He didn't seem like a doctor, much. He stayed here this spring, yes, sir," she said, flipping back through the cards. "First checked in May ninth. Checked out about two weeks ago. Hardly saw him. I think he was working nights."

When Jardine turned to speak to Theresa, she was gone. She was not in the car. He glimpsed her as she disappeared around the corner, heading back to the housekeeping units. He thanked Lee and Donna and went after her.

When he came around the side of the motel, Theresa was sitting on the playground merry-go-round, a flat disk, turning it slowly with one foot. It made a squeaking sound, like a pump handle. Trucks rumbled by on the highway, and the slow creak moaned in the air. He remembered times as a kid when he'd go down to the school playground and if there was no one there, late afternoon, dinnertime, all the other kids home eating, he'd get on the swings and pump up as high as he could go and get in the rhythm of it. Swings were mostly for girls, so he never went on them if there were other kids around. When he'd get off, the world felt clean and odd, as if he were aware of solid ground for the first time and was a stranger to it.

Theresa spun slowly on the wooden merry-go-round with the red paint chipped off the metal railings. Jardine watched her from a bench in the shade by the ice machine. He knew enough to just leave her alone.

THERESA STOPPED THE SPINNING by dragging her foot in the sand. She faced the sun. Her sense of the girl was strong here, and though she felt Tory had never been at the motel, she might yet come.

Images rose and fell inside her, seemingly disconnected, but she could feel them forming back there, gathering up into a voice.

Blank screen.

Go. She dropped down deep into the scene, as if she were right there behind Tory's eyes.

Sitting on the steps of the trailer.

Look at it, Theresa instructed.

Silver, cute as a little airplane. I love trailers. I always wanted to live in one and be a gypsy queen. It's much more fun than a house.

Airstream trailer, thought Theresa, *not airplane.*

He's inside, eating macaroni and cheese. That lopsided saucepan he cooks in.

Can't wander off. He says it's not safe, someone will see me.

Across the way, picnic tables, dark shade pines.

"What about the *Queen Mary*?" Doc calls out from inside the trailer.

Look at him, Tory. Notice his face.

She gets up, climbs the two steps into the trailer.

Looks like the Hulk, but not as funny.

Growing a beard now. Fuzzy red.

Took his earring off. Got his hair cut.

Mine's all tangled and dirty.

"Your nose is kind of round and you have squishy, hairy eyebrows and big teeth," Tory says aloud.

"The better to eat you with, my dear."

"You're wearing a T-shirt that says 'Coor-vo Gold.' What does that mean?"

"Cuervo Gold," he says. "It's tequila from Mexico."

He puts down the fork. I think he's mad.

"Why are you saying those things? Don't look at me, Tory. Don't look at me like that."

"It's her fault," she whispers.

"Whose?"

"She told me to tell what you looked like."

He jumps up, slams outside, yelling, "Who? Who told you that?"

"Just my friend."

She runs out after him, picks her doll up from the bench by the table. Got it just this morning at Kmart. Trailers are so cool. The seats lift up and you can hide in there, if you're playing hide-and-go-seek and making yourself very, very, very tiny, like a little bug. A doll-bug.

My dad calls me doll-bug.

"Doc, why can't I call my dad?" she asks. "He's going to be really mad. When my mom doesn't let me call him and he finds out, he yells at her on the phone."

Doc sits on the step of the trailer with a can of beer.

Tory, go out to the car and look at the license plate, tell me the number. Not out loud. It's a secret, Just think it, doll-bug. Think it quiet and hard.

"How come?" Tory asks.

Doc says, "I suppose he was just mad at your mom. He usually was, huh?"

"Yeah," she says. "They hate each other."

"I know how that feels. My old man used to lock my mother out of the house when they fought. Push her right out the back door wearing nothing but her nightgown and scuffs. But she was tough. Know what she did?"

"What?"

"She took the rake and started smashing all the windows out of his truck."

"They sound mean."

"They were."

She walks slowly toward the car.

"Hey!" he calls. "Where are you going?"

"I dropped something. My barrettes. Doc, why can't I call my dad? Just to let him know I'm okay."

"Your mom can tell him for you. She's the one paying me to baby-sit you until she's all set. She's probably going to take you down to Mexico, to get all better."

"But I feel better now."

"That's because I'm taking such good care of you, aren't I?"

"Not really."

"Why not?"

"You shouldn't keep me locked up in there."

"But you know why. I told you why."

"So no one'll see me and put me back in the hospital and stick needles in me and make me sick and maybe even kill me. Doc?"

"What, sweetheart?"

"Did your mom ever hurt you?"

"Sure. Lots of times."

"Why?"

"So I'd be good, I guess. And because she was nuts, drunk, mad, felt like her life was a waste. Anyway, she wasn't my real mom."

"Who was?"

"I was adopted."

"So you have two moms."

"You got it. Aren't you happier being with me, hon? Away from that mean old mom of yours?"

Standing at the front of the car now.

MLP, she thought, hard. *M. L. P.*

Suddenly, Doc stands up. "Let's hit the road, sweetheart. We're going to take a little trip. Maybe we'll win a million dollars."

"How are we going to do that, hit the jackpot?"

"You never know. Sometimes in life, you just get lucky. Now get back in the trailer, lickety-split. I think you're going to want a little pill for that motion sickness."

"No. I don't."

"Come on, here it is, wash it down with this water."

"It makes me sleepy."

"That's good. When you wake up, we'll be there."

"Only if you promise I can call my dad."

"I'll think about it. I'll have to check it out with your mom."

"I wish you didn't have to check with her."

"That's a good girl. Now why don't you lie down? I'm going to put stuff away and then we'll hit the road."

M. L. P. She focuses the letters into a beam of light and sends them out like a ray.

What about the numbers? Theresa asked. *And what state is it?*

California. M . . . L . . . P . . .

Doc comes up close to her, sits on the edge of the bed in the back room of the trailer. "You like Uncle Doc, don't you, sweetheart?"

"Sure," she says. "But I don't like being in here all the time."

"Mom's orders. You know I have to report to her everything you say."

"But you can't hear what I'm thinking."

"No, that's true, I can't. What are you thinking, Tory?"

Smiles. Shakes her head.

"Tory, are you keeping a secret from Doc?"

Turns over, closes her eyes.

He rubs her back. She clutches the doll to her chest.

"What's the little secret, sweetheart? You can tell me."

She smiles, thinking the letters and the numbers over and over. Chanting in the quiet place where no one can touch her, *California MLP 573. California MLP 573.*

Perfect, thought Theresa. *Now don't tell anyone you told.*

Theresa blinked.

The empty playground surrounded by weeds. Oliver on a bench in the shade. Sun going orange-pink over the palm trees.

30

As Theresa came up out of the trance state, everything seemed magnified and radiant—the shadows of the high grass on the dirt, a rusty lawn mower left at the edge of the parking lot. She'd gone in deep. Across the way, Jardine stood and started toward her. *Too soon,* she thought, and raised her hand. *Wait.* Something more was coming.

It was almost the sound of a wail, a cry of anguish deep in the psyche, like a molten core miles down in the earth. Not the sound of a scream, but the desire. Not an actual scream, but a life lived as the expression of a silent scream.

Mo-ther . . . Mo-ther . . .

Theresa stared toward the horizon, remembering that yellow-black absence at the center of Ellen's heart. That was this sound, this no-sound.

It was sunset, Wednesday. On Monday she'd heard "three days," but what did that mean? Monday, Tuesday, Wednesday? Or Tuesday, Wednesday, Thursday? *What difference does it make now?* she thought. *Now that Ellen has fled.*

Theresa closed her eyes again and imagined Ellen from memory—that first reading when she'd reached toward Ellen's heart, her light toward Ellen's absence of light.

A sharp pain stabbed through Theresa and she doubled over, her arms and wrists throbbing with slashes of heat, slow lines of pain down her fingers and across her cheeks, the held-back scream aching inside her.

"Let it out!" Theresa cried.

"Theresa! Are you all right?" She was aware of Jardine standing over her.

Pull back, she commanded herself. *Witness. Ground.*

She wanted to exit the dream, but felt torn. Ellen was breaking open, something was pushing out of that frozen hole. She wanted to stay, but she was afraid to be too close.

Theresa gripped Jardine's hand as the woman's cry escaped from her clogged throat. She shot up over the motel swing set, looking down from a distance, saw Ellen curled into a fetal position, weeping. An older woman bent over her, stroking her back, as Jardine was stroking hers now, gently.

Theresa felt herself snap back—admonishing herself for moving too quickly in and out of body. *Be patient,* she told herself. *Dangerous. Ground yourself.*

She opened her eyes. Jardine was perched beside her on the merry-go-round.

"What is it?" he asked. "What did you see?"

"Where does Ellen's mother live?"

"Not far from here. Huntington Beach. Her name is Ginny Carlin. DeLisi's mother gave me her name and address."

"I think that's where Ellen is. With her own mother."

"Anything else? You were out there a long time."

"Was I?"

Jardine glanced at his watch, then up at the sky, darkening to blue, stars dotting the darkness above the scraggly palms.

As they walked back to the motel office, Theresa told him about the images she'd gotten, trying to recall them precisely. "Remember when I got silver before, and I thought it was a plane? Wrong. It's an Airstream trailer. I got a license number: MLP 573, California plate. And I got more of a picture of him: 'Hulk, fuzzy red beard, no earring, he took it off, hair cut short, T-shirt that says Cuervo Gold. Another thing I picked up on was 'Queen Mary.' That's the second time I've gotten that. It led us to that landing site in Long Beach last night, but maybe the *Queen Mary,* the ship itself, should be searched. Or alert security there to the description of Tory and Doc."

Back in the motel office, Jardine made several calls, asking for a check on the license numbers, the one Theresa had gotten as well as the Pinto on the registration card for Whitney Park.

Theresa sat in Jardine's car, out in front of the office. She was drained. It was very strange to read like this. She couldn't tell whether she was really tuning in on an entire moment occurring between Tory and Doc, or whether she was just imagining the scene as a vehicle for picking up the information about the trailer, the license.

She sat breathing quietly, centering, bringing herself slowly back to this moment. Shadows on pink stucco, flies by the light of a soda-pop machine, Donna opening the door for Lieutenant Jardine as he came out of the office.

"Let's go," he said, starting the car. "You okay?"

"I'm fine," she said. She was silent for a moment. "I went in awfully deep. Sometimes it's hard to stay separate. I merge."

Jardine touched her shoulder, gave her a gentle pat on the back. "I know. I was watching."

"I think what's going on, aside from trying to do what I can to help find her, is that . . . " Theresa looked overhead, above one particularly scrawny palm tree, at a star, one brighter than the rest, perhaps Venus or Jupiter. She didn't know. "It's just that I feel so sad for Tory. While I was reading her, the emotional tone—how she is around Doc, that's how she is around her mom. Very dependent, believing he is protecting her. Simultaneously, she knows he is being mean to her, lying to her, he's locking her up, not letting her call her parents. He's probably sedating her off and on. It's horrible, Oliver. Because on the surface she's cheery and bright, she's surviving by not knowing. It's as if she can't afford to be conscious of her perceptions. If she were really aware of what was happening to her, she'd be too afraid. She's used to locking her fear away where she can't feel it at all."

They drove in silence toward Huntington Beach. After a while Theresa asked, "Shouldn't Rukheyser be doing this?"

Jardine kept driving. "I called him from the Seaside. He's meeting us down there. I just want to be there first."

Ginny Carlin was a seventy-year-old version of Ellen. Still very attractive, she wore her silver hair cut in a chin-length bob with bangs. Large, peach-colored glasses balanced on her delicate nose. Her eyes were puffy underneath, and her lipstick had faded over the edges of her thin lips. Though it was evening, she wore what appeared to be a golf outfit, white culottes above her thick knees, and a lime green shirt that made her skin look yellow.

She answered the doorbell, opening the inside door to the condo. "Yes?" she asked, reaching down to lock the screen door. She tried to do it inconspicuously, but it made a loud click. She smiled.

Jardine showed his badge to her.

"Mrs. Carlin, we're here to talk to Ellen. We have reason to believe she's staying here with you."

Ginny Carlin looked uncomfortable for a moment, then clicked the lock back and held the door open.

"This is Theresa Fortunato. She's with the Simon Foundation for Missing Children," said Jardine.

Mrs. Carlin clasped Theresa's hand. "How do you do?" she said. "I told her it's no use her trying to hide out down here." She shrugged and preceded them into a small, cluttered living room. Needlepoint pillows were stacked on a floral print couch. Dinner dishes had been left on the coffee table next to a pile of newspapers. "Ellen's not doing very well. Got here about six o'clock. Said people were coming after her, that she was in mortal danger, and that whoever took Tory was coming for her, too, and they'd already killed one man and burned up his store and that the psychic told her she was as good as dead."

Theresa cringed.

"I didn't know what she was talking about," Ginny Carlin continued. "Ranting and raving about someone following her so she couldn't drive her own car. She took a cab out to the airport and then rented a car. She claimed Joe was behind the whole thing. I gave her a sleeping pill, but she's up now. She's calmer, but . . . the stress is just too much for her. I'm going to take her to the doctor in the morning. Well, you'll see for yourself. I've had to have her hospitalized before. It's been like this ever since she was in her twenties. She'll be fine for a while, and then off she goes. It's the stress, it triggers the biochemistry. You just can't get into believing she'll be totally okay. That'll kill you. Every time I think she's going to be fine, my heart is broken to smithereens. You blame yourself, thinking you were a terrible mother—but what did I do wrong? I stayed home with her—my generation, that's what you did . . . "

"Mrs. Carlin," Jardine cut in, "where is Ellen?"

"Follow me," she said. She led them down a hall and opened a door to the left. Ellen sat in an easy chair beside an unmade bed, watching TV. She glanced up at them and blinked as if the hall light were too much for her.

"Ellen, this is Lieutenant Jardine from the police department. He wants to talk to you."

"What happened to Sergeant Rukheyser?"

"He's on his way, Ms. Carlin."

Ellen looked past Jardine to Theresa. When she spoke, her voice was flat, no affect. "You," she said to Theresa. "I thought I told you to stay the hell away from me."

Jardine sat down at the edge of the bed, pushing the pillows out of the way. Theresa turned to go back to the living room, but Jardine beckoned her to come in.

"Theresa is working with us, with the police, to find Tory, Ellen. It's time you cooperated fully with all aspects of the investigation. It won't do any good to run away."

Her eyes flicked back and forth between Theresa and Jardine. "I just don't want anybody in my thoughts, you understand? What I think is private." She addressed Lieutenant Jardine. "I don't mean to be rude, but she makes me nervous."

"Why is that, Ellen?"

"The way she climbs inside you, it makes you feel naked. And then, driving down, I hear my name on the news. I feel like everyone will be looking at me, looking right through me."

"What did you hear on the news?" he asked.

"Just everything coming out in public, all about Tory, me, Joe, our family. As if we haven't been through enough. What are people going to think, a mother who leaves her child alone at a hospital overnight and then she disappears. What kind of mother is that, anyway? I should never have left her—okay, I admit it—but could I ever get a decent night's sleep, sitting in that chair by her bed all night? No, sir. So it's my fault, right? Isn't that what everyone thinks? Isn't that what you think?"

Theresa caught Jardine's eye. She didn't think Tory's abduction or anything about Ellen or Joe had been picked up by the media yet. Rukheyser had said he wanted to keep the Munchausen thing quiet, until they located Ellen.

Ellen snapped off the TV. She bent over and put her hands over her face.

Ginny Carlin came over to Ellen and stroked her daughter's back, exactly the way Theresa had seen her do in the reading. Ellen leaned against her mother's thighs.

"Lieutenant, I don't think it's any use questioning Ellen any more at this point, do you? I think it really upset her to hear it on the news."

"Mrs. Carlin," said Jardine, "I don't believe the media have covered Tory's disappearance. They're often reluctant to report kidnappings that appear to involve parental-custody issues."

"Well, she must have heard something." Ginny Carlin pulled Ellen even closer to her as if she were a child and not a woman in her late thirties. "Just look at her."

"Just a few questions. Ellen, the snow shakies, those domes in Tory's bedroom. Where did Tory get them?"

Ellen wiped her eyes with the sleeve of her robe. "Those little snow things? She started collecting them. Someone in the hospital gave them to her. A nurse, I think. Why?"

"Do you remember the nurse's name?"

"Name? They're all a blur. All the nurses, doctors, anesthesiologists, lab technicians . . . they all run together."

"You were questioned about this before, Ellen, but I need to ask you again. How did you know Gerald Oslin?"

"I already told Sergeant Rukheyser I never heard of the man before this week. And I have no idea how he got her picture."

"Did you ever buy or collect antiques or folk-art toys?"

She shook her head. "I have some furniture that might be called antique, but they're things I've refinished myself, not anything terribly expensive. I got them at estate sales and secondhand stores."

"What about a genealogy—did you ever hire anyone to do ancestral research on your family?"

Again she shook her head.

Ellen leaned back in the chair. Her eyes were very wide and she seemed suddenly childlike. She's mercurial, thought Theresa, the way she shifts from anger to flatness to this bewildered child.

"Sometimes I just wish Tory had been adopted. Then I'd know her illnesses weren't all my fault. I begged the nurses to do a C-section, but they wouldn't. I must have pushed for ten hours. They had to pull her out with forceps. I think they damaged her at birth. There was always something wrong with her. And it's even worse finding out that there might not be an actual physical basis for her illness, whatever it is."

"Why is that worse?" asked Jardine.

"Well, that it could all be psychosomatic. That's what they were getting to last week, right before she disappeared. That's what they were definitely hinting at, bringing in Dr. Silver, that psychiatrist. I never, never wanted any of that for Tory, after what I've been through."

"And what's that?"

"I'm sure it will all come out now. My depressions, my breakdowns. Hospitalizations, shock treatments. Medication, the whole shot. I thought all that was behind me now. Joe brought it all out in the open during the custody case, to make me look unstable so I'd lose her. So the doctors started saying maybe Tory's sickness was mental, like mine. That I probably passed it on to her. All my fault . . . "

"Now, dear, it's not your fault," said her mother. "Sometimes these things are genetic." Ginny Carlin looked up at Theresa, then Jardine. "Her grandmother had a nervous breakdown, my husband's mother. The medical literature says that there can be a genetic propensity toward depression. I'm sure they just wanted a full workup on Tory. Lieutenant Jardine, could we stop this now? You can see for yourself that Ellen's in no position to answer these kind of questions."

Ginny Carlin continued stroking Ellen's back.

"I nearly lost her so many times," said Ellen softly, "but she always came back to me. She forgave me."

"Forgave you for what?" Jardine asked.

Ellen looked up at him. "She gave me so much in the short time she was with me."

"Are you talking about Tory or your first daughter, the one who died in infancy?"

Mrs. Carlin straightened. "Lieutenant, I am simply going to have to insist . . . "

"Mom, stop it." Ellen stood, pushing her mother away. She crossed to the bedroom window, peering out at the intense green of the shrubbery lit by garden lights. It had grown so dark. "Both of them, Lieutenant. Both my little girls."

"What was the baby's name, Ellen?"

"Vickie. Victoria. Both of them were named Victoria. Victoria Ann and Victoria Margaret. I'm not really a very good mother. My children keep dying."

"Is Tory dead?" asked Jardine.

"My little one . . . "

"What about Tory—Victoria Margaret. Is she dead?"

Ginny Carlin had slumped on the bed next to Jardine and sighed. "I can't say I blame Joe for trying to take Tory away from her. Can you?" Mrs. Carlin asked. "But I just wish he wouldn't hide her permanently, is all. Because Ellen does have periods of lucidity, brilliance, and emotional balance. Don't you, darling?"

"I'll bet you anything that Tory went to stay with Whitney." Ellen turned back and faced Theresa. "That's what you think, isn't it? Whitney Park?"

The doorbell rang, and Mrs. Carlin excused herself. Theresa could hear Rukheyser enter, low voices in the foyer.

"Oh, how she loved Whit," Ellen continued. "And he loved her. We all loved her as much as we could. And she loved us, I know she did. Tory loved me. I tried to take care of her. She was such a difficult child. She required so much of me. Everything of me. I couldn't leave her alone for a second, not since the moment she was born. That's when I knew something was wrong, her head all funny-shaped like that. When I first saw her, I didn't even think she was mine. Anyway, they're not really ours, are they? They belong to the universe."

Ellen's hands were shaking, her breathing shallow and fast. She pointed at Theresa. "She's the one who told me about the danger. 'Three days,' she said. And I don't know what I'm supposed to do. I can't stop my mind from thinking about it. All I can do is think and think and think about Tory and it's so loud in my head. What could I have done differently, what did I do wrong?" Ellen was holding on to the sides of her head, rocking back and forth, when Rukheyser entered the room.

Jardine stood and joined him and they conferred briefly. Rukheyser asked Theresa to leave the room, and she walked out into the yard. It was a relief to stand out in the warm evening air, to be out of the thickness of the house. Theresa felt almost physically ill in Ellen's presence. After a few minutes, Jardine came out to her.

"She's going to the hospital voluntarily. Rukheyser still doesn't have enough actual evidence to arrest her for child abuse or kidnapping."

Ellen appeared at the front door with her mother. She had changed into slacks and a sweater, and her hair had been combed. Though it was dark, she'd put on sunglasses, as if she were a celebrity facing the paparazzi on the steps of a courthouse.

She stopped as she passed Theresa, and reached out to touch her arm. Theresa could feel her trembling. She could barely see Ellen's eyes through the black lenses.

"Do you know everything, Theresa?" Ellen asked.

"You know more than I do, Ellen."

"I need to know what I did."

Ginny Carlin was insistent. "Sergeant, I just feel that I am going to have to call an attorney before we go one step further."

"This is not an arrest, Mrs. Carlin," said Rukheyser.

"Shut up, mother!" Ellen yelled. "Stop protecting me. Don't you get it?" She held Theresa's arm tighter, her thin fingers pressing into skin as she dropped her voice. "I need to figure out what I did. I did some things. I can't remember exactly, but I need to know what I've done to her. I need to know if I've killed her. Right now I honestly don't know. It's like a big hole in me. I want to know, I really need to know."

DOC COULDN'T BELIEVE they were really here. As they walked through the gates, the sign announced, DISNEYLAND, THE HAPPIEST PLACE ON

EARTH. The closest he'd ever come to this was Sunday-night TV, Donald Duck cartoons, and a ride on a Tilt-a-Whirl at a county fair one summer near Fresno. "When You Wish Upon a Star" was piped out on loudspeakers over the streets.

Tory was wide-eyed beside him as they strolled through the Old Town Square. Everything was smaller here, shrunk down, and Doc felt like a giant. *But it's just the right size for her,* he thought. Anyway, it was more the size that life should be. The world was filled with families here, having the time of their lives.

Wherever Doc and Tory went, happy music played. The entire place was one huge gift shop filled with snow domes of Disney characters. Tory picked out one with the Little Mermaid inside, swimming in iridescent glitter. It was a perfect world. There were even men dressed in white, moving quietly through the crowded streets, sweeping up trash as soon as it hit the pavement.

As they walked toward the castle, Tory tugged at his arm. "I didn't think the castle would be so small," she said. "It looks bigger on TV. And the roof is all faded. They should fix it up better."

As they walked under the tunnel through the castle, harp music was playing. "It's always like that," said Doc. "Like I told you. You've got to learn the difference between fantasy and reality."

"How can you tell?" she asked.

"Fantasy is in your mind, and reality is out here." Doc swept his hands around in a gesture of embrace.

"But this is real," said Tory, "and it is Fantasyland."

"Yeah," said Doc, "but you have to pay to get into this one."

"Can I go on one ride?" she asked, "since I missed out on the elephants?"

"Sure," said Doc.

The line at the carousel was long, but Tory waited contentedly. It began to rain, just a light mist, and when she finally got on a red horse and began to whirl around and around in the sparkling lights, she looked to Doc as though she had shrunk down, too. She looked like a toy girl on a toy horse in a toy world where rain fell through the lights like snow.

32

THEY DROVE NORTH, pressing through traffic, discussing all they had discovered about Tory DeLisi and Gerald Oslin. After that, Jardine was quiet for miles. He didn't even want the radio on. He drove all the way into Westwood, where Theresa had left her car in the hospital parking ramp, and dropped her at her car, on the third level. "Are you hungry?" he asked as she got out. They agreed to meet back in Venice at the Baja Cantina, just a few blocks from her house.

Theresa sat across from him at the small table, dipping chips into salsa that burned her tongue. Loud music covered their silence. Theresa looked around at the weathered and windblown patrons. Jardine was studying a dusty string of dried chili peppers. Little square lanterns and white Christmas lights illuminated the outdoor patio. The waitress set two Corona Extras on the blue-tiled table.

Theresa glanced at Jardine's watch, but couldn't read it upside down. "What time is it?"

"We're eating late. It's ten-thirty. Say, what ever happened to that actor you were seeing, anyway?" Jardine asked.

She felt herself blush.

"Wait a minute. I can't believe this—but I got it. I think I got it."

"Oh yeah? Okay, then, what happened?"

"Nah. It's just what flashed through my mind."

"Say it, Oliver." She laughed; his face was flushed.

He shrugged, drank his beer. "You didn't like, ah, sleeping with him. He—let's say he didn't—I got this image of—oh shit—I got this image of spilled milk. I mean, is that tacky?"

She laughed again. "I can't believe it, Oliver! That's good. That's exactly what it was, too. I mean, I couldn't hold it against him, he meant well, but . . . "

"But?"

"What can I say? I'm Italian, I'm very passionate. Anyway, I don't mind testosterone in a healthy dose. You know, a tattoo here, a Harley there . . . "

"Yeah, I know. I know you, Theresa. Better than you think."

She had an irresistible urge to take his hand, but ate some more chips instead. She glanced up at him as an old Marvin Gaye tune came on the jukebox, realizing how good it was that they were together at the Baja Cantina after the day's work. She always felt so easy with him. For a moment she even felt attracted to him, with his ruddy face and thick neck and dumb white button-down shirt.

"Did you know I've got a Harley?" he asked.

"You never told me that, Oliver."

"It needs some work. I haven't been on it for a while. There's a lot you don't know about me. You have ideas about me, but I'm an original."

"That's for sure. Like what else? Tell me five more things I don't know about you."

"Okay. I've got a collection of Cole Porter CDs. I make one great dish—chili. Otherwise I can't cook for shit. I play decent tennis. I once looked into getting my nose fixed."

She was nodding. "And . . . "

And I'm in love with you.

Theresa looked up at him, stunned. For a second she wasn't sure whether he'd said it. It had come through just as clearly as if he'd said it over a microphone. She said nothing. The waitress brought their food, enchiladas for her, burrito for him. She took a bite and it stung her mouth.

She took a sip of water. He was looking down, chopping his burrito up like crazy. Sure, she knew that. She'd known it for a long time. After they had started meeting regularly, having dinner, so he could work on his intuitive side. When he'd call late at night sometimes from a coffee shop on an investigation to ask her about a suspect, check out some imagery. When he'd bought her that book about roses. And last winter, when they'd gone together to that big fund-raiser for the Simon Foundation and he'd been the keynote speaker in that tux, and he'd asked if she'd go with him, and had even gotten his car washed.

She hadn't let it in and hadn't really wanted to. She didn't want to deal with him in that way, but why? Because he was sort of weird looking and a cop and he bowled and ate junk food and was the least spiritual person she knew and because he had that darkness in him that was his own fear of being there with her, which is why he'd never really asked her out but came around in this sneaky sideways kind of way, becoming her friend, so she'd start caring about him without seeing it was happening and running away herself.

"So," he said, "don't you want to know the other thing?"

"I don't know. It might be better if I didn't."

"Okay," he said, singsong. "But it's good."

She closed her eyes, motioning "come on" with her hand.

"You already guessed it. Tattoo," he said. "Left shoulder. Girl's name—Julie—on a banner with a heart. Got it in Amsterdam in 1968."

"You were in Amsterdam?"

"Yeah, with Julie, hitchhiking around Europe."

"But I think of you as so straitlaced, Oliver."

"It's just that I'm from Wisconsin. You've got an attitude about the Midwest. You're arrogant."

"I am, aren't I?" she laughed. "You're right about that."

"Yeah, real superior. A bit holy. It gets you in trouble and you could be having a lot more fun."

"I could? Oliver—is this a reading?"

He looked up. "Yeah, kind of. Hey—yeah—I'm giving you a reading. Damn!"

"Tattoo. So that's it? That was really the fifth thing?"

He chewed his burrito. "Yeah, for now. For now, that'll do."

After dinner, he walked her up the canal to her house. Osiris came out to meet them on the cracked sidewalk. "I'm going to Oslin's funeral tomorrow morning. You got clients in the morning?" he asked.

"Yeah, but I wouldn't come anyway. I've had enough funerals for one lifetime, remember?"

He nodded, rubbing his upper lip. "Sometimes I get confused," he said. "Differentiating between an intuitive flash, a hit on something, and my own obsessive thinking."

"There's a big difference. The intuitive hit is usually one phrase or an image. The obsessive wheeling is a lot of language repeating itself. The hit is almost childlike, simple. Sometimes you don't trust it, it's so clear."

His face was shadowed by the bougainvillea that dangled out over the sidewalk, and Theresa felt hot in her chest. She looked away before saying, "Good night, then, Oliver. Check in with me tomorrow."

"By the way," he said, reaching into his pocket. He handed her the snow dome from the Bahamas, the angelfish swimming in glitter. "You can have this back."

There were several messages on her answering machine, two from clients wanting appointments, one from Sarene, and one that made her very uneasy. "My name is Barbara, you don't know me, I live with Joe DeLisi in Cambridge. I'm terribly worried about Tory and I'm having a hard time getting hold of Joe to find out what's going on. Sergeant Rukheyser gave me your number. Could you please call me?"

Theresa sat at the table in the dark and dialed her number. When Barbara said hello, Theresa could tell she'd been sleeping. It was three hours later on the East Coast. She explained as much as she could to the woman, who was obviously very anxious and seemed to care a great deal for Tory. When Theresa had finished, Barbara sighed.

"This whole thing is so awful," said Barbara. "I was divorced myself when my kids were young—they're both in college now—but my ex and I raised them in a halfway civil manner. Ellen is so vindictive. She just has to try to make Joe's life unhappy every chance she can get. And Tory is her pawn, her way of getting to Joe. I really hope this custody suit is decided in Joe's favor and that Tory can come back here to live with us permanently. I don't see how a judge could rule against Joe, when Ellen is so untrustworthy and so dishonest."

Right, thought Theresa. And Joe is Dr. Integrity himself. Charm and lies, at least lies of omission. Jardine had been right about him, and she still didn't want to admit it.

THURSDAY, JULY 9

33

LIEUTENANT OLIVER JARDINE stood outside the chapel of the church in his navy blue suit. Since he'd been lifting weights, the suit felt tight around his shoulders and thighs. This was good, he thought. His face would melt down to mashed-potato lumps and his hair would fall out, but he'd have the body of a high school wrestling coach. And at least there were the endorphins. They were good for something.

Hearing the minister winding down and the people singing "Shall We Gather at the River," he followed the hallway alongside the chapel to a reception room, one wall of which was filled with oversize arrangements of gladioli and roses. Only one exotic arrangement, Oriental in design, seemed to be especially for Oslin. He went over and read the card. "In memoriam. Wes Young Associates." Two older women were seated at either end of a long table separated by plates filled with small ham sandwiches and sugar cookies. One held up a thin china cup. "Coffee?" she asked. The cup shook in its saucer. He went over to her and took it gladly. "The beautiful, the beautiful river," the mourners chorused from the chapel.

The double doors opened and people began to emerge from the chapel, eyes downcast, chatting quietly. Mary Oslin entered on the arm of her daughter. Jardine recognized the daughter from the portrait in Oslin's office, though she was older now, in her twenties. Right behind them, a tall older woman dabbed at her eyes with a handkerchief. Jardine assumed she was Gerald's adoptive mother. Next came Jane Wood in a short gray dress, black stockings, and gray suede pumps. She held a wad of Kleenex in her fist and looked stunning, though her eyes were red from crying.

*   *   *

Jardine spent the next hour hovering at the edges of conversations, listening to people discuss the deceased with reverence, admiration, and authentic grief. He overheard parachuting buddies, Oslin's travel agent, fellow antique dealers, a comic-book collector, neighbors, and even a friend who'd played football with Gerald Oslin back in high school. Without exception they agreed that Oslin's death must have been the result of a random burglary; no one could possibly have had reason to murder this lovely man. When he looked around for Jane, though, she was gone.

Jardine waited until the throng of people had thinned out before he approached Mary Oslin. She wore a black pantsuit and her feet looked squashed in tightly strapped sandals.

"Lieutenant," she said, extending her hand, "how kind of you to show up. This is quite a crowd, isn't it? A lot of people loved my brother." Mary Oslin looked composed, the shock and grief of the past few days shoved away for now. She appeared tired but perky. She's on hold, he thought. Coping, greeting friends and acquaintances, taking care of family, taking care of business, being the strong one. There was something very common, even wholesome, about Mary Oslin, like a good schoolteacher.

"I spent last night with the insurance investigators, reviewing the damage, going over records of inventory," said Mary. "They say it definitely looks like arson, someone trying to destroy records. But I can't imagine what or why. And then there's the will situation."

"What situation is that?" Jardine asked.

"It appears Gerald left a second will, dated more recently than the first, in which his wishes for his estate differ pretty greatly from his earlier thoughts."

"How so?"

"Well, of course, he and Jane never married, but he wanted her to be very comfortable. The will in the safe deposit box—Gerald had given me a key—left fifty percent to Jane and the rest to Mom, Hannah, and me. The second, more recent will does not provide for Jane at all. I think he drew the second one up during the time that he and Jane had broken off."

"Have you discussed this with your brother's attorney yet?"

"I'm meeting with him this afternoon. Here," she said, digging in her purse. "I have a copy of the second will right here. You can have it. I have others."

Jardine read it over quickly. It was one of those do-it-yourself wills that one could draw up using a special software program. It called for the residue of Oslin's estate to be divided equally among Mary, Hannah, and Mrs. Oslin. A substantial difference in the inheritance, dividing it in thirds, without Jane to consider. He wondered if Sondra knew about this. She was due to meet him at the church shortly.

"Of course, we've always loved Jane." Mary sniffed, her voice quivering. "I may be handling things badly right now, I may not be thinking quite clearly. I know Jane is very upset about this. Even if the most recent will does appear to leave very little—well, nothing—to her, it's obvious Gerald changed it when they broke up, and his feelings may have been cloudy then, too. Jane's not going to be totally left out, the family will see to that, but we also have to make sure we respect Gerald's final wishes. We'll just have to see." She attempted a thin smile.

It was possible, thought Jardine, even probable, that records pertaining to the estate could have been the target of that fire. He was anxious to learn what Sondra had found in going over Oslin's financial files from the hard drive.

Just then Gerald's mother joined them, and Mary introduced her to Jardine. She was a thin, horsy-looking woman with large teeth and white flyaway hair. Her tailored black suit looked expensive and her pearls genuine, but otherwise she appeared to be the kind of person happiest in old slacks and a hand-knit sweater, chopping wood at a cabin somewhere. Her face was sunburned and she looked robust for a woman who had to be in her eighties. Of course, she looked nothing at all like the round-faced Mary or the tall, rugged Gerald.

"I hope you don't mind my asking this," said Jardine, "but is anyone from Miss Tucker's family here?"

"Pardon me?" said Mrs. Oslin.

"Miss Betty Tucker," Mary said loudly. "Gerry's birth mother."

"Why, we wouldn't know," Gerald's mother explained. "We've never met them. At least I never have. Perhaps we could look at the guest book. They're all signing it right over there. Isn't it odd?" she thought out loud. "He could have brothers and sisters we know nothing about. Family is a strange concept. You know, I found out in all of this research of Gerald's that my grandmother was adopted. My great-grandparents were quite well off and they went to Europe and got a baby and sailed home nine months later and claimed it was their own. But they kept the documents in their safe-deposit box and my grandmother found out about it after her mother's death. Then history repeated itself and I adopted Mary and Gerald. Of course, it's all so different now, isn't it? Everything out in the open, no secrets at all. We tried to keep the semblance of things, but what was the use, really? Anyway, I can rest easier knowing I told Gerald the truth. He'd always sensed he was different, and I think it did him good to find that woman before she died and to get to know something about his roots."

Jardine reached in his pocket and pulled out the locket he had taken from Gerald's dresser. "Who is the woman in this picture?" he asked, clicking the locket open. "Is it you, Mary?"

Mary examined the locket, turning it over in her palm. "It does look a little like me, but it's not. I need my glasses to really see it. But I've never seen this locket before." She held it out at a distance to get a clearer look at it.

"It's engraved with the letter *L*." Jardine pointed to the flowery design.

"That's Linda," announced a man standing at Mary's shoulder. Jardine recognized him as the man who'd played football with Oslin in high school.

"Linda who?" asked Mary.

"The lovely Linda Lane." The man held out both arms as if he were announcing a nightclub act.

"Oh yes, I remember her," said Mrs. Oslin. "When did Gerry date her, Fred, was it junior year?"

The man smiled, thinking back. He was tall, like Oslin, with thick silver hair and bright eyes. "We used to tease him, and call her Lois and him Clark. She was even a journalism major and wanted to be a reporter. No, it wasn't in high school; he dated her in college."

"That's right," said Mrs. Oslin. "Now I remember. I never did meet her. Then Gerry went in the navy and he was real serious about her. They wrote, but she married somebody else."

"Where did you find this?" Mary asked, handing the locket back to Jardine.

"It was in his dresser drawer. I'm not sure why I picked it up. I'll return it to you," he said. "Sometimes you get curious—you're looking for connections to people, trying to get a sense of a person's past. I just wondered."

Gerald's mother spoke up. "She does look a lot like you, Mary, in that little picture."

Jardine was about to ask Gerald's mother some questions when a group of three or four people approached Mary, offering their condolences. They gathered around her in a flock.

"We never met you, Mary, but we heard so much about your family. And we just wanted to tell you how much Gerald meant to us all, how much he gave to us. He gave us our identities. Without him, there would be so much we'd never know about ourselves. What he did for us was truly a lifetime gift." A plain woman with long, frizzy hair seemed to be the spokesperson of the group.

Jardine intervened. "Excuse me, Mary. Would you mind introducing me?"

As she introduced him to the group and explained that he was the detective investigating Gerald's murder, Mary seemed to choke up a little, and Jardine wondered if his continued presence here was inappropriate. He also knew he needed to be here among Oslin's family and friends, getting a better picture of him.

"Did Mr. Oslin do genealogy work for you?" Jardine asked.

"Yes, all of us. We were all in a birth-mother support group. We're all adopted, and once we'd located our mothers, Gerald did genealogies for us so we also knew something about our real ancestry."

Jardine asked them if they had recognized anyone at the service or reception as belonging to Gerald's birth family. Among themselves, they agreed that they had never met one another's birth families.

"Were there any men in your group, doctors in particular, late thirties, forty? Stocky, balding, dark hair? Possibly a ponytail or pierced ear?"

They turned their mouths down and shook their heads. One said, "Gerry had a lot of clients for his genealogical work. He was good."

Jardine passed out his business cards to them and asked them to call him if anything came to mind regarding Gerald's birth family, anything that might be useful in the investigation.

"Is someone in his birth family considered a suspect?" one woman asked.

"We have no suspects at this time," he said. Then he remembered Tory's school picture. He took it out of his wallet and passed it around, asking them if they recognized the picture or knew how Gerald might have known her.

Mrs. Oslin held the girl's picture quite a long time, concentrating on it. "You know, she kind of favors you, too, Mary. Looks a lot like you did when you lost your front teeth."

Jardine took the picture back and studied Tory's picture again, the straight dark hair and wide-spaced eyes. Across the room, Mary's daughter held her toddler. She had the same hair, sleek and dark, although the baby's hair was short, springing up from her head as if she'd slept on it funny during a nap. But all three of them, Mary and her daughter and granddaughter, were big-boned, even the baby with her thick wrists and ball-cheeked face. Tory, in her pictures, was thin-boned and delicate.

Jardine had passed the food table and filled a small plate with sandwiches and cookies when he spotted Sondra Jackson entering the room. With a quick motion of her head, she gestured to him, and he followed her outside the church, where heat already radiated off the cement, the day gauzed in a yellow haze.

"I found something interesting going over the books," she said. "There's a discrepancy of approximately twenty-five thousand dollars. That's twenty-five G's missing. Bank records show a check made out to cash on the first of June for twenty grand. His June statement hasn't come out yet, so we'll get the check and see if we can get any prints. The ATM card for his Cash Management Fund was used July fifth at a number of different locations around the city, seven withdrawals totaling several thousand dollars. I'm checking to see if there were any sizable credit-card purchases or cash advances in the last week." She stopped, looking down at her notes.

"July fifth," said Jardine. "That was the day he was killed. Sunday."

"Correct. And the ATM card for that account seems to be missing. He had all his charge cards in his wallet, but he may have had duplicates. And sometimes people forget to sign the second card. We're in luck, though. One of the ATM withdrawal machines had video cameras filming whoever made transactions, so we're hoping to get a picture. It might take a day or two."

"Excellent, Sondra."

"The will—" she began, but Jardine interrupted.

"Have you talked to Mary? She claims there's a second will that cuts Jane Wood out altogether."

Sondra shut her notebook with a snap. "Yes, I saw it. It was signed by Oslin, but not witnessed or filed. Besides, both Jane Wood and Mary herself told me that Mary sometimes signed his name on checks and other business correspondence. And Mary also had plenty of access to her brother's computer. Who's to say he was actually the one who used the estate-planning software? The legality of the second will is questionable."

"Is Mary naïve enough to think that an unfiled will would be considered legal?" Jardine asked. Then he answered his own question. "She does not seem naïve to me. It doesn't make sense."

They walked down the sidewalk to her car.

"Okay," said Sondra. "I'm going to meet with the lawyer, and I'm getting an outside accountant to audit Oslin's financial records. At least we're getting into some kind of motivation here. It was a burglary after all."

"Just credit cards, cash cards, and snow domes," said Jardine.

He stared down the busy street. No trees, miles of storefronts and commercial signs. He wished for a moment he was out on his Harley, riding north on Highway 1 with Theresa at his back, her dark hair flying in the wind.

"I want to get a copy of Oslin's family tree, that birth family, Miss Tucker. If there's big money to be inherited, and controversy over the will, it might have something to do with his birth relations. I want to find out if any of them are alive."

"I'm glad you mentioned that. I've printed out all the genealogy material from the hard drive, and there is no family tree for Gerald Oslin. Adoptive family or birth family. Nothing."

"That's odd. Maybe he kept them in the file cabinets. Let's check again at his home. Surely he'd have copies of his own family tree." He paused for a moment. "So what have we got, Jackson?"

"A dead man who knew a girl who's missing. But no one who knows him can ID the girl. We've got a torched store and destroyed evidence, financial hanky-panky, and family jealousy with the deceased man's lover. We've got a crazy woman in the hospital who faked her kid's illnesses, and a frantic father who is also a suspect in his daughter's kidnapping. And, lest we forget, we've also got a psychic without whom we would not even know the cases were connected."

"And the victim's college girlfriend who looked just like his sister. Don't you think?" Jardine popped open the locket and Sondra studied it in his palm.

"Where'd this come from?"

"Oslin's dresser. Doesn't it look like Mary Oslin?" Jardine asked.

Sondra stared at the photo for a minute and frowned. "Well, she's white," she said. "But what's this picture got to do with anything?"

He shrugged. He didn't know.

They agreed to meet back downtown in the afternoon, and he walked back to his car, parked near the church.

Oslin's football buddy, Fred, stood on the steps of the church, holding a cigarette between his thumb and forefinger. He stamped it out and descended the steps toward Jardine.

"I always smoke at funerals," the man said. "I quit years ago, but I do it anyway. Tastes like shit."

Jardine asked him if he had any idea how to get in touch with Linda Lane.

"No idea. I wonder what ever happened to her. They met when she asked Gerry to her prom. He was a freshman at UNLV and she was still in high school. Her cousin was Gerry's roommate in the dorm. She was his first true love. Isn't it absurd how you remember all this stuff? It was, what, thirty-five, thirty-six years ago?"

Jardine stood in the near-noon heat, thinking about the Righteous Brothers and gardenias. How he'd found himself thinking about a homecoming dance, minutes after he'd picked up that locket at Oslin's. Another coincidence?

He looked up as the last of the mourners straggled from the church. Before he slipped the copy of the computer will into his jacket pocket, he read it over again. As in the first will, Oslin had made bequests to individuals and institutions prior to dividing the remainder of the estate among his relations and his girlfriend. The individuals were listed under the heading "Employees." But one name had been added to this list that had not appeared in the first will. The person apparently was not an employee; hers was the only name listed under "Other": Mrs. Wallace Knox, P.O. Box 590, Las Vegas, Nevada.

Gardenias, Jardine thought again.

THERESA SLEPT IN on Thursday and woke feeling groggy. She dreaded getting up, even wondered for a moment if she was sick. It reminded her of when she was a kid, those mornings she wanted to fake a sore throat, stay in bed all day and nap under her grandmother's afghan. Her sleep had been dreamless and blank, no voices filtering through. That was a relief, anyway. Tory was still missing, but at least they'd found Ellen. After lying in bed for a while with a headache, she finally got up and made coffee. It helped.

There were several messages from Joe DeLisi on her answering machine. "Could we meet sometime today, just to talk? I—I'm trying to take all this in, what's been done to Tory—it's . . . " His speech on the tape was broken, and she could hear the strain in his cracked voice. "I just need to talk. Please call me." She hadn't talked to him since he left the hospital the previous afternoon.

Theresa pulled her robe around her and opened the back door to the dazzling morning. The roses needed watering, and the patio was littered with dried eucalyptus leaves. She didn't want to speak to Joe just yet. He was asking her for emotional support, but she didn't feel comfortable giving it to him. That was what the foundation was for; he should be talking to Leslie Simon. Theresa could support him by giving him a reading—not only about Tory, but about himself. What was this all about in terms of *his* life, *his* growth? But that wasn't what he wanted, she knew that. And there were other things in the way—the chemistry between them, a not-so-subtle current that couldn't be acted on; the gap between his apparent sincerity and the conflicted entanglements and even alleged criminal activity of his past, personally as well as professionally.

Mostly, what Theresa needed this morning was to ground herself back in her own life. She couldn't allow herself to be swallowed up by one client, and at the same time she knew it was too late. She was in the belly of the whale already. She chose not to return Joe's calls, but to go for a run instead.

As she jogged down the boardwalk, two miles up, two miles back, she tried to clear her mind for the regular readings she'd scheduled for today. When she got back to the house, she fed Osiris and went out to tend her roses.

She felt an awareness of Tory back in her mind, humming as if she were a computer processing data, waiting, clock ticking. For the first time since she'd picked up on Tory, she felt intruded upon. *I don't want to carry this around with me,* she thought.

YOU CHOSE TO, she heard.

The American Beauty was wide open, velvety. "All right," she said aloud. "Okay, okay."

She hadn't heard from that Voice in a couple of days. She bent close to the rose, inhaling the sweetness. *Is Ellen still in danger?* she asked, internally.

She felt herself purposefully leaning into an answer, desiring the *no, now that you have discovered Ellen's secret, she will be healed; all will be well.* Theresa was aware of her own tendency to want resolution and good news, for her intuitions to help people, but she knew the difference between hope, fantasy, desire, and the clear precision of intuition. It felt different in her body. Those hopes that she was cheering for, she could feel them in her heart, wavering with anxiety. Hopes and fears were always closely connected. Intuition came right up the center of her body, straight up her spine, flowering into the center of her mind.

Go in again, she told herself. *Breathe. Blank screen, what do you see?*

Ellen on the phone, calling, calling.

Hello? Theresa answered, silently, within.

No answer. No one home.

Theresa stood back from the roses, admiring them. Her first client was due shortly. *I've got to let this go, for now,* she thought. *I'm obsessing.*

But while she was standing in the shower, letting the hot water spray over her shoulders, the Voice came again.

TODAY, was all it said.

Theresa leaned against the tiles, wrapping her arms around herself. That was it. What she'd woken up knowing, not wanting to know.

It was the third day.

It was during her second reading that Theresa began to sense Tory's presence in her thinking. She had to work harder to stay with the client's life. Amanda was a young woman trying to make a career choice: law school or an M.B.A. Theresa kept getting images of cages and boxes of different sizes. When she opened them, there was only black. When she opened the last one and looked inside, there was Tory on a bed in a motel room. *She gets up, goes to the door, and opens it. Stands there. Nothing is preventing her from leaving—but she shuts the door.*

Is this about Amanda or Tory? Theresa asked. She pictured Amanda stacking the boxes like bricks, walling herself in.

When she steps through the bricks, there is a road. She is running. After a while she stops. Lies down to sleep, and dreams. When she wakes, she's in a Japanese rock garden flowering with tulips, hyacinths, daffodils.

Theresa interpreted the images she'd received for Amanda. "The reason this decision is so frustrating is that neither choice has anything to do with you. It's like you're trying to live in a box, a cage. You're very determined to succeed, and you will be successful, but the context within which you're trying to create your life simply doesn't fit for you. There's a childlike part of you that wants to run away. You open the door, but you can't seem to move. You close the door."

"That's it exactly," Amanda breathed.

"Okay. What I'm getting is that you should defer this decision about outward success for a while. Leave it be. Simply move past the barrier of this decision. If you can travel, definitely do that, rest, be quiet, wander, even for a year or two. Things will be planted during that time—seeds, possibilities that need open time, wandering time in order to blossom. The need for a decision is your family's need and the culture's need. So even if you feel lost or bored by this wandering, that's good.

"Eastern influences—Japanese in particular—will be useful. But you don't have to go live in Japan. A design will be forming in you that will enhance your growth and flowering. So I'd say don't decide. Defer. Take some time off and go away."

"They'll kill me."

"Your parents?"

Amanda nodded.

Theresa went back in. She saw coins being poured into a hole in the earth and covered up. "Oh, I see," Theresa said. "They won't support you financially if you don't choose school at this point—and you see that as death. It is! It's the death of your dependency on them. This is good. It's the beginning of your planting."

"But that's what I'm afraid of!"

"Exactly," said Theresa.

After the readings, Theresa still felt restless and anxious. She decided to return Joe's calls; he was out. She didn't want to leave a message for Jardine on his pager. What was she supposed to say? *Today is the day?* She'd told him already, Ellen too. They could do with the information as they wished. I'm only responsible for the readings, she told herself, not for what people do with them. She wished she could believe that.

For the second time that day Theresa went over to the boardwalk. Passing shops, she heard snatches of music, Bob Marley, Dylan, Sade, each conjuring up a different era. The air off the ocean was cool, but the beach smelled of sweat and tar. A sailboat wheeled around out in the waves. She browsed in the vendors' booths along the way, T-shirts for sale acknowledging the riots: LAPD TREATS YOU LIKE A KING. Baseball hats and black leather hip bags with X's on them for Malcolm. She looked at granny dresses made of floral rayon and decided she no

longer wanted to dress like the sixties. Done that already. Regular
Venice inhabitants greeted her as she walked all the way up to the
mural of blue angel wings painted on the side of a building, a collage of
broken mirror fragments glued onto the mural in a circle.

For some reason it made her think of Michael, her ex-husband.
He'd died nine years ago this summer. Labor Day weekend. She had
never visited his grave. He'd been a funeral director. Once she'd had a
dream that he called her and told her that was what pissed him off the
most. You never went to my funeral! he'd cried in the dream. You never
visited my grave! There were times she still missed him, crazy man.
They'd had some times together.

Theresa took her shoes off and walked back along the sand, following the rhythm of the surf to where the waves just reached, ebbing
back into the blue gleam and tendrils of foam. When she reached the
rocks that jutted out into the water, she found a comfortable place to
sit and leaned back, listening to the roar of the undertow. Gulls
careened above in the bright haze.

The sun was hot on Theresa's shoulders. Nearby, a child raced
after a Frisbee. Theresa thought about the way she experienced Tory
from within. She perceived Tory as extremely intuitive; she even
seemed to "hear" Theresa, to be aware of Theresa's intuitive connection to her. Tory had been hearing her own voices, "friends,"
"angels," "stars," for some time now, and she was undoubtedly psychic herself, yet unformed, flooded with perceptions that normal people managed to suppress. Was Tory really like this, or was this just a
projection on Theresa's part? Maybe she had identified too strongly
with Tory's predicament and was reading things into her, instead of
reading *her*. In spite of her many years of practice, there were
moments where Theresa's boundaries were too permeable. She
would have to be careful to stay separate from Tory, not overidentify,
not merge.

What Theresa wanted was to find Tory, but also to be of service to
her—perhaps as a teacher. But all that was way out of line, she knew.
Even if they did find her—*and they must*, she thought; she had to keep
on assuming they would—Tory would go back east with Joe, with Barbara, back to her own life, to sort out what had happened with her
mother.

All Tory needed was to be psychic on top of all she would have to
deal with. Theresa thought of her own struggle to integrate this gift in
her life. Sometimes it only felt troublesome. *Stay open to her—that's
all you need to do.*

*   *   *

Walking home, Theresa stopped at a red traffic light and thought again of the tiny image of Tory that had intruded on Amanda's reading. Down in the box, standing at the motel door, not going out. She brought the image back, blinked on in her mind. The stoplight changed, but she stayed at the corner.

Tory, looking out a door, first to her left, then to her right. She walks down a street under neon trails, midway lights zapping in the rose dusk.

She turns and runs the other way where the lights end, toward the desert.

The light changed again, and Theresa was jostled by a man with a Great Dane on a leash. She stumbled off the curb. *Neon streets, midway. Let's hit the jackpot. Las Vegas,* she thought. *And she's gotten free.*

Theresa ran the several blocks back to her house, unlocking the door just as the phone began to ring. It was Jardine.

"Oliver, I've gotten a very strong picture of Tory in Las Vegas, and the feeling that somehow she's gotten away from her abductor. It may already have happened or it may be about to happen." Theresa gasped to catch her breath.

"I've got connections between Oslin and Vegas, too," he told her.

Jardine agreed to contact Rukheyser and said he'd get right back to her. The phone jangled again almost immediately.

"What did he say?" asked Theresa, but it wasn't Jardine.

"This is Ginny Carlin, Theresa. I'm down here at the hospital with Ellen, and she wants to see you. She knows that she's been very uncooperative and that she asked that you have nothing further to do with looking for Tory. But she told me to tell you she's sorry. She's been beside herself. We just heard from the police about your finding Tory's doll. You're our main hope, Theresa, you're the only one getting anywhere. Ellen wants you to read for her. To try, anyway. She says you've wanted to do that all along, and she'll even do it with Joe if you still want her to. Will you come? Please," Mrs. Carlin begged.

"Have you checked with Sergeant Rukheyser about this?" Theresa asked.

"He was here this morning and he'll be back later. But this has nothing to do with the police," Mrs. Carlin said. "Or the doctors. My baby granddaughter's life is at stake, don't you understand? You're the one who is putting things together. Even if somehow it is Ellen's fault, she wants to know."

"For a reading to be effective, Ellen has got to want it herself."

"She does. She truly wants to know where Tory is. Will you come? You've just got to help us."

Theresa held back. Ellen was very unstable. Rukheyser was preparing to confront her with the evidence of her abusive behavior in the form of a severe mental illness, and probably arrest her. Last night, Jardine had said that they had to make sure their facts and records were in order, that it was difficult to prosecute Munchausen Syndrome by Proxy abuse, simply because of the skill with which the deception had been carried out. Reading for Ellen at this time would be extremely intense, possibly even a risk to her health.

But it also seemed, last night, as though Ellen might be aware, at some level, of what she had done, that her denial was breaking up. If that was so, and if she was truly open to a reading, it could lead to finding Tory, but perhaps a reading wasn't the best way to find out.

"Mrs. Carlin, have you considered using hypnosis as a means of finding out what Ellen may have blacked out on? Psychiatrists do work with hypnosis. It might be more appropriate for Ellen than my seeing her while she's in the hospital."

"I spoke with the sergeant about that this morning, and it is something we're considering. But Ellen specifically wants a reading with you. She knows you're somehow connected to Tory."

Theresa had many reservations, not the least of which were her own negative feelings toward Ellen, but she knew she was going ahead with it. Ellen had finally agreed, and Theresa didn't want to miss this chance. Besides, there was Ellen herself to consider; if she could read for Ellen, she might come to know the meaning of those images of absence, of emptiness and death. If Ellen's life was at stake, Theresa had to do all she could to help her. And there was one more thing. Ironically, Ellen, who it seemed had arranged for her daughter's kidnapping, might be Tory's only hope for being found.

Theresa told Ginny Carlin she would come to the hospital and read for Ellen. Mrs. Carlin gave her directions to the hospital and for finding Ellen's room once she was there. "They're restricting visitors, so don't stop at the nurses' station. And if anyone asks, just say you're Ellen's sister. This is a private family matter as far as we're concerned."

Theresa changed quickly out of her shorts, showered, and changed into jeans and a cotton shirt. She left a message on Jardine's pager telling him what she was up to, then locked the house and hurried along the canal to her car.

35

A NURSE PADDED DOWN the white corridor in her soft-soled shoes, carrying a tray of medications and cotton balls. She didn't look at Theresa as she hurried past, and Theresa was relieved. Here it was, 312, Ellen's room, the one the nurse had just left.

Ellen looked drained but calm, even placid. She stood at a window overlooking a tarred roof and traffic below. Her robe was a yellow-flowered chintz material. *She matches her living room,* thought Theresa. The neckline of a hospital gown showed from under the robe, and her hair was pulled back, fastened with a barrette. She didn't acknowledge Theresa at all, even after she said, "Good morning, Ellen. Your mom said you wanted to see me."

"Thank you so much for coming," whispered Mrs. Carlin. "Did you have any trouble getting in?"

"No." Theresa set her bag on the chair next to the bed. On the bedside table, a handful of pink carnations leaned to one side in a thin glass vase. The tabletop was cluttered with Tums, Advil, Tylenol, and a disposable syringe still wrapped in cellophane. Several brown plastic prescription bottles were scattered amid crumpled tissues.

"What medication is she taking?" Theresa asked quietly.

"Just a sleeping pill last night. Tracedon. And they're upping the dosage on her Prozac. They also gave her a vitamin B shot for stress."

"Well, here we are again." Ellen finally turned to face Theresa. "Right back where we started."

"Are you sure you want me here, Ellen? Because I can only give you a reading if you're willing. If you're feeling a lot of resistance, like before, it's not going to work. If you still feel afraid, that's okay. We don't have to do this. We can wait."

"But I am willing," Ellen sighed. "Really." She sat in the chair by the window.

"It's not you I'm afraid of," she continued. "What scares me is the thought that I might know something about what's happened to Tory, and be unable to remember it. I've never had a blackout, even when I was drinking. It scares me to think that somehow I may have hurt her."

"How might you have hurt her, Ellen?"

Ellen dropped her eyes. "I don't know," she said sadly.

"I told your mother that a hypnotherapist might be better for this."

"I want to try this first. You *know* Tory."

This was tricky, thought Theresa. Ellen was still in heavy denial. Some part of her probably knew she'd been "caught," but Dr. Silver had said yesterday that such patients, when confronted with their abuse, often vehemently deny it and turn their anger on the medical staff. It wasn't Theresa's place to bring any of that up, at least not until Ellen was out of crisis. She would try to read for Ellen, but to communicate only those images that seemed to lead to Tory.

Ellen began to tap her heel on the floor, bouncing her leg in a repeated, exaggerated manner.

"Ellen," Theresa said, "if you're not up to this . . . "

"Please. Let's just go for it." Ellen fell back against the chair, as if a hand had shoved her.

"One more thing," said Theresa. "Sometimes when I'm reading, there are other voices. I hear them speaking, and lately I just say what they're saying. Out loud. I've gotten Tory speaking in this way. I wanted to let you know, if I shift into another voice—"

"She might talk to me?"

"It's not channeling. I don't claim that Tory is actually speaking through me. What happens in my reading is that I see and hear things, like a daydream or a fantasy. It's in the realm of what's called the imaginal unconscious, the place in us where dreams come from. Scenes and images well up; I don't consciously create them so much as wait and catch them as they rise up. I don't always know whether what I see and hear is an actual representation of a moment in time, or whether the images are a vehicle for information coming intuitively. What I'm saying is that when I 'hear' Tory, I'll repeat what I hear, but it's not Tory speaking. It's me. Okay?"

Ellen nodded. Mrs. Carlin had stepped back to a corner of the room and folded her arms.

Theresa closed her eyes. Red, a pulsing color-field. The plane of color began to retract into itself as if it were a funnel draining down thick liquid, twisting into a tight knot, then a garnet speck, a flake of dried blood blinking off into black emptiness.

There was that absence, that going away, only now the imagery was flooded with red rage.

"Don't leave us, Ellen. It is very important that you stay available, both for your own healing and to help Tory."

"I'm not going anywhere," Ellen said.

"Good."

Theresa felt drawn into the anger. She visualized the knot and magnified it in her mind's eye, pictured herself traveling into its tight threads. Loud voices, vibrating in her bones like a bass amplified, but she couldn't hear the words, just the tone of yelling, batting it back and forth, accusation. Insect on a pin, displayed, flayed.

"I'm hearing arguing," she said. "Physical confrontation. Someone grabbing your arm—stopping you."

She went on. "I'm hearing glass breaking, medicine bottles breaking, thrown away. Someone—a man—you don't want him around, he's someone close to Tory. He frightens you. You know he has seen you." *Be careful,* Theresa told herself. *Not your place to confront her.* "This is someone who tried to prevent you from doing something. To Tory."

Theresa felt the rash sensation on her skin, quickly burning to needling points. Injection. Ellen injecting Tory with something, sticking, pricking. She didn't feel free to say this to Ellen.

Theresa opened her eyes. "Someone saw you injecting her with something. A man."

"Who?" whispered Ellen.

"You feel tremendous shame. He sees you. You're breaking things. So is he."

Ellen was quivering now, a disjointed movement to her head, the leg still bobbing. "Is it Joe?" she cried.

"No," said Theresa. *Slow it down. Brake on.*

Theresa grounded herself in her breathing. "I'm going to go in deeper and open it up," she told Ellen. She slid back in her chair, her hands on the armrests, her attention scanning for Tory, not finding her. Voices, loud, pushing up her throat. She felt it inside her body, growling, sickness at the back of her throat. Gag. A man's voice, very angry. The voice wanted to come out, but Theresa held it down. It was hateful, and she didn't want to frighten Ellen. As it spoke in her, Theresa moaned in the back of her throat, trying to force the voice down: *You're going to kill her. What the fuck do you think you're doing?*

"What kind of mother are you?" The question had leaked out; Theresa couldn't stop herself from speaking it.

Ellen inhaled, a shuddering, sucking sound.

Theresa grabbed the arms of the chair. She did not want this voice. Doc's voice. Ellen started crying, bent over. It was too much, the scene exploding powerfully in her mind. *Bring it in silently,* Theresa commanded. *In silence.*

Then, in the image, Ellen came toward her, toward the *him* that

Theresa had entered. She pulled her clothes open, thrusting her neck back, her breasts arched toward him. He grabbed her hair, kissing her hard with his teeth. The picture abruptly snapped shut and the air around her was filled with ringing and alarm.

The voice coughed out again, as if it were stuck in her throat. *"You tell me to take care of her, and look what you're doing to her."*

"Please stop!" cried Ellen.

"What will you give me to shut me up, Ellen?" Doc saw, he blackmailed her.

Ginny Carlin stood over Ellen. "Who is it? Who is it, Ellen? Who said those words to you? You've got to remember."

"You had sex with him," said Theresa. "You gave him money. Someone you know, who was aware of what you were doing, who confronted you. You know him, Ellen."

"I didn't *do* anything. Can't *you* figure out who it is?" Ellen pleaded.

"*You* know him!" Theresa repeated.

Ellen shook her head back and forth. "But I don't remember, I don't remember . . . "

"There's a ringing all around you, like an alarm just screaming its head off. It's screaming to wake up."

"Maybe . . . maybe it's a telephone," Ellen stuttered.

As the phone jangled out of the stillness, Mrs. Carlin cried out and fell back against the wall, knocking her purse over, coins, combs, glasses scattering. Theresa picked up the phone. "Hello?"

"Ellen?" said the man's voice. "It's Whit."

"Just a moment," said Theresa.

Ellen held the receiver to her ear. "Oh God, Whit, thank God you called. No, they haven't found her yet. Yes . . . yes, there is. Would you? Yes, it would mean so much to me. I need you."

Mrs. Carlin took the phone from Ellen's hand and hung it up. She put her hands on Ellen's shoulders and pressed her back in the chair. "This is our only hope, Ellen. You have got to tell us what is going on. You've got to tell what you know, and that means everything. This is your child, Ellen, my granddaughter." She was yelling now, a mother scolding a child. "You have got to own up to your behavior! I will not allow this lying and this hiding to continue! Tory's life is at stake, do you understand!"

The door swung open and the nurse leaned in. "Is everything all right in here? I'm sorry, but there are to be no visitors other than family."

She glanced over at Theresa and at the mess on the floor.

Ginny Carlin straightened, smoothing the sides of her dress. "We're just trying to calm Ellen down a little," she said sweetly. Her voice had changed abruptly. She smiled at the nurse and bent down to scoop up the quarters and keys, the bottle of Tylenol and paper scraps, into her purse.

"I was just leaving," said Theresa.

Theresa looked across at Ellen, imploring. "Ellen, try to remember who spoke to you like that, who said those words. He fought with you, a lover, an employee. He may have hurt you. . . ."

"Joe hurt me."

"This man, he observed you, watched you. You gave him money, you had sex with him . . . "

Ellen whispered slowly, "It's the doctors who did it. Isn't his name Doc, after all?"

"Is it Whit?" Theresa asked.

Ellen was trembling, a series of tiny, quivering shakes. "No, please, it couldn't be Whit. He wouldn't hurt Tory, he wouldn't take her from me." She began to shake violently, almost a shock reaction.

This was a mistake, thought Theresa. *A terrible mistake.* She stood to go, turning back to Ginny Carlin. "If she thinks of who it could be, tell Sergeant Rukheyser."

"You can tell me right now." Rukheyser pushed in behind the nurse. "What are you doing here, Theresa? Is Jardine here?"

"No. I'm here because Mrs. Carlin requested that I read for Ellen."

He motioned with a jerk of his head for Theresa to step out into the hallway.

"What in the hell was going on in there?" he snapped.

"I was doing a reading for Ellen." Theresa tried to explain about the violent scene, the smashing glass, the sex.

Rukheyser interrupted her. "You have absolutely no basis for being here. This is a very complex and delicate situation. Ellen Carlin is a sick woman under investigation for child abuse, kidnapping, and possible homicide. She's being evaluated by psychiatrists to determine her sanity. It's shaky, Theresa. Very shaky. As much help as you've been to this case—and I'll admit you've brought a very interesting perspective, it has been useful—your presence around Ellen is obviously enormously stressful for her. Last night, now today. Every time you're around her, she's extremely agitated. We can't have her going off the deep end, Theresa."

"She's already off, Sergeant. I was just trying to see if there was anything else that I could do to help find Tory . . . "

"At this point, you're interfering, Theresa."

"I believe Tory may be in Las Vegas," she continued. "She's either gotten away from this Doc or she will, soon."

Rukheyser covered his eyes with one hand. "What makes you think so?" he asked.

His thin face seemed to grow thinner, she thought. He resembled a lizard. "I'm not going to go into detail, Sergeant. But it's the same thing that made me think she'd be down by the harbor in Long Beach."

He stared past her down the corridor. Things had quieted inside Ellen's room, low voices, soothing.

"Look, I'll have someone alert the Las Vegas police that the abductor and Tory might be in the area and they should watch for them. We'll fax them the sketches and Tory's picture."

"Thank you."

"But I insist that you stay away from the family and leave the investigation to us, Theresa. If Lieutenant Jardine wants to deal with you, that's his affair. But take my advice; keep it during off-hours. Stay away from crime scenes and known suspects. Whatever the two of you do in your personal time is none of my business, and police work is none of yours."

36

WHEN JARDINE ARRIVED at Rukheyser's office, Sondra Jackson was already there. She looked up from reading her notes on a clipboard, peered at him over her glasses. Jardine felt as though he'd stepped into the principal's office, Rukheyser tapping his pencil on the gray metal desk.

"I just came from seeing Ellen Carlin at the hospital," said Rukheyser. "I got there just as the nurse was throwing Theresa Fortunato out of the room. The patient was upset."

"I doubt that was Theresa's fault," said Jardine. He kept eye contact with Rukheyser, thinking, *So what?* He wondered why he'd ever thought the man played a decent saxophone. Now he was sure he memorized all his improvisational riffs. Probably practiced them at home, looking in the mirror to get his stage moves right.

"I asked her to stop interacting with family members, especially suspects. It's disruptive to my investigation and to the mental health of an already unstable woman. Jardine, call her off, will you? Consult with her at her office, if it makes you happy, but—last night, there she is at Mrs. Carlin's. And now, today, there she is again at the hospital. She's *in the fucking way.*" He chopped at the air with his palm as if conducting an orchestra.

"The family is free to work with Theresa if they want to," said Jardine. "She's affiliated with the Simon Foundation, so what's the problem? Besides, look what she's done. She's the one who alerted the foundation that the kid was missing in the first place. She identified key elements of the abduction in a series of drawings, culminating in a sketch that nearly matches the one our sketch artist came up with. She's given us at least a nickname of a possible abductor and details of a physical description above and beyond the drawing. Found the kid's doll under that bush in Long Beach and came up with a possible license plate number for the abductor's vehicle. Named the former fiancée of the kid's mother and a motel where he was registered, the same motel that Oslin got a postcard from. She's unraveled an insidious riddle of child abuse in the form of a mental illness that has eluded doctors up to this point, abuse that's been going on long enough for the mother to kill one child and make another disappear like a rabbit in a hat. Theresa Fortunato is a professional, Rukheyser. She's well known in her field, highly respected and, in short, your investigation would be diddly-squat without her."

Rukheyser shoved his hands in his pockets and grinned. "She's perceptive and intuitive, I'll give you that. But I'm a skeptic when it comes to this shit, and I don't mind saying so. So Ellen Carlin meets with a psychic; the psychic comes up with some sketches. She's just drawing what Ellen told her about the hospital room, what the kid was wearing. Now, if you were going to draw a picture of a child being abducted, how unusual do you think it would be to show the kid in a car with tears coming down her cheeks? Not too original, if you ask me. Or specific."

"But she made those drawings before she'd ever met with Ellen."

"Says who? They could be backdated. So they talked on the phone a while before Ellen actually met with her; Leslie Simon could have filled her in. When Ellen shows up for the session with the psychic, *voila!*—instantly channeled drawings for Mommy that her little girl supposedly made. Hell of a good way to suck in moolah from a vulnerable perspective client."

Rukheyser continued. "Okay, she comes up with a sketch after a few days of extensive meetings with the mother, the father, the police and people from the foundation, and her sketch purportedly looks just like one our artist drew. Why is that so surprising—when Theresa has been hearing a lot of descriptions of people in Tory's life? You might even have mentioned to her the person Oslin's girlfriend described. So Fortunato is good at observing, listening, filtering information, and throwing out possibilities that are great guesses disguised as predictions."

"How could she guess that Tory's doll was under that bush?" Jardine demanded.

"Don't forget that Joseph DeLisi is one of our primary suspects. While Ellen Carlin may have this syndrome thing going, that doesn't mean she necessarily nabbed her own kid. Let's say that DeLisi asks Theresa to see if she can name a site where the kid might be, they drive there, and while Theresa isn't looking, he throws a doll belonging to his daughter under a bush and waits until Theresa finds it. Very mystical. And the nickname 'Doc' doesn't mean anything, considering Tory DeLisi spent half her life in hospitals.

"And the Seaside Villa? You're talking with her every day about the case, Jardine. You mention a lot of details, including a postcard from a motel. Ellen tells Theresa in passing that she and her fiancé stayed at the Seaside Villa, a little vacation. Theresa puts them together and all of a sudden she magically knows the name of the motel where Whitney Park once stayed. I'm not saying her perceptions aren't helpful. But I have to question how she comes up with them. Excellent observation skills, creative mind, intelligent—I'd describe Theresa Fortunato as all of the above. Or does she have a mirror, mirror on the wall or a crystal ball implanted in her brain so she can see into other people's lives?"

Rukheyser was rolling now. Jardine sat back and waited until he'd gotten it all out.

"And aside from all that, there's still the issue of whether it is appropriate for her to be meeting with the family at this time. I maintain these are all legitimate concerns."

"What about Las Vegas?" asked Jardine. "Are you going to alert the department out there that Tory DeLisi might be in that area?"

"Why not?" said Rukheyser. "Can't hurt. But again, where did she get Vegas? You told me after Oslin's funeral that Oslin went to UNLV.

And that Oslin's girlfriend mentioned he made mysterious calls to Vegas. Is it odd, then, that Theresa made the connection? See what I mean?"

Rukheyser picked up a computer printout and slapped it with his other hand. "Besides, I've got to concentrate on this. A list of known sex offenders released from correction facilities statewide, and a second list, of employees, staff, patients, and families at Kettler Hospital in the last year. Three men from list number one also appear on list number two. One of them is a janitor, out on parole after serving time for molesting his girlfriend's kid. His name is Eugene Duckworth— that close enough to 'Doc' for you?—and he had three vacation days over the Fourth of July weekend, the days following Tory DeLisi's abduction. Now, this is what I call getting somewhere, not chasing visions across the desert."

He sat down, breathless from his speech. "We're getting ready to question Duckworth this afternoon."

Sondra Jackson uncrossed her legs, crossed them the other way, and adjusted her earring. She looked back and forth between the two men. "Are you finished with your debate?"

They both looked at her. "Yes, ma'am," said Jardine. He saluted. She didn't smile. Still looking at him over the glasses, a bad sign, thought Jardine.

"Do you have enough evidence to arrest Ellen Carlin for child abuse, kidnapping, or murder?" Jackson asked.

"We've certainly got evidence of child abuse in the form of this syndrome. We're working on the medical records and will be interviewing Mrs. Carlin as well as Dr. DeLisi in light of the recent findings."

"You mean the paperwork isn't ready to go."

"Correct. And I have word Ellen Carlin has hired one hell of a good attorney, so the evidence has got to be in A-plus order. What have you got, Jackson?"

She consulted her clipboard. "I checked Oslin's phone bills for any calls made to Las Vegas in the last year. You were right, Lieutenant. There were a number of them to Mrs. Wallace Knox. I tried calling her several times, and have left a message on her machine."

Jardine raised his eyebrows and addressed Rukheyser. "Mrs. Wallace Knox was one of the people Oslin listed in that computer-generated will. It could be that Jane Wood's suspicions about Oslin having a lover were right."

Sondra Jackson continued reviewing the notes on her clipboard. "Dr. Whitney Park," she went on. "We had local authorities down in

Baja check his condo. The manager let them in. No sign of the girl. The place hasn't been occupied in eight weeks. There were two weeks of rental in late April; March and May were rented, and Park himself was down there last February. No one reported any children on the premises in the last few months.

"I've been concentrating on Oslin's files, cross-referencing names: genealogy clients, buyers of both antiques and folk-art toys, the store mailing list, the birth-mother support group mailing list, skydiving club, and general addresses from his Rolodex and home telephone directory. I'm comparing all those with that list you've got there—the hospital personnel and patients. This afternoon Dr. Park is providing us with lists of his office staff, patient list, anyone who rented out his condominium in the last three years, as well as household employees and care-givers hired during the time he was seeing Ellen Carlin. We're searching for connections."

Rukheyser scribbled a note. "We should cross-reference what you've got with our list of known sex offenders."

"Right," said Sondra. "I'm also waiting for a list of hospital personnel fired or laid off in the last two years. Now, in going through Oslin's computer files, I have run into a problem. There are several items in his personal file directory that I can't open. They're locked, and it would take an access code to open them. I called both Mary Oslin and Jane Wood, and neither of them knows what that code is. I'm working on it. And when I spoke with Mary Oslin, going over some financial information with her, she said that in reviewing Oslin's books and bank statements for this last year, she found some substantial errors in his bookkeeping. We're talking twenty-five grand worth of errors. She's going to get back to me on it. He might have transferred funds from one account to another, or purchased an antique and not recorded the sale for tax purposes." She set the clipboard down. "That's it for me."

Rukheyser turned to Jardine.

"What have you got on Oslin that would be useful to me?"

Jardine stared at the toe of his black shoe. What he wanted to say was that Theresa had predicted, three days ago, that Ellen Carlin had three days to live. But he kept his mouth shut about that. "We checked on a couple of license plate numbers, including the number Theresa Fortunato came up with. Actually, we're still checking on that one. But the Pinto with the California plates listed on the registration card for Whitney Park at the Seaside Villa—it turns out the vehicle was registered to Gerald Oslin. Mary Oslin had no idea her brother had bought a Pinto in the last year. We've got APBs out on both vehicles."

"Oh," said Jackson, "the post-office box on that registration card? No such number in Portland, Oregon."

Rukheyser stood as Leslie Simon simultaneously peered in and knocked on the open door. "Mrs. Simon, thanks for coming down."

"Sorry I'm late," she said. She wore a bright coral suit and a patterned silk blouse. Jardine hadn't seen her dressed in a power suit before. She settled into a chair.

"Mrs. Simon will be meeting with the media later today," said Rukheyser. "We're going to review the case in preparation for a possible TV appearance."

"Yes," said Leslie Simon. "One of our main efforts is to keep missing-children cases before the media."

She brushed a speck off the sleeve of her suit. "I'm shocked—but ultimately not totally surprised—by the revelations regarding Ellen Carlin. The accusations of her abuse will air on all the local news programs this evening, and will receive front page coverage in the papers. The foundation has been featured on several prime-time news magazines, including '20/20,' and I'm going on 'Nightline' sometime next month. I'll bring Tory DeLisi's picture—and her story—with me. We have posters and flyers about our cases up all around the country; you can expect Tory's face to become recognizable nationwide. Our focus is not so much on investigation as on hopes for a sighting of these children based on people's familiarity with these pictures. In a very high percentage of cases, that is how our children are recovered."

"I hope it helps," said Jackson.

"We need to get ready for this press conference, Mrs. Simon," Rukheyser said.

As Jardine followed Jackson out of the office, he realized that Leslie Simon was not the only one wearing a new suit today; Rukheyser had looked unusually natty himself. The sergeant was taking his case to prime time, the Simon Foundation would become a household name, the LAPD needed some good press after the spring riots, and missing kids always elicited empathy. Everybody was getting a piece of the action.

"Let's go visit Dr. Park," said Jardine.

As soon as they got in the car, Jackson started in. "Oliver, I like the airwaves to stay cleared out between us, and things feel like they're building here, so I've got to get it out. While there's no question that Rukheyser is a pain in the ass, I think he has a couple of points. I believe Theresa Fortunato is doing some very fine work, and frankly I don't care how she comes up with the stuff as long as it contributes to what we're working on. But my biggest question about Theresa is how come she can't get anything for us on Oslin?

"I don't think Rukheyser's problem is actually with the work Theresa's doing. It's with the flow of information, the hierarchy. She ought to be communicating her findings directly to Rukheyser, but he doesn't want to work with a psychic. You want to consult with her, but she's not working the Oslin case. But I do feel that most of your attention is on the Carlin-DeLisi thing. Yesterday I wondered if I was working on Oslin by myself."

Jackson was silent a moment. "Well?" she asked.

"Yeah," he muttered. "I hear you. But I've got to follow my leads, and what I'm up to is focusing on where these two cases intersect. I'm not just helping out Rukheyser here. The DeLisi case feeds right into Oslin. Let's do this: let's set up regular, scheduled checkpoints between you and me. I'll tell you exactly what I'm up to, but I can't pull my attention away from the DeLisi kid. I have to follow my gut."

"You sure it's your gut, Oliver?"

"What do you mean?"

"Sure it's not some other, more basic part of your anatomy you're following?"

"Don't I wish," he said under his breath.

"You want my advice on Theresa?" she asked, then went on without waiting for his answer. "Tell her to work exclusively with Dr. DeLisi. Have her tape all sessions with DeLisi and give copies of them to you. Tell her the chain of command to both the foundation and Rukheyser should be through you, and set up regular report calls, morning and evening. Do not take her to any more on-site investigations, and tell her to meet *only* with DeLisi, not with Ellen Carlin or Ginny Carlin. That will clear things up with her and free you up to concentrate on Oslin."

Sondra Jackson removed her sunglasses and squinted at Jardine. "You want some more advice, Oliver? Take Theresa out for a very nice dinner, I'm talking bucks, here, nouvelle cuisine, not a bacon cheeseburger. The next day, send her roses. And get some decent clothing and some furniture, while you're asking me for my humble advice."

Jardine pulled up in front of Park's home and they got out of the car, slamming the doors behind them.

"Sondra," he said. "Did I ask?"

37

PARK LIVED IN A LARGE Tudor-style home, landscaped with camellias and hydrangeas. The slate sidewalk curved in an S through the close-cut lawn, and Jardine felt as though he were headed toward Oz down a yellow-brick road, but the road was gray.

He rang the bell and Park showed Jardine and Jackson in. They sat in the living room on a brocade couch that faced a massive fire-place. The house was cool.

Park handed a file folder to Jardine. "Here are the lists of people you asked me for. I'm getting some other names from Ellen. I phoned her at the hospital. Ginny called me last night and told me what was going on. I can't tell you how disturbed I am about all this. Being a doctor, being that close to her, and not seeing this. Of course, I came to know Ellen was a substance abuser: pills, booze. But she was subtle with it. It's not like she was an outright drunk or drug addict. I guess I saw what I wanted to see. In my specialty, I focus on people's exteriors. I saw Ellen's beauty, not her mental illness. At least not clearly. When I broke off our engagement I knew she was unstable, but I never imagined anything like this."

As Jardine flipped through the lists Park had provided, the doctor paced the room, moving from one view to the next, pausing at each French window.

The file contained a series of lists, some handwritten and others typed, titled, "Baby-sitters," "Nannies," "House Cleaners," "Yard Maintenance and Gardeners," "Day Care Providers," "Camps." His clinic employees were also listed separately, and finally his personal address book had been photocopied, page by page.

"Ginny thinks Ellen did something with Tory or hired someone to do something with her, but blacked it out," said Park. "That Ellen may have had a fugue state. She even hired a psychic to work with Ellen, but I gather the police came and threw the woman out. Now they want to try a hypnotist." Park finally sat down in a green leather chair and clasped his hands.

Jardine handed Sondra Jackson the file and stood. "Mind if I look around, Dr. Park?" he asked.

"Go ahead. Take a tour."

Jardine circled the living room slowly, then headed down the hall and turned into Dr. Park's study. A stately rosewood desk took up much of the room. It stood in the center of an Oriental rug. Diplomas and certificates, photographs and trophies were displayed on one wall. As he checked out the room—*field vision,* he reminded himself—Jardine nearly missed it. The doctor was using the object as a bookend, nudged between some medical books and the paneled wall: a small figurine of a Buddha seated on an elephant. Jardine pulled it from the shelf, and the line of books tilted toward the wall. Examining the bottom of the figurine, he found a small sticker on the felt base: OSLIN'S ANTIQUES, and the address.

Never met Oslin. Right.

His eyes were drawn to the gold and silver trophies lining one shelf, karate poses and ninjas posed in flying side-kick leaps. Framed awards for championship Tae Kwon Do tournament fighting. Jardine stepped closer to examine them. *So Park is a black belt. Well, well.* When Jardine returned to the living room, Dr. Park was still talking about Tory DeLisi.

"I'm just sick that I wasn't there for Tory," he continued, "that I was going to be her stepfather and didn't see what was going on. I will say this. I knew she seemed better away from her mother. Like the time Ellen and I went to Paris for two weeks, I hired not only a nanny to take care of Tory, I hired a nurse—two of them, actually, day and night rotation—because Ellen was so worried about Tory's health. But when we got back, Tory seemed fine. If I'd seen any of this—believe me . . ."

Sondra Jackson spoke up. "The nannies and so on—they're listed here?"

He nodded. Jardine handed him the Buddha. "Excuse me, Dr. Park. The sticker on the base of this says it's from Gerald Oslin's store."

Dr. Park turned the figurine over. "This was a gift," he explained. "I told you, I've never been to Oslin's store." Park held the Buddha out to Jackson.

"You maintained in a previous conversation that you'd never met Gerald Oslin."

"That is absolutely correct. That's what I'm telling you."

"But you know Jane Wood."

Park twisted his tongue in his mouth, let out a long sigh, and slumped back in the leather chair. Jackson peered over her glasses at Jardine, surprised.

"You're involved in martial arts with her, is that it? Got to know her during classes? Fought in tournaments together? That's an impressive display of trophies and awards you've got down there in your study. I noticed Jane's certificates when I visited her boat." Jardine stopped there, waiting. He was only guessing they knew each other. He'd wait Park out.

Park met his gaze directly, but his voice was subdued. "Yes, I know Jane. We . . . dated. We were lovers, off and on. We're still good friends."

"And you didn't see fit to mention this in our previous conversation?"

"See fit?" asked Park. "I thought of it. Of course I did. But you asked if I knew Oslin. I didn't. Never met the man. Jane and I have practiced karate together for years. When she broke up with Oslin, a year ago, she suggested an . . . arrangement. Nothing heavy. Fun, pleasure. Then, when she got back together with Oslin, we kept seeing each other. We continued through the time I was seeing Ellen. Ellen didn't know. I suppose Jane and I were keeping each other on hold a bit, in case things didn't work out with Oslin, with Ellen." He shrugged. "But mostly we were friends. It was . . . discreet."

"But Jane Wood did give you a very expensive gift," said Jackson, holding up the Buddha.

"She did. It was for my birthday. I appreciated it." Park stood and crossed the room to the fireplace. "I should have mentioned it. I was so used to keeping my relationship with her under wraps. Secret from Ellen. When you told me about Oslin, I felt sad for Jane. When you told me Oslin had Tory's picture in his office, I just thought, how weird. I couldn't think of any reason why he would have it. Oslin didn't know Tory *or* Ellen, as far as I know."

"Did Jane know Tory, did they ever meet?"

"No! I kept Ellen and Jane completely separate. I was very careful they never met. I'm not saying it was the most gallant behavior."

"Did Ellen give you a school picture of Tory, one that Jane might have taken from your wallet or your home?"

Whitney Park put his hand to his forehead, turned toward the mantel, then back again. "I'm sure Ellen did give me a picture of Tory. It's possible Jane might have seen it. I never noticed any pictures missing. Ellen and I had this very intense, whirlwind thing. It was extremely rocky. Knowing Ellen, you can imagine. I was caught up, obsessed. It was one of the reasons I broke it off. I would talk endlessly to Jane about it. Jane just listened. She was back with Oslin by that time." He held out his hands. "I don't see any reason why Jane would have taken Tory's picture out of my wallet and given it to Oslin. None! Can you?"

"And you know of no other connection between Jane and Ellen? They never met?"

"Ellen knew nothing about Jane that I'm aware of."

"Could Jane have met privately with Ellen, without your knowledge? To discuss your relationship with each of them, perhaps?"

"Well, obviously, you'd have to ask Jane or Ellen that."

"One last question, Dr. Park. Has Jane been involved with anyone besides Gerald Oslin—and yourself—during this last year?"

Park's face reddened. He shrugged. "Not that I know of."

Jackson nodded at Jardine. "Did you check the rest of the house?" she asked the lieutenant. Then, to Park, "Do you mind if we continue to look around?"

"Not at all. Look, I have nothing to hide but a friendly affair. It makes no difference if Ellen knows about this now. I can't believe I didn't say anything about it. I'm . . . embarrassed. If it could have anything to do with finding Tory . . . "

The phone rang and Dr. Park seemed startled. He quickly crossed the room to a small table.

"Dr. Park," he answered. "Oh, Ginny—how is she doing? No, the last time I talked to her was this morning." Pause. "When was this? The note said what? No." He hesitated again. "Have you called the police? Yes, I understand. Right. She could. If she does, I'll call you immediately. Please call me if you hear anything." A quiet click.

Whitney Park faced them, his hand still resting on the phone. "Ellen's left the hospital," he said. "No one knows where she is. She left a note that just said, 'I'm sorry.'"

AT FIRST THERESA didn't see him waiting at the edge of her porch, standing there out over the canal. She came around her neighbor's unruly bougainvillea, bending out of the way to avoid it, and was startled when he called her name.

"Joe," she said. "Have you been here long?"

"A while." He stepped off the porch, hair windblown, white shirt with the sleeves rolled up, wrinkled jeans, and sneakers. His shoulders were curled inward, Tory's absence wearing on him now, hope flaking away. He fingered his beard anxiously. "She's gone, Theresa."

She looked at him blankly. *So what else was new?*

"Not Tory," he said, as if he'd heard her. "Ellen."

She faced him now on the sidewalk, in the shade of a eucalyptus, its strong scent on the sea air, blowing cool through her hair. "What do you mean?"

"Rukheyser called from the hospital and asked if I'd been in touch with her today. He'd just been down there. Apparently she and her mother were waiting for a lawyer. Ellen asked to be alone for a few minutes, to take a shower or something. Everyone wandered away, went for coffee, whatever. Ginny fell asleep in a chair in the lounge. And then Ellen was gone. It couldn't have been fifteen minutes since someone had been with her. Maybe twenty. She didn't have her car and she didn't take Ginny's car. The police are waiting at both her house and Ginny's to see if she shows up at either place. They're watching this Whitney Park because apparently Ellen spoke with him earlier today. But I have this feeling . . . "

"What?" Theresa asked.

"Just what I've thought all along. That Ellen knows where Tory is, that she hired someone to take her away. That she's gone now to meet up with this person, to get Tory. I can't believe they didn't have some kind of surveillance on her. I should have hired someone myself, god damn it."

The thought bled through her, a hot ache at the back of her neck. "She's not safe," Theresa said quietly, and sat at the edge of the porch. "She's not safe out there."

"What do you mean? I'm worried about what she'll do, not what will be done to her."

A jet slanted down toward the airport, roaring as it descended through the yellow air. "Did you find anything new?" he asked.

"Yes. And I tried to tell Rukheyser, but he told me to get lost." She explained about her unfruitful session with Ellen. And Las Vegas. "But I've also gotten references to Arizona and Texas. It's not enough to mobilize police to search for her, I guess. I just don't have the authority. And Rukheyser doesn't really know what to make of me. He thinks I'm nuts."

"Is Jardine still with you?"

"Yeah, but I think he's getting flak that's meant for me. Rukheyser doesn't want him crossing too far over into his territory."

God damn it, Theresa thought. She felt so guilty. Shouldn't have gone to the hospital, shouldn't have tried to read for Ellen. Rukheyser was right. Would you read for a client who'd committed herself, a person under terrible emotional strain? Undergoing psychiatric evaluation? Never. Maybe make a meditation tape for them, visit them as a concerned friend, send flowers or a book. She *had* gotten way off base. What had she been thinking? She may have caused Ellen to break down completely, to bolt from an environment where she could begin to face her illness. Why had she even gone there in the first place?

Because she asked you to, thought Theresa.

NO, SHE DIDN'T. Voice inside.

That was true. Ginny had asked her to. But Ellen had certainly agreed to it. She'd wanted it.

Joe kicked at a small stone on the sidewalk, chased it, and kicked it again, into the murky water. Across the canal, a neighbor had tied up an old rowboat. Fat ducks lounged on the grassy bank.

He turned back to her. "I have an idea. Tonight on the local news, they're going to run a segment on the Simon Foundation. They're going to publicize Tory's disappearance. I think they're going to go into the Munchausen's thing and I'm sure they'll cover Ellen's taking off, too. I found out from Leslie Simon; they're interviewing her."

"That should help."

"Why couldn't they do that in Las Vegas, too? Put Tory's picture on the evening news and announce that there's a possibility she could be there? Give a number to call?"

"You could try."

"I'm going to call Leslie. May I use your phone?"

Theresa unlocked the house, showed him back to the tiny kitchen, then went to let Osiris out. She sat on a wicker chair, anxious thoughts wheeling: What if Ellen hadn't run off, either to meet with Tory or to escape arrest? Tory had disappeared from a hospital. So had Ellen. Someone may also have abducted Ellen. But it was broad daylight, a psychiatric ward in a major hospital. Surely, if Ellen had struggled, called out, someone would have heard her. Unless she had been drugged, sedated, wheeled out on a gurney, heading for an operating table or appearing to. Hospital staff? Who was on the floor? She thought again of the cluttered table beside Ellen's bed in the hospital room, the various medications, the unused syringe on the bedside table, the nurse leaving the room as Theresa approached.

Theresa could tell by the sour feeling in her chest that none of these were intuitions or psychic revelations. It was her rational mind cranking out scenarios, trying to solve and analyze. Behind her, through the screen door, she could hear Joe speaking with Leslie Simon, his voice emphatic. Where could Ellen be? Theresa closed her eyes, asking the question in her mind.

Blank. Dream dark. Sleeping. Ellen huddled under bedcovers. Shivering. Calling. Cold. Phone in her hand.

So she will be in communication. Is she hiding?

She saw Ellen lift apart at the waist, as if she'd been cut in two, like a magician's assistant sawed in half. Inside, a smaller Ellen, smiling. She, too, separated at the waist, lifted off. Another, smaller Ellen within, this one frightened. The image kept repeating, Ellens within Ellens like those wooden dolls she'd bought for Sarene in Chinatown on a trip to San Francisco long ago.

Hiding from herself, came the words.

Then a familiar image bloomed in her: *Bright lights blinking in a blur of neon, yellow, red, and green whirling through a night sky. The midway again. Or casinos,* she thought.

Joe appeared behind Theresa at the screen door. "It looks like they're going to go for it. It's being arranged now, and they want me to fly out. They're going to interview me on the evening news. They think it would be very helpful if they could interview you as well."

Theresa hated media coverage of psychics; they were always portrayed as hokey fakes. It was a setup to be diminished, and it was a distraction from the work.

"Would you be willing?" asked Joe. "Please. I'll pay all your expenses, plus a fee—hourly or a retainer, whatever."

"Are you sure I wouldn't be interfering, Joe? Maybe it would be best if you went out there by yourself."

But she recalled her initial impressions of Tory in whirling lights, blurred reflections on black tar. She'd seen a midway, a carnival, a theme park, perhaps. What was Vegas but a whole city of neon? And once there, she might pick up on something more.

"All right," Theresa said. Absence and emptiness. Maybe that was what that imagery was about: Ellen disappearing. Running away, not dying. Still . . .

"I'm worried about Ellen," Theresa whispered.

"Don't waste your time," Joe said bitterly.

She packed her bag, put food out for Osiris and lowered the windows. A damp breeze had come up, and then she realized it wasn't the weather. She felt clammy, a chilled shuddering like a fever beginning at the center of her bones and moving out slowly through her heart and her skin.

Theresa watched out the window of the plane as they rose up through the brown air, tilting now toward the bowl of the mountains and heading inland over the desert. How quickly there was emptiness, out of the clogged city, nothing but sand-colored hills and mud-brown rocks.

Joe was quiet, eyes closed, head leaning back on the seat, but she knew he wasn't sleeping. Once he put his elbow on the armrest between them and leaned toward her, warm against her side. It felt comfortable and she had an urge to put her head on his shoulder. After a while he pulled away, rearranging himself in the seat. In less than an hour they touched down in Las Vegas.

The television station was located in a white concrete building that resembled a warehouse. A receptionist gave them burnt-tasting coffee in Styrofoam cups while they waited on rattan chairs. The woman who met them had wire-framed glasses, cropped black hair, and tortoise-shell earrings that highlighted the warm brown of her face. "Mr. DeLisi? I'm Marilyn Blake, I'm the news director. Come on back to the greenroom, it's right this way."

They followed a linoleum-floored hallway with white cement walls, past rooms where cameras and recording equipment were set up behind glass doors. The greenroom housed another set of worn-looking rattan furniture around a coffee table cluttered with ragged magazines and an ashtray overflowing with cigarette butts.

"Ugh," said Marilyn Blake. "I hate this shit. I'll get somebody to empty this out." Theresa and Joe sat down, and she perched on the edge of a chair. "So you just flew out from L.A." She glanced down at her notes. "Your little girl was kidnapped? That's terrible. What happened?"

Joe began to explain, but after a rush of words, she cut him off. "Whoa, whoa, whoa," she said. "Slow down. Try to encapsulate. You're going to be on for two, maybe three minutes. We'll show your daughter's picture. You brought a photo?"

Joe handed it to her.

"She's sweet," said Blake. For the first time she seemed to focus on him as a human being instead of a news item. "You must be worried sick."

"That's why I'm here. Ms. Blake, this is Theresa Fortunato."

"You're the psychic?" she cooed. "This is hot. It really is. And you look good, too, not all goofy and bizarre." Marilyn Blake checked her watch. "Here comes Kathryn," she said. "Kathryn Chester, she's the anchor, the one who'll be interviewing you."

Kathryn Chester looked as though she had no intention of stopping. She swept toward them in her navy suit, palming her chin-length brunette hair. Theresa thought she seemed stamped out of a mold called *newscaster,* and when she spoke, she had a television voice, though her smile appeared warm and engaging. *She's a good person,* thought Theresa. *She only looks shallow.*

"Dr. DeLisi," said Kathryn. "And you must be Ms. Fortunato. Marilyn has filled me in only briefly, so you're going to have to help me out with this, but we're glad to help. Our station does a lot of benefit work regarding children. I'm so sorry to hear what you're going through. We received the fax description of your daughter, which I will read, we'll show her picture, and then I'll ask you a few questions. What would you like me to ask?"

Joe cleared his throat. "I'd like to describe her in more detail and talk about her illness. She was abducted from a hospital."

"That's a great angle," said Blake.

Kathryn Chester nodded, keeping eye contact. "And you're the psychic? Look, I've got to go on now. Marilyn will bring you in to get your mikes hooked up. See you in a few minutes."

They watched as local news sound bites were spoken crisply by the warm and engaging Kathryn Chester on a TV monitor mounted on the wall. As Chester broke away to an ad, she announced, "And when we come back, can psychics really aid in the search for a missing child?"

Marilyn Blake ushered them into the studio, where they sat at a round counter on a platform. Lapel mikes were clipped on, the wires hidden inside their jackets, and Kathryn Chester joined them. Voice check and cue and the cameras went on, red lights in the darkened studio. Theresa barely heard Kathryn Chester speaking. Joe described in a broken voice that Tory was ten, missing for a week, and very ill. That he'd hired a psychic. And Chester explained about the Simon Foundation, the LAPD, turning toward Theresa to ask only what had led her to feel Tory was here in Las Vegas. Chester summarized by reviewing the serial murder case on which Theresa had worked with the L.A. police nine years ago, looking seriously into the camera as they broke away to Tory's picture. Theresa watched Tory's face appear large on the monitor, and then it was done.

Kathryn Chester shook their hands. "I hope this helps," she said. She disappeared into the darkness of the studio.

Blake showed them out down the linoleum hallway into the too-bright light of the reception area. "You were good, both of you. Fatherly concern, very touching. The picture was very cute. People are going to be watching for her. And you," she said to Theresa, "you ought to think about having your own show. You look gorgeous on camera, not that you don't look good in person, but I'm thinking a talk show, where people actually come on with their psychic issues, before a live studio audience." Marilyn Blake handed her a business card. "It was real hot," she said. "Give me a call if you're interested." She nodded to both of them. "Peace," she called. "Hope you find her."

They took a cab back to the airport, rented a car, and spent the early evening driving around Las Vegas, cruising through the parking lots of small shopping centers, convenience stores, gas stations, handing out photocopies of Tory with a paragraph describing her and the Simon Foundation 800 number to call if anyone should spot her.

The sky glowed in red streaks at the edge of the desert beyond the neon. Theresa felt dusty and hot. Finally she said, "I need to eat something. And I need to get out of these clothes."

"You're right," he said. "Let's go check into the motel and grab a bite to eat. Marilyn Blake said they'd run the piece again on the ten o'clock news, and I want to watch it."

After registering at the motel, they climbed to the balcony facing the back parking lot. Theresa looked out over the aqua pool lit in the darkness, kids doing cannonballs while their parents were at the slot machines.

A minivan drove slowly across the parking lot with its lights off. Theresa took conscious note of it just as it rounded the curve in the driveway, heading toward the front of the building. She couldn't see the license number or exactly what color it was, gray or bluish in the dusk.

For the first time in all of this, she felt afraid. This was different from the fear that arose during a reading out of the intensity of the psychic work. It was not psychological, not internally provoked by imagery, but a sense of physical danger. Something wrong. More than a van without lights. Someone following, watching her.

Theresa unlocked the door and entered the anonymous room, the cold air welcome after the night heat. Clicking the lock closed, she tried to think it through: Ellen might be here in Vegas, having arranged to meet up with the person she'd hired to hide Tory. Ellen certainly—or someone—had a stake in the girl's not being found by the police. Theresa realized she'd exposed herself by going on television with Joe. If Tory's abductor had seen the news, he might recognize them, might look for them. On his own, or at Ellen's request. It occurred to her that she hadn't even told anyone she was coming here.

She pulled the phone onto the bed and dialed Jardine's pager number, leaving him a message to call. Then she did the same with the Simon Foundation's answering service.

She'd just taken off her jacket and shoes when she heard the knock. As she opened the door, it flashed through her that she should slip the chain lock in place, but it was too late. A burning sensation surged through her chest out of nowhere. But it was Joe. "Can I come in?" he asked.

He sat down on the edge of the queen-sized bed and bent over, his hands covering his face. Theresa sat next to him and put her hand on his shoulder.

"I just wanted to thank you," Joe said, looking up. "You're a friend, Theresa." They faced each other in the dim lamplight. His eyes moved over Theresa's face as if he were examining a map, where to go, lost again, no idea how to get there or where *there* even was. He brushed his mouth against hers.

No, she thought. *Yes.* She didn't pull away, but returned his kiss and knew the heat that had flashed through her wasn't all fear.

Joe drew her down on the bed. She could feel his chest flooding toward her, his hand under her shirt.

When the phone rang, Joe reached for it. "Yes?" he answered, his voice gruff and breathless. He waited a moment, then replaced the receiver. "They hung up," he told her. "Must have been a wrong number."

DOC SAT IN THE CHAIR across from the bed, watching Tory sleep. Listening to the hum of the air conditioner. All these rooms were the same in some way. One smelled of mold in the shower, another had fancy soap wrapped in tissue. Hard pillows or soft. But they were the same and he liked them. You could be anyone here, it didn't matter. It didn't matter what you had been or where you came from. The fresh glasses covered in cellophane, the ice machine always full, pouring out perfect cubes, whenever you wanted them.

Tory had fallen asleep easily. The large bed dwarfed her. He'd thought of giving her something to keep her asleep, but that was so much like what Ellen had been doing and he didn't want to do that anymore, not unless he had to. What he really wanted more than anything was just for Tory to *want* to stay with him. To love him, really, in that pure way that children were supposed to love their parents.

He called the number on the slip of paper he'd been carrying in his wallet. It rang only once and he waited a moment for her to answer, listening, then hung up.

Pulling the plaid curtains back slightly, he peered out at the parking lot, the vacancy light blinking red. Last night he'd gone to a different motel and removed the front license plate from a car, screwing it onto his dusty truck. He thought he'd do that just about once a day. People didn't look much at the fronts of their cars. Tomorrow he'd probably get rid of the truck, too.

He glanced at Tory before quietly closing the door of the motel room, then locking it. She'd been good lately. Not trying to get away. And she'd been asleep for two hours, hadn't stirred. Surely she wouldn't wake before he got back.

Get it over with. It will only take an hour, he thought. *Maybe less.*

40

THERESA PULLED AWAY from Joe and stood at the mirror, brushing her hair, all tangled from the heat and wind. Her skin felt gritty.

"Theresa, are you all right?" Joe asked. When she didn't say anything, he told her that he'd enjoyed kissing her, that he'd been wanting to do that since the first time he saw her.

She looked at him behind her, in the mirror's reflection. "I enjoyed it, too, Joe. But it's not cool."

He laughed, a short burst. "Of course it's not cool. How could anything be cool right now?"

"I just mean I'm working for you. With you. It's . . . complicated."

"So what? Life is complicated. It still felt good. You're a very beautiful and sexy woman, Theresa."

She pulled out the desk chair and sat down, facing him. "Joe, it's more than just messy. I . . . thank you," she said. "I'm flattered." Hesitating, gathering her thoughts. "It's not just that we're trying to work together to find Tory. Things I've heard about you, it's not such a good picture. Reports from your divorce and custody proceedings, about the restraining order. The police, Jardine, have filled me in. I've seen you blow up a few times myself in the last days . . . I know you're furious about all that's happened, and I know Italian men. I was raised by one, and I grew up with his anger in my face. And this stuff about being fired from a teaching position, dubious business contacts, financial investigations. All I want to say is that I know there's nice chemistry between us. In some other circumstances, I'd be very interested. But your references . . . " She tried to smile. "Is all that true?"

Joe DeLisi stood, checked his watch. "Look, Theresa. All we did was kiss. I'm not trying to have a relationship with you."

"Obviously not. And anyway, what would Barbara think about it?"

He shot her a sharp look.

"Didn't she tell you she called me, got my number from Rukheyser? We had a good talk. It sounds as if she really cares about Tory and is hoping to be her stepmom."

"Yes, I'm involved with someone," Joe said. "Future stepmother? That's Barbara's fantasy. We've been together since last winter, but I told her I wasn't ready for anything permanent yet. And, yes, Ellen did get a restraining order against me. She fell down the stairs when she was loaded one night, and hung it on me. It was bullshit. I've never hit a woman in my life. Weak men hit women. Italian or otherwise. And I was raised by a gentle father who never lifted a hand to any of his seven kids."

Joe shoved his hands in his pockets, pulled the curtains back. The rumble of a semi going by and loud laughing, drunken voices outside on the patio. He went on.

"I resigned a position at a university where there was a big scandal in the medical school. The deans and chairs were trying to pin anything they could on people who were involved in the financial records. I designed software programs; I didn't misappropriate funds. I was a target, a scapegoat. Again, total bullshit. I was never prosecuted, never even called as a witness. And dubious business dealings? Maybe some junk bonds. I jumped on that bandwagon for a while, then bailed out before Milken went down in flames. Those court records contain any goddamn thing my mentally ill ex-wife and her hotshot attorney could come up with to smear me and take my daughter away from me."

He rubbed his beard, quiet now, then added, "I thought you had a better opinion of me, Theresa." He picked up his keys from the desk and opened the door, turning back to her. "I'm going to go out and drive around some more."

The door shut soundlessly behind him.

Doc DROVE BY SEVERAL TIMES, circling the block, then parked one block over. She lived in a small yellow cement bungalow near the outskirts of the city. It was one step up from a trailer court. In one direction, the city lights filled the sky with an orange glow. God, it glowed. In the other direction, the desert stretched into night.

He rapped the flimsy brass knocker, and a rush of cool air thrust out at him as she opened the door. She was wiping her hands on a dish towel, the TV on in the living room. She seemed to be looking past him, out into the darkness. Mini-blinds were drawn against the night heat.

"Yes?" she asked. She looked much younger than he'd thought she would. Short brown hair, no gray, maybe she dyed it. Face tan, leathery from the Nevada sun, but not old. She was plump in a homey way. *Don't look at her,* he thought. *Don't look too much.*

"I never thought I'd get a chance to meet you in person," he said.

"Oh my God." Her face brightened. "Oh, my dear God, I can't believe it's you. It really is you, isn't it?"

"Yes, ma'am. It's me, all right. My name is Marty."

"I know, I know." She held the screen door wide and he brushed past her into the house. It was tidy except for one corner where there was a sewing machine. He didn't want to chat. Hurry up, he thought, as she shut the inner door. He didn't want to get to know her. Put his hand in his denim jacket pocket, the gun was there. It felt warm. He didn't know if he would use it or do it some other way, some quieter way. When he turned around to face her, he saw it in her eyes, the understanding from a million miles away. Her realization, one instant in time. That she shouldn't have opened the door, should not have let him in. That she was stupid, and hadn't thought, just swept away in the moment. She clasped her hands in front of her, holding the towel. She smiled nervously.

"So, Linda . . . " he said. "How about a beer or something?"

When he returned, the motel room was empty. The bed was empty. Fuck, he blew it. Now he wasn't sure of anything. The dark heat was pushing in on him. He turned and faced the mirror.

Tory had taken everything. Not that she had much. He could have been more generous, he thought. He hadn't provided very well. He had the money from the old man, but he was hoarding it. Now he wished he'd gone about it all much differently. Bought her nice clothes, and some toys. A boom box or a Walkman. All he'd gotten her was that goddamn doll. And he should have been clear right from the beginning instead of lying to her about her mother. She was too smart for that.

He'd become too complacent, too comfortable with her. Thinking, *She could be my kid, my daughter. That's all I wanted really. To have it work like that. But it doesn't. Just like it didn't work for me. Just because I was adopted, it didn't mean it worked. I didn't love them.*

Hell, they knew it. That's why they gave me back. And the foster homes. One after another. The detention center and finally the boys' home and then the army. Funny. The service was the only place he'd ever felt at home. Must have been the order and discipline, the meals. Maybe he should have been a lifer.

He knew she was gone, but he looked under the beds anyway, and behind the chair in the corner and the rubber-backed brocade drapes, and in the bathroom. Behind the bathroom doors, on the white tiled floor, he found her barrette. Purple plastic. He picked it up, turning it in his fingers.

Well, maybe that was the end of it, then. She was gone. They were all gone, now. He had thought he'd feel lighter. He didn't feel lighter. And he missed Tory already. It had been good having her around like that because he had to take care of her. Feed her, make sure she wasn't sick or anything.

He hadn't counted on her feeling imprisoned, though. When the plan was first laid out, that he would take her into hiding for a while until she was well, he was sure she'd understand, really understand why she'd been ill, what her mother had done. He hadn't counted on Tory missing the bitch. But then again, Ellen was a fantastic con, and even if you knew you were being taken in by her, you'd enjoy it. That was one way to relate to people. Let them use you and love it.

He could go look for Tory—or he could just let go. She'd try to head west, back to L.A. Maybe he'd go to Texas. Austin. He'd heard it was a good town.

Suddenly his life seemed as vast as the desert, without time or meaning. All that he'd been up to, what good was any of it if it wasn't for Tory? She was aiming right back to a life of cruelty in her mother's care. It was going to be hard for him to disappear completely. This week, with Tory, he'd seen just how difficult it was. And Tory knew him too well, she could ID him in two seconds. He could be on the run for a while, but he'd always be paranoid. He was in a different sort of prison. Why, nothing he'd done had cleared anything at all. There was nothing he was free of, and he really couldn't let Tory return to her mother. He felt rancid and pissed off and there was a hole in his gut, something she'd taken from him. It was late, she'd never had dinner. She'd be hungry. He needed a new plan. He needed something. He'd lie down and go to sleep in the cool blue room, get up in the night and start driving.

He decided to drink instead.

He packed up his things, checked once around the motel room to make sure he'd gotten everything, looked in the mirror, and decided to shave off his beard. Afterward, studying his freshly scraped face, he realized that he hated his face. It was strange seeing the woman in the yellow house. He could hardly say: *his mother.* In the instant she'd opened that door, he saw that he had her looks and hated her for it.

He backed away from the mirror, pulled on a black baseball cap. *I'm not a bad person,* he thought.

But he kept seeing the pillow over Linda's face, and his arms were deeply scratched where she'd clawed into him.

As he checked out of the motel, paying with cash, what he was thinking was that life was like TV. You could just turn the channel.

The bar was dark and loud, the bass went up through the soles of his feet. At the bar he ordered two shots of tequila and a beer, and when he opened his wallet, he discreetly flipped through the cash. He noticed the woman three stools down as she lit up at the sight of that wallet in his hand.

"Why don't you buy me a drink?" she called. "You look like you could use a little company." The woman had come to sit beside him now. She was drunk and not bad looking. She leaned in close to his elbow when he lit her cigarette, and crossed her legs. She wore tight blue-jean cutoffs, a red halter top, and black high-heeled sandals. Her toenails and fingernails were painted a flawless neon pink the shade of an orchid. He'd always had an admiration for the kind of woman who did her nails on a regular basis. It showed she cared about something and had some extra time. She said her name was Dani with an *i,* writing it on a napkin for him in childlike script and dotting the *i* with a heart. When she asked him, "Wouldn't it just be great to go stretch out someplace, have some fun?" he asked her how much. They walked arm-in-arm down a block and checked into a cheap motel. He watched her sit naked in a chair with her high heels on while he undressed.

It upset him that he couldn't feel much when she was riding him and making all that noise. It was like he was hovering above his body over by the TV, which was on low. After a while she stopped, rolled off him, and asked him what he'd find more exciting.

"Are you bored?" Dani asked. She fingered the scratches on his arms.

"She hurt you pretty bad, huh? You ain't an abuser, are you? I don't put up with any of that shit."

He played with her nipple and watched the TV, ten o'clock news coming on.

"You got about twenty more minutes, hon," she said, "so just let me know what you want. Maybe an X-rated movie would help."

That was when Tory's picture came on, all over the screen. He reached for the remote control and turned the sound up. "Authorities have reason to believe the child may be in Las Vegas and ask anyone who has seen her to contact this number."

How could they know? he thought. *How?*

He felt cold and scared then, and noticed that Dani was much older than he'd thought. She was on her back, her legs up in the air, stretching them like a ballet dancer.

"The Los Angeles Police Department has also issued two artists' sketches of a possible abductor," said the news anchor. The drawings loomed on the TV, and Doc gazed at them, horrified. No way, he thought. How could they know what he looked like? Someone at the hospital? "The second sketch was a creation of psychic Theresa Fortunato, of Venice Beach, California, who claims that the child drew the picture through her. It bears an uncanny resemblance to the police artist's sketch. Again, anyone who recognizes this man should consider him armed and danger—" Doc flicked the off button, and turned Dani over, folding her arm back in a wrestling hold, and she said, "Not too hard now, just play, okay, hon? I don't do rough stuff."

Massaging her shoulders as he entered her from behind. Thumbs in the muscles behind her shoulder blades. "Ooh, baby, that's nice. Where'd you learn that?" Caressing her neck lightly, then the pressure point on her neck, carotid artery. Bear down on it, cut oxygen to the brain, she'd black right out. A fellow medic in the army had showed him that. He fucked her quick, vaguely aware that the anxiety he felt about being seen in Vegas, the possibility he'd been seen with the kid, was fueling his sexual urgency. Like he'd had to be scared to do it. He couldn't remember really liking any woman since his wife, back when he was in the army. But she'd left him for a guy who sold tires, that she met at a bar somewhere. She'd told him, "At least he talks to me, Marty. There's just a lot of times when nobody in the whole wide world is home in there." She'd pointed to his head.

And then he was gone: back there with the old man, all oiled up and relaxed now, pressing into his neck, holding it until the man was out cold, limp, though his arms were muscular and taut. He worked out, but his tan skin was loose and crackly. *I fucking hate you man for everything you never did and who you never were.* Pushed the pillow down over his face, no resistance at all. Carrying him to that Jacuzzi, lifting him in, just letting him float there while the tub filled. Surprised how easy it was. Sat on the john for a while watching him before he realized he'd better get the hell out of there.

Lying on Dani now, he realized he'd gotten soft. Reached down to rub his cock, used to this, his own hands, not a real woman.

"Here, let me do that," Dani offered.

Afterward, he showered, paid Dani. He didn't really even want to talk to her, but he said, "Well, thanks."

"Sure, hon." Dani yawned, snapped the TV back on to a rerun of "Cheers."

Outside, he thought about it for a minute, then went around back to the parking lot. Found an open car, hot-wired it, and headed out going south, thinking, *Texas. Better yet, Mexico.*

The angels must have wanted it this way, was all he could think when he spotted her along the shoulder a short distance from a truck stop, just walking as the semis roared past her. She didn't recognize the car. He pulled over quick right next to her, got out and yanked the door open, grabbing her around the waist, throwing her in. He lucked out: a full minute of no traffic either way. He was sure he hadn't been seen. She was screaming as he jerked out onto the dark road and he told her to shut up if she knew what was good for her. She sucked those tears back quick.

"Just shut up, now," he said. "You run off on me, and that was not cool. Here I been trying to take good care of you, and you're not cooperating for shit."

"I just want my dad," Tory cried.

He accelerated, speeding past a semi. "You know, for a while there, I thought maybe I could be your dad."

"I hate you," Tory said. "You could never be anyone's dad."

"Watch your mouth, girl. I took good care of you before, didn't I? Aren't I your old Doc?"

"You're not my doctor. You're mean."

She was crying now, sobbing into her hands.

He wondered if she knew she'd been on the news. "Okay, okay," he said. "You're going to call your dad. But we're going to practice what you're going to say. He's going to have to come up with some money if he wants you back. You got that?"

She nodded, her hands still over her face. "How much?" she asked.

"He's got money, right?"

She nodded.

He drove south, out into the blackness. Tory cowered against the window. He didn't want her to be scared of him.

"This isn't the way I want it," he said quietly. "If we work at this together, a team, it's going to come out all right. I don't want to hurt you, Tory. But it's up to you. You know that, don't you?"

She looked straight ahead as white highway lines zoomed under the truck. Something was rising up in back of his mind, burning like shame. He'd forgotten something. What was it?

"I want there to be good feelings between us after all this. Right, Tory?"

Then he hissed, "Fuck." *The gun. The stupid fucking gun.* At the last minute he had decided it would be too loud to fire. He'd set it down on Linda's nightstand after he'd told her to lie on the bed. After he'd hit her with it once and she was still. *And fucking left it there, you stupid shit.* His throat burned down to his heart.

Tory kept her eyes locked straight ahead. They could drive all night if they had to. They had a full tank of gas. And he still had the Beretta.

FRIDAY,
JULY 10

42

She woke in total blackness, not sure where she was. Sat up and snapped the light on, glancing around the motel room, seeing herself in the mirror across from the bed, hair tangled. She checked her watch: nearly 2:00 A.M.

Theresa huddled back in under the covers and wondered if Joe had returned to his room. It would be strained between them now, he'd withdraw. But it had been good to break open the space of not-speaking between them. That air of silent communication was where things were the loudest for Theresa. The hell with it, she thought; there had been a charge between them from the beginning. He'd touched a hungry place in her, woken it up. Maybe now, with all that on the table, she could do her work without so much static.

Then she sensed the Voice near. It fluttered around as if behind her, hissing in the hum of the air conditioner. She closed her eyes to focus on her breath, but it didn't wait for her to center herself.

Theresa felt herself sink down like an elevator, a shudder of anxiety: *Too fast.* She counted breaths, imagined the ground, and slowed the descent, further, further. *By choice, not taking me, but guiding me.*

The Voice opened fully in her, no longer from behind, or from the right, but rising up from a deep core.

ELLEN DOES NOT KNOW WHERE THE CHILD IS. SHE KNOWS AT SOUL LEVEL IT IS RIGHT FOR THE CHILD TO LEAVE HER. NOW IT IS TIME FOR HER TO LEAVE SO THAT NO FUTURE HARM WILL COME TO THE CHILD.

Where is Ellen? Theresa asked.

She pictured Ellen condensing to a point of light and shooting off into space, hovering over the blue earth, drifting back into the atmosphere. A seed.

Theresa did not want to interpret the image. In fact, she resisted it profoundly, not wanting it to be so. But there it was, lodged in her chest: Ellen was dead.

She stayed with the falling seed, trying to intuit whether the image meant present or future. *Dead?* she asked. *Or dying?*

Eyes closed, Theresa imagined Ellen in a chair across from her in the motel room.

Tell me what you know, Ellen. The knowing that's unconscious. Bring it up for me to see. Who saw you making Tory sick?

What Theresa saw surprised her: parachute. A baby strapped in a white parachute slowly coming down. Buoyed by the chute, the baby grows older. By the time it nears the earth, it is a man in white.

The parachute snags in the branch of a tree. The man cannot touch the ground. He dangles there, swinging like a child, but he is not a child. Child-man.

Then the images shifted: Ellen in a bathroom in a red robe, staring into the mirror. Syringe in her hand.

The dangling man unstraps himself from the tree, jumps down. Ellen knows he's watching her. Knows he has seen her. He goes to her, opens the robe. His mouth on her white throat, hands cradling her breasts. He sucks each nipple. She leans back against the mirror.

She opens the mirror. Medicine cabinet. He reaches past her, sweeps all the bottles into the sink. She takes off her robe and lies down on the floor.

He is on top of her and it is as though Theresa can feel both of their bodies as her own. Money falls around them like leaves.

Ellen's voice: *I won't know this is happening. Won't know you saw. If I give you my body you won't see me. You'll see my beauty, not me. You won't see what I agree not to see in myself.*

She cannot feel his contempt for her in his gentle touch as he rocks into her until she gets everything she wants. He covers her with money until she disappears. Waves his hands over her like a magician. When he feels for her under the money, she is gone.

He returns to the mirror cabinet. On the shelf, inside a bottle, is a tiny girl. Tory. He takes her down and begins to close the mirror when he realizes there is a second bottle and she is also in that one.

He takes them both out, holds them in the palm of his hand, stroking them. They are so small. He will not hurt them.

One of them averts her eyes. She will not look up at Theresa, at her God-like eyes. That one stares off into space, rocking slightly, arms around her bent knees. The other Tory stands up in the palm, gazing up toward Theresa.

Can you see me? she cries.

"I see you, Tory," Theresa whispered.

In that moment, Theresa understood what "seer" meant. *See-er.* One who sees. One who does not. Both she and Tory had split into two. The deeply intuitive perceptive wise-eye who knew in the present moment exactly what the child-heart must be protected from, and so split them into *seer* and *sleeper.*

I will see it all for you. You will see nothing. You will be safe.

Theresa slowed her breathing. She didn't want this to be about herself. Tory was so close. Maybe too close. *Where are you, Tory?*

Tory runs down a highway. Trucks pass. Away from the circus of lights. Huge trucks all around her. Hands around her, over her mouth. She struggles to get free.

Theresa felt herself coming out. She focused on the sound of the air conditioner rattling by the window.

She fumbled for her notebook on the nightstand, scribbling notes: white parachute, child-man. Hanging in a tree. Family tree. Sexually involved with Ellen as some form of payment. She paid him with sex and money to be silent about what she was doing to Tory. Blackmail.

Theresa looked up toward the ceiling, remembering the image of Tory looking up toward her own psychic seeing. For an instant, Theresa had the feeling of some goddesslike watching presence observing *her,* witnessing *her.*

"Who is it?" she whispered.

ME, came the Voice inside.

JARDINE REHEATED A CUP of day-old coffee in the microwave. He rubbed his belly and thought maybe it looked a little flatter. For some reason he found himself craving a bran muffin and then was disgusted with himself. He could tell himself it was for his health, but he knew better. It was really some way he pictured himself with Theresa. He had found himself wishing he could wake up beside her. She'd have a bran muffin; he'd have a bran muffin. There was no way she would go have an Egg McMuffin. *Man, you would miss Egg McMuffins,* some voice in him argued. *Can you imagine the rest of your life without an Egg McMuffin?*

Maybe he should just call Marsha again, give it another shot. Marsha was more his type. Kind of boring, but his style. Did that mean he was boring? Yeah, he thought.

He answered the phone's ringing with a clipped "Jardine."

"Lieutenant? Mary Oslin here."

"Mary, what's up? Everything okay?"

"Sorry to call you so early. You said to call if anything new came up. I've been checking with the answering service for the store. Even though there was the fire, there still are ongoing clients, orders coming in and so forth. Anyway, this morning there was a message from a homicide detective in Las Vegas. They wanted to talk to Gerry about someone out there who hired him to do a family tree." She paused, and when she spoke again, she was crying. "It was so strange to get that message asking for him, as if he were still alive."

Jardine grabbed a pen and asked Mary Oslin to repeat the detective's name. He thanked her and hung up, immediately dialing the Vegas number. The switchboard rang him right through to the detective's office. The man answered with a loud cough.

"Mickelson, Homicide."

"This is Lieutenant Oliver Jardine with LAPD Homicide. I'm calling about a family tree drawn up by Gerald Oslin. He was murdered last Sunday, a suffocation made to look like a bathtub drowning. He owned Oslin Antiques here in L.A., and did genealogy work on the side. I just got a call from his sister, Mary Oslin. Apparently you've got some case you're working on where his name came up?"

Jardine heard the shuffling of papers on the other end, a match strike, then another rattling cough.

"Thanks for calling, Lieutenant. Yeah, you're going to find this very interesting. We got a homicide here, woman, fifty-three, white, divorced, lived alone. It appears to be a strangulation or smothering, but there was also a head wound. She was discovered in her bed this morning by a sister coming to pick her up to go to a flea market. No sign of forced entry. Doesn't look like a burglary. Anyway, we found this genealogy in the victim's bedroom along with a letter from this Oslin, and the name rang a bell; now I know why. It was in the *Times* a couple days ago, right? I read the *Times* every day for the sports section. Now that I know this Oslin's a homicide too, this family tree here looks even more interesting. There's got to be some kind of connection here."

"You want to fax the family tree to me?"

"Yeah, sure. He did it for her exactly a year ago, July tenth. The victim's name is Linda Knox."

Jardine slapped his hand down on the kitchen table. *Mrs. Wallace Knox.* "Her name came up at Oslin's funeral yesterday. Linda Lane—or Knox—was Gerald Oslin's girlfriend back in college in the fifties." *Gerald and Linda, UNLV. Theresa and DeLisi were in Vegas right now.*

"So they knew each other, huh?" Mickelson spoke in a nasal drawl, as if holding a cigarette between his teeth. "Both killed within one week of each other. Here's another thing. Even though the victim was not shot, we did recover a weapon. Smith & Wesson lying on the nightstand, beside the bed, plain as day. Her sister said she didn't think it was Linda's. We're running a check on the registration."

"The gun hadn't been fired?"

"That's correct, Lieutenant. It was fully loaded, but not fired. Probably used it to threaten her, knock her out. Inflicted a nasty head wound, like I said. Something else, too. One of the deputies brought it over to my office after I left the crime scene. Picture of a little girl, looks like a school photo, photocopied, enlarged. My deputy saw it stuck up on the woman's refrigerator with a magnet. This same girl's picture is all over the front page of the paper here this morning and on our local news last night. The girl's father is in town looking for her, and he was interviewed on both the six and ten o'clock news. We're trying to locate him now. The TV station hasn't been too helpful, say they don't know where he's staying, but they gave me the number of a"— again he riffled through papers—"Simon Foundation? You know anything about them? They're in L.A."

Jardine said yes, the family was working with the agency.

"Yeah," Mickelson went on, "my deputy said the girl's father was on with some psychic, said she had a vision the kid was in Vegas, so they come here looking for her. So now we got a photo of the kid on a dead woman's icebox. What do you make of it, Lieutenant?"

"I make of it that Linda Knox knew the little girl." Jardine explained to Mickelson the various connections between the Oslin and DeLisi cases, the same school photo, the snow domes, Jane Wood, the Buddhas.

"Well, I'm about to question the victim's sister," Mickelson drawled through his smoke, hacking again and clearing his throat. "See what she knows about that girl. What's her name again, DeLisi, Victoria? I'll give your Missing Persons a call and get right back to you if I come up with anything else."

Jardine showered, then dressed hurriedly in a dark suit and headed for the kitchen, where he heated up a second cup of bitter coffee. He sipped it anyway, standing at the kitchen window, staring out at the scraggly cactuses and the dying grass. He was about to call Rukheyser when the phone rang again.

He held the phone out from his ear as Mickelson hacked up a phlegmy cough. "Right. Mickelson here, in Vegas. We got something else here, thought you'd want to know right away. The Smith & Wesson? It's registered to a Dr. Joseph R. DeLisi, the little girl's father, the one was here in town on TV last night. You know how to get in touch with him?"

Cough again. Mickelson sounded bad, as if he were drowning in his own lungs. "We're going to want to question him." Jardine gave him the Las Vegas number Theresa had left. "Thanks, Lieutenant. You've been a big help."

Jardine tried calling the number first, but there was no answer. God damn it, she'd left him the number, all right, but not the name of the hotel where she was staying. Maybe Leslie Simon knew. He called her home number, but when he explained the situation, Leslie Simon said she had no idea where they were staying. "I opened up the *Times* this morning and was pleased that at last we're getting some media coverage on Tory, but I had no idea there was going to be coverage in Las Vegas, too. I had no idea, in fact, that Dr. DeLisi and Theresa were even going out there."

Jardine dialed Rukheyser's office next, repeating what he'd learned from Mickelson, leaving out, for the moment, that Theresa was with DeLisi.

"We've got something heating up here, too," said Rukheyser. "Still no sign of Ellen, but Ginny Carlin got a call this morning." Rukheyser paused, playing the moment out. "From Tory."

"She's alive? She's all right?"

"I don't know if she's all right, exactly, but she is alive. It was a ransom call. It was obviously rehearsed, and Tory said she'd be calling back with further instructions. What time can you get down here, Jardine? And get Jackson in, too."

Jardine checked his watch. He could be downtown in twenty minutes.

44

THERESA SAW THE COLOR photograph of Tory and her own sketch of Doc on the front page of the *Los Angeles Times,* a stack of them for sale by the cash register in the motel coffee shop. The headline read, PSYCHIC HAS VISION OF MISSING GIRL IN VEGAS. She bought a copy, spreading the paper open as she sat at the booth. The story continued on the fourth page with the police artist's sketch and a picture of Theresa supplied by the Simon Foundation.

"Damn it," she whispered. The waitress poured her coffee and grinned. "Aren't you that psychic that was on the news last night? I sure do hope you find that little girl."

Theresa faked a smile in return and went back to the ladies' room, where she brushed her hair off her face, wove a French braid down the back, wiped off her lipstick, and put on a pair of sunglasses. The last thing she wanted was to be recognized all over Las Vegas. She should have listened to her own intuitions the way she was always telling others to do, and let Joe go on television on his own.

She surprised herself by ordering eggs over easy and hash browns. She preferred a bran muffin and fruit, but she'd felt like something different today. It was strange that Jardine hadn't returned her call last night, she thought, climbing the balcony stairs to her room. Then she remembered that wrong number, Joe hanging up. She'd better call Jardine now.

Once she was in the room, she locked the door and placed the call. Jardine answered on the first ring.

"If you'd called two seconds later," he said, "I would have been out the door. Theresa, have you seen a paper yet?"

"I've seen it."

"Nice picture. Ought to bring you some new clients."

"For God's sake, Oliver, I didn't do this for publicity. I came out here to help find Tory. Joe asked Leslie Simon to arrange media contacts here in Las Vegas, and we did a short interview on last night's news. Joe has been driving all over, distributing flyers. Why didn't you call me back last night? Did you get my message?"

Jardine hesitated. "I did call. Your client hung up on me. I thought about calling back, but I figured the two of you were busy."

"Come off it, Oliver. We were not *busy.*" *Yes, we were,* she thought. Theresa twisted the phone cord around her finger. "I'm getting this weird feeling about Joe, like I had with Ellen. When you called, he told me it was a wrong number."

"I told you to watch it with him, Theresa. And listen, I just spoke with Leslie Simon. She did not arrange that TV interview. She started getting all kinds of calls from Vegas last night, people claiming to have seen Tory or Doc, based on the photographs and drawings they'd seen on the evening news. Leslie was surprised as hell, said she knew nothing about you and Joe going to Vegas."

Theresa was silent.

"When are you coming back? There's a lot going on." As he told her about Ginny Carlin hearing from Tory, she almost cried out. *She is alive, she is,* Theresa thought. But when Jardine told her about a woman murdered in Vegas last night, a woman who had Tory's picture, it brought her right back down.

"Maybe I should stay here," she said. "If Tory might be here."

"Get back to L.A., Theresa, and call my pager number as soon as you can. I might need you. And I don't like you hanging out with DeLisi."

"I know," she said.

She packed quickly and took the next shuttle out to the airport. It was ten-forty-five. A flight to Los Angeles had just left; the next one departed at noon. She read *Vanity Fair* until the boarding call.

There were a number of empty seats on the plane, and she was glad to find a window seat. Outside the small window, the luggage was being loaded from a trailer, the sun already intense on the tarmac. It was not until he'd slid into the seat beside her and fastened his seat belt that she looked over at him.

"Good morning, Theresa," said Joe. "I appreciate your keeping me informed of your travel plans."

She removed her sunglasses. "You lied to me, Joe. You told me that was a wrong number last night. And you said Leslie had set up the interview on the news. She didn't even know about it."

He unfolded the Las Vegas paper in his lap, Tory's photograph prominently displayed. "I couldn't get hold of Leslie when I called yesterday. I set up the interviews myself."

"Why did you lie to me about it?"

"I didn't lie. I told you I'd called Leslie and that the interviews were being arranged. That was true. And I told you that the news director thought it would be great if you came on with me. That's exactly what Marilyn Blake said. She wouldn't give 'a missing-child item'—as she called it—the time of day until I mentioned that a psychic working with the Los Angeles Police Department had predicted my daughter was in Vegas. Turns out she'd heard of you. Heard you on some radio talk show a few times when she was visiting her sister in Anaheim. Suddenly the evening news was a go. Miracle of marketing."

"You used me, Joe."

"I hired you." He handed her a check for a thousand dollars.

Theresa thought about tearing it up, but she said, "Thanks. I'll donate this to the Simon Foundation. Joe, why weren't you just straightforward with me? Why did you manipulate me?"

He couldn't keep eye contact. The plane began to back out and taxi toward the runway. "I apologize. I guess I'm not used to dealing with women in a straightforward way."

"I guess not," she said.

JARDINE STOPPED IN at his office to pick up a file, then hurried to the elevator, heading up to meet with Rukheyser and Jackson. When the elevator doors slid open, Whitney Park was standing there, hands in the pockets of his wrinkled khaki raincoat.

"Dr. Park, what brings you down here?" Jardine asked.

Park pulled a cassette tape out of his pocket and handed it to the lieutenant. A name was scribbled on the tape's label in handwriting that was fitting for a doctor's prescription: illegible.

"It says 'Ellen,'" Park explained. "This is a tape of a message I received from her on my answering machine at home. I first listened to it about an hour ago, although I'm sure it was made last night sometime."

The elevator stopped, and Dr. Park kept pace with Jardine down the hall to Rukheyser's office. "I decided to come down here with this in person because, after you questioned me yesterday, I realized I was much more involved in all this than I thought or than I wanted to be. It looked bad, didn't it—my withholding the fact that I knew Jane, that I had some tangential connection to Oslin?"

He paused at Rukheyser's door. "Lieutenant, do you consider me a suspect in Tory's disappearance?"

Lieutenant Oliver Jardine had learned many years ago in talking to suspects that being direct always paid off. "Absolutely, Dr. Park," he said.

Sondra Jackson and Rukheyser stood simultaneously as they entered. Jardine told them about the cassette, and Park added, "This isn't the actual microcassette from the answering machine itself; I recorded this on another tape player right next to the phone." Rukheyser unearthed a tape deck from under a pile of books on the floor behind his desk. He snapped the tape in.

Ellen Carlin was obviously drunk, drugged, or both, her speech garbled and halting. "Whit, Whit? Are you there? Oh God, please pick up if you're there . . . " Her voice shuddered, then trailed off.

Park looked out the window, facing away from Rukheyser, Jackson, and Jardine, as they listened to a sob, choked back, followed by rapid breathing, almost a panting sound.

Ellen resumed. "So tired, Whit. Can't take it. All I ever wanted—wanted to be good—good mommy . . . " Her voice broke again, gasping as if she couldn't get her breath. "What they're saying I did to my baby—Mother says—she says I'll probably go to jail if I don't—or prison for the rest of my—locked up where I'll never see my baby ever again. My baby . . . my baby . . . Whit, I still love you . . . Remember?—Paris that day we—Monet's garden and the time we—" There was a silence, a clattering, the phone crashing to the floor.

When Ellen spoke again, her voice was far away, nowhere near the receiver. "I took some pills, Whit . . . By the time you hear this . . . "

There was a long silence on the tape, but Park turned back to them, raising his hand. "Wait, there's more."

"Whit? Find my baby, please, I—know who took her, he saw me, the psychic told me, he's the one. He saw me . . . Doc, he knows . . . "

Park looked down. "That's it," he said. "The tape goes on, but all you hear is air. She must have passed out."

Rukheyser rewound the tape and they listened to it a second time. "Dr. Park, I have to say it sounds like more than a binge," said Rukheyser. "It sounds like a possible suicide attempt to me."

Park was nodding over and over. "Yes, I agree. I didn't want to think so, but that's what it sounds like. Yes."

"Do you have any idea where Ellen called from?"

Park shook his head.

"Any idea who this 'Doc' is?" Rukheyser asked.

"I know one hell of a lot of doctors. She could be referring to any number of my friends, colleagues, or acquaintances."

"Anyone specifically who goes by the nickname 'Doc'?" Jardine asked.

Dr. Park thought for a while. "No. Is there any way to trace where her call came from?"

Rukheyser turned to Jackson. "Let's run a search on Visas, MasterCards, and Discover Cards for Ellen Carlin, Virginia Carlin, and Joseph DeLisi. Check for any payments to hotels or motels in the past twenty-four hours." To Jardine: "We should check with the Westwood Plaza Hotel, where DeLisi's staying. See if anyone looking like Ellen checked in there. We may have to get a look in his room."

Jardine followed Jackson out into the hall, where she sat at an empty desk. "Lieutenant," said Jackson. "I've got something this morning, too. Nevada Motor Vehicles found an Airstream trailer abandoned at a KOA campground in Jean, Nevada. California license plate, matches the number Theresa gave us. There's a maximum-security prison there, by the way. They've impounded the trailer. Should we have somebody pick it up, or send someone out there to check it out?"

"Jean, Nevada?" said Jardine. "We better send somebody from forensics out there." Jackson turned to the desk to begin making calls to MasterCard.

God damn it, Ellen knew, thought Jardine. *She knew who Doc was.* Theresa's reading at the hospital had brought something up to the surface of Ellen's mangled psyche. Whoever Doc was, he was someone who knew what Ellen was doing to her daughter. After Theresa read for her, Ellen had disappeared, fled the hospital or left with someone. Possibly someone had taken her out, either helping her get away, or taking her against her will.

If she'd left on her own, Jardine wondered, where might she have gone? They'd all assumed that she'd run to escape arrest, but if she had finally realized who 'Doc' was, she might have gone to where she thought he might be. Where would she go to find him? Jean, Nevada?

Then it came to him, and he grabbed the phone book on the desk next to Jackson, flipping through the pages so fast that he ripped one page right out. He dialed the number quickly. "Donna? Lieutenant Jardine, Los Angeles Police. I was down there a couple of days ago, looking for a man and a little girl."

"Lieutenant, I've had you on my mind all morning. I was going to call you just as soon as I finished up with cleaning out the pool."

"We're looking for a woman named Ellen Carlin who may have stopped in yesterday, asking about the same man I mentioned. She's in her late thirties, white, dark hair—"

"She didn't just stop in here, Lieutenant. She checked in. Yup, here's the registration, but the name says Virginia Carlin, not Ellen. Virginia Carlin on both the registration and the MasterCard slip. I put her in unit 6, back in housekeeping. She checked in sometime in the afternoon, yes sir. Lee was watching Oprah, but I couldn't stop to watch because we found a wasp nest over the door of 12A. Well, that woman asked if I knew some man who stayed here a while back and it wasn't until this morning while I was cleaning out that pool, why it crossed my mind, that sounds a lot like the man the police were here looking for. I ought to call the lieutenant. I asked Lee and he said I watched too much TV and just keep my nose out of it. I was just about to go look for your card."

Jardine instructed Donna to check Ellen's room and call him right back. He motioned to Jackson to come back into Rukheyser's office, and filled them in, not only about what Ellen had said, but about Theresa and Joe DeLisi in Las Vegas and the homicide of Linda Lane Knox. Whitney Park slumped in a metal chair. When Rukheyser's phone rang, Jardine snapped it up before Rukheyser could touch it.

"Lieutenant? This is Donna. I'm calling from number 6. She's in here all right, and at first I thought she was dead. She's not hardly breathing and I got a pulse, but just barely. There's pill bottles all over, and an empty bottle of vodka on the floor. The phone was off the hook and she was half off the bed, like maybe she was trying to call someone. But that may have saved her because when she vomited, her head was down. I heard of people choking on their own—"

"Donna!" Jardine spoke sharply. "Call 911 immediately and then call me back."

"I already did, Lieutenant. And I can hear the sirens coming now. I got to go flag them down."

"Tell them that police officers will be on the scene as soon as possible. Donna, don't let anyone besides the medics in the room."

Jardine grabbed his file. "Seaside Villa, south of Long Beach," he said. "Jackson, call Long Beach and have them send a couple of squads over there. Tell them to consider the room a crime scene and have them seal it. Let's get the hell down there."

As THEY PULLED UP, Jardine saw Donna out in front of the pink stucco office next to the candy machine. She waved them on toward the back of the motel. A Long Beach officer stood by a squad car outside number 6; the ambulance had already left.

"They took her to the hospital down in Huntington Beach, sir," said the officer. Jardine entered the housekeeping unit first, Rukheyser elbowing past him. Dr. Park stood just outside the door, staring into the disheveled room.

The patrol officer continued. "First they pumped her stomach. There are a lot of pill bottles on the nightstand there, even some on the bed. There are some in the bathroom, too. Demerol, Halcion, Prozac, Tylenol. The motel owner, she found an empty bottle of vodka down on the floor there. There's an empty orange juice carton in the trash in the bathroom. She must have washed down an arsenal. I did remind the paramedics to treat everything as possible evidence, including bodily fluids."

"Don't touch anything in the room," Rukheyser instructed. "I'm going to want all the names of these medications, where they were filled, and the doctors who prescribed them. Did the medics think she was going to make it?"

"Touch-and-go. Her breathing was real shallow." The officer shrugged. "She's not dead yet."

Not dead, thought Jardine. *But she can't talk.*

He walked across the room slowly, scanning the top of the desk, behind the TV, under the bed. In the kitchenette along one wall, the counters were clean. He pulled open the wall cabinet. It held only one Melmac plate and a battered saucepan.

The bathroom vanity was cluttered with makeup and hair gels, sprays, shampoo. A prescription for codeine cough syrup, another for Tylenol with codeine. Jardine thought of all the years of Ellen's medicating Tory, not to heal her, but to make her sick. Now she had turned that same destructive behavior on herself. Swallow your medicine and die.

The shower curtain was pulled closed, and Jardine yanked it back. The bathtub was full of clean water. He stuck his hand in it: cold. There was the juice carton, in the wastebasket by the vanity. He riffled through the trash under the carton, and at the bottom of the wastebasket he found a plastic syringe. He picked it up with a piece of tissue and returned to the front room. Rukheyser was busy with the crime-scene investigators who had just arrived, the photographer asking what all they wanted pictures of, where he should start.

Outside the open door, Jardine could see Sondra Jackson crossing the parking lot toward number 6. He stepped out into the noon heat to join her, holding out the syringe as she approached, and told her where he found it.

Jackson raised her eyebrows. "You think Ellen Carlin shot up in addition to taking all those pills?"

"She never seemed like the junkie type. Besides," said Jardine, "it's too neat. If you were going to take a truckload of drugs to kill yourself, would you carefully shoot up in the bathroom, either before or after you swallowed the pills, and discreetly throw your works in the trash? And another thing—why is the orange juice carton in the trash in the bathroom? Wouldn't you mix your drinks in the kitchenette by the refrigerator? The ice bucket is sitting right there. Anyway, I can't see Ellen getting ready to commit suicide and tidying up the room first. Also, since she was drinking, where's the cup?"

"What cup?"

"That's what I'm saying. There isn't one. There are no cups in the room, clean or used." Jardine called to one of the crime-scene investigators, asking him to look for a cup.

"So what are you saying?" Sondra slipped her sunglasses on.

"Maybe someone was here with her," Jardine suggested. "Maybe somebody shot her up to make it look like a suicide. I don't like the bathtub. It's very close to how Oslin was killed. Only Ellen never made it to the tub."

Rukheyser called Jackson into the unit to speak with her, and Jardine strode across the grass to the playground merry-go-round where Theresa had been sitting two days ago, off in her mind somewhere. The back window of a Cutlass parked by the petunia bed was filled with Disneyland souvenirs. Jardine thought again of the snow domes, of Tory's hair found on Oslin's pillow. Who was Doc? How did Doc know Oslin?

White shoes, two pairs of white shoes. He thought of Royce Billings's mother, in her white uniform. Doctors didn't usually wear white shoes. Nurses did. Who gave Tory the snow domes? A nurse gave them to her, Ellen had said. But she couldn't remember which one, there had been so many.

Oslin had included Linda Lane Knox in a will he made out a year ago, one that was never filed. Left twenty grand to his college girl-friend. Jardine remembered wondering if Gerald Oslin and Ellen Car-lin might have had an affair, but what about Gerald and Linda? Maybe they had renewed their relationship during the time he and Jane had split up. But why did Linda have Tory's picture? Gerald gave it to her, but why?

Jardine checked his watch. Theresa should have called his pager by now. What flight did she say she was coming in on? She was sup-posed to be back in time for Camille Taylor's radio program; she was Camille's guest today. The flight from Vegas took less than an hour. Where the hell was she?

Jardine stalked around the corner to the motel office and Lee looked up as he entered. The dachshund on the green chair yapped.

"Can I use the phone?" Jardine asked. Lee set it on the counter. He called information and got the number for KESP. "Camille Taylor," he said gruffly.

"Sir, you can use the direct-dial number to call in to the show. Camille will be on the air in about five minutes and she'll be happy to answer your questions."

"I can't talk to her on the air," he said. "It's a private call and it's urgent. Tell her this is Jardine, with the Los Angeles Police. She'll talk to me."

The receptionist was silent. "She isn't going to be real happy to talk to the LAPD, but here goes."

He waited while some Third World drum played in the back-ground, then Camille came on the line.

"Hi, Camille. Is Theresa there?"

"No, and she's supposed to be. She's late. You got her all hung up in something again, don't you?"

"Don't blame me. Theresa makes her own choices."

"You can say that again. All I know is she ain't here now, and my cue is in about two minutes."

"Damn," he muttered. "I've got to reach her, Camille. Has she told you anything about what's been going on?"

"Bits and pieces, bits and pieces. Told me she was hot for this little girl's daddy and all in a state over it."

Jardine rolled his eyes. "That's who she was with last night in Las Vegas, and the man is suspected of murdering a woman while he was there."

"Vegas? What was she doing there? Lieutenant, tell you what. Resa never misses listening to my show. We always talk on Friday, and she gives me feedback. I know she'll be listening if she can get near a radio. She better be. I'll put out a message for her on the air."

"What are the call numbers, Camille? I want to listen, too."

He gave her several numbers where he could be reached, then shoved the phone across the counter toward Lee. When he turned to go out, Dr. Park came in.

"I'm going to go down to the hospital in Huntington Beach," said the doctor. "Sergeant Rukheyser says he's heading down there to talk to Ginny Carlin. He says there's a chance that this guy might be calling in with a ransom demand. Somebody's got to stay with Ellen. I'll ride down there with the Huntington Beach officers.

"Do you still think I'm involved in this?" asked Dr. Park.

"I'm working on it," said Jardine.

Park reached in his pocket again. "I have something else for you," he said, pulling out a thick white envelope. "That list of clinic employees you wanted. I went back three years."

The list was alphabetized by last names, so he almost missed it: Glendocker, Martin P., LPN. *Martin.* The name Jane Wood had seen on a genealogy at Oslin's.

Jardine pointed the name out to Park. "Tell me about Martin Glendocker. He was a nurse in your clinic?"

Park's brow creased. "No. I can't place him. I never had a male nurse at the clinic."

"Did he ever take care of Tory?"

He snapped his fingers. "That's it. Martin Glendocker. Marty. He didn't work at the clinic. He was a home-care nurse. He helped take care of Tory when Ellen and I went to Paris and another time when I had to be gone for a week. That's what she was trying to tell me on that tape—'Remember Paris . . .'"

"Why didn't you think of him, Park? I specifically asked for names of any care-givers."

"I paid him out of the clinic payroll. That's why he's on the list of clinic employees. He assisted a nanny we'd also hired. I think he was there some of the time and on call some of the time. I honestly just didn't remember him."

"What do you know about him? Can you describe him? Why would he register down here at this motel, Dr. Park, using your name? Did he bring Tory down here? Ellen obviously knew where Martin Glendocker lived, registered in her fiancé's name. That's why she came here to kill herself, right?"

"Jesus Christ." Park glanced up at Jardine, white-faced. "Martin Glendocker knew Gerald Oslin. It was Jane who recommended Martin Glendocker to me, and gave me his number. I'd been complaining to Jane that a trip Ellen and I had planned to Paris was going to be called off because Tory was sick. Jane said that she knew of an unemployed nurse who was looking for work. I didn't like the idea of hiring a male nurse, but Jane said he was a friend of Oslin's and we did have a nanny staying with Tory full-time. Glendocker was just supposed to check in with Tory once a day and be on call in case anything came up."

"Thanks," said Jardine. He ran back along the sidewalk to the housekeeping units. Jackson was still there, taking notes on her clipboard as the investigators examined the room.

"Sondra, do you have all those lists of employees from Kettler Hospital with you?" She flipped back the pages on the clipboard and removed a sheaf of lists: Kettler staff, patients, doctors, nurses. No Martin Glendocker, LPN.

"Oh, here's one more list," said Sondra. "Recent applications for jobs at Kettler. What are you looking for, Lieutenant?"

There it was: Martin Peter Glendocker, followed by his Social Security number and the address of the Seaside Villa in Huntington Beach. The date of application and interview was July 2, the day before Tory DeLisi disappeared.

"This is our man," said Jardine. "Now all we have to do is find him."

47

THE PLANE IDLED out on the runway and the pilot finally announced that they were going to have to go back to the terminal. There was a minor problem that needed servicing. The minor problem took over an hour, and they did not take off for L.A. until two o'clock.

Theresa tried to sleep on the flight, but she couldn't. Joe was silent and withdrawn. Clearing the air with some people backfired, she thought, and usually it was the people who were used to keeping a lot in the unconscious, the "unsaid." But Theresa also noticed that she, too, was withdrawn. The energy between them had flattened into something cold and dry, as if they'd gone on ahead and had sex, and it had gone badly.

By the time the plane descended toward LAX, circling out over the ocean, then back in for a landing, it was just after 3:00 P.M., Pacific time. Theresa felt anxious, checking the overhead bin and under the seat. Had she forgotten something in Vegas? Joe DeLisi walked beside her down the concourse, still aiming his silence at her like a fume. He needs to be angry for an audience, she thought. *But don't spew it all over me. Spare me.*

As they pushed through the glass doors of the terminal, DeLisi floundered toward an apology. "Theresa, I want to thank you for all you've done to help find Tory," he said. "I hope you won't let the things you've heard about me stop you. The stress of all of this, well . . . I'm not myself. I hope you understand."

She told him fine, fine, don't worry, but all she wanted right now was to get home, beyond the range of his energy field. They found her car in the parking lot—he'd left his parked on Washington near the canal—and as she pulled out onto Sepulveda, Joe turned on the radio. That's when it flashed through her: *Friday, Theresa. Camille's show.* She'd lost track and blown it completely. "Life Lines" had started at 2:00 P.M. and she'd promised Camille she'd be a guest today. Camille had even said they'd talk about issues concerning childhood, and that Theresa could discuss Tory. *Damn.*

"Do you mind if I switch to another station?" she asked, pressing Scan until she found KESP. "My friend's program is on."

"And if you've just joined us on 'Life Lines' this afternoon, we're talking about abandonment in present- and past-life contexts." Camille's caramel voice filled the car as Theresa turned the volume up. "Does what happened to you in the childhood of a former life affect you in this one? What seeds are you planting for your children right now that will affect them in future lifetimes? I'm going to be taking some more calls, and coming right up I have Angela on the line, calling in from Azusa. She says she has recurring and very distinct memories of a death experience—from three hundred years ago.

"But first I want to repeat a very important message that you may have heard me announce earlier. In a current case of a missing child, my good friend and frequent guest on 'Life Lines,' Theresa Fortunato, has been helping a family look for their daughter, Tory DeLisi."

This time it was Joe who cranked the volume up. Theresa wove through the afternoon traffic toward Venice.

"I'm sure many of you are following that case in the news," Camille continued. "Theresa, if you are listening in this afternoon, here's a message going out to you from Oliver Jardine. He urgently requests that you get in touch with him as soon as possible. Theresa Fortunato has been assisting families for some time now through an agency called the Simon Foundation for Missing Children and has been helpful to several families in locating their children. So, Theresa, I know you are out there somewhere and hope you will receive this urgent request for a phone call to Oliver Jardine or just call me here at the station. And now, Angela from Azusa. Go ahead, Angela."

Theresa pushed down on the accelerator, wheeling into the parking lot of a convenience store where a pay phone had been installed in a patch of weeds by the curb. "You stay in the car, Joe. See if she says anything else about Tory." She slid coins into the phone slot and dialed Jardine's pager, leaving her home number and the message "Call in five minutes." Then she called Camille and was put through on the private line into the studio.

"Resa," Camille answered, "hold on." She heard Camille put on a tape of rain, thunder sounds, and flute. Then she was back. "The lieutenant is all in a state, not knowing where you are. I don't know what all's going down, but he wouldn't try to track you down like this if it wasn't for real. Are you okay? Who's with you?"

"I'm okay, I'm with the girl's father, we just flew in from Las Vegas and we're heading back to my house."

"What are you driving?"

"My car, what else? Camille, call Jardine and tell him I'm on Sepulveda heading north and I should be home in a few minutes. Have him call me there and keep on trying until I pick up. And Camille," she said. "I completely spaced out the show. I'm sorry."

"Jardine told me you went on somebody else's show in Vegas and, honey, I will never forgive you." She laughed. "Don't worry, you can come on next week. But hey—somebody else really ain't going to forgive you if you don't take her out to celebrate her birthday."

Theresa closed her eyes. The smell of the traffic was making her lightheaded. "Sarene . . . " she whispered. "I'll call her. Thanks, Camille."

"Talk to you when I get done with the show."

Theresa slammed back into the car. "I got hold of Camille," she said to Joe, jerking out into traffic and swerving quickly around a slow truck.

"There wasn't any more about Tory on the radio. What's happening?"

"Camille didn't know. Just that Jardine was looking for me and something important was going on. I left word for Jardine to call me at home in a few minutes. We're almost there."

She took the corner at Washington with the tires whining, heading out toward the beach, and was signaling right when the siren blasted close up, then another bleating beside the car. Glancing at the rearview mirror for a second, she hit the brakes to avoid crashing into the squad car that squealed at an angle in front of her, then another next to her and another, her car surrounded by the squads now, red lights whirling crazily.

Her heart went black hot, fear stinging through her chest, as she noticed the rifles aimed at the car. Directly in front of the windshield, an officer assumed a stance, handgun held straight toward her face. The voice, loud, instructing her, "Put your hands on the wheel." She reached down to pull up on the emergency brake and the voice on the megaphone shouted, "Hands on the wheel! You, too, man! Bring them up slow!" Joe raised his hands. On the passenger side, the point of a rifle tapped against the window and the car doors were yanked open. An officer closed his grip around Theresa's arm, led her firmly out of the car, and began searching the front seat. Three officers dragged Joe from the car, he was spread-eagled against the hood. They patted him down under gunpoint.

Someone was screaming from a passing car, "Get down, lady! Get down!"

Theresa stepped up on the sidewalk. "What's going on?" she yelled. "What are you doing?!" She felt invisible, no one heard her. For a strange instant she wondered if she'd been shot, if this was death, a sudden exit where you got to stay and watch the rest of the show.

Joe was handcuffed. One cop was up close, reading him his rights. Roughly they escorted him to a squad car and shoved him in the back seat. Joe looked over at Theresa once, then away as the squad wheeled out, red lights spinning, the siren silenced now.

The cops finished searching her car. They'd opened the trunk, taking out her flight bag and digging under old beach blankets. An officer came toward her and handed her the keys. "All right, miss. You can go."

"Do you mind telling me what's going on?"

"Yes, ma'am. The man you were with was just arrested."

"No kidding. For what?"

"Murder." The cop turned and walked a few steps.

"Who? Who did he murder?"

"To tell you the truth, I don't know. They're bringing him in to question him. Somebody in Las Vegas."

"A child?"

"I don't think so."

"What about me?" Theresa asked.

The officer shrugged. "You're free to go, ma'am. The detective in charge will be getting in touch with you to take a statement."

Theresa got back in her car and drove the three blocks down Washington to the canal. She parked by the green water and waited to get out until she had stopped shaking.

Osiris wound around her legs, purring, as Theresa stood in the kitchen by the phone, waiting for Jardine to return her call. She couldn't get it out of her head: the black hole of that rifle barrel in her face, Joe's turning away in the squad car. What had happened in Las Vegas last night? She felt sick, not only at how he had used her, but how she kept accepting his explanations and apologies. Joe and Ellen never should have divorced, she thought. They were made for each other.

When Jardine called, she nearly yelled, "What is happening, Oliver? Who do they think he killed?"

"Gerald Oslin's college girlfriend," said Jardine. "Linda. Oslin had done a family tree for her. And she had a photocopy of Tory's picture on her refrigerator, the same one we got out of Oslin's office, only enlarged."

"Why? How would Joe even know this woman?"

'We don't know that yet. But a Smith & Wesson registered to

DeLisi was found next to the bed where she was murdered. DeLisi is in very big trouble unless you can provide him with a complete, iron-clad alibi for all of last night."

"No, I can't do that. He had his own room."

"Did he stay in it?" Jardine asked.

Suddenly she was angry, heat flooding her cheeks. "There were a number of hours last night when I was not with Joe DeLisi."

"Which hours, Theresa?"

"Most of them. He left my room just after ten, Lieutenant, not too long after he hung up on you. I didn't see him again until he sat next to me on the plane. That was about noon." Osiris had jumped up on the counter, and she ran her hand over his fur.

Jardine went on to tell her about the tape Park had brought in, about finding Ellen at the Seaside Villa, about finding out Doc's real name and how he was connected to both Oslin and Tory.

"It still doesn't fit," said Theresa. "Why would Joe murder Oslin and his old girlfriend?"

"He might not have. He might have hired Martin Glendocker to do it for him."

"But why?"

"Maybe Gerald Oslin and Linda Knox knew, for some reason, that Joe DeLisi had hired Glendocker to kidnap Tory. Glendocker might have told them what he was up to, or they found out, and he wanted them quiet."

Theresa pulled the phone over to the table at the center of the kitchen and sat down. She could feel the adrenaline crashing in her body like too much caffeine.

"We'll find him in no time now, Theresa. We've got his Social Security number and the photograph off his driver's license number."

Finally, Theresa asked, "How about Ellen? How is she doing?"

"I called down to the hospital about an hour ago. Her mother is there with her. She's in intensive, in a coma."

"What did she take?"

"There was a whole pharmaceutical company in the room when we got there—sleeping pills, antidepressants, even a big bottle of Tylenol. There was also a used syringe, an empty fifth of vodka, and an orange juice carton in the trash. We're waiting to hear from the lab to see just what she took. Look, Theresa, I have to get downtown. We're going to be interviewing DeLisi. What are you up to?"

"Somehow I'm just not in the mood for a wild Friday night."

"I can't imagine why."

"I'll probably go over to Camille's." *Don't forget to call Sarene,* she reminded herself.

"Stay where I can get in touch with you, will you?" Jardine asked.

Theresa still felt lightheaded, and she realized she hadn't eaten since breakfast. What she really needed was a hot bath and then she'd take herself out to eat at the Island Café.

In the tub, she kept picturing pickup sticks, those little colored plastic ones she'd had as a kid, all crisscrossing in a jumble on the floor. Trying to pick them up one by one, to avoid making the others move. Which sticks were touching? Which was under, which over? How were they interconnected and what was the pattern?

After her bath she lay down in her robe on the couch, and listened to an old Flora Purim tape, and was startled to awaken later in the semidarkness. In her bedroom, she dressed in jeans and a white silk T-shirt, a string of amber beads around her neck. There on her dresser were the pillbox and the angelfish snow dome, sitting on the file that held the drawings, the original sketch of Doc, and Tory's snapshot. She never had gotten all those things back to Ellen. She brought it all back out to the patio table, along with the brown bag of Tory's things. Pink Christmas lights glowed in one of the cedars, casting a pale light on the table where she examined each object, holding them for a moment, trying to quiet herself, make herself receptive to Tory, but all she felt was an eerie stillness inside her. She didn't know what it meant, but it made her lonely.

Theresa looked again at the drawing of Tory in the car, the one with the images circling around in the sky of the picture like funny clouds: some kind of animal, a ship, a castle with fireworks, a unicorn. She didn't know why she hadn't noticed it before: this drawing, which had come to her the night Tory disappeared, matched the missing snow domes exactly. But why these particluar ones? Why had Tory ended up with these domes?

A brown animal in a cage, the snow dome of a monkey. Zoo. Of course. A ship, the *Queen Mary*. The castle surrounded by stars. That had to be Disneyland. And the unicorn, the unicorn on a carousel, the merry-go-round, a midway . . . All the places a child on a trip might ever want to go, to have the perfect happy day, to make all the bad things seem to disappear. All the places you'd take a child if you wanted to relive your childhood again—not, perhaps, the way it was, but the way you wished it had been.

She placed the items in a brown bag one by one with a feeling of sadness. It was almost as if she were saying good-bye to Tory, the child in her imagination whom she had never met.

It was not until she was getting ready to head over to the Island Café that Theresa again remembered Sarene. Some surrogate auntie, she thought; her birthday was almost a week ago. She picked up the phone to leave a message for her at her mom's, and was surprised when Sarene answered.

"I haven't been ignoring you, I promise," said Theresa.

"You have too!" Sarene said. "But it's okay, because I figured out where I want to go. My friends all went yesterday and said it was so fresh. We could go tomorrow!"

"Where?" asked Theresa.

"The Orange County Fair, it opened yesterday. And I want to go on all the rides my friends went on, Quasar, Gravitron, Ultra Mirror Maze. There's even a funhouse called Superstition Mountain. And Resa? Do you think it would be all right if I brought my boyfriend, Quinzy? I know you'll like him and I need you to talk Mom into liking him. Please?"

Theresa promised they would go the next night. When she hung up, she felt a dead-still calm come over her, the lucid knowing she felt only at the center of her deepest readings. The realization went through her in a slow, light space. Ellen had not tried to commit suicide; someone had tried to kill her. Theresa knew who it was.

And she knew exactly where to find Tory.

48

THE FAIRGROUND PARKING LOT was crowded. A wave of screams from a roller coaster rose up over the midway lights. Beyond that, the red edge of the sky glowed, a last shred of daylight. Doc held Tory's hand as they wound through the cars. They were wandering in a maze, he thought, looking for cheese. Like a couple of dumb rats.

Tory seemed happier since she had talked on the phone to her grandmother. *Thinks she'll be home soon.* Just his luck to call her parents, trying to demand ransom money, and neither of them ever there to answer. *Leave your name at the sound of the fucking beep. I'm sorry, sir, Dr. DeLisi does not seem to be answering. Right.* That's why Doc had called Ellen's mother this morning and put Tory on the phone with her. He'd met her once or twice at Ellen's when he'd stayed there. But he still didn't know exactly how he should proceed. He hadn't planned on this at all.

For a long time, Doc had felt separated from everything he'd ever done. Part of him was just off to the side, always giving him shit, saying, *Now what have you done, you stupid idiot? Now you're really in trouble.* But tonight he didn't think he was. He'd call Ellen's mother again and have her mail the cash to a post-office box. Or another idea was to have her put the money in a brown paper bag and drop it in a trash can on Venice Beach. He'd dress as a homeless person, so they wouldn't be able to identify him. He'd have Tory with him, and if any cops were around, forget it. Something like that. He'd figure it out.

He paid for their tickets and, just after they pushed through the turnstile, there was a pay phone against a white wall. "Want to call Grandma again?" he asked. *Keep them hoping, give them time to come up with the cash.* Ellen's mother didn't live far from the fairgrounds, Doc realized. Just over in Huntington Beach. "Tory, all I want you to do is say, 'Hi, Grandma,' and tell her you'll be home real soon."

Tory held the phone to her ear for what seemed an awfully long time.

"What, isn't anybody home?" Doc asked. "No answer?"

"Hi, Gram," Tory said flatly. "I'm all right and I'll be home soon."

Doc reached over and pressed the lever, cutting the call off. "What was that about?" he demanded.

Tory looked down, shrugged. "I did what you said."

"Damn right, you did." When Tory cringed visibly, he felt bad. He saw that if you were going to kidnap a child for ransom or to hurt them, you couldn't have a heart. You couldn't care about them. If you were doing it because you cared about them, it was worse, because you could feel their sadness and fear. It was clear now that he was no different from his parents, all four of them. He'd tried to be good to Tory, but he had betrayed her. Was that the secret of being a father, was that what he was doomed to?

Tory seemed resigned. Patient. She was a good kid. He would have made a shitty father, he saw that now. He was good with the treats and the fun stuff, the zoo and the *Queen Mary* and Disneyland, all of that. Even this, a night at the Orange County Fair. Free rides. All the junk food she could want. He was going to win her something, too, he'd promised. A great big dog, a shaggy one in some fluorescent color. But the day-to-day stuff, breakfast, lunch, and dinner, laundromats, combing hair. Not to mention they didn't even have a house and she'd have to start school in September. Make bag lunches, earn Girl Scout badges, practice the piano, make valentines. And try to hide forever, with her wanting her mom or her dad the whole time. So it wasn't going to work, Tory being his kid, his daughter, his baby girl. She wouldn't go for it, and he didn't blame her. She wasn't a baby. And she wanted to go home.

As he bought a cherry rainbow snow cone, Tory stared at the fat man in the booth. He had a dragon tattooed on his hairy shoulder. "How do they get the ink to go in between the hairs?" she asked.

The blacktop under their feet was still warm from the sun. He always wanted childhood to be like this, banners whipping in the wind, yellow lights by the Texas Taco booth, pink lights by Dog on a Stick. Maybe that's what he would do next, see if he could get a job with the midway, head out of town when the fair moved on. Get an Airstream trailer like the one they'd abandoned in that state park.

They walked through the Parade of Products, looking at the hard-boiled-egg dicers and birdhouses that would keep squirrels off. Tory asked if she could put something in the Time Capsule, a message maybe, a letter to someone.

"To who?" Doc asked.

"Mom."

"I thought you hated her."

"No, you do," Tory said.

"You don't hate her?"

"I'm kind of scared of her, but I miss her anyway."

She wanted a Texas Taco, then, and she sat eating it on a bench by the band shell, American flags fluttering all around the gazebo roof. Next she asked for a souvenir, and Doc handed her a ten. She came back with a white stuffed unicorn.

"Look!" she said. "Just like the one in my snow dome."

"All the places in those snow domes that are in California—we've been to them all. The *Queen Mary*, the zoo, Disneyland, and now here. This unicorn means we came to the right place," Doc said. "But if we're going to go everywhere in the snow domes I gave you, we'd better get busy."

"We never went to San Francisco, Phoenix, the Bahamas . . . "

"And what about Graceland?" Doc asked. "Don't you want to go see the mansion where Elvis lived?"

"I don't really like Elvis that much. He's dead. Anyway, you never gave me that one."

"Right. That's the one I wanted."

"And anyway, you said I could go home soon. I don't want to go anywhere else."

"Come on. Let's go on some rides," he suggested.

"Goody," she said, hugging the unicorn.

"You can keep them," Doc said, "the domes. But promise you'll think of me when you look at them. You know, I got those domes from my dad."

"You did? The dad that adopted you?"

"No. My real dad. He had a whole collection of them. He gave them to me, and I want you to have them. So you can remember me."

Tory looked down at her feet in blue thongs. Her feet were awful dirty, he thought. She needed a bath.

"Are you scared of me, too?" he asked.

She nodded. "Ever since last night."

"You weren't afraid of me before that?"

Tory thought about it. "Sort of, but I pretended I wasn't. Then I forgot I was pretending."

"I'm sorry I had to scare you," he said. "Do you forgive me?"

She looked past him, toward the Ferris wheel. "What happened to your real mom and dad?" she asked.

"They died," he told her. "Come on." They meandered toward the midway, browsing at the souvenir booths selling flags with skulls and crossbones and fuzzy black rugs with pictures of Jesus or a red motor-cycle woven right into them.

Tory seemed very small beside him, close up against him while he bought ride tickets. "I want to walk all the way around first," she said, "so I know which ones I want to go on." They strolled past the Gravi-tron, the Tilt-a-Whirl, the Ninja Slide. Club Fun, Fantasma.

"That one first," she said, taking a ticket from Doc's hand and get-ting in line. He told her he'd wait for her right here, and he'd hold her unicorn.

When he was about twelve, he'd had a dog, a ratty black mutt he'd found at the quarry. His father hadn't liked the dog much, he used to shove the dog out of the way with his foot when the mutt came sniffing and wagging. Sometimes his father would kick him. He bullied the dog

and he bullied Doc. He was mean to his wife. The sad thing was that
the dog always tried to nuzzle up close to his father. Sit right at his
feet and just look up at him, begging for some tidbit of affection. Tory
reminded him of that.

He watched as Tory climbed onto the ride and found a seat. *How
did I get into this mess in the first place?* he wondered. It was that letter from Gerald Oslin, sent to him in care of the nursing home where
he'd been working part-time, nights. How long ago? A year? How
bizarre to hear from some total stranger out of the blue, announcing,
*I'm your father, your real father, and I'd like very much to get in touch
with you.* He'd never known he had a son, the letter said, until six
months before. He'd been searching for him ever since.

It was curiosity more than anything else that made Doc call the
number on the letter, some antique store in L.A. He wondered if he
would look like his father. What kind of life would he have had if this
man had been aware he'd had a son? And how come he hadn't known?
It gave Doc a weird feeling, as if he had a second life, running parallel
to his, one where he was happier, richer, and more loved.

They arranged to meet over lunch at a Big Boy in Torrance, and
Doc couldn't stop studying the man's face for some sign of himself.
They were both big, that was about it. Maybe a little something in the
eyes was the same. Gerald Oslin told him that he'd recently been back
in touch with a college girlfriend he'd had before he went into the navy,
back in the fifties. His girlfriend had read about him in the alumni
newsletter, about how Oslin had started doing genealogies, research-
ing family trees, how Oslin had found out he'd been adopted and had
contacted his natural mother. That he'd always had a feeling something was missing because he'd never been told, until he was an adult,
that he was adopted. The old girlfriend, Linda, knew that wasn't the
only thing missing from Gerald Oslin's family tree.

She wrote to him and told him she'd given birth to a son after he'd
gone in the service. Never told him about it; they'd broken up or lost
touch and she'd gone on to marry someone else. The baby had been put
up for adoption through an agency in California. Linda thought he
would want to know.

Gerald Oslin told Doc it hadn't been all that hard to find him.
He'd joined a birth-mother support group, and used the same methods
that had led him to find his mother—adoption agency records, Social
Security, the army. And what a coincidence, both of them living right
here in Southern California. He'd never had any other children. He
wanted to make it up to him; throw a baseball around in the back-

yard, go fishing, do all the things that fathers and sons were supposed to do.

They started hanging out together. At first Doc liked it. He saw Oslin had money, a nice big house. Maybe he could move in with him. Oslin wasn't too hot on that idea, but said there was a possibility he could come up with a down payment for a house for Doc. He really wanted to be there for Doc, he said. Doc was laid off from the nursing home and Oslin helped him get some jobs, including the one with the doctor. Where he'd met Tory, where he'd met Ellen.

Maybe it was all that family feeling that made Doc like Tory so much. He took care of her for two weeks while Park and Ellen went to Paris. He wondered how he'd gotten to be in his late thirties and never had kids. Maybe he had a kid out there somewhere. Maybe *he* should adopt. He and Tory got on great, and Doc started bringing her little presents, things he found around Oslin's house. She especially liked those snow domes. Whenever he brought her one, they'd pretend they were going there, and they'd make up stories about the fun they'd have. She'd shake the dome, watching the snow swirl inside the glass.

A month after she came back from Paris, Ellen hired Doc to take care of Tory, even though Ellen wasn't going away on a trip. Doc thought it was strange that Ellen didn't just take her daughter to the hospital, but after he'd been in the house a few days, he observed Ellen giving Tory an injection of something. Watching her closely, he saw what she was up to. He ought to have called the cops, but he had this idea. The main thing was to stop her from hurting Tory, but why not get something out of it, too? When he confronted her, she paid him all right, a grand in cash. The real surprise was fucking her. He didn't know what to make of it, but she wanted it, and he sure didn't mind.

It was like a grimy secret that, when they thought about it, made them want to hurt each other, but for a while it seemed a kind of love. He'd never had a woman of her class after him like that. He stayed at her home another week, taking care of Tory and having sex with Ellen. Another fake family. Maybe she thought if she went to bed with him, that would bond him to her and he'd stop asking for money. He didn't.

She brought the next grand down to a motel where he'd checked in, south of Long Beach. He thought it was funny, registering in her fiancé's name. He stayed on, renting a housekeeping unit by the month. The next week she called and said she'd found out he was working without a license and she'd turn him in to the state if he ever tried to get money from her again. He didn't bother. He was sick of her anyway, she was crazy.

And he'd made out okay—not just the money she'd given him, but some other things he'd wanted. Some silver and jewelry. Her Smith & Wesson. This and that. Things he found stashed away. Steal what people have hidden, he'd discovered; they wouldn't notice it.

He did feel sorry for Tory, though. They'd become friends. She'd even given him one of her school pictures and he put it in his wallet.

Meanwhile, Oslin started in on him. He was no different from any father, adopted or natural. Wanted Doc to get his hair cut, stop wearing an earring, get some decent clothes, go into treatment, go to AA, go to NarcAnon, quit smoking weed, lose weight, the whole shot. Get more of an education. It was worse than his adoptive father, because Oslin was a perfectionist. Oslin kept telling Doc to get his life together, criticizing him all the time. On his ass every time they got together, calling all the time to see if he'd put in that job application, seen that counselor, taken the test to renew his nursing license. The hell with that, Doc thought. He was going to tell Oslin to fuck off. He liked his life better before Oslin had tracked him down, but he started thinking. *Play along, Marty, play along. Lay low, wait for opportunity to knock.*

There were little ways he started planning ahead. For what, he didn't know. He watched carefully when Oslin shut off the security system in the house or the store when they went in, and he memorized the code numbers. Found spare keys in a desk in Oslin's study at home and had copies made, put them back before they were noticed. Extra set of credit cards, lower right-side desk drawer. He didn't take those, but he knew where they were when he might need them. Got the old man to shell out for some classes at a community college. Then he withdrew and kept the money. He was trying to figure a way to get the big bucks he knew Oslin must have; that's when he got the idea that old Dad might give him the down payment for a house.

The other idea hit him one day when Oslin looked over his shoulder as he was paying for some beer. Oslin saw the picture of the little girl and asked him who it was. It was brilliant, the way it flashed through him. Oslin was a sucker for family connections. "Well, that's your granddaughter," Doc had said. "That's my little girl. Her mother lives in Hawaii, and I'm trying to get custody of her. I'm way overdue on my child-support payments." Maybe Oslin could help out. Maybe Oslin would start coughing up for her college fund, too. He took the school photo out of his wallet when he was visiting Oslin at the store one day. Oslin was pissed he'd stopped in there, but he took Tory's picture and stuck it right up there with his sister's portrait.

Doc began to see that Oslin was ashamed of him. Oslin never had a family reunion dinner, introducing Doc to his sister and mother and all. Wouldn't let him stay at the house, much less move in. Finally stopped having him over to the house at all. Never introduced him to his girlfriend. He knew he wasn't welcome in the stuffed-shirt antique store. Doc knew Oslin had started to mistrust him. Maybe he'd started missing things around his house, the snow domes, a camera, this and that. Oslin began to recoil from him, as everyone he'd ever been close to had done. He began to feel Oslin's disgust, his fear of him, and he hated Oslin for that.

So Doc decided he'd had it with all that shit. He'd never been part of a family that had ever felt good and happy. It always soured, love gone rancid like a thing left in the back of a refrigerator, once nourishing. But he began to wish he did have a daughter in Hawaii. Maybe he even half believed that he did. If Tory was his kid, by God, she'd be a lot better off than she was with her own mother. He'd raise her up right, give her the home he never had. The one that fucker Oslin had never provided, and all because of him and Linda, Doc had spent his entire childhood in foster homes, boys' homes, detention centers, not to mention the scum that eventually adopted him and treated him worse than that wagging dog.

The army was the only place he'd ever felt he belonged. Only place with some order to it. He'd liked the guns, and afterward he'd gone to nursing school on the GI bill; he'd been a medic in Vietnam.

So he'd known it was coming to an end with Oslin. The old man would confront him soon, maybe even call the cops. Doc sent him a postcard saying he'd found a house and thanks for the down payment. Gave him those roses for Father's Day because Oslin liked flowers. He tried to string him along a little while longer.

When Doc went over to Kettler that day to apply for a job, and saw Ellen Carlin stepping out of that elevator, he had a feeling like crossed destiny, another parallel life opening up before him. If he could do one thing right, it might cancel out a lifetime of error, starting with the very fact of his mistaken birth. He knew which floor Tory would be on, and he searched until he found her. When he saw how sick she was, he knew he was an angel sent to save her. He knew she'd save him, too. Then and there he decided to make a decent life for the two of them. He'd find a good woman to marry, buy that house. Give Tory a good home. That was the idea. Take her and disappear into a fresh, clean life.

It wasn't until afterward, out at the truck motel in the desert, that Doc remembered Oslin had Tory's picture. Oslin would read about it in the paper and he'd know who took the kid. If he wanted to really make it work, Oslin would have to go.

Anyway, Doc hated him.

Oslin had been surprised to see him last Sunday. Brought my little girl by to meet grandpa, Doc had said. She's visiting from Hawaii, fell asleep in the camper, so tired from the trip. Oslin had gone out to look at her. Brought a bottle of wine to celebrate buying the house, Doc had said. He stirred the chloral hydrate into the wine and Oslin was out.

Seeing him in the water, his father's face submerged, blank eyes looking at nothing. *You never existed for me. Just like I never existed for you.* It wasn't until a few days later that he thought of Linda. Remembered Oslin mentioning he'd sent a photocopy of Tory's photo to Linda.

Now they were both gone, but it was all another error. Everything he touched was contaminated.

It occurred to him now, watching the Fantasma slow down, maybe he should just walk away. The hell with the ransom money. He had taken plenty from Gerald. Anyway, it was too hard, the way they knew how to mark cash and all that. What he should do, Doc thought, was just give Tory some money and the rest of the tickets, put her on the next ride, and he'd be history. Drive out to the airport, buy a ticket for Cancún. They'd never find him down there. That's what I'll do, he thought. She'll always remember I tried to save her, even though I failed.

No one would be able to track him down. Now that Gerald and Linda were gone, no one could trace him to Tory.

Doc stood in the night breeze, smelling popcorn and grease, listening to heavy metal blasting out of the next ride over as Tory skipped down the Fantasma exit ramp. She ran to him, reaching up for the unicorn. He would miss her.

"I'll go on one ride with you," he told her. "Then the rest of the tickets are all yours."

"The Ferris wheel!" she cried.

As they stood in line, he realized that Gerald and Linda were not the only ones who could trace him to Tory. Not at all. There was the man in that used-car lot. The cashier at Kmart. Maybe even Dani-with-an-*i*.

There was Ellen.

There was Tory herself.

And last—that picture on the news last night in Vegas, that psychic, the one that had drawn that picture that looked exactly like him.

Whoever *she* was. She knew.

49

THERESA ENTERED THE FAIRGROUNDS, pushing through the turnstile into the world beyond the gate. A Dixieland band was playing in the gazebo ahead, and from her right came the roars, squeals, and din of the midway. Now that she was here, it all looked terribly familiar, as if she were returning to a place she'd been in childhood. But this was Tory's childhood, and Theresa was walking into *her* present as she had foreseen it. For a moment she felt a panic in her chest like birds rising up off a salt marsh, hundreds of them flapping wings, wind brushing her breath. Theresa sat on a bench by the bandstand, waiting until the wing-drumming anxiety in her heart slowed down. Scanning the crowd, she shifted into field vision, not a staring or a looking-for, but an opening up of attention to the periphery of sight, letting her seeing float freely, allowing details, objects, and perceptions to draw her gaze.

It was Friday night, and the fair streets were packed with visitors. She needed to be as receptive as possible, without picking up on every person that passed her by. She took some time to imagine a filter in front of her eyes, like an odd pair of sunglasses. *Only let me see what I need to see. Light-shield around me.*

Passing a pay phone on a white wall, she stopped to call Jardine again. She'd left a message on his pager before leaving the house: *Meet me ASAP, Orange County Fair midway. Theresa.* Now she tried him again, leaving the pay-phone number so he could return the call. Ten minutes, fifteen: she watched the passersby with their children, waiting for a muscle man and a little girl with a pageboy haircut. Her panic had subsided; her mind was now lucid and prescient. She imagined floating down to the midway in a translucent bubble, like Glinda in Oz. *Wish I had a wand,* she thought. She had only this listening and the voices and images that came to it.

Theresa could no longer wait for Jardine. It was pulling her forward. She felt compelled to walk along the blacktop strewn with the litter of snow-cone cups and popcorn boxes, past the aisle of snack booths. It was as if a string were unreeling out of her chest, her heart following. As if she had no choice. *But I do,* she thought. *There is always a choice. Fate is no more than the moment showing up and you being present to it. Doc won't recognize me, he's never seen me before. Neither has Tory.*

The wind was warm; it shook the souvenirs that hung in bunches from the side of a vendor's shack. Theresa blurred her vision slightly, all lights spiraling into soft focus. The crowd shifted around her in one bright, rhythmic body swaying into the midway.

Where is she? Theresa walked slowly, trying to feel for her now, not just with eyes but body-seeing. *Carousel,* she thought. *A merry-go-round with a unicorn.* She wandered past the Ultra Mirror Maze and Club Fun, Gravitron, Quasar. She had heard those names in the vision, and when Sarene had rattled them off on the phone, she had known this was the place she saw the first night that Tory came to her. She passed a fun house called Superstition Mountain, a large mural of an Indian on one side of it, an evil-looking prospector on the other. There did not seem to be a carousel.

Stop, stop here. She watched the Gravitron spin, a giant wheel, people inside a cylinder, pressed back against the white grid walls by centrifugal force. The Gravitron tilted on its side, and everyone screamed with pleasure.

The ride slowed and the people unstrapped themselves, laughing, holding their stomachs, coming down the exit runway. *Here,* she thought. Theresa backed up into the space between the Gravitron and the Ferris wheel, stepping over electric cords into the sticky spill of ice cream and syrupy snow cones on the blacktop. No child, no girl. *Tory,* she thought, *Where are you?* She did not see Tory on the ride.

Around her, the world slowed. She'd felt this way once in a car accident, as if time had spread out. A surge of adrenaline released in her brain, saying, *This is it. Stop.* A man passed her hiding place and she stepped out into the crowd to follow him. No child with him. He wore a tan business suit, tall and thin, nothing like she'd imagined, pale hair nearly white. *Not him,* she thought. *Then why . . .*

It was the way he was walking, different from the rest of the crowd, stopping now ahead of her, his coat flying open as he turned. She glimpsed it, one second, black against the white of his shirt, a gun in a holster under his arm. He was wearing sunglasses. She swerved over to the edge of the blacktop, stood against a guessing-game booth where you could throw coins on plates to win cheap jewelry. He squinted behind his glasses. She knew he saw her. Theresa looked down as he came toward her through the crowd, and then he broke into a run. She spun back, scrambling between the two rides, their generators buzzing out hot air as she stumbled between them. Her foot caught on an electric cord and she fell, hitting her head against the metal stairs that went up the back of the Gravitron.

She looked up above her at the Ferris wheel, one of those new ones with boatlike cars, people facing each other inside them, oohing and ahing. *And there she was.* Tory, wheeling down, a stuffed animal clutched against her chest. Across from her sat Doc. He was muscular, square jawed, wearing a black cowboy hat. The Ferris wheel lifted them up again through the music and the sparkling lights.

The thin man she'd thought was Doc stood over Theresa now and yanked her up by the arm. He removed the sunglasses.

"Rukheyser!" she snapped.

"*Sergeant* Rukheyser, Fortunato. Where is she? Where's Tory DeLisi?" He reached inside his coat, unsnapping the holster.

No, she thought, *no guns.* Years ago, when she'd helped Jardine find that serial killer, it had come to this. The police closed in and shot, but they killed the wrong person. Michael had died in her arms. She had heard his last breath, the sucking in his chest as he'd tried to whisper her name.

"Don't use that," she pleaded.

"We're dealing with an armed and very dangerous man," said Rukheyser.

"Who has a child with him."

"Where, Theresa! Tell me where she is."

"Where's Jardine?" she demanded.

"He's here, he's looking for you, too. We tapped Ginny Carlin's line and traced a call that Tory made from a pay phone here at the fair. Jardine got your pager message about the same time. Now, if you know where the kid is, you goddamn well better tell me." He grabbed her arm again, hard.

"Leave me alone!" Theresa yelled.

A large Black man in a Lakers T-shirt approached them. A small crowd had paused behind them, straining to see between the rides. "Having some trouble, miss?" the man asked in a loud voice.

"Los Angeles Police Department," Rukheyser snapped back. "She's working with us."

"Is that right, miss? You a cop?"

"No!"

"You got an awful lot of witnesses here," the man said to Rukheyser.

"We don't need no kind of police brutality scene going down. We had enough of that in this town. Sir," he added.

Rukheyser let go of Theresa's arm, turned and stalked back out onto the blacktop.

"Was he harassing you?" the man asked Theresa.

"Yes. Thanks," she said. "I'm okay."

Glancing up, she saw Jardine striding toward her in his gray suit and tie, looking like the most obvious cop in the whole world, sticking out in the jumble of T-shirts, shorts, and halter tops. He spotted Theresa, and as he ran toward her, she glanced back as the Ferris wheel spun Tory by one more time. Tory was gazing straight up at the faint suggestion of stars.

"She's on the Ferris wheel, right there," said Theresa. "Doc is with her."

Jardine watched the brightly lit Ferris wheel spin by. When Theresa looked again, she saw Doc scanning the crowd below as he pushed his hand into the pocket of his jacket.

"I think he's armed," said Jardine.

Sondra Jackson seemed to appear from nowhere, out of the shadows. She nodded a greeting and Jardine told her Tory and Doc were on the ride.

"Go tell the operator to keep the Ferris wheel going," Jardine instructed. "Don't stop and don't let anyone off until I signal you."

"What are you going to do?" Theresa asked.

"I want you to go." Jardine took her by the shoulders. "I don't want you getting hurt."

"Be careful, Oliver. Be careful of Tory."

"She's our primary concern, believe me."

Jardine took a position at the side of a ticket booth, watching as Sondra discreetly flashed her badge to the Ferris wheel operator in his orange jumpsuit. Theresa was not going anywhere. She bolted across the blacktop between two RVs and waited there in the darkness, praying Tory would not be hurt.

The shots cracked out above the screams that rose in unison from the Gravitron. Two shots, like a car backfiring. The man in the orange jumpsuit looked up, not understanding what had happened. The chest wound was staining through his uniform, and he staggered back.

Now the screams changed from delight to terror as the crowd began to realize what was happening: *gunshot, cops, dead.* Someone screamed, "There's a sniper up on the Ferris wheel!" Theresa watched as a little boy fell and a woman ran over him.

The operator slumped limply over the controls. The Ferris wheel sped up, spinning faster through the dizzy lights, the boatlike cars lurching and swinging crazily back and forth as the ride went out of control.

Shots again—two, three—and the crowd trampled back, fleeing until there was an empty space around the Ferris wheel. Theresa could not see Sondra or Jardine.

But there was Tory, spinning around on the giant wheel. Doc had her in his lap, his gun held near her face, against her throat. She was still clutching the unicorn. The Ferris wheel zoomed up again, the cars clanging against the metal support girders.

And then she saw Jardine, high up, climbing a support beam, on metal rungs that protruded like a ladder to climb for repairs. He crawled up, poised there a moment, then leapt into the car just behind the one Doc and Tory were in. Doc doesn't see him, Theresa thought.

Rukheyser bent over the jumpsuit-clad man, and jerked the brake down. The Ferris wheel lurched to a sudden halt, the cars swinging wildly. Some of the other rides had also stopped now, but the ones farther down the midway kept going, blaring rock and roll. But a circle of silence surrounded the Ferris wheel. The people on the ride crouched down in the cars. A teenage boy bounded from one of the lower cars, and Rukheyser shouted, "Stay where you are! Everyone stay where you are, and stay down!"

The car Tory and Doc were in had come to a stop halfway down the wheel. Doc leaned toward Tory's ear, yelling something. Jardine crouched over them in the car above, taking aim. Tory cried out in a shuddering, high-pitched wail. The midway had become nearly silent. Suddenly she shouted, "Please don't shoot! He's my friend!"

"Let her go, Glendocker! Drop the weapon!" Jardine shouted from the car above. The wheel descended, bringing them down.

Startled, Doc looked up and Tory broke from his hold, throwing herself to the other side of the car. The car tipped and swung to one side. Doc half-fell, half-lunged toward Tory. As he grabbed for her, she ducked and pushed up.

Doc lost his balance and hurtled out of the car, arms pinwheeling as he fell to the blacktop, facedown. Sondra Jackson was at his side immediately. She held her gun on him as he tried once to get up, then collapsed on his chest.

Rukheyser eased the control bar up and brought Tory's car down to the loading platform. He opened the door and she crouched on the floor of the car, holding the fuzzy white unicorn. Theresa walked toward them, moving through the crowd.

She wanted to go to Tory, to hold her in her arms, stroke her hair, tell her everything would be okay, but Tory didn't know Theresa as anything but a distant listening star.

TORY STAYED CROUCHED DOWN in the Ferris wheel car. She had frozen the way small animals do when threatened; even her eyes were still, downcast. Rukheyser knelt by the open door of the car, displaying his badge for her to see, speaking to her gently, reassuring her that no one was going to hurt her. Everything was all right. She would not come out. Theresa watched from the crowd that had gathered, a sea of quiet witnesses, craning to see. As another officer covered Doc, Sondra Jackson grabbed his gun from the pavement.

Sirens screamed from a distance and an ambulance appeared, pulling up at the base of the Ferris wheel. The crowd split apart to make room for it. Fair security guards and uniformed officers pushed through the packed midway, holding the crowd back from the man who'd been shot and the man who'd fallen.

Medics scrambled to minister to the Ferris wheel operator. They lifted him onto a stretcher and then into the ambulance. Jackson handcuffed Doc where he lay facedown on the ground. He'd seemed unconscious for a few minutes, but had come around. Two uniformed officers brought him to his feet and escorted him to a squad car. He got in calmly, glancing once over at Tory. As the door was slammed, he looked directly at Theresa, but did not seem to recognize her.

Theresa took a good look at him, at the face she had imagined. A real human face was so substantial, so complex. Yes, he resembled the image in her mind, but her inner vision seemed airy and vague now that she saw him in the flesh. All the details had been there in her readings, but she couldn't say it had coalesced into this exact face. The squad car pulled away, driving out toward the far end of the midway.

Sondra Jackson joined Rukheyser at the Ferris wheel. She spoke with Tory for a while, and gave her a stick of gum from her hip pouch. At last Tory stood, and Sondra held her hand as she walked down the exit ramp.

Another operator took over the controls of the Ferris wheel, bringing the rest of the cars down and unloading the passengers, including Jardine. A second squad car had emerged from the parted crowd, and Ginny Carlin climbed from the backseat. "Tory!" she cried, and the child ran to her grandmother, burrowing into Ginny Carlin's shoulder and neck, hiding her face. But it was Ginny who was crying, saying over and over, "Thank God, Thank God . . . Oh, my little precious . . . Thank God . . . "

Rukheyser put a hand on Ginny Carlin's arm and motioned for them to go to the squad car. Theresa felt the anxious wings in her chest again, birds flying up out of the black dream where she knew things. She broke out of the crowd and held a hand up to Rukheyser to get his attention. Jardine and Jackson came over to join Theresa as Rukheyser shut the squad car's door. Inside the backseat, Tory put her head down on her grandmother's lap.

"Good work, everybody," said Rukheyser. "Excellent teamwork. I wish I could say we could call it a night, but our job has just begun. We'll book Glendocker, and then I think we should start in tonight with some questioning. He indicated he has a car out in the lot; we'll impound that and search it.

"And Tory will have to be taken to the hospital. Mrs. Carlin asked if Tory could be admitted to the same hospital where Ellen is, but I think it'd be better for everyone if she went back up to Kettler. On the surface, she does not seem to have been beaten or anything, but she'll need a complete physical, of course, and we won't want to question her until Dr. Silver has had a chance to evaluate her. So we'll meet downtown in an hour. Anything else?"

"How's Ellen?" Theresa asked.

"Bad," said Jardine. "She's still in a coma. They're going to do tests to see how much brain activity there is. There was a severe drop in body temperature, and really whacked-out blood sugar and acetone levels. You know, we thought that she took some godawful mixture of pills? Tests on the stomach contents and blood indicate she took an overdose of Tylenol. Plain old Tylenol."

"And Joe?"

"Still in custody. It has yet to be determined what role he played in this, but it's likely he hired Glendocker. The Vegas detective, Mickelson, flew in to question him, but DeLisi wants to wait until Monday, when his lawyer will fly out from the East Coast. It's going to take a while to weave this whole thing together."

Theresa let out a sigh as she watched Ginny Carlin stroking Tory's hair in the backseat of the squad car. "Where will Tory go when she's released from the hospital?"

Rukheyser said, "I'm sure both the grandmothers are going to try to get custody. There will probably be a big fight all over again, and she might end up in foster care. Why?"

"You can't let Tory go with Ginny Carlin."

"Why not?"

"What's up, Theresa?" asked Jardine.

"I think you had better have the plastic syringe that the lieutenant found in Ellen's room at the Seaside checked for fingerprints. I believe you'll find Ginny Carlin's prints on it, and other evidence that she was in that motel room with Ellen. I suggest you look in her purse right now for other syringes just like that one, and for a bottle of Extra Strength Tylenol that's probably about empty." Rukheyser, Jardine, and Jackson were silent, as if they didn't know what she was talking about. But to Theresa it was obvious. "Ellen Carlin didn't try to commit suicide," she said. "Ginny Carlin tried to kill her."

Rukheyser spoke briefly to an officer, instructing him to stay with the squad car and keep Mrs. Carlin and the girl inside. He drew Theresa over, away from the car. "Go on," he said. Actually listening for once, she thought.

But she addressed Jardine and Jackson. "When we went down to Ginny Carlin's house that night and Ellen was there, remember how out of it she was? I mean, she was always a very intense and strange woman, but that night there was a real personality change. We all attributed it to the stress and the fact that she was being confronted with the Munchausen Syndrome by Proxy. But do you remember that Ginny said she'd given Ellen a sleeping pill? I wonder what else Ginny gave her.

"And the next day, when Ginny called me over to the hospital to read for Ellen, again Ellen was very strange, alternately drowsy and placid, then explosive. There were a lot of medications sitting on the nightstand, including a large bottle of Tylenol. I also noticed a syringe, still wrapped in its cellophane package. I thought it odd that the nurse would leave it sitting there but Ginny said that the nurse had just given her a vitamin B shot so I thought maybe the nurse had just forgotten it. A while later, Ginny knocked her purse over and everything in it fell out. As she was hurrying to put the stuff back in, I noticed another bottle of Tylenol. And Lieutenant Jardine found that syringe in Ellen's motel room.

"My feeling—and it's not even particularly psychic—is that Ginny Carlin also has Munchausen Syndrome by Proxy. Didn't Dr. Silver say that if there is not an intervention in the family, Munchausen Syndome by Proxy often repeats itself generationally? Look at Ginny and Ellen; Ginny got her right into that hospital, just as Ellen always did to Tory. Twice in these past few days. And now it looks like Ellen will be there quite a while. Unless she dies.

"Ellen's father, Ginny Carlin's husband, was a pharmacist. The family had access to a lot of drugs and knowledge about what those drugs would do. Ellen has a long history of prescription drug abuse, probably initiated by her parents in childhood and adolescence. Ginny said she had to have Ellen hospitalized a number of times thoughout her youth and as an adult, that you never could tell when she'd be sick again, that it was cyclical. She claims it's depression and maybe that's part of it. Who wouldn't be depressed, in that family? Not to let Ellen off the hook, but I think it's essential that you examine Ginny Carlin's role in all of this, and until Ginny is completely cleared of any involvement, I beg you not to let her near Tory. It is very common in other types of abuse, violence and sexual abuse, for adults to repeat what was done to them as children. And I believe Ellen Carlin was trained by an expert."

Rukheyser cleared his throat. The fairgoers had begun to disperse now and the rides were all going again, their lights flashing in the darkness. The screams were once again expressions of elation and delight.

Jardine whistled. "I think we have to take this into account, Sergeant."

Rukheyser returned to the squad car and asked Ginny Carlin to get out for a moment. He requested that she empty the contents of her purse onto the front seat of the car. She said, "Why, of course," and dumped the large bag out. Rukheyser sorted through the mess and picked up several plastic syringes from the pile of keys, money, papers, combs, and gum wrappers. There was also a large bottle of Tylenol. He shook it. Empty. He picked up a matchbook and handed it to Jardine. Theresa glanced over and read the cover: Seaside Villa. So the matches had turned up after all.

"What is it, Sergeant Rukheyser? Whatever is the problem now?" asked Ginny Carlin. As he led her to another squad car, Theresa could hear her hissing irritably, "Those syringes? I have diabetes. Those are my insulin syringes. I have to carry them with me. I've never heard of anything so ridiculous in my life. I demand to speak with my attorney. You can't arrest me, I have done absolutely . . . "

Rukheyser slammed the car door.

Tory had rolled the window down, the unicorn on her lap. Theresa took the angelfish snow dome out of the small embroidered bag that was strapped over her shoulder and handed it to Tory. "I know your dad," Theresa said quietly. "I'm sure he'd want you to have this back."

Tory shook it, staring into the small glass world where everything was magic, where snow fell on angelfish and unicorns and nothing ever went wrong.

FRIDAY, JULY 17

EPILOGUE

CAMILLE'S VOICE CAME OVER Theresa's cordless phone through a tinny opera and a slight buzzing sound. "You're sure you're going to make it to my show today?" asked Camille. "I'm counting on you, and I know a lot of people are going to be listening in."

Theresa sat out on the patio, Friday morning. Osiris purred at the center of the glass table as she rubbed his belly. "I'll be there."

"No sudden jaunts to Vegas with interesting but unavailable men, you hear?"

"Yes, Mother."

"Ooh. I sound that bad?"

"Just keep all the mother-love focused on Sarene, Camille."

"Who are you going to give yours to—Osiris? And speaking of Sarene, honey, you outdid yourself, taking her and that boyfriend of hers to hear Bobby Brown. It beat the Orange County Fair hands down. Anyway, I know you weren't too excited to go back and ride on a roller coaster."

"You've got that right, Camille. I want off the roller coaster, not on."

Theresa assured Camille she'd be at the radio station this afternoon, a half hour early. It had been a week since Tory was found, an odd and empty week of returning to her daily schedule, client readings, bike rides down the boardwalk, breakfast at the sidewalk café, and fussing over her roses. The American Beauty was over the hill, but gorgeous, her white edges browning slightly in the heat.

When the chimes sounded, Osiris leapt off the table and padded ahead of Theresa toward the wooden gate at the side of the house.

Lieutenant Oliver Jardine and Sondra Jackson greeted her. They were both out of cop uniform, Sondra in beige leggings and a matching tunic, Jardine wearing faded Levi's, a black T-shirt, and black high-tops.

"When I parked out on Washington," said Sondra, "I pulled up right behind Oliver here, who rode up on his . . . " Sondra paused, peering over her glasses at the lieutenant. "Red Harley."

Jardine grinned.

"You fixed the bike?" Theresa said. "Oliver, that's great."

She led them back to the patio, where she brought out muffins she'd baked the night before, a bowl of fresh fruit, and a pot of French-roast coffee. Jardine bit into a muffin. "Hmmm," he said, his mouth full. "Bran. I love bran. Bran is just so . . . "

"You know bran is an aphrodisiac?" Sondra laughed as Jardine slit his eyes at her. She pulled a file out of her bag and set it on the table. "Thought you might want a copy of this, Theresa. Gerald Oslin's family tree."

There were two of them: his adoptive family's genealogy, including Mary and her daughter, Hannah, and the genealogy that showed the ancestry of his birth mother, Betty Tucker, and his father, who was Betty's cousin. There was a line drawn between Gerald and Linda, and a line down to Martin Peter Glendocker. The dates of death for Gerald and Linda had been filled in.

"Remember the locked files on Oslin's hard drive?" asked Sondra.

Theresa shook her head and Sondra explained. "It was strange that neither Mary nor Jane knew the secret code to access Gerald Oslin's personal files. Mary said she thought Gerald had probably created coded files when he suspected her of snooping around the hard drive while working on his financial records. Jane had no idea what the code might be, either. We kept trying different words, free-associating. It was the lieutenant who came up with it."

" 'Past,' " Jardine said. "Oslin's favorite topic. And that's what was in the file—his past. Family trees, correspondence that detailed his search for Betty Tucker and eventually Glendocker, letters to Linda, including some in which he confessed that perhaps it had been a mistake to make contact with Marty, that he was afraid Marty was a very disturbed man. That Gerald thought he might be stealing from him.

"Also, Mary Oslin did find a number of checks made out to cash over the last year," Jardine continued. "Checks that Oslin had recorded in his checkbook as gifts to an organization called 'Adoption International,' but the returned checks were made out to cash and endorsed by Oslin. We think the checks were actually gifts to Glendocker. The lab has them now, and we'll be able to tell if he ever had his hands on them. Not that we'll need it to convict him," added Jardine.

"Glendocker also left a whole scrapbook of evidence in a duffel bag in his truck," said Sondra. "A portrait of Oslin in his navy uniform, taken from Oslin's office, the keys to both Oslin's home and the store. An empty kerosene can that had fibers on its base from an Oriental carpet, a very particular one, Afghani. The rug just inside the antique store's front entry was water-damaged but not burned, so we were able to match it."

"And I'm glad I remembered to have them screen the tub where Oslin was found when they drained it," said Jardine, "because we also found fibers that matched a shirt in Glendocker's possession, the one he must have been wearing the day he killed Oslin."

Theresa pushed her chair back and sipped her coffee. "I went down to Huntington Beach and visited Ellen," she said quietly. "I don't know, it just felt incomplete without some contact."

"I hear she's about the same," said Jardine.

"Still in a coma. They have no way of telling how long that might be. She could be down in it for another week or a few months or for the rest of her life. I tried to . . . " Theresa stopped, considering whether to talk freely with Sondra there, and then went on ahead. "I tried to make contact with her, psychically. Tried doing a reading for her. Needless to say, I've never read for anyone in a coma before."

"What happened?" asked Jardine.

"It didn't surprise me. It was just emptiness, that black-yellow feeling with an undercurrent of hostility. It's strange to feel an emotion around her, but, well . . . there it was."

"Puts me in mind of a hornet," said Sondra. "Trapped between two panes of glass."

Jardine poured himself another cup of coffee. "All charges have been dropped against DeLisi, by the way. Thought you'd want to know. Though the gun was registered to him, it did not have his prints on it. He'd reported it stolen five years ago. Insurance claims and police records backed up his statement. It appears that Ellen took it with her when she separated from DeLisi, and Glendocker must have stolen it from her when he was staying at her house. His prints were all over it. He admits that he acted alone. He also admits using Whitney Park's name when he registered at the Seaside Villa."

"And Ginny, what will happen to her?" asked Theresa.

"She hired Ellen's attorney and she's out on bail. Of course, she denies the charges and says she'll do everything in her power to take Tory away from Joe. But she's living in a fantasy. You know that her prints did show up on the syringe found in Ellen's room, I called and told you that. And there was other forensic evidence that Ginny Carlin had been in the room at the Seaside Villa—hair samples and gravel from Ginny Carlin's car port. A nurse on the psych ward where you went to read for Ellen will give testimony that she saw Ellen's mother actually giving Ellen an injection. They also had to take several urine samples from Ellen because blood kept showing up in the tests. But the blood was not Ellen's type; it matched her mother's blood type. A doctor examining Ginny Carlin found tiny prick scabs on her fingers—she was squeezing her own blood into Ellen's urine samples to contaminate them. Dr. Silver said that is classic Munchausen Syndrome by Proxy behavior. He said he doubted that Ginny had done this sort of thing to Ellen as an adult, but under all the stress, they'd both reverted to behaviors established in Ellen's childhood. And another thing: upon checking further into Ginny Carlin's background, we found she also had a 'stillborn child' who died just hours after birth. And a two-year-old who died of 'influenza.'"

"And she still denies all this?"

"Oh yes. She maintains that Ellen framed her, then tried to kill herself. When confronted with the forensic evidence that she was at the Seaside Villa, she maintained that Ellen had called her and asked her to come to the motel. Ginny Carlin said Ellen was hysterical and drunk. She says she tried to get her to return to the hospital or go into a treatment program, but that Ellen was out of control, so she left, thinking she'd return the next day, when Ellen had calmed down.

"But Ginny couldn't resist taking those nice plastic cups that Donna had so kindly provided the housekeeping units with. She had them in the backseat of her car, along with a receipt in a brown paper bag for vodka and orange juice. So Ellen couldn't have been drunk when Ginny got there. Ginny got her drunk. She either convinced or forced Ellen to swallow about a hundred Tylenol tablets, or maybe she dissolved the Tylenol in the orange juice and poured it down Ellen's throat or made her drink it. On top of that, she shot Ellen up with insulin until she went into insulin shock."

Osiris jumped up from his spot in the shade, and Theresa knew that Joe and Tory were at the gate before she heard the chimes. "Do you think Tory has any chance of recovering from all this?" she asked.

"Dr. Silver says that it will take a lot of therapy and a lot of love."

Theresa passed the spot where she had heard the Voice speaking to her of Ellen. It was cool there in the shade, but nothing else. The Voice had subsided, replaced by a stillness and a sense of both satisfaction and sorrow. Theresa was deeply pleased that Tory had been found. And, as she knew was always true in such cases, there was still much tragedy to be dealt with.

"Joe." Theresa smiled. He paused, then leaned over and brushed a kiss on the side of her face.

"I'd like you to meet my daughter, Tory. Tory, this is the lady I was telling you about."

Tory was holding her father's hand. She seemed so small in person, her dark eyes as intense as her father's. She carried a purple backpack.

"Thanks for finding my doll," she said.

"You're welcome, Tory. I'm glad you got it back."

They followed Theresa back to the patio. Jardine and Sondra stood as DeLisi and Tory arrived, and the adults tried to make small talk while Tory played with the cat and wandered up the stairs to Theresa's studio. When Tory was out of range, Joe DeLisi thanked them all for their help. "I appreciate your putting me in touch with Theresa, Lieutenant. I know you had your doubts about me after you read all those bogus court records."

"Ellen's lawyer made a good case against you in that custody suit, Dr. DeLisi."

"Yeah, well . . . I'm not saying I haven't made mistakes. But I was a good father to Tory. I can't thank you all enough for your help."

Sondra checked her watch and said she had to be going, and Jardine stood, too. "I'll see you, Theresa. By the way, when is our next meeting?"

"You mean our dinner?" she asked. "How about Wednesday? Where should we meet?"

"I don't care," he said. "I know a good Korean place with entrees under five bucks."

Theresa thought it strange the way Sondra Jackson glared at Jardine. They said good-bye. "We can show ourselves out," said Jardine.

When she returned to the patio, Joe was gone. She climbed the stairs to the studio, assuming he had gone up after Tory. Tory was seated on the couch, playing with the divination artifacts on the table, the crystal ball, the sand tray, several decks of tarot cards, the I Ching coins in a dish.

"Where's your dad, Tory?"

She shrugged. "I don't know."

Theresa sat next to her on the couch. She had wondered if it would be overpowering to see Tory in person. When she had been with Tory in her mind, the connection between them was palpable and intense. But sitting here with Tory, she was aware she was with a shy ten-year-old girl, a deeply traumatized child who nonetheless exhibited enormous resilience. Her survival skills, if nurtured in a healthy environment, would give her a brilliant core of depth and compassion for others, particularly other children, other survivors.

"You know last week, when I was on the Ferris wheel with Doc?" Tory looked up at Theresa, then held the crystal ball to her eye. "Doc made me say that. That he was my friend."

"Well, he might have been, to begin with. But not afterward, after he took you away."

"How did you ever find my doll?" Tory asked.

Theresa wondered how much Joe had explained. It was always better to be direct. "Do you know what a psychic does?"

"Read the future?"

"Kind of. I imagined that I was talking to you and I kept asking you to tell me where you were, what you were seeing, what you were doing. In my mind I saw a picture of a park in Long Beach."

"Does 'imagined' mean that you made it all up?"

"Imagining isn't lying," said Theresa. "It's creative and playful and mysterious."

Tory carefully put the pack of cards down. "These are cool. I like the pictures on them."

"Would you like to keep them?" Theresa asked. She remembered years ago, fourteen years old, being given her first deck of cards by a gypsy fortune-teller on the Lower East Side of Manhattan.

Tory said, "Really? I could keep them? Will you teach me what to do with them?"

"Sure. If your dad wants me to."

"I want you to," said Joe. He stood in the doorway to the studio. "I was in the house using your phone," he explained. "I hope you don't mind. Theresa, you'll have to come out and visit us on Martha's Vineyard. You could teach Tory ways she can use her imagination. I'm sure you'd inspire her."

"Will you?" asked Tory. "Will you come, please?"

*   *   *

Joe DeLisi embraced Theresa at the gate when they said good-bye. He held her briefly, resting his beard against her hair. Tory was down by the canal, looking at the ducks. Joe kissed her, then.

"Thank you," he said. "I hope you will consider coming out. We have lots of room at the summer house."

"That would be nice," she said. "And give my greetings to Barbara."

Theresa waved to Tory and blew her a kiss. Tory ran back to her, opening her backpack. "I almost forgot to give you this." Theresa unfolded a drawing of a black-haired queen riding a red bike through a garden of roses.

"Hey, I almost forgot to give you something, too." Theresa went into the house and fetched the brown bag of Tory's things. She had put Tory's blue glittery sneakers in the bag as well, and when Tory saw them, she beamed and held them up for her father to see. Theresa kept the snapshot of Tory, though, that Ellen had given her. It was on her refrigerator, along with the drawings. She would put the queen right up there next to them with a magnet. Then Tory and Joe were gone, under the bougainvillea that hung over the sidewalk by the canal.

Theresa stayed looking out over the canal, and Jardine reappeared where Joe and Tory had just gone. "Hello, again," he called.

"Hello, Oliver. Did you forget something?"

He shoved his hands in his pockets as he came up the sidewalk and stood beside her, taking stock of the ducks, the white bridge, and the stripes of summer clouds. "Yeah," he said. "I almost did, but Sondra reminded me."

"What's that?" Theresa asked. She shook her curls back over her shoulders.

"How about Friday night instead of Wednesday? I was thinking," he said. "There's this little French bistro I found last week over on Melrose. What do you say, Theresa?"

"Which Friday, Oliver?"

"I was thinking this one. Tonight."

"Is this for work?" Theresa asked.

"No," he answered. "Pleasure."

Theresa looked at the drawing of the queen on her red bike in the roses.

YES, said the Voice.